PRA

"Demonstrates Mr. Peters ... a novelist. . . . *FLAMES OF HEAVEN* . . . successfully makes the difficult transition from military techno-thriller to literature."

—*Washington Times*

"In this novel of contemporary Soviet life. . . . Peters demonstrates not only a talent for characterization but a formidable knowledge of the former USSR."

—*Library Journal*

"Winning. . . . Peters knows more about the Soviet Union than most Russians. . . . [a] stunning picture of political disintegration."

—*Grand Rapids Press*

"[Peters is] as lucidly literate as he is humanly insightful. . . ."

—*Chicago Sun-Times*

"Ralph Peters is an excellent novelist with an extremely clear and readable style. . . ."

—*Los Angeles Daily News*

"Peters writes with a style that is lucid and so direct that it seems to be almost effortless."

—*San Diego Union*

"Ralph Peters is the Tolstoy of the genre. . . . [His books are] rich . . . always challenging. . . . You'll end up reading them again and again."

—*Army Times*

PRAISE FOR RALPH PETERS'
THE WAR IN 2020

"... the military counterpart of Orwell's *1984*. . . . *The War in 2020* is not for the fainthearted. . . . Ralph Peters brilliantly contrasts a future world of frightful technology with the very human reactions of the men who use it. . . ."

—The New York Times Book Review

"Extremely well executed. It's big, it's textured, yet it manages to be fast, a rare and winning combination."

—Washington Post Book World

"*The War in 2020* is several cuts above the average. . . . It is, in fact, of considerable literary merit. . . . Intimate knowledge of the military shows in every line."

—Los Angeles Daily News

"Mr. Peters, who proved himself a master storyteller in his previous books, is better than ever in this one. The plot of *The War in 2020* is as sweeping as the steppes of Central Asia. . . ."

—Washington Times

RED ARMY

"Going Tom Clancy one better. . . . without question the best of its kind. . . . It is hard to imagine a better portrayal of modern war."

—*Newsweek*

"*Red Army* is a tour de force . . . written by someone who is expert at his topic—warfare. . . ."

—*Chicago Sun-Times*

"Unique. . . . From the standpoint of both technical accuracy and human emotions, Peters has provided us with a provocative and illuminating book."

—*Milwaukee Journal*

"A stark, gripping tale. . . . Powerful, unsettling."

—Stephen Coonts

BRAVO ROMEO

"Ralph Peters . . . writes about as tough a suspense-espionage-chase thriller as any of the Ludlum–le Carré school. In fact, he just may be a little bit tougher."

—*San Diego Union*

"*Bravo Romeo* puts what Graham Greene calls 'the human factor' back into spy fiction."

—*The New York Times Book Review*

"An uncommonly intelligent and exciting caper, with a likable hero. . . ."

—*Publishers Weekly*

"Peters has an acute ear. . . . So many of the passages come off so well that one knows this is a serious writer. . . ."

—*The New Republic*

Books by Ralph Peters

Bravo Romeo
Red Army
The War in 2020
Flames of Heaven

Published by POCKET BOOKS

RALPH PETERS

A
NOVEL
OF RUSSIA

POCKET BOOKS
New York London Toronto Sydney Tokyo Singapore

To Volodya Yarin
and Leonid Semeiko,
whose paintings
inspired me

This book is a work of fiction. Names, characters, places and incidents are products of the author's imagination or are used fictitiously. Any resemblance to actual events or locales or persons, living or dead, is entirely coincidental.

POCKET BOOKS, a division of Simon & Schuster Inc.
1230 Avenue of the Americas, New York, NY 10020

ISBN: 0-671-73739-2

Pocket Books printing May 1994

10 9 8 7 6 5 4 3 2 1

Cover art by Ben Perini

Printed in the U.S.A.

The views expressed in this book are those of the author and do not reflect the official policy or position of the Department of the Army, the Department of Defense, or the U.S. government.

"The strength of a man is no more
than the strength of muscle and bone . . .
but love's strength has the power of God."

—Sufi proverb

PART ONE

Moscow, Moscow, Moscow . . .

1

THE GENERAL WAS HAPPY. HE WAS HAPPY BECAUSE HIS wife was happy, and his wife was happy because of Sasha Leskov, who had painted her with a youth, grace, and near-beauty she neither felt nor possessed. Sasha was a master at reading human expectations from a nervous smile or the way a hand smoothed down the front of a blouse. And he was accustomed to painting generals' wives. It was the semi-official part of his work, quietly paid off with a resalable Japanese cassette player or cartons of Western cigarettes. Occasionally, the portraiture even became the most important aspect of his job, depending on the general and his wife and the garrison. This portrait had been just important enough for the general—acting under his wife's orders—to delay shamelessly the artist's return home to Moscow.

This general was the Potsdam garrison commander, and his wife had heard from the wife of another general that Sasha had done an absolutely marvelous portrait of the wife of the Leipzig garrison commander, a woman who had not had the good manners to shed her attractiveness to men with the years and who was regarded as a brassy, uncultured bitch who had married above her station.

It was unthinkable to the wife of the Potsdam garrison commander that such a woman should achieve any unique distinction. Also, the women involved were all dear old friends, and in Russian circles, friendship could not endure without either equality of advancement or equality of suffering. This was a difficult problem. The wife of the Potsdam garrison commander could not very well take a kitchen knife to the portrait of the Leipzig garrison commander's wife—although she would have been steadfastly ready to weep and share the sorrow had some anonymous avenging angel defaced, shredded, and burned her friend's portrait. So the only possible solution was to have her own portrait done by the charming, still-youngish man in the jeans and leather jacket.

It was the ass end of a series of frantic, boring jobs. Sasha didn't mind so much. He had grown used to these little delays, and he never told his woman of the moment precisely when he would be coming home. Just keep feeding the cat. See you sometime in November. He didn't mind so much, but he was tired. This tour had taken him all over the German Democratic Republic, to almost every key Soviet garrison, a one-man storm splashing paint on oversize canvases or plaster. He painted big, handsome, clean-shaven figures all triumph and self-sacrifice. Sasha had never been in a war, and he had done his mandatory service behind a typewriter, but he knew instinctively that the heroes he painted to salve the military's wounded vanity bore little relation to the way men looked when they fought and died. Neither did the titans in his paintings resemble in the least the pimply, rotten-toothed boys in ill-fitting uniforms who composed the present Soviet Army. But he painted to please, blessed with the ability to work quickly when the work didn't matter to him. He had almost reached the point where he could paint exactly what they wanted without thinking at all. It was all howlingly dishonest, of course, but that didn't really trouble him. At worst, the whole business just made him tired.

There had been a time, early on, when he had laughed over his work in secret. The worse he painted, the better his military clients liked it. He painted the outrageous, the ridiculous, the impossible, and the generals and graying colonels mistook it for glory. But the same joke could only be funny a limited number of times, and he eventually settled down to a flat, efficient routine, amazing his sponsors with his ability to work hard. They found him so unlike their preconceptions of how an artist must behave that they confused his desire to finish his work and be shut of them all with exemplary dedication. That, too, had been amusing for a while. But after a decade, it was just gray and occasionally pathetic.

Recently, he had been working on a mural in the headquarters of the Third Shock Army in Magdeburg, painting a battle scene rotten with cheap sentiment only to turn from his work and find a potbellied colonel weeping like a boy who had lost his father.

The greatest challenge at the moment was to endure the near-panic of his workday masters. There was a constant inarticulate nervousness now, as the men in Moscow who did not wear uniforms relentlessly traded away the privileges and positions of those who did. It was a new, unexpected age, thrilling for Sasha's friends in the arts, but a nightmare for the old war-horses who had just botched a war against a bunch of blackasses in Afghanistan and were trembling for their perks and pensions. Just being around them day after day wore you down emotionally. And he felt physically down, as well. He missed his rigorous daily swims and regular sex. It was time to go back to Moscow, back to his real life.

Painting the murals in the foyer of the Potsdam officers' club was supposed to be an honor. Because of the historical associations. But it was just a little rathole of a place, with burnt-out lights and dirt in the corners, far better in the evening than by the light of day. Thankfully, it was evening now. The last evening of the last day. His work was done. For a few months there would be no more drab garrisons, no more generals' mighty wives or mole-pocked, nervous-thighed daughters. There would be time to paint seriously, to make love, to swim in the big indoor pool, to sleep late and rub the cat's belly. Time for friends and time to be alone. Moscow.

The general smiled like a fool and raised his glass in Sasha's direction. Tonight, at least, the man was happy. He had called for a party, supposedly to celebrate the birth of the oh-so-lifelike, oh-so-heroic new murals out in the entranceway, although Sasha knew the old bugger was simply taking advantage of a tactical opportunity to have a bit of a roar. The sorry bastards found so few excuses for throwing parties these days, and it was hard on an officer corps in which the level of sustainable drunken exuberance was a crucial measure of competence.

The general was happy. And his officers were happy, too. They had eaten well, drinking valiantly all the while, in a warm acid haze of cigarette smoke. Bored, Sasha experienced it all from a remove, the range of emotions running from the simple animal joy of being inside, warm and soundly fed, on an autumn night, to the desperate need of some to briefly shatter reality with alcohol, to rinse away the stink of failure from lives of small, empty successes. He watched the party-makers with an informed artist's eye that he never brought to bear on his military paintings, cataloging faces, postures, single features: the way a great hippopotamus of a man lifted his vodka glass with angelic delicacy, the various, highly individualized ways in which uniforms became disheveled, the protruding brow that gave a lieutenant colonel the look of a deep-eyed saint in an old Novgorod icon. A rakish young officer worried his fingers over a blemish on his forehead whenever he imagined that no one was looking. An engineer officer's work-mashed fingers coiled purple over the neck of a bottle, and two young officers, idiot twins with identical Guard's mustaches from the army of the czars, balanced their cigarettes in a manner effeminate and impractical, lacking only monocles to complete their anachronistic absurdity. At the end of the table, a lieutenant's eyes shifted as if receiving little electric shocks as he struggled to get his social bearings. It was all simultaneously original and instantly familiar from the experience of hundreds of garrisons. Had he not been the nominal guest of honor, Sasha would gladly have spent the evening elsewhere.

Straining to top off his neighbor's glass, a major who had been introduced as the garrison's political officer lost control of his bottle of vodka. Liquor pulsed out over shattered glass and howls of disapproval shot up like flares above the long table. A marginally more sober hand quickly locked onto the bottle, rescuing what liquor remained, while another officer clumsily guided the major back down into his chair.

Given the tenor of the times, Sasha figured the political officer had plenty of justification for slamming himself with alcohol. Once the man who whispered in the ear of the king, earlier in the evening the major had drawn only a grudging response with his ornate toasts. He remained a tolerated guest, but no one bothered to pretend to love him these days, and the sins of generations of his predecessors were quietly held against him—even by those officers who still claimed to be good Communists. Everyone needed a scapegoat.

A wiser or more sober man than the political officer would have kept his seat and his temper. But the major would not be stilled. He struggled with his delinquent limbs, wanting to rise again, challenging them all:

"You think I'm drunk? You piss-cutters? I'll show you."

His hand grabbed the nearest vodka bottle. He lifted himself clumsily, dragging the opened flaps of his jacket over the wreckage of his dinner. His tablemate shoved the major's sleeve out of his face, and the major lurched to the other side, toppling a pair of bottles of mineral water.

"Sit him *down,*" the general commanded from the end of the table, voice balanced between authority and raw good humor.

"Give him the penalty mug," the officer with the spot on his forehead demanded.

The other officers followed suit, chanting, "Penalty mug, the penalty mug." They hammered the table with their fists, stinging the china with loose cutlery.

The general smiled. It struck Sasha as the smile of a man who was sexually naive, physically crude, and sentimental. The man's wife had surely recognized the possibilities offered by that smile upon their first meeting. Her own smile, unpaintable, was merciless and sexless.

The general waved his hand, summoning one of the warrant officers' wives, who traditionally worked in the clubs for a few extra rubles and the chance to steal food. A blonde marched obediently forward, good looks straining to survive against late nights and bad diet.

"I serve you, Comrade General."

A Moscow girl, with the unmistakable singsong accent exaggerated now for the powerful little man with the stars on his shoulders. Sasha could tell by her every movement that she had the general sized up perfectly.

"More vodka," the general called with sudden vigor, as though ordering another wave of soldiers to their deaths. "And bring . . . our special mug."

The officers grouped around the long table roared.

Sasha knew what to expect. He'd seen the stupid game played before, one of the many childish rituals that comforted men whose lives were dedicated to killing and dying.

But the political officer had no idea what was coming down on his head. He had squandered his last capabilities and sat dead-eyed in his chair, staring at the gravy smeared on his plate. He had disintegrating features, skin half-dead from alcohol, and a boy's yellow hair. His mouth hung open, and his shoulders had lost their shape. He might have served as a model for a painting of a man shocked by a terrible and unexpected loss.

"*More music,*" a colonel barked. This was the general's chief of staff, responsible for knowing what the general wanted in the split second before the general knew he wanted it. The colonel had a mean voice that no amount of alcohol or mortal love would ever soften. "Where in the hell are those little drizzle-asses?"

The lieutenant with the nervous eyes scurried toward the back room where the three enlisted musicians were undoubtedly ramming the scraps from the officers' dinner down their throats. The serving woman reappeared with a huge tin tray of vodka bottles, small plates of cucumber and graying olives, bread, and a crude ceramic beer mug of the sort tourists loved to take home as a souvenir of East Germany.

The assembled officers yelped like bad, happy children. Applauding. Tonight there would be plenty of vodka. Tonight, as bad as things were, there was plenty of everything. And the general was happy. It was a rare, wonderful hour of opened collars and friendships reborn.

Now and then one of the officers seated near Sasha offered him a polite compliment on his work, a shred of thanks. But he was largely forgotten. A half-emptied glass of beer stood before him, its head long since faded. He always pleaded a stomach ulcer, lying, since it was easier than trying to explain to his countrymen why he did not drink liquor. He sat resignedly, musing over things he wanted to do on his return to Moscow, a bit disappointed that he could not bring more enthusiasm to the prospect of seeing his current girlfriend again. It was odd how a minor detail could bother you, hanging with you, becoming exaggerated in the memory. She had such thick lips. Like kissing a sponge. Vera. Christ, he'd almost forgotten her name. But then, she wasn't one of the serious ones. To the extent that any of them really affected him. No real impact on his life. She did take good care of the cat, though. Fresh milk from the state farm north of Moscow, where her father was some muckety-muck. And it wasn't just the cat who got taken care of. She brought tomatoes, fresh eggs, and homemade sausages of a quality that *never* made it to the stores. Vera was far from the most exciting or intelligent woman he had ever known, but she did have her virtues. Didn't complain much. Worked hard. And she was grateful for the hours he could spare for her. He thought of her coming in after work with her basketful of good things she had gathered for him like a peasant-girl heroine from a fairy tale. He would miss that when it came time to send her on her way.

Why did they always think that the goal of every relationship had to be marriage?

God, he loved women. Not just the look of them, as did most men. But the taste when you licked them behind the shoulder blades on a hot day. The smells. The tides of muscle under sweating flesh, the words they chose to reach for you, the harmonies their flesh sang with yours. The way they whispered in your arms on a winter afternoon. Even their vanity and their anger. When he painted them, he tried to get all of that in, and more. When he was really painting. And when the stars were right, even the most arrogant of them wept to discover that a man could see them that way. Not just tits-for-sale or a proffered butt the way most painters wanted to do it. But a collarbone all light and fineness, arms empty and anguished, eyes full of history and apartness, that transient, terrible joy that came over them. Some of them took winter colors when you re-created their flesh, others were of the earth: brown and green stirred together to report the shadow of a thigh. There were so many unexpected colors hidden in them. Vuillard had gotten that right, but nobody noticed. Light, oil, flesh. Getting the special perfection of each one down on canvas. Forever. Thumbing your nose at God. Sasha thought of the smell of his apartment-studio in the winter when he was making love and painting and then making love again. The colored oils and the oils of the body. Extravagance of life.

Motion caught his eye. A big captain with transport facings on his jacket thumped the political officer on the back, smiling down at the bleary major.

"Seryosha, my dear man. It's time."

The political officer alerted slightly, as though he had heard a dog bark in the distance. The brotherhood gathered around the table laughed.

The general stood up. Yellow smile, half lord, half fool. He seemed hardly taller than when he had been seated. Little man with a weight lifter's neck. He wavered slightly, soaking with drink. Two places away, Sasha could smell the man's breath, mark the long day's whiskers. Yet the general managed to project an incontestable authority.

How did they learn that?

"Major Miladov," the general called mischievously, "attention."

Aided by his tablemates, the political officer rose to his feet. But he could not maintain himself and the other officers had no sooner released their grips than they had to take hold of him again.

Sasha could not see the least conscious knowledge in the man's eyes.

The musicians bumbled back into the room in their sweat-stained wool uniforms, dragging an accordion, a violin, and a guitar with them. The chief of staff met them with a brusque wave. Warning them not to start playing just yet.

"Major Miladov," the general continued, "you have, in my presence, committed a most serious crime against your comrades, against the People, and against the state. I must personally bear witness . . . that you are guilty of the wanton waste of vital resources." Set deep in ruined skin, the general's eyes were those of a prankster brat. "Have you anything to say in your defense?"

The major did not even realize the general was speaking to him. He could not hold up his chin.

"*Guilty*," the other officers answered for him.

The general shook his head in exaggerated sympathy. "Comrade Major, I have no alternative. My hands are tied. I must sentence you to trial by fire and water."

Approving grunts. Feigned solemnity. Mean smiles.

The major's face did not change. He wore the expression of a drugged soul in a psychiatric clinic. Totally unknowing.

Sasha could feel it. Unmistakably. They had reached the point in an evening of drinking when a man is equally ready to love or inflict physical pain on another. These men felt the need to touch, even if to touch was to hurt. The air was overheated and fouled with smoke, and Sasha wished he could slip outdoors into the cold clarity of the night. To leave the shut-in world of his own kind for a last go through the scrubbed German streets. He wanted to walk himself clear, to start becoming the other man again, the one who had no part in all of this. He feared one of his depressions coming on, the rare black moods that led him into folly. He needed to walk, to burn himself out with exercise.

But he could not leave. They would not understand. All things had to be shared—especially this tepid debauchery that so captivated Russian men, that made them click off their brains and crowd together. It was no wonder their women were forever so unhappy and so ready to take solace elsewhere. Of course, to be honest, Sasha told himself, the women would have missed their routine suffering. Misery was as addictive to his countrywomen as empty speech was to the men.

"Colonel Brukov," the general said to his chief of staff, "prepare the rite."

The colonel ceremoniously filled the big beer mug with vodka. Then he carefully handed the drink down the table. Each next officer accepted it, placed it before him, saluted, and passed it on again without drinking from it. Across from the puppet figure of the political officer, a motor-rifle captain relit a candle that had gone out and pushed it across the tablecloth until it almost touched the nap of the victim's uniform.

"In accordance with the glorious heritage of the Workers' and Peasants' Red Army," the chief of staff announced icily, "any officer found to be in so shameful a state of disability that he cannot be trusted to carry out this hallowed ritual on his own has the right to call on the generosity and forbearance of his comrades in arms—who will assist him, with all necessary force."

The smiles were ever meaner now, the eyes narrowed until you saw the traces of Tartar blood.

"In any event," the chief of staff went on, "the subject must redeem himself through a show of inner strength and physical courage." He smiled without separating his lips. "There is no other path."

Sasha had seen this game played half a dozen times before. With the poor bastard gagging and puking, strong arms locked on him all the while. On one occasion, the object of the sport had needed to be rushed to the military hospital, dying of shock and poison. Where did they find the joy in it? Sasha sat still and withdrawn, recalling his stinking, shouting father bashing his mother with closed fists. Man in all his glory.

Four officers attended the major now. Two held him upright, while the third held the mug of vodka at the ready. The last man, the motor-rifle captain, held the political officer's left hand clamped in his big paws, just above the reach of the candle's heat.

At last a reflection of intelligence showed in the major's eyes. He turned his head slightly, heavily, trying to read the flushed, eager faces of the men beside whom he served.

"Comrades . . ." he muttered.

The general held up his hand. Wait. It was the last part of the ceremony, a vestige of antique bonds and incense-ridden churches, so odd in this godless world of missiles and tanks. Sasha watched the political officer. The man looked dully frightened. And sick.

"If there is any soul here," the general said, "with sins to expiate . . . any soul clouded in darkness who aches for the light . . . he may take Comrade Major Miladov's place in the ritual."

Silence. No one made a move to take on the political officer's appointed role. They longed for his suffering now, for the public display of his humiliation and pain.

Tribal, Sasha thought. We're still living in the swamps and hunting with spears. He looked around the table, able to see most of the faces. The meanness of it all made him want to turn his back, and for a moment, he imagined himself standing up and volunteering to take the major's place. He could handle the alcohol, although it would make him sick. But he did not believe he could master himself sufficiently to take with the required discipline the physical pain of being burned. Anyway, he told himself, it wasn't his battle. Let them kill each other, if they wanted.

Not one of these bastards has the basic humanity to put a stop to this, he thought. Not one.

The political officer had arrived at a speechless awareness. The alcohol had even exaggerated the danger he was in. Sasha thought the major was about to break into tears. Face of spoiled green. His jaw, his lips, moved slightly, but he was unable to move the muscles sufficiently to make words.

The air changed. At first, Sasha lost his feel for what was happening. Then he saw the other man standing at the lower end of the table. He had been seated on the same side as Sasha, making it impossible to see him until he rose.

A senior captain. With rich blue airborne facings and shiny black hair left behind by some long-forgotten tribe of horsemen. Features distinctly Russian, though. Good-looking, he had a fleshy nose that would swell as the years went by. Muscled, he would grow heavy. But tonight he looked bright and dangerous.

The captain's chest was heavily armored with colored ribbons and enameled badges. It was surprising, and very impressive, on such a young officer. Only the general had more nonsense dangling from his uniform.

Afghanistan, Sasha told himself.

The captain spoke, voice surprisingly quiet:

"Comrade General . . . I request the honor of carrying out Major Miladov's mission for him."

To Sasha's astonishment, there was no swell of bitterness or resentment. This airborne glory-boy had just spoiled their fun, yet Sasha could not feel the least annoyance on the part of the other officers.

The general's face registered a twilight mix of indulgence and something else that Sasha could not quite catalog. The old man's eyes settled on the young officer who had broken ranks and betrayed them all, but his look was almost fatherly.

"Mikhail Nikolaievich," he said, voice ripened with drink, "you have my permission."

The table exploded with enthusiasm, gaiety.

"Show us how it's done, Samsonov," a little puff with a Guard's mustache cried out.

"*Mi*sha, *Mi*sha, *Mi*sha," a voice began, followed by others. Sasha did not understand any of this. It did not fit the pattern. It was almost as though all of them had been waiting for this the entire evening.

"Show us how a *Russian* drinks, Misha."

It all went quickly. The captain took charge of the room by force of presence. Sasha began to see it now: the acknowledged hero, the natural leader. Another tribal response. The captain's face was a shade too good to waste on the propaganda murals. But there was no call for heroes in serious painting anymore. How could you use a man like that? Sasha wondered, intrigued by the technical problem.

The captain stood at the major's side. He was a man of medium height, but one of those who always seemed taller until you got a direct physical comparison. With one economical gesture, he forced the political officer back down into his chair. The only man who looked unhappy, unappeased, was the motor-rifle officer who had been clutching the major's hand, waiting to enforce the infliction of pain.

The black-haired captain seized the mug of vodka. His comrades began to clap in rhythm, cheering him on. With a quick sideward glance, he positioned his left palm low over the candle flame, holding the flesh steady at the exact height where the pain would be the greatest. Without any further ceremony, he began to drink.

The chief of staff signaled the little orchestra to play, and they strummed and stroked their way into a happy song from even sadder times. The captain drank steadily, without lowering the mug or moving his burning hand.

He won't spill a drop, Sasha thought. And what will the poor bastard prove?

Sudden diamonds appeared on the drinker's forehead. His head cocked back and his Adam's apple thrust forward. A crowing rooster. Or a drowning one. The hand over the flame wavered slightly. But it did not retreat.

One after another, the officers got to their feet, leaning forward, crowding in, shouting encouragement. The captain was drinking for them all. In any tribe he would have been the chief. Or the priest. Capable of shouldering the collective burden, of bearing the cleansing pain.

The air smelled of alcohol and a thousand years of cigarettes.

The captain's fingers began to curl involuntarily over the flame. You could see him struggling with himself, with the universe. The mug was almost fully inverted, it was almost over. The captain forced his hand out flat above the candle again.

He made a sudden noise like the beginning of a choke. The man who tried to drink down the stars. The waitresses had all drawn closer, excited by the chance to see a male suffer.

The captain slammed the empty mug down on the table so hard the flimsy legs trembled. Dripping a single bead of liquor from the corner of his mouth, he wiped his face with the back of his hand, gasping all the while to catch enough of the fleeing oxygen to remain conscious. Hands slapped him on the back and shoulders, knocking him against the chair in which the forgotten political officer sat drowsing. Then the pain from his hand reached up through the alcohol stun and the captain grunted like a hurt animal. His jaw dropped, showing good white teeth, and he slowly clasped his tormented hand to his breast.

One of the serving women ran for ice. Sasha thought that he could smell burning flesh. But it was either faint or imaginary, impossible really to capture. There were too many other smells in the room: tired working women, naphtha, unwashed uniforms, the ruined, mildewed carpets, with the reek of liquor and tobacco binding it all up in a cloud.

The airborne captain was a hero, the eternal hero.

But not everyone was content. The big motor-rifle officer who had been so eager to hold his victim's hand over the flame stood up again. He was markedly taller than the airborne officer and even better muscled.

"That's shit," he said. He stood erectly, though his voice smeared with drink. "Give me the mug." And without waiting, he reached across the table and seized it, simultaneously grasping a bottle of vodka.

Sasha caught an odd look in the airborne officer's eyes. Instead of the death of intelligence the alcohol and pain should have caused, the man looked almost superhumanly alert, as though he would never need to sleep.

The musicians scratched their instruments, beginning another familiar, inconsequential song. They wore carefully subservient smiles, but Sasha knew from his own brief service how much they relished this chance to watch officers hurting themselves.

The big motor-rifle captain cocked his torso to the side to get his hand down over the flame and began to pour liquor into his mouth, struggling to capture his audience. But the moment was gone and only a handful of drunks paid him any attention. He had not even drained the mug halfway when he began to choke. Doubling forward, he doused the candle with his hand, knocking it over as he coughed, and spat vodka over his comrades.

His face reddened, swollen, as he tried to suck down all of the oxygen in the room. Eyes of a horse strained to death.

"Again," he shouted, wobbling. "Again."

He was finished. The power quickly went out of his voice. He briefly continued to roll with an imaginary sea under his feet, then he sat down hard, collapsing inwardly with the shock of the alcohol.

The airborne captain had disappeared. No. He had merely returned to his seat. Retreating into a private quiet.

The general levered himself back to his feet, finding his own body less cooperative this time. He got his balance, then raised his glass. And he lowered it again, trying to recall the planned words. Experienced, the musicians lowered their volume until the minor chords were merely a frame for the coming toast.

None of it ever changed.

"A fine night," the general began. "Such . . . a fine night. Comrades . . . my brother officers . . . raise a glass with your commander." He looked slowly around the table, fading eyes checking compliance. "I want to drink . . . to one of our own this time. To one . . . who will be leaving us . . . all too soon." The earlier look of beatific intoxication was gone from the general's face and he looked very old. "These times . . ." He shook his head. "These times are difficult for us all. And who knows where it will end?" His mouth hardened. "When an army must part with an officer who possesses the qualities . . . the level of military culture . . . of our Senior Captain Samsonov . . . simply because some fool of a bureaucrat signed a treaty . . . and because some other coddled bastard in a comfortable office produced a list of names without regard . . . without regard . . ." The general's swollen fingers tightened around his glass until Sasha felt certain it would snap into bits. "I tell you . . . when an army must lose a veteran, a hero . . . such a man . . . because of such foolishness . . ."

The general stopped himself. Even battered with alcohol, every Soviet officer still knew the limits of open speech. He sighed, looking down at the tablecloth as if counting the burn marks on the grayed linen, and the power went out of him. The transformation was remarkable. From God in epaulets he became a little, overweight man slumping toward old age. Waving his glass at the darkness. "Comrades," he said softly, "let us drink . . . to Senior Captain Mikhail Nikolaievich Samsonov."

It was different this time. There were no raucous shouts. Instead, all of the officers who could still make it to their feet rose solemnly, turning their faces and their liquor glasses in the direction of the man who had come to the rescue of the drunken political officer.

Sasha did not mistake the heaviness in the air for love. This was fear. He understood it now. The hero was being turned out. Along with tens of thousands of other officers. Because old enemies were enemies no longer and cuts had to be made. Sasha had seen the same thing elsewhere, if not so dramatically presented. It was as if an epidemic had come, striking indiscriminately. Each of the other officers would be thinking to himself, yes, well, if it can happen to Samsonov, with all those medals on his chest . . . And the once-secure careers suddenly looked fragile. The guaranteed housing for wives and children, the accustomed access to slightly more and better food, each last precious privilege could be lost overnight. They had all heard the stories of cashiered officers' families living in abandoned boxcars, in tents, on the street.

"To Samsonov," a lone voice echoed.

"To Misha," another man added quietly.

The captain with all of the ribbons and medals simply looked off into the distance, clearly uncomfortable with this attention. There was still no trace of the effect of alcohol in his eyes. To Sasha, the man's expression would have been better suited to a young, unspoiled priest than to a drummed-out officer at a drunken party. The mouth, the eyes, had gone soft with compassion for those around him, for their own unknown fates, with his own loss discounted.

Sasha recognized the type now: *trouble*.

The officers ceremoniously drained their glasses. And the alcohol helped immediately. It always helped. A few men managed smiles.

"Misha. Give us a speech."

The lady-killer with the pimple on his forehead leaned forward. "Damn them all, Samsonov. Tell us how you feel."

"Speech."

"Stop the music, you little bastards."

"Speech."

The man with the medals smiled—still the naive young priest—and rose to his feet. His movements were not as unsullied as his eyes. But he was in control. His eyes burned.

"Speak your mind, Misha. Don't hold back."

But this man would always hold back, Sasha knew. He would speak honestly. Yet he would hold so much back, keeping the real misery to himself, all dignity and loneliness. Not a bad sort, of course. But a dreamer and a fool. You could pick his kind out on the streets of Moscow by the aura of failure. There were tens of thousands of them, eternally baffled at the meanness of the world. Most of the older ones were alcoholics.

The airborne captain nodded to himself as though he had just come to an agreement with another man hidden behind all the ribbons and badges.

"I haven't been with you long," he began, clear-voiced despite the amount of vodka he had just downed. "What has it been? A few months?" He settled his clear eyes on the general. "I'm grateful to Comrade General Major Gorchenko, without whose help I would have . . . lost my right to wear this uniform even sooner. So many others . . ." He bucked away from too sentimental a line of speech, and he smiled. He had strong even teeth not yet ravaged by either the deprivations of sainthood or the common diet. His eyes briefly met Sasha's, then moved on. "I always wanted to be an officer. For as long as I can remember. And on the day I first put on my uniform, I assumed I would wear it forever." His smile deteriorated, hiding behind heavy lips. Sasha, who prided himself on his ability to see everything at one glance, was surprised to finally notice how meaty the man's lips were. The entire mouth was almost womanly. The power of the eyes had tricked him, and now he told himself wryly that the captain's fleshy lips were almost as bad as Vera's.

The captain shrugged, continuing, "Well, I had my dream. I've been an officer. And let's be honest. I'm lucky. Compared to so many others. I have no family to worry about. And thanks to Comrade General Gorchenko, I at least have a job waiting for me. Even if it isn't exactly soldiering."

Another goddamned Russian saint, Sasha told himself. The kind of poor sap who would be a martyr no matter what sphere of endeavor he chose.

The most important rule in dealing with saints, of course, was to keep enough distance between you and them so that you didn't get in the way of the pagan arrows or the executioner's ax. It always made Sasha laugh to think that the Russian soul had a far greater proclivity for martyrdom than for an honest day's work.

"Anyway," the saint-captain concluded, "I'm still a soldier tonight." He raised his glass. "Comrades . . . to the Soviet Army."

This was not cheap emotion, Sasha realized. Just stupid, unexamined love for a thing that would have killed him, given enough time. Pity the girl who falls in love with an idealist.

Motor functions decayed, the officers were a cartoon of dutifulness. Lurching out of their chairs like fools. Imagining themselves to be standing straight-backed and strong.

Suddenly, the general hurled his emptied glass against the nearest baseboard. It was a rare gesture these days. Even glasses had grown scarce and were not to be wasted. But this was a very special night.

It was as if the only adult present had given a roomful of children permission to misbehave. The officers shouted, howled, and cocked their arms, firing their glasses through the air, striking the floor, the wall, an ill-placed chair. For a few moments they were all bold, strong, and confident again. Ready to fight the stars down out of the heavens. It was a level of emotion very close to tears.

This is how I should have painted them, Sasha thought. Not in the pose of faked heroics, but like this: afraid, struggling to be courageous, aching for comradeship, generous to the point of sacrifice, tired, drunk. He found them all vastly more appealing in their clumsy, revealed humanity than when they were swaggering about yapping orders at every living thing. But such a canvas would have pleased no one. The military would have taken it for a mockery, getting it all wrong. And the man on the street merely would have shrugged.

Sasha was the first person in the room to realize that the party was over. He heard the end off in the distance, canting his head as if it really might help him capture more of the sound. Around him, the conversations flickered on, shifting between gaiety and melancholy. The three-man ensemble played a sloppy cossack song, and a charge of officers exploded into laughter at the detonation of a ribald joke. None of them heard the other sound yet. But Sasha heard it unmistakably now, coming down out of the darkness, chilling, the kind of sound that gathered physical mass so that you felt it coming toward you in your bones. One of the officers with the affected manner of smoking a cigarette spoke to him, asking his opinion, and Sasha responded automatically, vacantly, straining to hear through the heavy air, the walls, the distance.

There was no mistaking it. *They* were coming. As they had come every Monday night in Leipzig and then in Dresden. Sasha was carefully nonpolitical. But the first time he had heard them, seen them, *felt* them, he had nearly been swept away by the power.

Couldn't the others hear it? Were they so drunk? The general sat slumped in a reverie, briefly at peace. Three slack-faced officers attempted to sing along with the musicians, dancing, stumbling, dancing again in the unbreathable air. They had goaded the musicians into playing a harsh Vysotsky tune about a bad girl who had been bad once too often. The lieutenant who had looked so nervous earlier in the evening was scouring abandoned place settings for the last edible bits.

How magnificently Russian of us, Sasha thought. Our world is coming to an end and we drink and sing.

But he was wrong. Someone else heard the avalanche, as well. The priest-eyed airborne captain had moved to the front window, his profile crisp and still impossibly sober.

"My God," the officer who had been attempting to talk to

Sasha said, almost dropping his cigarette, "those scum are coming down our street."

Other officers perked up. It was impossible to hide from the noise any longer.

The chief of staff shook his head with an ambushed look, then mastered himself and said flatly:

"Impossible. They know enough to keep their distance."

But he was wrong. The massed voices swelled and echoed down the canyon of the boulevard. Officers stood up, joining the airborne captain by the window, lifting back the heavy drapes. The general shook himself back to life and stumped across the room, with his subordinates clumsily making way for him.

But the view through the window did not match the sound. The broad street remained empty, with bare black trees down the center island and squat East German autos parked under the streetlamps. Just in front of the officers' club, centered on a tiny lawn, a statue of Lenin hailed the windows in the old apartment blocks opposite. But there was no motion, save a last few leaves skidding down the sidewalk. The night simply looked cold, with a promise of still colder weather to come. This visual stillness made no sense. Reality was broken. Thousands of disembodied voices chanted with the force of bombs.

The enormity of the sound made the window glass shiver.

"What are they saying?"

"Can't make it out."

But Sasha knew what they were saying. You didn't have to know much German to understand.

"What's that? What?"

"Be quiet."

"German scum. We've already let them go too far."

The chief of staff turned abruptly to the general. Both men had exhausted eyes.

"Shall I call out the guard force?"

The general shook his head. "No. Not yet. I don't want any incidents."

"You can't reason with them," a graying major said angrily, speaking to no one in particular. "The German only understands an iron hand."

"What are they saying now?"

It was growing difficult to understand the words of the man

next to you. The chanting of the crowd was a huge, animal thing. Frightening. Although none of the officers ever would have admitted to being afraid.

"It's the same shit," one man said. " '*Wir sind das Volk . . . Freiheit . . . Freiheit . . .*' "

"And what does that mean?"

" 'We are the people . . . freedom . . . freedom . . .' "

"I'd like to show them who they are. The ungrateful shits."

But the little knot of officers had become a fragile, inconsequential thing. Capable of being devoured by the approaching beast without the least fuss. And they all knew it.

"Lock the doors," the chief of staff barked at the waitresses.

The first demonstrators strode into view, banners and homemade placards lofting and bobbing above their heads. Seconds later, the boulevard had been inundated by a wave of humanity. They sounded so fierce, so angry and powerful. Yet they were only young men in jeans and housewives in scarves, bundled children carried in the arms, workers, dreamers, rock music fans, and shopgirls. *We are the people.* It sounded so incontestable in monosyllabic German.

Pale faces turned toward the officers' club and a few demonstrators raised their fists. But they did not stop. The crowd flowed by, disorderly, dully dressed, and spiritually brilliant. A few peripheral figures strayed briefly into the club's front garden, but there was nothing purposeful in it. They were all so much more peaceable than the unison of voices implied.

Sasha felt relieved. He was glad that there was no confrontation because he worried about which side he might find himself on. He didn't want to be on any side—politics was for dreamers and fools—yet this was more intoxicating than alcohol could ever be. The demonstrations put him in mind of those rare women you *knew* at first sight you had to avoid at all costs.

The mass began to thin in passing, and a young, punk-dressed group of demonstrators briefly changed its slogan to: "*Kolya raus, Kolya raus . . .*" Using the East German nickname for the Soviet soldier.

But this crowd, too, carefully kept its distance from the little military enclave.

The last stray banners buckled in the middle, their demands unreadable in the poor light. A teenaged boy ran from nowhere to nowhere, and a blond head shone and disappeared. Another line of young people locked arms and swayed festively across the street, singing the "Internationale" with exaggerated pompousness and laughing. A long-haired young man with a light-catching earring held up one finger in the direction of the officers' club, and just as he disappeared, a dark object came flying through the air and exploded wetly against the plinth of Lenin's statue.

"Sons of bitches," an officer muttered. But the others remained silent. It had been an impressive spectacle, unexpected on this street, in this town. The big demos happened in the industrial cities, not in pleasant little backwaters such as Potsdam. Something was wrong, wrong, wrong.

"They need a good lesson," a major said slowly. "Every so often, the German needs to be taught a lesson."

The officers had instinctively inched closer to the general. The father. Waiting for his words, his judgment. In the background, the chanting faded to a ghostly echo.

The general stared out at the darkness. He snorted a bit of wetness high up into his nose, almost spoke, then found the words inadequate. He shook his head, then shook it again. "I'm amazed. I just can't believe the order hasn't come down. Why on earth is Moscow waiting so long?"

"We've waited too long already," an officer said, sensing the direction of the general's feelings.

"Perhaps," the general said, "perhaps. I only know that the longer we wait the more . . . difficult it's going to be." He was talking more to himself than to the others. "How much blood do they want to see spilled?"

"So long as it's German blood . . ."

The general nodded. But he wasn't agreeing. Sasha felt the old man's pickled thoughts sloshing. "I don't believe . . . they understand . . . how dangerous hesitation can be. Our new leadership . . ."

"Our new leadership," a voice echoed, full of contempt. Talking about snakes or Gypsies.

"This new leadership," the general went on, "simply may not understand. Do they have any idea what it's like to put tanks in the streets? I was there, in 'sixty-eight, in Prague, and I know . . ."

In the background, a telephone rang. Sasha looked at the

general's tired face, thinking how much better an easel subject he would have been in this hour than his swollen shrew of a wife could ever be.

Unexpectedly, the general smiled, coming to himself again. "Well, it was nice of our German brothers to arrange a bit of entertainment for us, don't you think?"

The officers laughed. Dutifully. Tentatively.

One of the waitresses hurried toward the general, then paused at the last moment and turned to the chief of staff. Whispering in his ear. The colonel turned quickly and followed her, marching off with enforced sobriety.

"Anyway," the general said, "we've been here for almost fifty years, and I expect we'll be here for another fifty. This will all blow over."

"Moscow's to blame," an officer said. All bravado. And liquor.

"We just have to be patient," the general said. "It'll all be put right in the end."

But he didn't believe it. Sasha was certain. The general was like a man struggling with all his heart to believe in the fidelity of a sluttish wife.

Across the room the kitchen door swung open and the chief of staff reappeared. His face was inhumanly pale. It struck Sasha that it would have been impossible to paint a face that white. No, he corrected himself, El Greco had done it. Men all purity and rapture. A different thing, though. The chief of staff wore an expression of horror, not transcendence.

The colonel marched toward them. Dead, dead face.

"What is it, Boris Mikhailovich?" the general demanded, electrically sober.

The chief of staff shook his head, mouth open. He could not speak. He came to a halt too soon, as if his feet had lost their strength to go on, and he stood apart from the assembled officers, separated from them by a cold river of knowledge.

"What is it?" the general repeated.

The colonel raised his eyes. He was a hard man. Everything about him was hard. Sasha had no sympathy for the type and now it startled him to see the sheer bewilderment in the man's eyes. Bewilderment and tears.

"They've opened the Berlin Wall," the colonel said.

2

THE PARTY WAS OVER. ACCOMPANIED BY THE CHIEF OF staff and an aide, the general hurried off down the street to the commandant's office. Two witless lieutenants were detailed to lug the political officer home, while the other officers faded away in small groups, slipping half-empty vodka bottles into the pockets of their greatcoats and crunching broken glass underfoot. A last few continued to curse the Germans and the current regime in the Kremlin, while others snickered about an absent officer's wife. Forgotten, Sasha sat in the shadows and watched them go, making paintings in his head that would never find their way onto a canvas.

Alone, he glanced down the length of the table. Mottled cloth, crumbs, empty bottles, smeared crockery. Very little went to waste. Even the officers were hungry these days. The dead smell of smoke and stale air gave the room a tawdriness that made him long for the morning and fresh air. Yet he found himself unable to move, unready to leave. He felt as though something of great importance remained unresolved. Now that the officers were gone, he had only himself to mock. And it wasn't as much fun as it had once been. He didn't know where any of this was going. He didn't know where he himself was going.

Paris, he told himself. Hollywood. Goading his doubts with names that had no reality or genuine interest for him.

I am going to Moscow.

His hand moved a pencil over a scrap of paper. Absently, he sketched the sole remaining waitress as she went about her cleanup chores. She had been quite pretty once, he could tell, with good hair and eyes that had trusted life to deal her a better hand than it had offered her parents or sisters or friends. In the weary lifting of a plate, Sasha saw the ghost of the faith she had once offered her man, the childish belief that, somehow, *he* would make it all different and better. They all believed in miracles. Now she was in her late thirties and undoubtedly slept around out of boredom. There was nothing else for which she could hope except the absence of brutality.

He had started out to sketch her frankly as she appeared: a character piece. But his fingers decided otherwise. Instead of drawing the hair half undone and the eyes exhausted to the point of illness, he made her the way she might have been, rescuing the spoiled potential in the good line of her profile and in the eyebrows that promised an ever-famished sexuality.

The woman said nothing. She loaded tin tray after tin tray, hauling the evening off to the scullery. Leskov understood. She was ignoring him so that he would leave without further demands, so that she could lock the door and go home to her sleeping man.

And there would be a child or two waiting. She had given birth, Leskov was certain. The line of surrender in her shoulders telegraphed her struggle to raise children in a series of garrison towns. Typical woman, typical life.

She worked her way toward him from the bottom of the table. He could feel her annoyance rising. Figuring him for yet another drunk she would have to fend off. A small red plastic heart dangled off a tin necklace. As she came closer, he saw that her skin had been waxed over with sweat.

She slapped a plate of wilting cucumbers onto her tray and drew herself up before him, punching a small fist into her hip. Glaring.

Then she saw. She opened her eyes and saw the little miracle he had worked on the torn paper.

"Is that *me?*" she asked. Afraid to hear the answer. Aching to hear his answer.

Sasha nodded. "Hold still for a moment."

She obeyed, but only briefly. Then she moved around the table to his side, bending over the sketch with the eagerness of a child.

"I'm not that pretty. Not really."

"That's how I see you," Sasha said. He measured his voice exactly so as to make her a little gift but without any hint of personal desire or expectation.

"Really?"

Sasha nodded again, gently, looking into her eyes. They had lost all of their practicality and impatience. Thoughts far away. In seconds, she had re-created her life, flying across borders, annihilating years.

She said, "I really was pretty like that once. I'm not now. But I was." In the simple, quiet voice of a good girl waiting at a Moscow tram stop for a heartbreaking boy. Years away from this life of small, constant insufficiencies, of dishes dirtied by strangers and stockings rolled down in haste.

He held out the drawing. "For you."

She winced, as if he had raised a hand to slap her. Then she took the paper in her hands and strained to see.

"You've made me beautiful."

"I just drew what I saw." His tone withdrew slightly, going carefully with her.

She shook her head. Disagreeing. And she smiled. It was a wonderful smile, despite the ill-cared-for teeth. It was the first time all night that he had seen her smile like this, and he always watched the women in his surroundings carefully.

"I heard you painted a picture of the general's wife."

Sasha nodded. "That was work. This was pleasure."

"Would you sign it? Like artists do?"

He took the fragment of paper and scribbled across the lower right-hand corner. He briefly considered asking her name so he could write a dedication, but rejected the notion. He knew better. Anything that sounded too personal would only bring her trouble when she showed the drawing to her husband or lover. Or when a drunk found it in a drawer.

"It's so lovely," she said. "Even if it isn't really me."

She carefully placed the sketch on an adjacent table and

went on with her work, so close Leskov could smell her. He knew she expected him to rise and touch her, and for a moment, he thought about how it would be. He'd certainly had worse. But he was different now, trying to be different, trying to force things to make sense, and he knew without doubt that he had given her all he really had to give her. He had enough. Let other men have theirs. It was more and more difficult to bring the old fire to bear on women who did not matter. At thirty-five, he was not tired of sex. But he was tiring of all the inadequacies and disappointments that surround it.

Recently, for the first time in his life, he had experienced some difficulty performing after he and a fresh acquaintance had tumbled into bed. The ordeal flailed his pride until he calmed down enough to realize that he had not even liked the woman, not her smell, nor her manner, nor her voice, not the way she felt under his fingers or the way she moved against him. He had simply felt obliged to put her in his bed because she was pretty and available. Then it occurred to him that he was doing a great many things in his life that he really did not want to do, out of habit or vanity or to meet a stranger's expectations.

So he did not touch the waitress, but contented himself by watching the lines of her back and buttocks under the tight-stretched cloth of her dress, wishing her well. He took a last sour sip of beer to wet his mouth, then set the glass on the tray for her.

She looked at him again. Eyes unmistakably disappointed. Yet, not so bad, not so bad. It was only that he had disarranged her view of the world when he failed to run his hand up between her legs.

"Can I get you anything?" she asked. Her voice had none of the artificial veneer it had worn throughout the evening, as she served. It was quiet, a little nervous, and wonderfully real.

"No. Thanks."

"A bottle? We always have some tucked away."

He began to say no, that he did not drink. Then he understood her. She wanted to give him something, anything. Not out of a feeling of debt but from a reawakened desire to give.

"That would be lovely," he said. "But just one."

She smiled again, and it was a far handsomer gift than any bottle could ever be. Then she hurried off to the kitchen, trotting awkwardly on high heels uneven with heavy wear. She returned after only a moment, still smiling, with a bottle of premium vodka.

"It's from the general's personal supply," she said. "But he'll never know."

She presented it to him as though it were a high award for his services. He smiled, thinking to himself that not so long ago he would simply have followed her back into that darkened kitchen.

"It'll keep me warm," he lied.

As the bottle changed hands, her fingers briefly touched him.

"I bet you have lots of girls," she said suddenly. Not smiling now.

"I'm married," Sasha lied. It always amazed him that you had to be so much more dishonest when you meant well by others than when you didn't give a damn.

The waitress flinched. But she had made up her mind to go on, ready to risk spoiling it all.

"I know I'm not so pretty. Not anymore. But I'm prettier than the general's wife. And younger."

Sasha laughed. Like so many of his words, the laugh was measured. The perfect brushstroke. "All I did was paint her portrait."

"That's not what they say." The first sullenness. The situation was about to turn bad. And he had not wanted that at all.

He touched her. He took her by the upper arm with a grasp distinctly empty of sex.

"What's your name?"

"Natasha."

"Natasha, I've only been married four months." Lies, and still more lies. "We're in love."

Natasha pouted. "And does your wife know? That you go around painting other women? And giving them drawings?"

He nodded.

"*I* wouldn't let you do that," she said. "If you were my man."

"It's my job." He fit the bottle of vodka into the pocket of his jacket. Jutting, it barely stayed put.

The woman gathered herself. She had given up. He could feel it. It was going to be all right after all.

"Anyway," she said, "thank you for the picture." She lowered her eyes, a shining little Moscow girl again. "It's the nicest thing anyone's done for me in a long time."

"I'm glad you like it."

With grace and accuracy, he moved in on her and left a kiss on her forehead. He was back out of range before she could respond.

"Time to go," he said. "It's late." And he moved toward the door, going quickly and lightly, as though it were a fine, fresh morning.

He waved one last time. The woman stood alone, drawing a cigarette from a rumpled pack as she watched him go.

There was an old leather sofa under the murals Sasha had inflicted on the foyer. The airborne captain, the hero of the evening, sat there with an amused smile, absently nursing his burned hand against the lining of his greatcoat.

"I admire your restraint," he told Sasha.

Suddenly confronted with the garish inconsequence of his work, Sasha was too jarred to get the captain's meaning at once.

"With Natasha," Samsonov went on. "I was frankly surprised."

Sasha smiled pleasantly, inexplicably drawn to the man, yet cautious, not sure what the captain was after. The warning signals came up again. And he noticed that Samsonov was one of those men who were not as handsome up close as from a middle distance. But the strength was still there, commanding even in the lassitude of his posture in this late hour. The strength of the believer. Dangerous.

"I figured an artist wouldn't be the type to pass up . . . a free meal. But I suppose she's not really your type."

Sasha shrugged. "You're a soldier. You know you have to pick your battles."

The captain brushed his jaw over his collar. Sasha could detect no visible trace of the alcohol the man had put down. There was only a smell of cologne gone sour. Samsonov fretted his burned hand on the wool of his uniform, suddenly impatient.

"Listen. I've been waiting for you. I wanted to ask you a question."

"Why I didn't yank down Natasha's knickers?"

Samsonov waved his damaged hand, dismissing the theme. "No. That's your business. Except that you and I are probably the only two male creatures in town who haven't had a run at her." His eyes had a way of cutting through, of asking their own questions even as the voice took a different course.

Sasha could not begin to explain it to himself, but he was glad that this man had waited for him. He imagined now that he had sensed the beginning of a bond when their eyes met earlier in the evening. One of those unexpected convergences between radically different human beings who nonetheless shared a few flakes of the same greater soul.

Dangerous, Sasha thought. Yes. But at least not as damnably dull as everything and everyone else. At least worth talking to on a dead night in Germany.

"So what's the question?" Sasha asked.

"I just can't understand it," Samsonov said earnestly. He flicked his hand up toward the murals. "Why does a man with your talent paint this kind of shit?"

The two men walked. The night air was cold and acidic with the smoke of brown coal. Clusters of people remained in the streets, despite the late hour. Celebrating the opening of the famous Wall. Sasha would have liked more details, but he knew only a few words of German. And he did not think that many Germans would be in the mood to speak Russian on this particular night. It was strange, too, walking with Samsonov. It was as if the Germans could not see the officer, conditioned to look right through the uniform and the foreign flesh inside it. There was no overt hostility, even when the revelers were drunk. Samsonov was simply a ghost, and Sasha became invisible by association.

They crossed over the marketplace. Signs of a rally lay everywhere: discarded placards, scattered handbills, jewels of broken glass. Elsewhere, though, the streets were ruthlessly clean. Very German. Buildings might badly need a coat of paint, but the garbage containers stood at attention along the curbs—the demonstrators had not toppled a single one. How they must despise us, Sasha thought, remembering Moscow, the dirty, half-broken city he loved.

He drew the zipper a bit higher on his jacket then pulled out the vodka bottle that had been bouncing off his hipbone. His fingers were cold.

"Here," he said, offering the bottle to the man in uniform. "You want this? I don't drink."

Samsonov automatically raised his hand to fend off the generosity, but a moment later, a change came over him and he accepted the secondhand gift.

"Your ulcer?"

"No," Sasha said, tired of lying. "I don't have an ulcer. I say that to keep your pals from pouring that swill down my throat."

"You don't like to drink?"

"No."

Samsonov smiled. Amused.

"You're a bad Russian," he told Sasha.

Sasha shrugged. "Half Latvian. On my mother's side."

"And Latvians don't like to drink? The Latvians I know—" The officer checked himself. "Anyway, it's better. Liquor is unhealthy."

"But you drink."

"Yes. I'm a good Russian." Sarcasm. And something more.

"Always drink the way you did tonight?"

"I'd be dead."

"All right, then. Let me ask *you* a question. Why did you come to that sorry bugger's rescue? A fondness for political officers?"

Samsonov smiled. All teeth and shifting muscles and the unmistakable sense of apartness you saw in brokenhearted women.

"Maybe I'm just a compulsive rescuer."

Below the band of his cap the officer's black hair glistened in the light of the streetlamps.

"Tell me," Sasha said. "Is a sense of shame part of being a good Russian?"

Samsonov laughed. "By no means. We're a shameless people."

"Then you're not a very good Russian after all."

"No. I'm a very, very good Russian. A shining example."

"Who can drink all night. And not show the least sign of it."

"There are effects," Samsonov said after a moment. "I really should give it up. Like you." He considered the prospect for a few more paces. Laughably earnest. "It's a bad habit. We pick up so many bad habits. I started drinking when I was stationed out east. There was nothing else to do. I'd read every book I had twice."

"But . . . if you give up drinking . . . you won't be a good Russian anymore."

The captain laughed again. "I'll always be a good Russian."

They entered a showcase street where no automobiles were allowed. It reminded Sasha of the Arbat, only cleaner and newer. With wrought-iron lamps curling overhead and full shop windows. It was difficult even for Sasha to understand why these people were so terribly discontented. Moscow housewives would have fainted at the sight of such abundance.

Samsonov would not come too close to the displays of consumer goods. As though he feared infection.

"Amazing, isn't it?" he asked from behind Sasha's shoulder. "You'd think they'd won the war." His voice was sad, and old. A man who had watched one of his children go wrong. "They have no spiritual values." Then the words began to pour out, as though he had been waiting a long time for someone to whom he could talk. "Cleanliness alone isn't civilization. These Germans . . . I find them educated, but uncultured. Obsessed by material things. Perhaps because they have so much. I think . . . that possessions must be addictive."

"You don't have any possessions?"

"Only my books," the captain said. "And they don't count. But I'm not the issue. It's these Germans. They have so *much.* And they cry for more. The best of them don't have the soul of a Russian girl from the countryside."

Sasha began to recognize the speech from a lifetime of similar encounters. Whenever a Russian found himself trumped by the great world beyond his borders, he invoked the superiority of the Russian soul and its capacity for suffering, making a national glory of fecklessness.

"Listen," Sasha said, "I was in Leipzig. I *saw* them and

heard them. Tens of thousands of them, filling the boulevard in front of the train station. And there was more to it than the dream of a new refrigerator."

Samsonov alerted. "You were in Leipzig? I've heard it's really bad."

"Bad? No." Sasha decided to trust his companion, despising himself all the while for his foolishness, his *Russianness,* in doing so. "It wasn't bad. It was . . . inspiring."

The two men paused to look in the window of a beauty salon displaying glossy oversize photos of models in extreme Western hairstyles. Frozen by a lens, a little tart licked her lips at her admirers.

"I saw it coming," Samsonov said, stepping away. His voice was slow and sad, as though all of this was very personal. "You could feel it without even trying. But we locked ourselves in our barracks. We shut the drapes, bolted the doors, plugged up our ears." He brushed Sasha's sleeve with a sweep of his hand that went a bit out of control. "You saw how it was tonight. You saw the general's face when he heard about the Wall. The poor bastard. And he's one of the best of them. He really believed that all we had to do was to drink ourselves sick in order to make time stand still." He kicked a frozen rag across the pavement. A cat shadowed around a corner.

"So . . . what are you saying? That we should send in the tanks?"

The captain thrust his hands down into the pockets of his greatcoat. Made of high-grade wool, it was cut to fit him beautifully, with broad epauletted shoulders and a tight waist. *Exact,* Sasha thought. He looks so *exact.*

"No. Of course not," Samsonov said. "Absolutely not. I know that's not a solution. I'm not a fool." He looked down at the pavement just beyond his stride. "The truth is that I don't know what we could have done differently. I just feel that . . . we've gotten it all terribly wrong, somehow." He straightened suddenly, brightening. "Come on. Let's go up this way. I'll show you something interesting."

They turned into a street that was not on official display and therefore had not been polished and painted. It reminded Sasha of the small cities of the western Ukraine, with their best years almost a century behind them. The world was so much of a piece.

The two men stepped out into the street to get around a mound of brown coal briquettes that had been dumped against the side of a building. It was cold enough for their shoes to leave trails in the frost on the pavement.

"Tell me, Mikhail Nikolaievich—"

"Misha, please."

"Tell me, Misha. What is it exactly that you *do* believe in? Since you don't believe in sending in the tanks."

The captain replied very quickly, almost as if the response had been drilled into him:

"In Russia. In the future of Russia."

"Not the Soviet Union?"

Samsonov looked ahead, into the distance. "I believe in the future of Russia."

Sasha pulled in his shoulders, trying to coax a bit more warmth from his jacket. "These days," he said, "when somebody tells me he believes in the future of Russia, he usually means he believes in the past."

"I believe in the future," the captain said obstinately. "In a better future."

"And . . . what form does the future take?"

Turning his face to Sasha, Samsonov smiled. "I don't know. I'm still thinking it through."

"Well," Sasha said, grinning in response, "a man of faith." But he was thinking seriously: I was right. I had him pegged from the first. Only purity and innocence could be so dangerous. Samsonov was the kind of dreamer with whom cynics made revolutions, then discarded.

"Don't mock me too much," the captain said with mixed humor and great earnestness. "Faith is very important. You know, I think there are times . . . when a man must simply have faith."

"In what? In God?"

This time the priest-captain took more time before replying. Their footsteps tapped along the freezing cement.

"Once," Samsonov began, "the notion would have made me laugh. But now . . . I don't think it matters so much what a man believes in. As long as he has faith." No trace of humor remained in his voice. "Sometimes . . . I think that faith is everything. Don't you have any kind of faith?"

Sasha rolled his head to the side as if he had taken an

invisible blow. "I suppose you're a member of Pamyat? That you figure everything would be just grand if only we could dig up the czar and kick out the last half dozen Jews?"

Sasha thought of Rachel Traum, her heart full of visions and dreams even more naive than those of this airborne captain, an inexhaustibly generous soul caged in a hopelessly inadequate body. And Sasha thought of Lev Birman, with his big, saintly love of art and his little talent, always painting and apologizing.

"I have nothing against the Jews," Samsonov said quietly. "I've grown out of that kind of nonsense."

"You didn't answer my question. Are you a member of Pamyat?"

"No. I know people in it. But I can't accept their platform. It's too silly. Anyway, it's technically forbidden for officers to join."

"But many do."

Samsonov shrugged. "Perhaps I'm timid. But I always went by the rules."

Sasha could not let it go. "But those assholes have your sympathies. Be honest."

Samsonov remained calm, as though the subject was not really of much importance. "They're not all fools. And they're not all bad men. Anyway, who are we to say that all of their answers are wrong? They're just stumbling around in the darkness like the rest of us. At least they have faith in something."

"Still a Party member?"

Samsonov laughed. "Yes."

"Covering all your bets?"

"Oh, I'm not *that* cynical. Everyone had to belong. And some of the things—at least the words—are still good. The problem isn't with the words, it's with the way human beings applied them."

"So . . . you're sympathetic to Pamyat *and* to the Party. I'm impressed with your breadth."

The captain dismissed the sarcasm. "I know the Party's dead. But to be frank, I've hung on because I thought it might help me stay in the military. Fighting one bureaucracy with another. Perhaps that was cynical. But . . . there's nothing I wouldn't have done."

They turned into a street where all of the houses had been freshly restored. Row houses faced in brick lifted stepped gables into the sky. The early-morning emptiness made it feel as though the world had gone hollow.

"This is the Holland quarter," Samsonov said, relaxing into the role of tour guide. "Dutch artisans came here at the invitation of the Prussian kings and they built these houses for themselves. As a reminder of home."

And what memorials will we leave behind? Sasha wondered. But he said nothing. He felt that both of them had been glad to turn the conversation at least briefly toward an easier theme.

Damn it, we're so Russian, Sasha thought. We'll talk away the night and be useless for anything tomorrow.

"The Germans have only cleaned up this one street," Samsonov went on. "The rest of it's a ruin."

It was definitely time to go back to Moscow, Sasha thought. Sleep. With Vera. Or with somebody a bit livelier. Pet the cat. Fuck some more. Until you fucked the stupid politics out of your brain. Screw away the world. Then paint.

Sasha blew out a long frosty breath.

"Cold?" Samsonov had drawn out a pack of cigarettes. Spikes of harsh tobacco. Soviet wares with a little Cossack horseman on the wrapper.

"A little. I'll survive."

"Cigarette?"

"I don't smoke."

"Even when the cigarettes are free? You really *are* a bad Russian."

"Half Latvian," Sasha repeated.

The captain stuck a cigarette between his lips and hunched to light it. "I admire you, really." Bouncing the cigarette on his lips. "You don't smoke, don't drink. You're clear-eyed and fit. A man without vices."

Sasha laughed. "I have my vices."

They walked again, working through the heavy tiredness to the stage of physical vacancy where a man could go on for a very long time, motor skills diminished, mind rich and acute. The captain led the way down an empty boulevard guarded by high yellow lights.

"All those ribbons," Sasha said. "Afghanistan?"

"They gave them out by the handful."

"No, they didn't. Not all of them."

"Ribbons mean nothing."

For the first time, Sasha sensed dishonesty in the man's voice. He knew the type. The ribbons meant a great deal to this man, although he would never have pursued them. If earned, he would cherish them until the day he died, like the old war veterans hobbling through the streets of Moscow with their faded accomplishments pinned to their faded lapels.

"How long were you there?"

After a few paces, Samsonov said:

"Three years."

"You volunteered to go back?"

"I stayed. Until the end. Except for a little break in a Samarkand hospital."

A cat charged across a vacant lot, stretching to its full length as it sprang over a mound of rubble. Sasha could never see a cat without thinking of his own animal. Vrubel, the furred art critic. Snoring under the easel. Vera would be taking good care of him, she was that kind of girl. Possessed of the overwhelming desire to serve. Not like the last cunt, who had thrown parties in his apartment and locked the cat out on the balcony with its piles of shit and no food.

Sasha laughed. It had occurred to him that Vera would be a splendid match for this earnest, decorously haunted captain. She had faith in the Church, and Samsonov had faith in Russia. Between them they could save the world. Why were virtuous women so dull?

"It didn't really affect me," Samsonov said abruptly. His words chimed through the frozen air. "I'm not like some of the others. Afghanistan didn't leave any deep scars. So don't imagine that I'm one of those veterans who parades around expecting to be pitied. I did my job, and that was that."

The voice of a talking mannequin, Sasha thought. The sincerity, the openness, was utterly absent.

"And you," Samsonov continued. "You still owe me an answer. You have so much talent. It's evident. Why are you painting such crap?"

"My paintings glorify the motherland."

"Don't shake me off."

"It's a job."

"But you don't believe in any of it. You hate it. I watched you painting. You know how you look when you're painting? Like a man washing windows."

"I'm not like you, Misha. I'm not a believer."

Now *he* was lying. He believed in his painting. In his real painting that was the only thing left that had the power to get him out of bed in the morning. But you could never explain something like that to another human being.

They came to a broad intersection. Off at an angle, the tall hard-currency hotel dominated the cityscape.

"You're embarrassed by what they make you paint," Samsonov went on. "You despise yourself. But you keep on doing it. That's prostitution."

"Arrest me."

But the captain was nakedly sincere. What kind of country did he imagine he served? What kind of a world did he think he was living in? The Soviet Union was a great big bag of shit wrapped in a see-through myth, and you accepted it and got on with your life. It struck Sasha that this man's brand of incorruptible, pigheaded, blind idealism was exactly what had gotten them all into such a mess in the first place. The old Bolsheviks who went to their executions still believing that Stalin was Father Frost.

"I paint what they want," Sasha said, annoyed. "And I get to travel. I've been here half a dozen times. I've been to Hungary, to Poland. I've even been to Damascus. And I've got my own apartment out in Textilshchiki where I can paint whatever I want on my own time. And all my friends who turn up their noses at what I do spend most of their time trying to figure out how to survive and the rest of their time pitying themselves and each other, and all they paint is shit, anyway. Great theories, lousy art. And they come to me when they need decent-quality canvas, and if they're lucky, maybe they sell something to some Westerner who wants to buy 'Soviet art' the way somebody else wants to buy a toy balalaika. Would that suit you better?" Sasha shook his head in wonder at the other man's chastity of spirit. He suspected that Samsonov had never taken advantage of a single unearned benefit in his life—and that he had passed up most that were his due. "Wake up, Misha. We live in a world where only a fool refuses to paint the general's wife."

They had come to a bridge over a black river. The water threw off a special cold that came up into your face and worked its way through the concrete and leather into the soles of your feet.

"You know," Samsonov said quietly, "the air is very bad here in the summer. It's bad now, with the brown coal. You can smell the sulfur. But in the summer, with the heat, it's poison. You have to take it easy on the soldiers." He looked down into the oily water.

"What river is this?" Sasha asked.

"The Havel. A branch of it. Can I see them?"

Sasha looked up from the black, swirling water without understanding.

"Your pictures," Samsonov said. "The real ones. I'd like to see them."

Sasha shrugged. "If you're ever in Moscow . . ."

"Give me your address. Please. I'll be in Moscow after the New Year. After they muster me out, I'll be going to work for the Interior Ministry. With the internal troops. There's a transition course I have to take in Moscow." The captain looked away. "I'm going to learn how to be a glorified policeman."

With stiff fingers, Sasha drew a small card from his wallet. He had plenty of the cards, printed up by the Artists' Union to impress the generals. It was, apparently, the way things were done in the West, and the Artists' Union wanted to help him. Really, the officials were wonderfully helpful. As long as it was to their benefit to be helpful. They were so happy that Sasha made the generals happy, who, in turn, made the Ministry of Culture officials happy, that they were willing to do anything for him. Except organize a formal exhibition of his serious works.

After watching the success of fools with Western gallery owners and auction houses, Sasha had renewed his pleas at least to have his work shown as part of a multiartist showcase. But just before his departure on this last trip, an exasperated bureaucrat had told him, frankly and secretly, that he would never have his own exhibit. And he would never be part of a group show. The men at the top of the Artists' Union did not want his energies diverted from his military painting. His work was simply too important for smooth relations between ministries. It was a sacrifice for the good of the collective.

"We all have to make sacrifices for the good of the collective," Sasha told the captain, employing the official tone that every Soviet child came to know as well as the voice of its mother or father. Then he softened. "Honestly. You're welcome to drop by. If you ever have time."

I'm like a goddamned woman, Sasha thought. All you have to do is show a serious interest and I'm flat on my back. Please come look at my pictures. Even if you're some poor mixed-up bastard who's just lost his job and wants to save Mother Russia. Admire me. Praise me. And I'll be yours forever.

Anyway, he did not really believe the captain would show up. All of this was so Russian: a late-night conversation after a party, the sudden, sloppy intimacy born of the loneliness of liquor. The Russian talking disease. Promises to be expunged from the memory with only the faintest trace of guilt. An entire nation talking and talking and talking and doing nothing.

Talk was the opium of the Russian people. Liquor was only the match that lit the pipe.

Sasha suddenly longed to sleep. His last energy had evaporated, and it amazed and irritated him a little how wide-awake, almost electric, Samsonov's eyes remained. Strange bird, Sasha thought.

Under an arcade of bare trees, the ground-floor lights still burned brightly in the commandant's office. Sasha imagined the shaken officers sending messages to everyone they could think of, begging for information, for guidance, and hoping with all their hearts that the early bulletins from Berlin had been a mistake or a hoax. A shivering sentry gave Samsonov a perfunctory salute.

"I won't really be a policeman," Samsonov said. "It's not a militia assignment. The Interior Ministry has regular formations, organized along the same lines as the army."

"I know. I've worked for them, too."

Samsonov turned his head quickly. The eyes under the visor of his cap were more alive than anything else in this town at this hour.

"You've worked for them? How are they?"

Sasha was too tired to beautify the general's wife now. He

grimaced. "Scum of the earth," he said. "If that isn't too generous. Stupid little thugs. Convicts in uniform."

"It can't be that bad."

The poor bastard, Sasha thought. His new friend had the earnestness of a good child. Well, farewell to the gleaming boots and glory.

If he doesn't find a worthless cause to help him throw away his life, Sasha told himself, he'll find a worthless woman.

"Wait and see for yourself."

Samsonov brooded for a few paces, then said:

"I hear they're trying to clean them up, though. Bringing in former regular officers and the like."

"You'll have your work cut out for you. From what I saw, the officers are just happy when their men aren't selling off their weapons on the black market."

"It can't be that bad," Samsonov said with determination.

They approached the officers' club again. Time for good-bye.

A shadowy movement caught Sasha's eye. Behind the statue of Lenin, with its base smeared dark. He felt Samsonov tense beside him. Ready.

It was a man. Drunk. German. Grinning like a fool. He stood swaying and pissing on the dead flowers at Lenin's feet, surging now and then to hit the great revolutionary's shoes.

Sasha half expected Samsonov to lunge forward and collar the man. But the captain simply stood flat-footed on the sidewalk.

Shocked, Sasha figured.

Belatedly, the drunk saw them. His grin didn't falter in the least. He simply turned a little toward the interlopers, happily spraying the frozen grass. Then he began to speak, in alcohol-soaked German, waving his little white flag in the direction of the two Russians.

"What's he saying?" Samsonov asked. "Can you make it out?"

"My German's not very good," Sasha said, "but I think he's saying something about the piss of a lifetime."

3

SAMSONOV MARCHED ALONE. NOT A SINGLE LAMP burned in the spoiled mansions of Potsdam. Protests, celebrations, the washing of dishes, and the rub of mortal love . . . all of it was done. He imagined the Germans close under their bedding. Then he heard, in perfect memory, the sounds of his soldiers sleeping in the barracks bays—the snoring and the rustling of blankets stiff as bark, the sudden cry of a dreaming boy. The barracks always smelled of sweat and ammonia, while here the air reeked of sulfur. But a sleeping man was a good man, no matter the language he spoke upon waking. Samsonov always felt an aimless affection for humanity in these early-morning hours, thinking how innocent men and women could be with their ambitions shut off, doing no one harm, warm, careless, adrift.

But surely that was an illusion. Surely there were other men, or women, who were painfully awake in this town, afraid to shut their eyes. Surely he was not alone.

He tried to shape his burned hand so that it would be less painful and nudged the bottle of vodka the artist had given him. Later, he told himself. Can't open it yet. Must be patient. Then drink it down hard.

He was one of those human beings who feel far more deeply than they can ever express to another. Thus it was a terrible sin to him that the artist so misused his talent. Samsonov had been cursed with the ability to experience profoundly while being denied the gift of diverting his soul into paint or music or words arranged on paper. He could only wander down foreign streets with an inarticulate sense of the world's cares, of men haunted by a difficult past or uncertain future, of women trapped in dead loves, and of children frightened, frightened, frightened.

He had been a weak boy, dropped from his mother's lap into the roughneck eternity of Siberia. His sickliness had been aggravated by a mother who held him close, close, close, unwilling to lose him the way she had lost her man, a military transient. The first great challenge of Samsonov's life had been to break away from all that love, from the ceaseless avalanche of selfish affection, and to force his reluctant body to obey him. He tormented himself with physical trials, aching to strengthen himself until he could hold his own with the other boys, until he could walk down the street without fear of swooping bullies. He exercised in light clothing in the colossal winter, wanting to become strong with a kind of total strength for which no one had a word. And when his body could endure no more, he hid himself from the world and his mother's infuriating pity by reading. Books were such wonderful friends. They made it clear that he was not alone, that others had felt and were feeling the things he felt. And then, one day at school, the sports hour was dedicated to wrestling. He found, to his astonishment, that he had grown stronger than any of them, that no one could throw him and hold him down. Preoccupied with the details of a body he perceived as deficient and weak, he had not noticed the total change. It was a revelation from above the clouds, cut short only when one of the other students took advantage of the instructor's turned back to kick Samsonov in the crotch, then slam him to the mat and pile on top of him with the comment:

"You might be strong, fuckhead. But you don't know shit."

His mother died. And his long-absent father reappeared in a colonel's uniform and did the sole good deed of his life for the boy, securing him a place in one of the Suvorov military preparatory schools. Samsonov, unlike the other cadets, who wept for home and cursed the stringency, found the environment satisfying, the studies almost a joy. When his teachers spoke of the ideals of service, his heart swelled. Yes. He would be a protector of the weak, of the downtrodden. Against enemies dark and dangerous. There was no higher calling. He dreamed of sacrificing his life, with countless heroic variations. He was going to be an *officer,* and he would always do his duty, take care of his men, and make good decisions.

The veteran sighed in the raw cold of Germany.

It was time to find a new dream. His burned hand twinged and he thought again of the artist, whose work was so much better than it should have been, whose words were so much more cynical than his eyes. Why was everyone so afraid?

He marched along the chapped facades of the old royal and imperial buildings, thinking peevishly that the Germans had lost all of their ideals of service. His path still led him away from the barracks and his bed. A man could do with very little sleep, really. Until he grew so weary that the sleep that came over him was a metal oblivion immune to dreams. His heavy feet followed an incline. He could feel the old palace waiting for him, low and long above the many terraces, patrolled by a single ghost. But he did not choose the winding street that would have taken him to the gate where grenadiers and carriages had passed. Instead, he turned down along the perimeter of the great park, footsteps tapping out code in a frozen world. Back where the shrubbery had been allowed to run wild and the tourists did not go, a broken gate hung rusted and forgotten. Only the occasional pair of lovers went that way, and then only in warmer weather. Samsonov had passed them by in the darkness before the season turned, going silently, not wanting to intrude yet wounded by their small glowing cries.

Leaves and dried brush crackled powerfully underfoot, marks of a different month. There were ghosts in the trees, hanging from the shaved limbs. His ghosts, other ghosts. In Siberia, there were many different spirits, some from the lakes and rivers, others from the boundless forests, still others that caught fire from the stars and tumbled burning from the sky.

Far from any light, Samsonov instinctively skirted the rococo horrors of the teahouse, the devil faces flecked with gold. He came out onto the main path and followed it under a deep gloom of trees until it opened into the garden at the bottom of the terraces. The perfect, impractical palace stood above him, hundreds of stairs away.

Sans Souci. Without care. An impossible dream.

If there was a watchman, Samsonov never encountered him. But then he never went too close to the palace itself. He always needed a little distance. It was good to sit at the foot of the stairs, alone with the sky. It was the best sky he could find here, where the air was haunted by coal smoke and chemicals. He had loved the sky in Afghanistan. He had hated almost everything else. But he had loved the endless, brilliant sky.

Beyond a palisade of trees the small city glimmered. Frederick had been no friend of the Russian people, fighting them hard and writing of them viciously. But the old king had been a soldier, and that bound men together, despite everything else. Anyway, the old Prussian's ghost was the only company left at this hour of the morning.

Samsonov drew out the bottle of vodka, tore off the cap, and raised a silent toast. Then he drank so hard that it hurt the muscles in his throat.

He sat down hard at the foot of the grand staircase. It must have been impressive, he decided. When Old Fritz brought home his victorious armies, with the dead buried and the crippled hidden away. Fife and drum and the shock of boots on cobblestones. Sabers and sharp commands. God, being a soldier could be such a wonderful thing. It made no sense, and you could never explain it to someone who did not feel it themselves. But there was something so addictively beautiful about it. Even when it terrified you and you hated yourself for your folly and swore that, if you lived, you would leave the army forever, even then a side of you loved it, and you soon forgot your promises, remembering only the thrill of being more alive than any other man could ever be. You even loved it when it broke your heart.

He thought of the day earlier in the year when the last official combat units had come out of Afghanistan, with General Gromov crossing the Termez bridge under a cold sun, so handsome and dignified that you didn't notice how small he really was, a hero posing for the cameras, assuring them that everything was in order, while behind the reporters' backs the raggle-taggle border town squirmed with relatives desperate for the sight of a son, with young soldiers mustered out on the spot, foodless and confused, with beggars and thieves. The shabby hotel was overfilled, and the street vendors charged astronomical sums for stringy bits of shashlik. Spread over a twenty-kilometer fan to the north, the bivouac sites of the returned units broke down into carnivals as traders and whores materialized out of the sand, selling everything from videocassettes to hashish. There weren't enough rations, the water was bad, and waste covered the ground where units expecting to remain only a few hours had been careless, only to find themselves sulking without orders for a week, waiting for the trains to come with the flatcars for the tanks and infantry fighting vehicles, waiting for mustering-out papers, for inspections, for the end of the world.

In Termez itself nothing was safe. If it could be stolen, eaten, or fucked, it had to be guarded with live ammunition. The brass toasted one another with ice-cold vodka, red-scarved children adorned returning vehicles with carnations, and women who had made long, impossible journeys from Tula or Smolensk wept at the inexplicable absence of their husbands. Nobody cared. You were as apt to find your orders blowing down the dusty streets as on the desk of the temporary commandant. The foreign press was hustled in for Gromov's crossing, for his embrace of his son in the middle of the bridge, then they were whisked away before the stench of dysentery from the campsites could hit their refined nostrils.

The whole business was an unspeakable chaos, with entire units simply disbanded on the spot. It was the end of the great Fortieth Army, which could have provided a backbone of officers and warrants with combat experience for the Soviet military. But this was a war everyone just wanted to forget, and the bureaucrats took control and drummed as many veterans as possible out of the service because it was easier, quicker, and cheaper to make the required reductions that way. Samsonov remembered one boy, his tunic bedecked with medals that he could only have won in half a dozen brutal combat actions, sitting in front of the train station and crying like a baby because the ticket he had been issued to go home was no good. And he remembered a battalion commander skimming off commissions from the hustlers and prostitutes working his unit. Samsonov had only been able to feed his company by forcibly diverting rations headed for another unit. And they had been lucky. As airborne troops, they had been spared the instant dismissals. They had been deemed too precious to throw away. Until now.

He had become a statistic, a nameless integer in a quota filled by distant men taught over generations to revere quantitative factors above all else.

Samsonov took another hard drink of vodka. Ass on the cold German concrete, soul back in the dust of Central Asia.

Boris Gromov, who had been the best of the lot of generals, had slept safely on the Soviet side of the Amu Darya the night before his famous crossing. A helicopter had lifted him back to the Afghan side for the public ceremony. He dismounted from his troop carrier on that bridge and opened his arms to his teenaged son, symbolizing this homecoming for the entire nation, for the world, while a hundred meters away his soldiers took turns with a festering whore in the back of a field ambulance.

Afghanistan. What would Frederick have made of such a war? Frederick, who entertained captured officers at his own table, trading compliments. What would he have made of the castrated corpses and poisoned valleys? Old Fritz had been a ruthless bastard. But had he ever seen a comrade—still alive and conscious—whose skin had been peeled from his body? Had he ever seen steel birds full of men tumbling from the sky, spilling living bodies as they fell? Perhaps he had seen worse in the slaughters at Kunersdorf or Hochkirch. Surely every war had its own horrors. But Samsonov could not help feeling that Afghanistan had been something special, something terribly beyond the bounds of European experience.

Samsonov did not want to hate anyone. But hatred had taken over him like a wasting sickness. Hatred growled inarticulately in his soul, vexing his reason. Afghanistan had done that. One of his lieutenants had lost both eyes to gonococcal conjunctivitis picked up down around Tarin Kowt. But Samsonov's illness merely clouded his vision. He knew, objectively, that it was all wrong. But the sight of any of the brown-skinned men of Central Asia—Afghans, Persians, even his Soviet countrymen—made him go instantly cold and very compact inside. The way he had begun to feel on the edge of combat, after he had seen a lot of death. In the final stages of the war his company had taken very few prisoners. Facing the Dushmani with their rags and rifles, Samsonov had seen only the hacked corpses of his fellow officers, heard the screams of a young soldier blown legless by a mine. After the first few times, killing men became the easiest thing imaginable. By the final days he had not even been able to walk through the bazaars. He was much too volatile. Ready to snap a man's neck over an accidental brushing of elbows. And when he saw Soviet soldiers in those stinking alleys, furtively trading military goods for drugs or pocket-size radios, he wanted to kill them, too. It was *his* kind against the other kind, and there was no middle ground. And now, so far away, the disease was slowly worsening, deepening, no matter how hard he fought against it. This illness would not respond to the medicine of reason. He had hated the war. But now he was sorry it was over.

The war was over. And all of the dead were for nothing. All of it had been for nothing. He would not even be a proper officer anymore. He finished the vodka and put the bottle tidily back into his pocket. He could feel the alcohol working on him at last. It took so much. If he was lucky, he would doze off heavily, dreamlessly, until the sounds of the city coming to life woke him. Then there would be time to hurry back to the officers' billets and shave. And then there would be duties to occupy his mind, the final duties of the final days. The night wrapped its frozen arms around his shoulders. It was still black, but Samsonov had spent many nights under the sky, and he could feel the beginning of the slow climb back up out of the depths, the new day rising with an old man's slowness toward the first gray light. A small animal skittered over the frosted grass and Samsonov gathered his greatcoat in over his chest, regretting his burned hand. He would need to see a doctor.

There was never enough vodka.

He remembered how they had come in by helicopter, a stripped-down company of airborne soldiers wrenched from their protective armored machines and lifted over mountains of such beauty it jarred the soul. The plan called for them to land and establish a patrol base on a plateau between snow-capped peaks and the juncture of two river valleys where suspected rebel infiltration routes came together. An old stone fort dominated the elevation. The fort was a patchwork affair, demolished and rebuilt by dozens of armies—Greek, Persian, Afghan, Mongol, Mogul, Sikh, and the evanescent might of nameless tribes who had not left behind so much as a chip of beaten gold for the scholars who might have granted them immortality. Samsonov, who had read his history, imagined erect British officers parading before their shivering brown soldiers of the line whenever duty took him to one of the thousands of such *kowts* pocking the landscape of Afghanistan. In a way, they were all the same—ghostly, windy, unhappy places, with excellent observation and field of fire. Practical. And morbidly romantic.

The rebels held their fire and let the paratroopers land. Nobody, not even Samsonov, who was by then very experienced, noticed a thing until all of his men were on the ground and the nearby saddles and opposing slopes erupted with fire. The rebels had behaved with startling discipline, not loosing their American-made antiaircraft missiles at the helicopters until the aircraft were on the way out, struggling desperately to gain altitude. The missiles quickly knocked two of the birds down into the sheer valleys, announcing to the landing party that they were trapped.

Samsonov's company held on for five days, under constant shelling and sniping, their perimeter punctured again and again by gruesome night assaults. The wounded bled to death for lack of attention or screamed in pain or raved in the delirium of infection. The air force supported as best they could with fixed-wing fighter bombers. But the aircraft had to fly very high because of the missiles and they rarely hit their targets. The Dushmani responded with mortars and rockets, identifiable by pitch as Soviet in origin, looted from army stocks or purchased from rear-echelon soldiers on the Kabul black market. The nights were cold, the days hot and sandpaper dry, and despite brutal discipline and rationing, everything eventually ran out—food, bandages, water, bullets. For the first time, Samsonov saw men go mad from thirst, while others, hardened, drank their own dwindling piss back out of their canteens. Samsonov himself had wounds in the right buttock and thigh, and the last time he tried to reset a bandage he found his leg ricey with maggots. But it was as though he were looking at a queer clinical example from a distance, as though it were someone else's body hanging out of his torn-off trouser leg, and he matter-of-factly replaced the bandage, telling himself that the maggots were probably saving the leg by eating out the rot. Then he laughed with a dried-out gasp, realizing that it did not in fact matter whether the maggots saved his leg or not.

He took a last roll call, crawling from position to position, and found that his company had dwindled to an undersized platoon, with not a single man unwounded. A little later the hallucinations began. Giants came stalking up the hillside toward the battered fort. The sky was overprinted with indecipherable texts. And there was singing that stopped as soon as you really tried to listen. There was nothing left but madness and a very bad death. The air force had already lost three more helicopters trying to relieve the position and there was nothing left to do. In his lucid moments, Samsonov could feel the rebels preparing for a final assault. And he knew what they would do with any wounded paratroopers they captured.

He crawled into the trench where they had shielded the last functioning radio with corpses for want of sandbags. It took all of his strength of will to enter the hacked-out ditch. He had no reservations about what he intended to do. But the mind was never totally inured to horror, and the last time he had belly-crawled down into the nest of corpses he had created just enough of a disturbance to bring a snake slithering out of a dead sergeant's mouth.

He switched on the radio set, hoping the battery still had some life in it, and eye to eye with a decomposing boy from the Ukraine he begged the distant authorities to send the fighter-bombers back to inundate his own position. As he spoke, he visualized the officers back in the rear, crisp uniforms and clear eyes, drinking tea and debating the admissibility of such a course of action.

A radio voice answered him. But it was very weak. And Samsonov could not even be certain that his own words made sense. Everything was so difficult now. So unclear. He could not get at the reality of the tiny metal voice. Automatically, he clicked off the radio, conserving the battery, as though he might need to use it a hundred more times, on a dozen more missions, and just as automatically, he crawled back to his fighting trench and hunkered down to save himself from the bombs he had just summoned to kill him and the rest of his men.

The specificity of memory was an astonishing thing, and no act of will could blot it out. Samsonov clearly remembered hearing the sky tear open as the jets came in, and he was clearheaded enough to think that the pilots were very brave because they were coming in low, despite the missiles. The light was failing and the jets shot down through valleys already deep in shadow, taking unjustifiable risks for the sake of the doomed men on the ground. Samsonov buried his helmeted head under his forearms, crying and thinking how sorry he was to leave a world in which there were such brave, good men. How unreasonable it was to be lying in a ditch so far from anything that mattered. It was all so senseless after all.

The explosions climbed the hillside, coming for him, and he began to shake. His legs twitched. Or perhaps it was the earth shaking beneath him. The mountains were shaking themselves apart. They were all going to tumble down into the valley, tumbling forever. Why did any man ever want to be a soldier? Someone screamed. *He* was screaming. Or was it only a voice in his ears? He floated above the earth.

The bombs came down on top of his position. He felt heavy blows on his back and he could not breathe. He wanted to live so badly. He buried himself a millimeter deeper in the trench, thinking, *Damn you, damn you all.*

Something broke inside his skull. His nose felt warm, burning. It was raining and he licked the wetness from his lips. Warm rain. Someone laid a heavy blanket over his legs and he could not move them. It was either impossibly loud or silent, he couldn't tell. I'm dying now, he thought. This is dying. But he continued to clutch his helmet to his head. Something raised him off the ground and smashed him back down. Then everybody he ever knew piled on top of him as though this were all nothing but a rough game. He choked. The breathing was the hardest part. The air had gone away and there was only hot dust. The earth quivered underneath him like a woman in orgasm. *Kill me,* he told the bombs, *kill me, you bastards.* He did not want to be buried alive. He began to twist and tear and turn, unsure if he was actually moving at all or only dreaming. He imagined that he was rising to greet the bombs. But that much was only a dream. A dream in which you watched yourself. He was still flat down upon the earth, swallowing fumes, and it occurred to him that, in the end, no way of dying was any good.

"I'm sorry," he cried. "I'm so sorry. I'm sorry." There was no specificity to it. Only a beaten child at a mother's feet.

A very near miss knocked him unconscious.

His own choking and gagging woke him. It was day again. Hot. His mouth was impossibly dry and his lips felt very close over his teeth, as though the cheeks had grown into the gums. Then he saw the sky.

He had never really seen the color blue before. This sky was so empty and blue that he thought for a moment that this was eternity, nothing but a deep, still blueness. It was so beautiful that he was ready to accept it, to embrace it, to rise and take the empty air in his arms. Then he saw the skull.

Jawless, it had perched against his cheek like a snuggling lover. He yanked his face away, but the blanket of earth held him for a long moment before he could claw and twist his way free. He sat up and found himself piled over with dry brown bones. He was in the middle of a deep hole, surrounded by long yellow femurs, jagged rib cages, scraps of fingers, and loose bone chips withered to the consistency of a cracker, with skulls everywhere. Scraps of old leather and bits of faded cloth clung to some of the remains. It made him think of an icon he had seen in Pskov. The Day of Judgment. With the dead rising from their graves.

He launched himself up out of the pit, going dizzy with the intensity of his effort, trying to reach the clean blue sky without giving an instant's thought to the possible presence of the enemy.

The last walls of the fort had been blasted down to the foundations. History erased. Amid the litter of gray and ocher rock, the bodies of his men lay, some barely distinguishable as human, others amazingly intact in death. Everywhere, the abundant old bones lay interspersed with the fort's most recent victims.

He hobbled among the ruins, weaponless, head throbbing, weirdly numb to the other pains in his body. Aching to find someone else alive. But everyone and everything was dead. The carrion birds had not yet begun to circle, perhaps put off by the reek of so much high explosive. Everything in this world was dead. Except him.

Then the helicopters came. Flying in perfect echelon. Unafraid. The plateau and the surrounding valleys had literally been bombed to death. The first snub-nosed aircraft hovered and turned, looking for a spot where its landing gear wouldn't snag. Finally, it settled in where the bastion of the fort had stood. Samsonov sat down on a stone, watching himself sit down from the remove that always seemed to be with him now, and he observed the little tan figures dropping from the bay doors of the aircraft without any special interest.

"My God," a distantly familiar voice called. "It's Misha. He's *alive*."

Then other helicopters landed and there were officers and men all around him, while still more of them searched the devastation for additional survivors. A lieutenant vomited noisily, while two veteran officers argued about the old bones as they picked up souvenir brass buttons. It was obvious that the mass grave unearthed by the bombardment had been British, a relic of some campaign in the last century, but the officers could not agree on the likely circumstances of death until the medical officer looked up from examining Samsonov and settled it. The dead men, he pronounced, were victims of some local epidemic, probably cholera, since battle casualties either would have been buried in separate graves or would not have been buried at all. He scrubbed at the blood on Samsonov's forehead with an alcohol swab and muttered:

"I'll bet those poor bastards didn't know what the fuck they were doing here, either."

4

THREE DANCING MEN HELD THEIR ARMS ALOFT, CIRCLING a gold-toothed woman, while a band of dark-haired, dark-eyed musicians clanged through the arabesques of cigarette smoke that filled the restaurant, their smallish amplifiers turned up so that every speaker distorted. Arms extended, clutching invisible braces to keep from swooning, the woman turned, slowly and rhythmically, slowly, slowly, hard eyes half-closed as she considered the strutting, pleading gestures of the males. Perspiration fixed her black hair to her temples. Her fingers let go of the imaginary props and began to snake. The broader, wilder movements of her partners appeared juvenile against her intensity. Her lips shut as she felt something stir within her. Perhaps thirty, what her body had lost in sleekness it had gained in depth of feminine power. With each slight twist of her torso she threatened to rob any male who came too close of his strength, his reason. Her cheeks sucked in with a silent gasp and she began to roll her head from side to side. The Asian scales and rhythms strained for volume, weight. But the woman had transcended them. The men smacked their heels on the floor, slapped their thighs, preened their chins back over their shoulders, alley cats attempting to seduce a lioness.

People's Deputy Ali Talala thought of Ashi as he watched

the show put on by his homesick fellow Uzbeks in the Moscow restaurant. His beloved bore no physical resemblance to this dancing woman. Ashi was as delicate as the stem of a flower, as the petals. And she could barely walk, let alone dance. Yet Talala recognized the same inner intensity, the hunger, the desperate, half-buried explosiveness of a feminine being that shocked unprepared men into incapability—the wife who could not be quenched but only forcibly contained. When such a woman joined the right man, the two could fashion a mortal ecstasy so sublime it verged on blasphemy. But such women rarely found the right man because so few men possessed both the necessary courage and the strength for them, and their lives usually collapsed into social ruin, brute violence, and sometimes death. He had rescued Ashi from all that. Ashi, his beloved, limping by the fountain, rehearsing poetry for his arrival. He longed to return to Tashkent, to sit bundled where they might anticipate next year's roses and to listen to her sing, delaying the first real embrace until they were both half-mad. Ashi, his great love, the jewel of his middle years, God's blessing. It gave him a fine bittersweet pleasure to think how badly she might have ended had he not rescued her.

Then he thought, helplessly, of Shirin. His eldest daughter, shot from the loins of an imposed wife, a good enough woman, whose sole purpose had been the transmission of his children. Shirin should have been born a man. That was God's joke. Because Talala could recognize her, too, in the sweating, half-fainting dancer, and whenever he let such comparisons go too far, it brought him near despair. His Shirin, his princess of princesses, among the Russian swine. Of all his children, he could not help loving Shirin the most, the girl child with a man's intensity. Perhaps because she was the eldest, perhaps because his only son was so small and weak. Perhaps simply because Shirin was so much like the devil who had sired her.

He would not think of Shirin now. Nor of Ashi. There was business to conduct.

Suddenly, the female dancer exploded in broad, swaying movements, opening her eyes wide and parting her lips to reveal the rows of gold teeth again. Fatal, not beautiful. She rolled her head back, showing a long slender throat as if drinking rain or thanking God.

Yes, Talala thought, smiling. The men were irrelevant. Such a lioness would not even feel their meager touches. Far better to bed alone. Until the advent of the true beloved. The old poems were full of that, although you had to know how to read them. The poetry of Samarkand was a secret drawer that opened only to knowing fingers. Desperation hidden in the flowers. The young did not read poetry anymore, could not recite. While he had known the strains by heart long before he first laid eyes on a book, before he first comprehended that such music could be jailed in paper cells. He still preferred to hear Ashi's deep, soft voice shape the words to reading them in silence. Poetry was meant to be sung, as women were meant to be embraced.

The music ended abruptly. The woman slumped, looking suddenly worn and overweight. She followed one of the male dancers, a weak-chinned man, back to their table, husband and wife. Talala read their history in an instant.

"Any woman who can dance like that . . ." Talala's dinner guest remarked, voice coached by alcohol. "*That's* why you keep them locked up."

These Russians, Talala thought, understand nothing.

"My dear Colonel Losov," Talala said, "you know that one of the many glories Soviet power brought to Central Asia was the liberation of the woman from medieval conditions, from the tyranny of the neotheocratic state. No one is 'locked up' today. We simply have a different social manner."

The policeman laughed, then drank off his glass of wine as though firing vodka down his throat.

"Whatever you say, Ali my boy. Whatever you say. Listen, maybe I'll have you fix me up with some little Uzbek dolly sometime." Losov grinned with a self-satisfied stupidity that Talala found uniquely Slavic. "But no gold teeth, all right?"

Talala could just overhear the conversation at the next table. One of his countrymen, young and very handsome, was explaining to a middle-aged Ukrainian homosexual what might happen if additional gifts were not immediately forthcoming. If the policeman heard it, you couldn't tell from his features. Of course, Talala told himself, Losov wasn't interested in small game. And Soviet policemen of all ranks were adept at hearing only what they wanted to hear.

Across the room, a drunk rose from his chair, swinging at

a waiter and howling, while nearby tourists cringed. The waiters posted near Talala's table swiftly converged on the man, pinioning him then punching him hard in the belly before handing him off to a pair of militiamen entering from the vestibule.

The senior waiter on duty hastened to Talala's table, straightening his jacket as he approached, bowing before he was really close enough, then bowing again. He apologized for the disturbance and asked, in Uzbek, whether the most honored people's deputy might not prefer a private dining room after all.

"Thank you, Mohammed," Talala answered in Russian. "That won't be necessary. Colonel Losov and I are at home among the People."

The headwaiter backed away, bowing again, then with considerably less obsequiousness, hustled his subordinates back to their posts by Talala's table, letting the irate demands for service from a half a dozen other patrons go ignored.

There would be no private dining rooms tonight. Nothing conspiratorial. Talala wanted to be seen publicly with this officer of the Interior Ministry police, whose too-fine civilian suit fooled no one. Everything had been foreordained, blessed by guiding hands.

The band began to play again, hurrying the melody of some Western pop song as if surging to fulfill a planned norm at the last minute. Despite himself, Talala recognized the piece, electronic syrup poured over heavy drum blows. It was the hit of the moment, you could not go anywhere in Moscow without hearing it. The musicians had copied it painstakingly and phonetically, without real understanding. Talala disliked it when the band here played Western or even Russian songs, but it was not a matter in which he would interfere. He knew very well the importance of allowing men their tiny vices.

A group of shining young foreigners rose to dance, their unfocused frenzy a total contrast to the hypnotic eroticism of his own kind. Blond, northern, and recognizable as the spoiled and invulnerable offspring of diplomats, the foreigners had festooned their evening clothes with dozens of Soviet medals and ribbons in a caricature of the high officials and veterans who had, for decades, marked Moscow's public life. A few years earlier, such behavior would have created a scandal. Now no one who mattered cared.

A blond young man and his blond companion—so similar they might have been brother and sister—turned the dance floor into a mock bedroom, hips colliding, nuzzling. Far from erotic, Talala found the display vulgar and pornographic: the sexuality of dogs. But the young foreigners felt no shame. They laughed, then kissed for all to see.

Talala turned his eyes away, briefly surveying the crowded room, with homesick Uzbeks, Tadzhiks, and Kazhaks gathered close under the stucco ornamentation the way their parents or grandparents had crowded into the hospitality of a neighbor's tent, their restaurant tables laden with all that generosity could afford. Then there were the black marketeers doing business, in every accent, with every skin tone the Soviet Union had to offer. And there were always celebrants—tonight a Russian name-day party had swum deep into the vodka. Goggle-eyed tourists watched it all with faces so idiotically naive it was difficult to imagine how they had ever earned enough money to pay for their splendid clothes. A strolling rose-vendor worked the tables, a grandmother intentionally pathetic, followed by two teenagers peddling lacquer boxes, watches, and caviar from their coat pockets, all under the careful eyes of waiters calculating their cut. Finally, there was this police colonel, who understood nothing at all.

The new mark of a prospering Soviet bureaucrat was a suit that fit. Colonel Losov's suit fit him very well, draping over a big chest padded with fat. Above a yellow-rimmed shirt collar, the policeman's wattled skin chronicled years of too much liquor. His lips and the tufts of hair in his nostrils were discolored from tobacco, and he had eyes more mean than intelligent. To Talala, the colonel appeared identical to tens of thousands of other officers of the state, all greedy prisoners of the moment.

Losov was certainly greedy when it came to food. He ate with both hands, pausing only to slosh more wine into his mouth. Routinely, the tables in the Uzbekistan were crowded with dishes of elaborate appetizers, cold chicken in ginger, smoked fish, cold meats, pickled garlic, with plates of olives, leeks and cucumbers, tomatoes and dill. Orange-red salmon eggs appeared in small mountains, while true caviar, gray and black, was available to those with hard currency or influence. Flat loaves of hot bread lay over the plates and dishes balanced one on the other, while sentinel bottles of wine, vodka, champagne, and mineral water stood at nearby attention. Talala had once heard a tourist remark that such ostentation was obscene in a hungry city. The tourist had spoken in carefully constructed Russian, for all to hear. But no one took notice. For the patrons, this was the natural order of things. Those who could afford it ate here and ate well. Fools ate elsewhere or not at all. And this police colonel, guardian of the People's trust, had been perfectly happy to elevate himself from the ranks of the fools.

"I hope, my dear friend," Talala said, "that everything is to your satisfaction." He leaned over the food to be heard above the ringing of the band.

"Superb," the Russian said with a full mouth. "Absolutely superb."

"Please," Talala went on, "have some more wine. This is very special, from a vineyard that used to belong to Rashidov himself. I ordered it in your honor."

"Good," Losov mumbled, swallowing and reaching for his wineglass.

Talala took a sip of mineral water.

"Colonel Losov, I beg you," Talala continued, "please accept my hospitality in the future, as well. There will always be a table for you here. And you will, of course, pay nothing. I would be insulted."

The Russian spooned up as much black caviar as he could manage in one go, mashing the delicate eggs in his carelessness. He loaded the caviar directly into his mouth, chewed twice, then gulped, leaving a trail of shiny beads on his lips.

"Very kind of you, Ali my boy. Very kind." The Russian smiled the smile of an old policeman. "But I'm afraid I can't be bribed quite that easily."

Talala put down the slice of cucumber he had selected and raised his hands to the heavens, appealing for understanding.

"Please, my dear friend. Give me just a bit more credit. I do not for one moment underestimate the gravity of our relationship."

The Russian finished off another glass of yellow wine. Then he sighed and interrupted his eating, leaning over toward

Talala, elbows on the edge of the table, sleeve in a beige pool of ginger sauce.

"You see, Ali," the colonel said heavily, fixing Talala with his bloodshot eyes, "we've got all the cards. Times have changed, and you boys are simply going to have to face up to it. Nobody's afraid of the Uzbek mafia anymore. That's history. Gone with Rashidov and his cronies. Long gone." He could not resist helping himself to another spoonful of caviar. He wiped his mouth with his hand and said, "The trials . . . why, the trials barely missed you. You're lucky you're not sitting right now." He smiled. "And of course, not all of the outstanding issues were settled in courts of law. In exceptional cases we have to take exceptional measures." He opened his smile, showing brown teeth speckled with fish eggs. "Why, there are friends of yours I haven't seen walking around for over a year."

Talala lifted one eyebrow and one hand, extending the palm. "Everything is as Allah wills." He was not a religious man, but he instinctively appreciated the utility of such hand-me-down expressions. Dealing with Slavs, you could wear them like a mask. And certainly, this was not a country where a man needed to believe a thing in order to say it out loud.

"Now listen, Talala," the policeman said. "It's like I explained. There's enough for everybody. We work together. But you play by our rules, from now on. Your people don't have to know." He nodded at the waiters and a concentration of Central Asian patrons. "To all these blackasses, you'll still be the big man, the shrewd customer who outlasted all the others. We don't give a Polish fart what your people back home think, that's your business." He licked his lips, then set his face in a tough expression made a little absurd by all the alcohol he had consumed. "But you're going to have to play by our rules. And you're going to have to pay your 'taxes.' On time. We find you cheating us one time, you just might have a reunion with some of those old friends you haven't seen around lately." The colonel was sweating with all of the food and drink he had forced into himself. "And don't forget you've got a family." He smiled grotesquely. "Like that daughter of yours who goes to the university, the looker. What's her name? Shirin? Am I saying that right? I'm sure we all want to protect a girl like that."

Talala delicately cut a slice of tomato into four wedges, then laid down his knife and fork without eating. He spoke calmly, in a voice just loud enough to be heard by his guest. "My dear Colonel Losov, my friend, I'm a *businessman.*" He used the English word so much in fashion. "And I have read that it is most important for the businessman to be flexible. Today . . . the wind is blowing from the north." Again he held up an empty palm to heaven. "And I would rather bow with grace before that wind than be broken by it." He edged in so close that he could smell the policeman's ripe breath. "But don't think I'm so weak that I have no pride. I expect to be treated fairly."

The Russian guffawed, then drank in delight, as if he had been told a potent joke. "Naturally. Of course. I told you, Ali—there's plenty for everybody. We all just have to co-operate." He refilled his vodka glass, sloshing the liquor. "Let's drink to that. To plenty for everybody."

Smiling, Talala raised his vodka glass, which he had filled with mineral water. The Russian followed the vodka with a hunk of smoked salmon gathered in his fingers.

"These are," Talala said resignedly, "troubled times. It's difficult to see the future."

The Russian chewed and grinned. "The future belongs to men like us. And I'll tell you what else. I think my future just might hold one of those little Uzbek girls of yours. I mean, I never had much interest. You know. Figured they're dirty and all that. But I got to admit some of them look pretty good. Like that daughter of yours. And you only live once."

"Yes," Talala agreed quietly. "You only live once."

"You know," the Russian went on, eating and talking, "it's times like these when the real opportunities come. Sure everything's a mess." He laughed. "Hell, I can tell you this—*you* don't even have an inkling of how much of a mess things are in. You should just read some of the reports that come across my desk. The whole country's turning into slop." He dug for a clove of pickled garlic with his fingers. "But that just means 'businessmen' like you and me can make our own rules." He gulped his food, laughing all the while at his own joke. "Now isn't that a fine thing for a policeman to say?"

"You know," Talala said deliberately, "I don't believe you."

"What?"

"I don't believe you."

The Russian's fingers stopped halfway to his mouth. "What the hell do you mean, you don't believe me? *What* don't you believe?"

Talala smiled a friendly smile, only joking after all. "I don't believe it about all that liquor. We were never able to bring in so much. In a single shipment. It's never been done."

The Russian nodded his chin down into the swell of his neck. Smug and pleased. "We have resources you never even imagined. International connections."

"The power of the State," Talala said softly.

"Yeah. The power of the State. Listen. You name a liquor. Go ahead. I don't care what kind. Finnish vodka. French cognac. Scotch whiskey. Just name it. I'll have a case delivered to you tonight." He snorted. "Hell, I'll send you *ten* cases."

"You truly have so much?"

The Russian shook his head at Talala's ignorance. "In one Moscow warehouse I've got over four thousand cases, imported and domestic."

Talala lowered his eyes as if he still could not believe his new partner. "I really would like to see such a thing. Just once in my life."

"*Done,*" Losov cried. He was happy, crafty eyed. "I'll take you there myself."

Talala took another sip of mineral water.

"When?"

The policeman frumped his chin, thinking through the alcohol. "What the hell. We'll go tonight. Right after dinner." Then he smiled knowingly. "After all, I don't want to give you time to set up some kind of tail on us. I still don't quite trust you, Ali my boy."

"To what extent," Talala asked, "can any man ever trust another? Only when interests coincide."

"Damned right. And I just hope you've got it through your little brown head that your interests coincide with mine."

"As Allah wills."

At a slight gesture from Talala, a team of waiters converged on the table, lifting off emptied plates and bowls to clear a space in front of each of the diners. A moment later, oversize platters of skewered lamb appeared, followed by boats of red sauce and still more wine. The Russian started to eat immediately, tearing at the crisped-off chunks of meat then glossing his throat with wine between mouthfuls.

Talala nudged his water glass and said:

"Please, my dear friend. You must excuse me. I must make a personal venture."

Losov grinned, revealing one lamb's fate. "It's all that water you drink. You'll be pissing your life away."

Talala rose and walked quietly away through the smoke, with waiters shoving other patrons out of his path.

In the vestibule, a small group of Russians argued with the receptionist about a purported reservation, while the doorman loitered with a pair of militiamen in ill-fitting uniforms. Two young blond women in exaggerated makeup sat smoking on a bench, facial expressions utterly disinterested. Talala's purpose actually had nothing to do with the toilet, but a longer than usual line of his fellow Uzbeks and other Central Asians outside the door complicated his journey. Annoyed, he pushed to the head of the line. As the men recognized him, they hastily burrowed against the wall to make way.

"What's going on?" he asked, opening the door.

He caught the stink of the room in his nostrils and heard moans. Off to the side, a heavy Russian woman sat perched on the sink, with a slender Uzbek ploughing between her legs while half a dozen other men waited their turns, smoking. The woman's exposed flesh rolled with each thrust, but her eyes were dumb and distant.

Talala turned away. The Russians, he told himself, had degenerated beyond redemption. Both the men and women were for sale, if in slightly different ways.

He turned into a doorway marked STAFF ONLY. Reaching familiarly for the light switch, he still had the sewer smell of the men's room in his nostrils. With the years, Moscow had grown ever more hateful to him, and he ever more actively sought excuses to return home for extended stays. He picked up the telephone to make sure that his orders had been carried out to the last detail.

On his way back to the main dining room, Talala stopped at the receptionist's desk. As soon as she saw him standing above her, the Uzbek woman completely ignored the Russians clamoring for a table. Talala bent low and spoke quietly and very harshly to the woman. He turned away without waiting for a reply, but he knew with absolute certainty that the two idling militiamen would shortly break up the party in the men's toilet. He felt nothing at all for the Russian whore. But he hated to see his countrymen lowering themselves to such a level.

Sitting down again, Talala noted that the policeman had already finished his entire plate of lamb. The man's lips and chin gleamed with juice.

"Perhaps," Talala said, "you'd like to take some of mine?"

The Russian finished drawing the curtains inside the rear compartment of the automobile. Normally this was done so that the citizens on the street could not see in. Tonight it was so that Talala could not see their route.

"Don't be offended," Losov said. "The location's a 'state secret.' " The smell of alcohol breaking down in the man's stomach filled the car.

"But we're partners . . ." Talala said.

"That time will come." The Russian dropped heavily into the seat, then readjusted his black kid hat with a gloved hand. "After all, our partnership is still new. And you've got your own secrets, I'll bet."

Talala sighed, expelling a cloud of breath. "I suspect, my dear friend, that you know all there is to know about me by now."

"Oh, we know plenty. But there are always a few things a policeman wants to hear in person."

"The water is sweetest straight from the fountain."

"What?"

"An Uzbek saying."

"Oh."

They rode in silence for a time, with Losov breathing so heavily it sounded almost like snoring. The monster of a car hurtled over the broken Moscow streets. Now and again a streetlight's frozen glint would find a gap in the curtains. But Talala made no effort to spy out their trail.

The policeman bent down heavily, fighting the bulk of his overcoat to get at his briefcase. Finally, he produced a bottle of vodka and pulled off the cap.

"Drink?"

Talala shook his head. "Thank you. I do not have a Russian stomach."

Losov drank from the bottle then considered the smaller man with eyes that barely focused. Talala hoped the Russian would not drink too much more. It was important that he remain at least partially sentient.

The car struck a particularly deep pothole then rebounded over a set of streetcar tracks. The policeman spilled a great deal of vodka over himself and the car. He cursed the driver robustly. But Talala did not mind. Compared to the reek of the Russian's breath, the fresh acridity of the vodka was perfume.

"Should have brought a loaf of bread with us," Losov said. "No good drinking without something to cushion the blow."

"You know, my dear friend," Talala said, "I cannot help feeling envy. A man in your high position . . . a colonel of the militia and well placed within the Interior Ministry . . . you've got connections—and protection—of which I could only dream."

"Yeah. Well, it's like it is for you when you go back to Uzbekistan. You're a big fish. This is our pond, and we're the big fish here."

"To do what you have done . . . you must have protection from the highest levels."

The policeman nodded smugly. "High enough, my boy. High enough."

"Perhaps," Talala said thoughtfully, "I shouldn't trust you. Here I am, riding alone with you in the night. How can I know where you are truly taking me?"

Losov laughed heartily. "Oh, I haven't loaded a bullet for you yet, Talala. You're much too valuable. At least for now." He was in marvelous spirits, holding the half-empty bottle of vodka on his lap like a king's scepter.

Outside, a trolley hissed and thumped by them, close, invisible. The passenger compartment was growing quite warm and it stank. Old socks, alcohol, sweat.

They truly are animals, Talala thought.

After half an hour, the car braked to a stop. The driver, a uniformed militiaman, hurried to open the door for the colonel.

Outside, the night was breathtakingly cold after the swampy

interior of the car. It was very dark. The car's headlamps were the sole source of illumination amid a clutter of warehouses, junked machinery, and piled building materials. A scrap of rag blew against Talala's leg and he recoiled, imagining for a moment that it was a rat. He did not care for rats.

The driver cut the lights and the world reduced to very black shapes low against a slightly paler sky. The Russian clicked on a flashlight.

"Come on," he told Talala. "Follow me."

Swaying, Losov led the way between freezing puddles of bad water and oil. They crossed a plank bridge, with the big Russian's weight crushing the boards down into the muck. It was so cold that the earth and everything exposed upon it should have been frozen hard. But this was a poisonous place and the soles of Talala's feet found grease and slime.

The Russian turned down a narrow alley between two warehouses, then stopped by the vague outline of a door. Unsteady, he shone the flashlight toward the handle and keyhole.

It took the policeman a long time to open the door. Accustomed to drink, he could carry on a conversation and walk with only a little distress, but as he fumbled with his keys, it was clear that he was far gone.

Let his eyes and his soul remain awake a bit longer, Talala thought.

At last the door groaned open. After letting Talala through, the Russian switched on the overhead lights, then made a second ceremony out of locking the door behind them.

The warehouse, cement floored, was colder than the night outside. It was more or less neatly filled with crates. But Talala saw no foreign liquor. Only vodka of Soviet manufacture, enough of it to alleviate Moscow's chronic shortage for at least a week.

"You have impressed me," Talala said.

The policeman snorted. "This is nothing. Just wait."

He led the way again, rocking sideward like a huge, top-heavy doll. They went down between canyons of vodka, all of it bound to go to waste if it was not more warmly stored. It never ceased to baffle Talala that the Russians could be so wasteful, throwing away fortunes. Perhaps only a poor country on the edge of collapse could behave so insensitively. Squandering its resources. Squandering its people. The Russians were devils who, first and foremost, plagued themselves.

The policeman halted at a set of steel doors. He raised a gloved fist and pounded dully on the metal.

The two men waited in the cold. Their surroundings had a graveyard quiet. The big Russian wheezed as though he had been climbing a mountain. He cursed and struck the door again.

Nothing.

"I'll have their asses," the Russian swore. "If they're fucking off on me, they'll be inspecting reindeer shit in the Arctic Circle." He looked at Talala, face red and stupid with liquor and the cold. "You can't trust anybody anymore."

He pulled off his right glove and began fumbling with his keys again, sunk into a bad humor. Each tiny failure brought a fresh obscenity with it.

Finally a key slid into place. The policeman grunted and clicked the lock over twice. But he still did not open the door. He paused, pleased with himself again, and smiled down at Talala with a colonial ruler's contempt for a tribesman.

"Now you're really going to see something."

The Russian yanked open one of the big doors. It had not been oiled in a long time.

The fan of light from the outer warehouse caught a few cases with foreign lettering. The rest lay in darkness. Brushing past Talala, Losov felt heavily for the light switch.

Someone helped him.

"What the—"

The lights were bright enough for a man to read the finest print on the thousands of cases of foreign liquor. But the spectacle of merchandise only formed a backdrop to the real drama.

A middle-aged blonde's distorted body hung by the neck from a ceiling beam. She was a heavy woman, and every part of her body seemed to feel the misery of gravity even after death, straining toward the floor. Her eyes focused at the wrong distance and her mouth and extended tongue were black, as though she had been eating charcoal. Her skin had turned the pale blue you sometimes encountered in fresh farm milk, except where a badly dressed appendectomy scar showed bloodless white. On the floor beneath her lay a splash of waste.

She was not alone. Two children, a girl in her early teens and a boy slightly younger, hung naked on either side of her with the same eyes and green-black mouths. The girl's pale legs were smeared with blood and feces.

Two uniformed militiamen hung a little way off, guarding the family.

"No," Losov said in a very quiet voice. "No." He stood with his mouth open, hands at his sides.

"No."

A club against the back of his knees dropped him to the floor. He began to cry, a weeping little child. "Oh, no," he said. "No." He was barely whispering.

Talala's men worked quickly, searching the big man for weapons. He had an automatic pistol in one pocket, magazine in another. He put up no resistance.

"Anya," the Russian whispered. "I'm sorry. I'm so sorry."

Talala glanced at the Uzbek who held the seized pistol. "He makes too much noise. It offends my ears."

Obediently, the Uzbek grabbed the policeman by the hair, yanking back his head. With a sweep of his other arm, he brought the butt of the pistol down on the Russian's jaw. A knife shone as a second man moved in, reaching for the pulp of Losov's lower face. The policeman made a terrified, grunting noise, then gagged. Quick as a magician, the second Uzbek thrust his fingers into what remained of Losov's mouth. A moment later he had cut out the man's tongue.

A knee behind the shoulder blades sent the policeman flat on the floor. He made a braying sound, spitting streams of blood.

Talala walked over to him and looked down. He turned the policeman's face with the tip of his boot until their eyes met. Losov was a very different man now. His eyes had the look you saw in the eyes of trussed sheep as they waited their turn to be slaughtered. He bleated in shock and pain.

"You Russians," Talala said. "Always so greedy. Always in a hurry." Narrowing his eyes, he stooped so close that the bloody spittle almost touched him. "Your protectors in high places? They sold you out." Talala laughed peacefully. "In fact, they sold you out surprisingly cheaply. I will not tell you how little you were worth. I'm not that cruel."

Losov began to cry again. It was evident that he wanted to

speak, to plead for his life. But his organ of speech had been destroyed.

Talala sat restfully on his haunches, regarding the ruined man before him. The eyes were incredibly good. He could see in Losov's eyes that he had gained his full measure of revenge.

"Do you know why this is happening to you?" Talala continued. "Would you like to know what you did wrong? I'll tell you. Never threaten an Uzbek's family. Never." He smiled. "I don't think you'll forget that lesson, will you? My dear friend. I would have spared your family. And you yourself would simply have gotten a bullet in the back of the head. But you went too far. I could not permit it." He shook his head in genuine pity. "I had to treat you like this. To do to your family in fact what you had already done to mine in words. You gave me no choice in the matter."

The policeman bleated and bled.

"So I have to kill you," Talala said matter-of-factly. "And everyone who loves you."

He nodded in the direction of a shadowed aisle. Three more men appeared, one Central Asian and two brutal-looking Slavs selected from the work-for-pay killers who had emerged from the war in Afghanistan. They half carried, half dragged a young woman who had been attractive only hours before. She was gagged, but her eyes said everything Talala needed her to communicate.

"Get up," Talala told the bleeding policeman. Immediately, other hands brought Losov back to his knees, steadying him so that he could see.

He began to growl, to struggle, raging with new life. The Uzbek had to strike him several times with the pistol and hold him very tightly in order to control him.

Her three escorts dropped the young woman a body length from the policeman. Then one of the hired Slavs took her by the neck and sat her up against a wall of crates.

She was conscious. But her eyes did not really see at first. She looked as though she had spent the last few hours experiencing things of which she could not have dreamed in the blackest night. Her face was bruised and swollen. Yet an unmistakable attractiveness remained.

"Take off the gag," Talala ordered.

The nearest Uzbek cut away the rag with a knife. The woman's mouth fell open. Her front teeth were gone.

She said nothing. She did not cry. Slowly, her eyes adjusted to the sight of Losov. But her face did not really change. She looked as though she had already given up. If there was anything in her expression, it was a tinge of pity for the broken man before her.

Losov surged again, trying to break free, to reach the woman. The animal sounds had become those of a fouled machine. He was crying and his bloody cheeks were brilliant with tears.

"Finish it," Talala said.

The Uzbek who had cut the gag drew out his knife again. Taking the woman by the hair he pulled backward and exposed her throat, which he slit through as though it were soft cheese.

The woman did not even react. Her eyes remained on Losov until they appeared to become sleepy and her executioner let her fall against a stack of cognac cases.

"A true man," Talala whispered in the policeman's ear, "would take better care of his mistress."

He cut the Russian's throat himself, deftly, not even soiling his hands.

As the wide-eyed man bled to death, Talala squatted by him again, taking one last look, offering his victim a good-natured, close-lipped smile.

"By the way," he told the dying man, "that's a very nice suit you're wearing tonight."

People's Deputy Ali Talala's Moscow residence was a large apartment in a building constructed under Stalin for members of the Soviet elite. Unlike more recent structures, which had begun to decay before their completion, this grumpy ocher tower concealed wood-paneled hallways kept immaculate by a service staff, brass fittings, and elevators that worked. There was no trace of the leaky-plumbing smell otherwise characteristic of Moscow architecture, and entrance to the building was so carefully controlled that a resident needed to fear nothing common as he took the last muffled steps toward his private world.

The men who lived in this building sought a careful measure

of anonymity from one another. In their steaming, overcrowded blocks of flats, the People knew each neighbor's odor, and they drank together and helped each other, when they were not fighting over the possession of a corner of a communal cupboard. But the residents of Talala's building still had things worth hiding. Although two neighbors might build a friendship on swapped influence, it was at least as likely that they would live across the hall from one another for years without exchanging names. This was the world of the near-mighty bureaucrat, where whispered rumors moused along the hallways as though the ghost of Stalin himself still had an eye narrowed and an ear cocked.

To enter one of these apartments as a privileged guest meant leaving the dolor of the Moscow winter behind you. Icons, so prized by nonbelievers, glittered from the walls beside paintings looted by an earlier generation from an estate in the Ukraine, from a manor house in East Prussia, or from a rectory in Silesia. Video recorders and compact disc players trumpeted the importance and connections of the host to his carefully selected guests. The vodka never ran out and there was always plenty of food, and it was only very recently that some of the residents had begun to suspect that the current czar of all the Russias might be serious about disrupting their once-immutable privileges, bringing a grace note of fatalism to the parties attended by men and women who had lived so well so long.

The door to Talala's apartment was identical to the others in the corridor, solid and polished, with a worked handle of a quality no longer produced anywhere in the Soviet Union. But as soon as Talala stepped inside, he left more than the Moscow streets behind. There was relatively little furniture. Instead, the floors and walls displayed antique rugs and carpets of a quality that could no longer be found in the museums of Central Asia. Bokharas ran from crimson to purple-black on the floor, layered one over the other, their smoking, brooding tones shocked to life by a litter of hot-colored tribal rugs, all knotted or woven by women striving to create a small woolen paradise in the desert or amid the crags of barren mountains. In place of the infidel's icons, Talala had hung a collection of prayer rugs worn to velvet by centuries of knees and foreheads. Swords and axes of the sort once used to draw blood from white-coated Russian soldiers or unsuspecting caravans caught the lamplight and flashed it to the ceiling. Persian filigree and coats of Khivan chain mail covered long, low tables. The rooms even smelled of the irrigated gardens of the south.

When Talala came in at midnight, his transplanted chieftain's tent welcomed him with color and familiarity, canceling the grime and squalor through which this day's fate had led him. But most welcoming of all were the faces of his family, grouped around a large low table set for dinner hours before. Two women, wife and sister, sat on piled rugs in brilliant Uzbek dresses, lozenges of yellow, red, hard green, and purple running through the cloth. They had bound up their hair under flaming silk, but their faces remained bare with the fierce remembered independence of nomads. Three children, two blossoming girls and a thin boy, lolled sleepily. All together, they formed a human bouquet of welcome, showing their love and respect by waiting for the head of the household to break the first bread of supper. It was a mark of Talala's enlightened views that, in private, male and female family members sat side by side.

The two older women rose at Talala's approach, while the children lowered their heads. It was a time for smiles and generosity. But Talala was unusually weary and disgusted by all that necessity had forced upon him. He feared that creeping age—he was newly fifty—and the endless stress of dealing with the Slavic filth all around him were beginning to wear him down. He was anxious as never before to return to his real home. To go beyond the cities, beyond the soft green hills that gave pasture, past the poisoned gigantism of the cotton fields, to cross the last clogged irrigation ditch and leave behind the powdery, dying soil of the new man-made desert and to reenter the timeless world of the great, true desert where his family's blood had trickled down the centuries. He had been born in a yurt the year before a distant state had called his father to war, and he had ridden ponies long before his first ride in a motor vehicle. Fate had decreed that he should grow wealthy and powerful, that lesser men should drive him and his kinsmen through the streets of a great, if derelict, capital. But it was only during his journeys back to Tashkent and Samarkand that he felt even half-alive—Tashkent with its government assemblies and the poetry of Ashi's being, and Samarkand, the base of his power, the earthly mansion of his kind. Those cities lifted his heart. But even then, it was only Ashi or the high desert that could bring him real joy.

"I have no hunger," Talala said. "Eat without me. I'm tired."

He moved past the wilting feast, heading for the sanctuary of his bedroom. His wife rose, following to be certain that the lord of her life had no special needs.

Suddenly, Talala stopped. He glanced over the caramel faces of his children.

"Where's Shirin?"

"She stays at her dormitory tonight," his wife answered. "The Russians give her so much to study."

Talala nodded and turned back toward his rest, his face a sketch of disappointment, tolerance, and love.

5

SASHA HAD NEVER SEEN RACHEL SO ANGRY. IN PRIVATE conversation she might be passionate, but she never attacked—every last fool received the benefit of the doubt. In public she was usually retiring, conscious of her bent spine and small stature, forever trying to make herself smaller and less visible, happy to arrange things behind the scenes then watch from a corner as events unfolded. But tonight she was in a near rage, lashing the foreigner with English sentences that flowed so swiftly Sasha had some difficulty following.

The argument was about him and his work. A crowd of artists and hangers-on surrounded the debaters on a staircase landing in the apartment building whose residents Rachel and her friends had persuaded to allow the unofficial exhibition. Borrowed photographer's lamps, mounted to light paintings and graphics, made faces very white and threw exaggerated shadows. Grinding rock music sounded from a cassette player turned high, and from the floors above and below, the laughter and barking of packs of art lovers, punks, black marketeers, and bored Muscovites randomly punctuated Rachel's speech. The stairwell smelled of cabbage and mildew, and the Englishman on the receiving end of Rachel's verbal blows repeatedly opened his mouth to speak only to have Rachel slam in a conjunction where he had anticipated a period. He was a young man, with an old man's mannerisms, constantly massaging his throat.

"*And* what's more," Rachel said, waving an index finger like a knife, "you understand *no*thing. Your beloved Furmanny Street prima donnas—*they* aren't artists. They're *scavengers*, chewing little tiny bits off the corpse of Russian culture. Not one of them has a pair of *eyes*. They don't produce *art*. All they do is turn out snide little commentaries for each other so they can feel superior to anyone with real talent. And *now*—now they're turning out what *you* want, to please *you*. To make *mo*ney. At least they weren't cor*rupt* before you and your like appeared, with your auctions and patrons and your pockets full of dollars. No, they might have been foolish and lazy and untalented—but at least they weren't cor*rupt*." She paused for a breath so quick the Englishman could barely get his lips apart before she continued her assault. He resumed rubbing his throat with his fingers going in little circles. It reminded Sasha of masturbation, as though, should the Englishman continue stroking himself harder and harder, his head might explode in a gush of brains.

"*You* corrupted them," Rachel went on. "Oh, perhaps you didn't mean to. But do you have any idea what effect international attention has on a Russian with a tiny little talent and a great big ego? *Do* you have any idea? And all this going-on about 'schools' of artists. Why should an artist have to belong to a 'school' to be taken seriously? Do you think artists are *fish?*"

There was a moment of silence. The Englishman's lips moved in a wordless stutter, as if he could not believe he might actually receive a chance to respond. Then he slipped his hand down over his heart, massaging his trench coat, and said:

"But . . . but my dear Miss Traum . . . you must understand . . . it's simply impossible to paint like this." He gestured at the nearest of Sasha's pictures, an urban wall with one faded poster, all of it washed in light that gave the wall the depth of the sea. "It's just not done. . . . I mean, I mean . . . it's almost representational. But without the calculated veracity of photo-realism, which is, in any case, a fully discredited movement." He turned suddenly to Sasha, eyes pleading for help from the artist whose work he had been gleefully and publicly disparaging before Rachel's counterattack. "I ask you, Mr. Leskov, what ex*act*ly were you trying to articulate in this work?"

"What did he say?" Sasha asked Rachel in Russian, unsure of his English.

Rachel grimaced, twisting her small face in disdain. She had wonderful eyes; he had painted them once, only the eyes and the bridge of her nose, the eyes of a great beauty, in an undersized body that barely functioned.

"He wants you to justify your painting in theoretical terms."

"Oh."

"You don't have to tell him a thing. He's worthless."

It was the first time Sasha had ever heard Rachel call another human being worthless.

Sasha turned back to the Englishman, speaking slowly in the other man's tongue. "Mister . . . I just want to paint the light. How is the light. I think this light is very beautiful and then I paint it. That is all."

The Englishman beamed in triumph, unspeakably grateful to Sasha. "You see?" he demanded of Rachel. "You see? He wants to paint the *light,* for the love of God. Does he imagine he's the reincarnation of Monet?" The Englishman shook his head in disbelief. "One cannot paint *light,* my dear man," he told Sasha in a voice he might have wielded against an innocent but exasperating child. "This is the end of the twentieth century, not the nineteenth. The artist dare not allow himself to be distracted by the ephemeral vagaries of the external world. In order for art to suffice, it can only exist as a manifestation of a theoretical system successfully divorced from the mundane. Of course, in the Soviet example, one might allow for a certain political aroma"—he spoke exclusively to Sasha now, sneaking out from under Rachel's barrage—"but that is, of course, a historical exception. Do you understand what I'm telling you, Mr. Leskov?"

Sasha shrugged, bored and annoyed. In his experience people who theorized too much about anything never produced anything of merit. Yet this Englishman was a well-known critic, a powerful man. And Sasha had been in an unaccountably bad mood all afternoon, even before the exhibition opened.

"I think only that the light is beautiful on this wall," he said. "It is not so important."

"But it *is* important," the Englishman insisted. "It *is* important. You are not totally without talent, Mr. Leskov, but you must seek to transcend this emotionalism I detect in your work." In his disappointment at Sasha's mental turgidness, he mistakenly turned back to Rachel. "Tell him, for the love of God, that it simply isn't done. Explain to the fellow. An artist can no longer paint something because it's 'beautiful.' It's totally unacceptable. Why . . . the denial of mundane beauty is the very fundament of contemporary art."

"Beauty is unac*cept*able to you?" Rachel demanded in a voice of fire. "Beauty is unac*cept*able? And why should we get out of bed in the morning, if not in the hope of discovering some small sliver of beauty? When art denies . . ."

Sasha quietly slipped back into the crowd and went down the stairs to the lower corridor. He wanted to be alone for a few minutes, to put himself back in order. It had been a bad day, not dramatically bad, but stupidly bad. He had lost his temper and shouted at Vera over a minor matter, and she had wept like a child, never before exposed to that side of him. Only a good, exhausting swim had kept him from kicking the walls. But his mood was as gray as the weather, and his temper as short as the winter days. Even Moscow seemed disappointing to him this time, after he had so longed to be home. It was as though something had changed in his life, or wanted to change, but he could not yet identify it. It wasn't really Vera. Women were not of that much consequence. But a hidden page waited to be turned, and the dull, heavy sense of it made him feel turbulent and uncharacteristically skittish. He spent most of his energies in trying to keep his behavior even, but those around him had begun to sense that something was wrong. Even the cat stayed out of his way.

The corridor was hung with colorful, bad works all of which incorporated the number 53. The Englishman had liked the series very much and had tried to speak to the artist, Genia Tomkin, but Genia was too drunk for the Englishman's questions, sorrowing over the death of his brother, a militiaman, in a warehouse fire a few days earlier. No one had explained to the family what the brother, whose duty was to chauffeur high-ranking officers, had been doing in a warehouse, and

Genia was convinced it was all a KGB conspiracy to punish him for his art.

Sasha tried honestly to lift himself out of his black mood, looking at Genia's pictures for the merit the Englishman had seen in them. But the slovenly canvases only reminded him of a schoolboy's hasty takeoff on Malevich.

Maybe I'm the fool, Sasha thought. Maybe I'm kidding myself about everything.

A big arm settled over his shoulders, wool that smelled of sweat and tobacco. It was his friend Lev Birman, a big, big man with a whopping paunch and heaving breath, a first-rate soul and a second-rate painter, unlucky in love. Almost wanton in his generosity, the fourth-rate women who occasionally dotted his life went at him like dogs at a chained bear.

Lev was panting and smiling. "Sasha, you should go back up and pay attention to that asshole. Court him a little. He's very important. He writes books about Soviet art, and if he says you're good, you make a killing."

"Not interested."

Lev's great paw squeezed Sasha's biceps. "Come on now. Wouldn't you like to be famous in the West?"

"For painting numbers? Or maybe for smearing dogshit on a wall?"

It was impossible to explain, even to another artist. The canvas children he sent into the world mattered to him. Some more than others. But what mattered most was the process, the good days when you drowned in the color and light for a few hours, when you tumbled into that hyperreality so good, so addictive, you could only compare it with sex. Painting was a solitary celebration. The only freedom. He wanted people to like his work, of course. And he wanted to exhibit successfully, in order to free himself from his other life. But more than anything else, he just wanted to paint.

"So," Sasha said, changing the subject, "you're really going?"

Lev nodded, crushing his beard down into his chest. "I'll miss you, my friend."

"I'll miss you. Who will I have to tell me what a great artist I am?"

Lev chuckled. "You'll always have Rachel. And some

woman or other. But who will *I* have, in America, to tell me what a *bad* artist I am?"

A young woman pranced by them followed by her long-haired boyfriend, a moderately well-known rock musician. The woman wore a Soviet air force peaked cap over a tumult of chestnut hair. In place of an officer's badge, the cap bore a Madonna fan button. Her leather jacket hung open, and above the standard miniskirt, a hand-lettered sweatshirt said in English ROCK FUCK GOOD TIME.

"Hello, Tanya," Sasha said.

"Piss off, you bastard."

The woman turned up the stairs, showing a great tear in the back of her stockings. Torn hose were also fashionable this year.

"Who was *that?*" Birman whispered.

"One of life's little detours."

"I never saw you with that one."

"Didn't last long. So you're really going?"

"Yes. It's a miracle."

"I'm glad for you. You'll be a great success."

"You know, I really didn't think they could arrange it. But foreigners can get anything done in this country."

Nearby, a middle-aged art professor Sasha recognized had two black marketeers in tow, lecturing them on the contemporary resonance of traditional Russian painting. Black marketeers, fiercely uncultured men, had recently started coming to the informal exhibitions organized by Rachel and her friends, always with a hired expert to approve their purchases. A small minority of the population was becoming so rich so fast that they had to seek places to put their money, and Rachel's crowd, God only knew how, had talked some of them into investing in art. Everyone was happy about it because, although the men who made their money on the left knew nothing of art and couldn't even be said to like what they bought, they paid in hard currency. And such types were good to know whenever you needed something.

"Maybe it's a good thing you're leaving," Sasha said.

"Yesterday's criminal is today's capitalist," Lev responded. "And today's budding capitalist is tomorrow's great collector."

At one time Rachel's exhibitions, for which she never took

any commission, had only included those artists who could not receive approved shows or whose works could not be displayed prominently in the state commission gallery where she worked during the day. Lately, however, with the black market money and the foreigners, already established artists knocked on the door of her parents' flat, where Rachel lived in a cramped room on her workday salary.

"I don't believe it," Sasha said. "I don't believe anything good is going to happen to this country. We're incapable of staying on track for very long."

"Then you should come with me to America. If they could arrange it for me, they could fix it up for you."

"You're Jewish. America only takes Jews."

"I can teach you how to be Jewish. Or how to be a Russian Jew, anyway. You just tell the immigration authorities that your grandfather was at Lenin's side during the Revolution and that Stalin sent your father to Siberia. Then tell them the KGB regularly confiscated your paintings. Seriously, I'm sure the Americans could fix it up for you. They're starving for Soviet artists, we're all the rage. And you're ten times the artist I am. It's all so easy for them, they're so rich. They just bought everything they could carry out of my studio, then I got an invitation to come to America and a private appointment at the American embassy. I didn't even have to stand in line."

"I'll miss you," Sasha said again. It was a black day. "You'll have to write to me. Tell me about how famous you become."

"Why stay here, Sasha? What is there for you in Moscow? You want to paint those military masterpieces of yours until the day you die? You're not one for all that mystical Mother Russia crap. You'd do better in the West than I ever could. Let me talk to the Americans."

Sasha shook his head. "I'm happy enough here. And I don't even speak English well."

"You speak it better than I do. And think of the girls. American girls. The girls of this California. Do you know that in San Francisco all of the men are homosexuals and you can pick any girl you want?"

"So that's why you're going."

"I think that American women must be the most beautiful in the world," Lev said dreamily.

"All right. When you write to me, you can tell me all about the wonderful American girls. Just be careful in San Francisco. Everybody has AIDS."

"There are deadly women everywhere," Lev said. Then his eyes fixed on something over Sasha's shoulder and he laughed out loud. "All you have to do is turn around."

Sasha turned around. And his life changed. He did not realize it at the time. He did not feel love at first sight. If anything, something about the woman put him off, aggravating his foul mood. But who among us is capable of thinking clearly when the hand of God reaches down and slaps us on the back of the head? Perhaps what annoyed Sasha about her was the realization, on a still-subconscious level, that fate was walking toward him. While the more sophisticated side of his subconscious insisted that fate no more had a place in the contemporary world than beauty did in contemporary painting. So he turned around and his life changed and all he felt in that instant was a faint thud in his soul akin to the effect of indigestion.

She looked as though she could leap on a wild pony and gallop away, and she looked as though she would never smile for anything so trivial as a man. Small and very fine, she looked fearless and strong. Sasha thought her eyes were masculine, and only much later did he realize they were the most nakedly feminine eyes he had ever seen. She had paled in the northern winter, but her skin still had color enough for a drunk to mistake her for a Gypsy. A heavy sheet of black hair fell down over her dark fur coat, and hair and shoulders gleamed with a wetness that had been snow before she entered the humid building. Sasha could not see her body under the big coat, but he could sense it, he could have sketched its contours with great accuracy. He knew that two kinds of Central Asian girls came to Moscow: those who came to sell things at the market and the daughters of the powerful, who came to study at the university. Of those who went to the university, there was a further subdivision: those who timidly kept to themselves as though their fathers and older brothers were watching them every minute, and those who went wild in the sudden freedom of a great city far from home. Sasha had no doubt into which ultimate category this girl had fallen.

Her eyes met Sasha's, dismissed him, and moved on. As

she passed by, she trailed a scent of spice, salt, and almonds that lingered as if she had wiped it across his face.

Only as he watched her climb the stairs toward Rachel's still-thriving debate did Sasha notice that a man was with her. Or a boy, to be more precise, following her like a dog. Blond and handsome, he nonetheless had no real presence compared to the girl. His stylish Western clothes were by far the most powerful thing about him, and Sasha figured him for the offspring of some big shot in the Foreign Ministry or the Ministry of Trade—a little puff of smoke trailing after the winter fire of the girl.

Sasha turned to face Lev again and found himself eye to eye with Vera.

"I saw you looking at her," Vera said with a little laugh and a smile that was not altogether forgiving. She was still pouting a bit about the verbal lashing he had given her for moving a pair of oil canvases while attempting to clean his apartment.

"And here she is," Lev declared with a big bearded smile. "Your guardian angel. Verushka, my darling, I'd stay in Russia if you'd have me. I'd convert to Christianity."

"You look hot," Sasha told her, widening his smile with an invisible paintbrush.

"You'd be hot, too, if you were cooking all night. Anya's kitchen is so tiny, it's one big oven. Here." Vera held up a plate piled high with little deep-fried turnovers. "Take some before this batch is gone, too."

"Cabbage?" Lev asked, already reaching.

"Cheese."

Lev's eyebrows went up. "Where'd you get enough?"

"Vera's got connections. Her old man's a big shot on a state farm up past Space City."

Birman, wheezing, got down on one knee, clutching a fistful of piroshki. "I swear it. I'd give up everything, if you'd marry me. Or you could come with me to America."

"And who'd take care of Sasha?" Vera asked.

She was a girl with a genius for saying the wrong thing. Men described her as beautiful because they never really looked at her. She had blond Russian hair that lofted off her shoulders like angel's wings and a good figure, the flesh generous here and there on a body that gave an impression of frailty that Sasha knew would not hold. She was pretty, not beautiful. A delight to see and touch now, in ten years she would begin thickening until the changes in her body killed all sober desire.

She was a nice girl, almost laughably demure in this crowd of plume-haired punks and overdressed criminals. She wore an orange sweater over a pink blouse, both of which might have been hand-me-downs from her mother's generation, and the only makeup on her face was a smear of crimson lipstick. She looked innocent and warm and decent to the point of stupidity.

Sasha helped himself to one of the cheese pies, admiring the complex coloration that seemed so simple if you didn't really look, the random blisters on the fried crust, the feel of the thing, the weight. He would have liked to paint some cow of a general's wife stuffing her maw with the pies, eyes piggy huge. Above all, they wanted you to paint them thinner, the oil-paint diet.

"You won't get piroshki like these in America," Vera told Lev. She stood straight-backed and proud. "In America they eat only hamburgers."

Lev shrugged. "I like hamburgers."

Vera settled her free hand on her hip. "And when did you eat all these hamburgers? To like them so much?"

"I don't have to eat them to know I like them. In America everything is wonderful."

"America is godless."

Lev shook his head and looked at Sasha. "Who's she been reading? Solzhenitsyn?"

"Vera was raised in the perfect Soviet family," Sasha said. "Her father's a Party member and her mother belongs to the Church. She's blessed on earth and in heaven."

"That's the trouble with you," Vera said earnestly. "You two don't believe in anything. None of you do around here. If you believed in God, you wouldn't paint the things you do, Lev Adamovich. Those disgusting pictures of two women . . ."

"Vera wishes I'd paint something sensible," Sasha said. "Like icons." Then he took another bite of crust and cheese. He had not realized how hungry he was. His muscles wanted food, after the blessed rigor of his afternoon swim. Swimming saves sanity, he thought. But it makes you hungry as hell. For an instant he slipped back into the big indoor pool, half-deserted in an off-hour, going deep into the silence, away from everybody and everything, into a world of straining muscles, water, and sudden, gorgeous air.

"That's not *true,*" Vera said. "Sometimes your painting is wonderful." She turned to Lev. "He's doing my portrait. He's making me absolutely beautiful."

Sasha helped himself to another turnover. Other hands came sneaking in as well, magnetized by the golden reek of the food.

"You're lucky," Lev said. "Sasha's a great painter. Someday, when these shits get their heads screwed on straight, your portrait will hang in a museum." He smiled like a bad boy. "I *do* hope it's a nude."

A crashing sound triggered a chaos of voices up on the landing. The next sounds were unmistakably those of a fight.

"Your pictures," Vera cried.

For an instant, Sasha imagined that little Rachel had lost patience and attacked the Englishman. Then he figured that one of the tenants had decided he'd had his fill of art and had come out of his apartment full of vodka.

He went very quickly, deft on his feet. He leapt the stairs two and three at a time, weaving between the islands of metal-music fans and art lovers. With a light touch he slipped past the woman in the miniskirt who had told him to piss off and their eyes connected for a slice of a second. As he moved higher, he could feel her eyes trailing him, another story that might not be finished.

As he approached the landing, one of his works came tumbling end over end to meet him. It was an oversize pastel sketch. The makeshift frame caught on a winter coat, and one of the rockers put his foot through the stretched paper in an attempt to rescue it.

Sasha let it go. He shoved roughly through the ring that had formed on the landing and saw Rachel and the Englishman trying to shield his remaining works with their bodies while Genia Tomkin, slump-bellied and drunk, swung lazily at the pretty boy who had followed the Asian girl up the stairs. The pretty boy poked out his fists, ineffectual and ridiculous, and Sasha saw instantly that both of the combatants were too afraid of hurting and being hurt to do any real damage to each other. They were only good for destroying artwork.

Sasha shoved the drunken artist out of the way with both hands, bringing so much force to bear that Genia stumbled backward and crashed down against the wall. Without pausing, Sasha wheeled and caught the pretty boy by an outstretched arm, spun him around and smashed him into the opposite wall so hard his breath emptied out with an involuntary cry. He pinned the boy by the neck and upper arm, pressing his cheek into the masonry.

"Just who the hell do you think you are, you little snot?"

The boy gasped to refill his lungs. From the corner of his eye Sasha saw two men in identical overcoats watching the show. They were long-recognized secret policemen who were always detailed to attend art exhibitions. Dumb-eyed and silent, they had become a fixture everyone would have missed. Years before, they would have called for the police to close the show after an hour or so, but times had changed.

Tonight they wore little smiles of amusement.

Fuck them, Sasha thought. He renewed his grip on the boy's neck and shoved him into the wall again.

"Daddy going to pay for the damage you did, you cat turd?"

"Lemme go."

Sasha gave him a knee in the ass. "You think you're such a tough guy, maybe you'd like me to kick your nuts down the steps and drag you outside?"

The boy struggled to turn his head, sizing up what he could see of Sasha with eyes inherited from three generations of successful bureaucrats. Finally he said:

"That pig insulted my girl."

Behind Sasha's back, Genia laughed like a happy madman. "All I did was ask his nigger bitch if she wanted to fuck."

"Shut up, Genia."

"What's wrong with that?" Genia's voice was puffed with liquor. "They all want it."

"Genia, just shut up," Sasha shouted, losing the last band of control over his temper.

His ears told him what was happening. He could hear the wheeze and scrape of the artist trying to rise from the floor. Drunk and ready to take on the world.

Sasha turned, gave the pretty boy an elbow in the kidneys that dropped him to his knees, then side-kicked Genia in the stomach, almost losing his balance as the sole and heel of his boot sank into fat. Genia gasped and thumped back down into a slouch against the wall.

Sasha stood between the two fallen warriors, looking for someone or something else to hit.

"You two stupid shits," he said, breathing heavily. "You'd be scared of your own pricks, if they ever got hard."

He saw another picture where it had fallen, the low-quality canvas torn through. He spun and kicked the fallen boy as hard as he could in the meat of his backside, knocking him flat. Stepping closer, he kicked him again, in the side of the hip this time.

"*Sasha.* That's *enough.*" It was Rachel, the only one with the courage to come forward. The Englishman stood pale as milk behind her shoulder.

Sasha shook his head, suddenly embarrassed, only now realizing what he had done. Instead of looking at Rachel, he focused on the Englishman.

"I suppose," he said in Russian, "it's also impossible for artists to beat people up where you come from. Well, this isn't fucking England and you can take your fucking English opinions and jam them back up your ass."

The Englishman was astonished. "Good lord, Miss Traum, he isn't mad at *me,* is he? What's he going on about?"

"Fuck the load of you."

The pretty boy had gotten back up to his knees. Canny, he looked up at the two plainclothesmen and said, "Look at this. He tore my jacket. It's from Italy."

The secret policemen shrugged. It was a changed world.

Genia, too, began to whine. About the harshness of the world and his recently deceased brother.

Sasha turned his back and headed for the stairs. The spectators hurried to give him room.

He wanted to see if the pastel sketch could be rescued. Technically, it was a minor piece, but he had felt a great deal of affection for it, had not planned to sell it. It was an attempt to capture roses without sentimentality, gray, white, and black on pale blue paper, working with grouped objects as mass, as a unity, to get at the essence of roses. The work had happened because a woman had left roses at his door and he had laid them on the kitchen table without thinking, only to discover how thoroughly beautiful they were in their accidental array. Roses sketched because there happened to be roses.

Someone else had beaten him to the frame with the torn paper.

"Your work?" the Central Asian girl asked calmly.

Sasha nodded, appraising her in the remnants of his fury.

"How much?" she asked.

She was so beautiful that it made him angry. With a different kind of anger.

"It's ruined," he said. "And it's not for sale."

"But I like it. I want to buy it. How much?"

"It's not for sale." He felt angrier now than he had felt when he was kicking the boy on the floor.

Vera stepped up beside the Asian girl. She looked big and clumsy, cow-eyed in comparison.

The Asian girl produced a small black purse of buttery leather that caught the light of the studio lamps. She counted out bills from a thick roll, balancing the torn picture on end against her leg. It looked even better that way, fruity, black roses falling from heaven, a bouquet from God.

"Here." She held out a fistful of rubles.

Sasha took the last two steps very quickly. He grabbed the frame, held it out, and put his foot through the middle of the roses, exploding the original tear. Then he tossed the ramshackle frame back against the girl's fur coat.

"You can have it for free," he said.

To his surprise, the Asian girl picked up the frame, stooping slightly with a grace that made him hurt inside. She mothered the torn paper against her breasts.

"I'm in your debt," she said.

6

DID YOU THINK SHE WAS PRETTY?" VERA ASKED.

"What?" Sasha had been drifting toward sleep.

"That girl. The one who wanted to buy your picture."

He had not made love to Vera. As he'd left the exhibition, his anger had turned inward and he had barely spoken. In bed, he had taken the woman in his arms automatically, thoughtlessly, but had carried intimacy no further. He felt empty. And lonely. With a loneliness that Vera would never mend. They lay awake, in a miserable silence. He could feel the woman's inarticulate alarm, sense her wakefulness by the slight vibrancy of spirit and flesh that lulled when sleep finally came, and he felt sorry for her. But he was paralyzed, incapable of comforting her with a word or an active hand. He simply lay there, suspended in unhappiness. Then, as his thoughts finally began to smear toward unconsciousness, Vera spoke.

"I don't remember," he answered, lying.

"The dark one. The Uzbek or whatever she was."

"Don't remember," he insisted. But he did remember. With a clarity that woke him again.

"She wanted to buy the torn picture. You threw it at her."

"What about her?"

"I thought she was beautiful," Vera whispered. "I thought you liked her."

"I almost knocked her down the steps."

There was a moment of silence between them, a measure of inadequacy.

"Do you love me?"

"What?"

"Do you *love* me?" Her voice wavered. The familiar distress.

"Vera . . . please. I've always been honest with you. I don't love anybody. I never have." He pulled her a bit closer against him. Round breasts that would fail, a stomach that would distend, fate. "But I *like* you. I'm glad to have you in my life." And it had been true, although it seemed much less true now.

He could tell she was crying. There was no noise, no shivering. But the tension of her body changed slightly and she pushed her face a weight deeper into the pillow.

"I wish," she said slowly, "that I could be beautiful for you. Like that girl."

"Vera, you *are* beautiful." It was astonishing how easily the words could emerge, in a tone of absolute sincerity. "You're a very beautiful woman." He held her about the waist. Taut, unmistakably young in its resilience, the flesh nevertheless begged for children and age.

Vera nestled closer against him. It was a child's gesture, free of sexuality.

"I'm so afraid," she said. "I love you so much."

"You need to sleep." He stroked her gently. He knew that the best thing would be to end the relationship immediately. But somehow, the canvas was not quite finished. Perhaps, he thought, it was only that level of selfishness that decent men and women pretended did not exist.

But he liked the way she cared for him. And the way the morning light fell like cream upon her face.

He felt a slight bounce on the mattress. The cat. Come to sleep now that the sound of soft voices had replaced the electric tension.

"Vrubel's here," Vera whispered.

"I know."

"You love *him*."

"People don't love cats."

"*You* do. You love your cat. But not me." She said this in a tone of voice that resented nothing but simply wondered at the way of the world.

"I don't love the goddamned cat." As if to prove it, he pushed Vrubel with his foot, making the animal give up part of its accustomed sleeping space. "I don't love anybody or anything. The last human being I loved was my grandmother. And she's dead."

The cat inched back to its familiar spot, settling warmly against the back of Sasha's calf.

"I wish I could have met her," Vera said.

"Who?"

"Your grandmother."

"You wouldn't have liked her. And she wouldn't have liked you."

"But why? If she was such a good grandmother, she would've liked me just because I love you so much."

"She was Latvian. She hated Russians."

"Well," Vera said slowly, "you wouldn't have to tell her I was Russian."

Sasha smiled in the darkness. He could hardly imagine a woman more instantly recognizable as Russian than Vera. And his grandmother had possessed such fine eyes. Eyes alert to the faintest of an artist's lines, eyes for small birds in the green, green marshes low behind the sand flats and the sea, eyes full of a century's horrors.

"You wouldn't have liked her," Sasha said flatly. "She was a snob. Very much the grande dame. If you spoke Russian to her, she'd answer in Latvian. If you spoke to her in German, she'd answer in French. She could be very cruel."

But she loved me, he thought. It was one of the few certainties in his life. She loved me and she put the brushes in my hand and the colors in my eyes and the faith that I could make a record of how beautiful it all was before other men managed to destroy the last of it.

"But why would she hate Russians?" Vera asked in perfect innocence. "Why would she hate me without even knowing me?"

"Because," he began, talking to himself, "Russians killed her father at the end of one war and took away her husband at the beginning of the next one. Because a Russian married her daughter—or because her daughter married a Russian. Because two officers of the great liberating, heroic Red Army raped her in the middle of the day in the entryway of her apartment building because she was too well dressed to be one of the People."

Vera turned it over for a few seconds, but Sasha understood exactly what such tales meant to her: history lessons, not quite real.

"But . . . she didn't hate you. And you're half-Russian."

"No. She didn't hate me."

The cat stretched and groaned and settled its long back against his leg. Vera began to weep audibly.

"Can't you just say you love me? Even if you don't mean it?"

"Vera, we've been through all this."

"I'm sorry. I'm so sorry."

"Come on now." He tightened his hold on her again. The eternal Russian woman, either throwing herself on the tracks over a man who couldn't be bothered or rehearsing to be a grandmother. Even the ones who weren't religious luxuriated in penitence.

"I'm so sorry you weren't the first. I wish you could've been the first. So you could have loved me forever."

"My God, Vera. I told you. That makes no difference to me whatsoever. People have sex. It's normal."

"But I want you to be the only one. I love you so much. I didn't know you existed, or—"

She had confessed to a single lover in a child's affair that had turned out badly. It was nothing. But convinced that God had seen her, she would not let it be. She had given up, at least for the present, on trying to insinuate religion into Sasha's life. But its most perverse and superficial aspects haunted her at odd hours.

"Vera, you're a good girl. Come on now."

"I'm so bad. It's bad even that I love it so much when you touch me."

He tried to choose his women as sensibly as possible. But you made mistakes. The best bets were generally shopgirls convinced they were too pretty and clever by half for so lowly a position. They were predictable, dependable for a while, and they loved to fuck and have their portraits scribbled off. They were also well situated to keep his apartment supplied with scarce goods that never found their way from the stockroom to the public shelves. A steady woman, well chósen, meant never having to stand in line, meant more time to paint.

He was always amazed at how easy it was to make Soviet girls and women happy. Almost invariably, their sexual experiences had been so abysmal that it was an overpowering shock to them when a man took a little time and understood even the most elementary aspects of pleasing them. More often than not, they didn't really know how their bodies worked. Saddest of all were the too-young girls who had already come to think of themselves as nothing more than a bucket for a man's residue.

The important thing, of course, was never to let the relationship drag on too long, and to end it artfully. The dangers were always the same—visions of marriage, lies about the sexual safety of a given night. He had stopped counting abortions.

It was not a world his grandmother would have understood. To the very end, she had barricaded herself behind culture, manners, elocution, and musty notions of social and personal honor. She had only survived so long because she had been overlooked, never quite important enough to elicit a special effort from the avenging angels of the State, who had carried off the men in her life one after another. Or perhaps allowing her to age in her brittle iron separateness had been the most refined punishment of all. It was impossible to say.

Blessedly, Vera faded into sleep, cried-out and deliciously ravished by her misery. Sasha knew the type so well, although Vera was a particularly fine example: the girls and women who couldn't ever really lose, who were contented enough when a man actually loved them and who were spectacularly, gloriously miserable when he didn't. No real passion, and no unbearable pain.

The tension went out of the female muscles beneath his hand and arm, and Vera's breath steadied. Her warm, tolerable smell seemed stronger, the darkness darker. Sasha was very much awake now, but with the special late consciousness that frees itself briefly from the prison of time.

He thought about his grandmother. He credited the proper,

inviolably neat old woman, with her fine posture that not even Russian rapists could spoil, with teaching him about sex. She had never uttered the word in his presence. Women of her generation, no matter how well satisfied they might have been in their personal lives, never brought such matters to speech. But in her patience, dignity, and pride, she had managed to convey to him that women were more than dogs with kitchen skills.

He had spent long summer vacations in her splendid, threadbare treasure house of an apartment in Riga, enchanted with the proximity of the sea and the odor of foreign history. They had visited the survivors of other good Latvian families, in one-room flats crammed with old photographs and books, or in the green countryside, and he, a restless boy, had unwittingly absorbed a consciousness different from the stew of selfish deceits and intoxicated intimacies that fed Russian lives. When the old woman told him tales of Riga between the wars, free and blossoming with culture and national credibility, her carefully chosen words and dreaming pauses had filled him with a sense that the world was a far richer and more beautiful place, more abundant in possibilities, than he had ever imagined. She spoke of friends and relatives, of men and women who had actually lived together without ruining the other's life, of a reality that did not require the decoration of official lies to make it bearable.

The old woman with her smell of last year's flowers had managed to hold on to her apartment with its impossible curving art nouveau windows and its library and porcelain perched high above Gailissa Street. In the fervent, fertile years of Latvian independence between the world wars, Gailissa had been the most beautiful residential street in Europe, a small, perfect jewel, with each fanciful apartment building straining to outdo the rest. Built in the artistic riot on the eve of the first war and polished in the peace, the street had matured in the years of lacquered automobiles, pearls, and dinner jackets. The residents of Gailissa Street were the men and women for whom Vidbergs had done his splendid erotica, before the arrival of Soviet power turned him into the Baltic Goya, chronicling his nation's murder in black and white. The brilliant national theater played first and foremost for the lovers, dowagers, and dreamers of Gailissa Street, and the interior design that outpaced the best of Scandinavia or Berlin found its reward in their parlors. Across two magnificently free decades, never untroubled, a tiny people had erupted with energy, talent, and joy.

Then the world changed the rules. The dreadful overture began when the Reich summoned all of the Baltic Germans home, and they left the universities and decaying estates and small shops, the grainfields and forests and swamps where they had been at home for the better part of a millennium, lugging overstuffed suitcases aboard white steamers with harsh black insignia in the center of their flags. Fools celebrated their leaving, declaring that Latvia was well rid of them at last. But more thoughtful men and women kept their silence. Then the Soviets marched in with lists of those to be used, those to be deported, and those to be shot upon apprehension.

And the golden people of Gailissa Street who had not booked passage in time, who had counted on their miniature army to fight, who had not believed that a civilized, modern world could permit such transgressions . . . those golden people died in sandpits beyond the edge of the industrial sector, with a single bullet in the back of each head. The slender women with their exact, shining hair found themselves knocked to the ground in an alley by gangs of Red Army men or went mad in the bed of a truck full of soldiers, or watched their teenaged daughters, educated to good books and good manners, disappear screaming into a uniformed mass. The wonder of Gailissa Street had to be destroyed in the name of the People, and commissars with old Brownings broke through the doors and beat the women before and after raping them, forcing their husbands to watch until the saviors of the world got bored and cocked their pistols. The new Soviet man poured his sickness of soul and body into Latvia. Drunken soldiers shot down every man who wore eyeglasses because all men with eyeglasses were intellectuals and enemies of the People. The secret police took over the block of flats on the far corner of Gailissa Street for a headquarters, choosing the only ugly building in the row, an ocher faux-rococo horror. The names of the streets and buildings changed. And the cattle cars and trucks continued to roll east with their human cargo.

Then the *Nazis* came. And then the Soviets came back.

Years later, a small boy with his name written on a piece of paper and pinned to his chest stepped down from a train in the Riga station to be met by a rigid, unsmiling woman in black who briefly looked him up and down then said by way of greeting:

"That suit will never do. Whatever could your mother be thinking of?"

His mother, who, unreasonably, impossibly, had fallen in love with a young Russian officer in the postwar years, who had married him despite all that the man's blood had done to those of her blood, had followed her man back and forth across a continent, from dusty garrison to drab city. His mother, who had learned to forget all that she had absorbed at her mother's side, had become more Russian than the Russians, a heavy, bent, prematurely aged woman in a kerchief and bad shoes. The two women had not exchanged one spoken or written word since the daughter's marriage. Then, suddenly, Sasha's mother had sent a telegram to Riga, announcing that one Alexander Ivanovich Leskov would arrive in Riga at such and such a time, on such and such a train. Looking back, Sasha realized that his mother had wanted to give him something better than her own life, something his older brother had already missed. It was the act of a woman whose pride had been exterminated. Yet, on that bright, billowy summer day, Sasha had only felt fear, the loneliness of separation, and hunger.

His grandmother, still without a smile, had taken him directly to an ancient tailor who worked out of the tiny room where he lived with his wife. The man bowed and addressed Sasha's grandmother as "Madame." Only after an eternity of measurements in the stinking-sweet torpor of the tailor's lair did his grandmother offer him a prim lunch in an apartment where the air was the color of amber and where eating meant ceaseless, increasingly impatient criticism of his table manners. That first stay was a dull agony, with long silences and little terrors, until, one day near the end, the old woman slapped him hard across the face for chewing with his mouth open. A moment later she collapsed in tears, falling to her knees and hugging him so hard he could barely draw a breath, weeping out the pain of decades and calling him, "Alexander, Alexander, Alexander . . ."

He had longed for that "vacation" to end. Then, when it was over, he had cried, too, waving at the straight-backed black figure with the white hair left behind on the boarding platform. He went back to Riga the following summer, over his officer-father's drunken protests. When he thought of it all now, it was hard not to grow sentimental, recalling the shrill family fights and his mother's willingness to accept his father's blows without giving in. He saw her now as a drowning woman struggling to hold her child above the swirling water.

His older brother had never been sent to Riga, nor had he ever been invited. Pavel was his father's son. But there was no point in thinking about Pavel now.

Sasha lay between Vera and the cat, drenched in yesterday. In his teenage years the trips to Latvia had changed pitch. Once the outings to country cottages or remote stretches of beach had been brilliant highlights of his vacation, but now his thoughts turned more and more to the broad-faced girls laughing together in the streets of the old town, where medieval churches cast long shadows of disapproval over the giddy conversations and the first secrets of desire. He had loved to listen to the music of their voices, to find a reason to talk to them in his formal grammar and dreadful accent. They laughed and would have turned away had he not been blessed with good looks. He kissed his first girl in a narrow old-town passageway, both of them trying to ignore the too-human smells of their surroundings. Rummaging through his grandmother's library, he found a sheaf of startlingly sexual etchings from Sigismunds Vidbergs. He already had good enough eyes to recognize a master's hand, but there was something else here, too. In those secret pictures sex took on a dazzling, unexpected range. There was much he did not understand. But he *felt* it, like hearing your first symphony after a lifetime of folk songs. These women offered a lithe readiness a world away from the clumsy grapplings of schoolboy and schoolgirl. The exposure of slight, white flesh from beneath inked silk stirred him as nothing else had ever done. The images had a purity of line and wantonness of purpose that made him feel enriched and lonely at the same time. And he felt a terrible sense of loss, imagining from his grandmother's tales that all such perfect women must have been murdered or had grown ruined and old. He looked at the curving, slim bodies, the mouths split in ecstasy and alarm, and feared that he would never find such a one in his lifetime. Later, of course, he discovered that such women remained into his generation and beyond, as capable as ever of stunning a man with desire. But on that dead-air summer day, he had believed only that he was condemned to spend his entire life dreaming of beauty irrevocably lost.

There was other art, as well. Like all well-brought-up girls of her generation, his grandmother could draw a bit and played at watercolors. And as soon as she saw the easy facility with which her grandson condensed the earth and sky to paper and lead, she produced a fine wooden painting kit of a quality unavailable for decades—and fresh paints and an aged instructor to go with the gift.

Sasha still had the battered painter's box. But he had never managed to capture the Vidbergs etchings. Informed belatedly that his grandmother had been found dead of natural causes, he had moved heaven and earth to get to Riga. But by the time he arrived, her apartment had been stripped of every possession and new occupants had moved in. Standing in the familiar threshold, blocked by a heavy woman with a mask of blackheads across her nose, he had only managed a last glimpse of the eccentrically shaped windows, their womanly curves corrupted by cheap draperies. A baby howled and stank against a backdrop of stewing cabbage and scruffy furniture, and the woman claimed that she and her husband had been living there forever and that she knew nothing about any old cow who might have lived there before.

Three or four years later, a neighbor experienced a fit of guilt and sent Sasha a Meissen figurine looted from the old woman's apartment. But the figurine had been poorly packed and it did not survive the mailing. So now all he had from his grandmother was the wooden painter's kit, memories of floral perfume masking an old woman's sweat, a small, unsatisfying portrait he had painted from memory, and the abiding faith there would always be beauty in the world.

Pretending to be asleep, Vera lay awake in quiet terror. She did not know how to reach this man. Convinced that she loved him, she could not imagine life without him. She could not think of being away from him forever without stirring herself into a panic. She did not care for his paintings, finding them negligible and unnecessarily gloomy, except for her portrait. But painting didn't matter. Nor was she much impressed with the material things his associations might provide. And their lovemaking, while pleasant, was not the focus of her longing. But she loved to look at him, to feel him against her and in her not so much for the physical power of it but because she had him then, he was hers and no one else's. She wanted him to marry her, and she wanted it more than she had ever wanted anything else, although she could not say why.

She had lied to him, of course. She had lied to him from the beginning and she found herself telling ever more lies. But he never suspected, as far as she knew. And the lies were all right because, in her heart, she knew she was an honest person. God wouldn't mind little lies like that. If it meant you got married.

She had lied when she told him she had only one lover before him. But she did it for him, because that was what men wanted to hear and his nonchalance about the matter didn't fool her for an instant. She had also lied about the number of her lovers because she could not believe she had been so weak and wicked. It seemed to her that, if she could fool this man, she could almost fool God. Or at least make Him forget. She was a good girl, everything that went before had been a mistake. She was meant to be this man's wife and a mother.

She had been trying for two months to become pregnant by him, lying about that, too. But God would forgive her. Once she was pregnant with his child, Sasha would not be capable of turning her out. She knew him, recognized his goodness. Oh, he might be angry at first. But he was a good man at heart, a good, good man who needed to be rescued.

He frightened her at times. The way he unthinkingly associated with absolute scum, with vagabonds and Jews. She was glad that dirty Birman was going to America. Now she had to pry Sasha away from that little freak Jewess. Vera knew what Rachel wanted, oh, she knew it beyond doubt. Sick. The creature was sick to imagine that a healthy man like Sasha would ever . . .

And then the cat could be gotten rid of. It was a dirty, spoiled thing, and Sasha paid it far too much attention, stroking it, pretending to carry on conversations with it, allowing it onto the bed. It was repulsive.

But she had even taken care of the cat for him, while he was away. To prove her love. She was ready to sacrifice anything.

Those Jews were all devils. They just wanted to get Sasha in their clutches.

It was preposterous. How that revolting little Rachel could be in love with Sasha. And she made it so obvious. It was disgusting, unspeakable. With those little Jew eyes popping out and those grotesque dark circles and the Jew pallor. Almost puking her love out for all to see. God only knew what went through the imagination of such a horrid little beast.

She was safe, of course. Sasha would never dream of having physical contact with such a monstrosity. With all his going-on about beauty. It was only that Sasha was so trusting. He pretended to be so cynical, but he believed everything that people told him. It would be all too easy for some slithering creature to take advantage of him in some horrible, unimaginable way. Sasha was weak because he did not have faith in God to guide him, to protect him. Of all the men who had left their traces between her thighs, Sasha was the most naive and the most in need of God. He was, finally, such a weak man.

Whenever they made love, she tried to hold him inside her as long as possible. And when he slipped away and she felt him starting to flow out of her, she would lock her thighs and turn, tightening her intimate muscles to hold his love inside her forever, to make him grow inside her. She was, in fact, not so enthused about having a child for the sake of having a child. But it was the price of changing her last name to Leskova.

Vera Petrovna Leskova.

She imagined a smoky church filled with deep musical voices and the presence of God, two crowns suspended above two heads. The words, the irrevocable words . . .

But God was punishing her now. For the abortion. That was why Sasha was not yet growing inside her. She had sinned and God had seen it. How long would it take Him to forgive her?

She decided that, when she next took the train up to visit her family, she would go out to the woods to see Old Luda. Yes. The old woman might just know a way. Maybe she could get one of her old girlfriends to go with her. It scared her to be completely alone with Old Luda. She could promise to have her girlfriend's fortune told, and she could ask Luda if she didn't have some lotion to help her become pregnant, or some charm.

Anything for Sasha's sake.

Shirin Talala eased herself out from under her lover's weak arm and wiped herself with the bedsheet. She knew with cold certainty that she would never share this one's bed again.

It was a shame. Had he been more physically capable or at least more imaginative, they could have had a good arrangement. He belonged, in his way, to the same level of society as she did, with hard currency, influence, tables in restaurants, tickets, good clothing, even trips abroad. It would have made everything so easy. But the boy's stupid, whining brevity was intolerable.

He snored, a satisfied coward. She loved the thought of men so much, the anticipation. A shame that the reality was always so unsatisfactory. She put her fingers between her legs and began to touch herself.

The Talalas belonged to a border tribe that had roamed and ruled between Uzbekistan and the Tadzhik hills, changing alliances as readily as they changed horses. They had existed in their own microcosmos, practicing female circumcision well into the twentieth century, until the enlightenment of Soviet rule finally convinced them that the mutilation of their female children was needlessly cruel and unnecessary—and strictly punishable by law. Shirin had been born into a race that despised women, where the men, proud of each manifestation of their sex, still slept in rooms apart from the contaminating odor of femininity, where the women were expected to work themselves to death for the privilege of bearing children until their insides collapsed. While their men sat drinking tea and playing dominoes under a shade tree. The Soviets were bloody bastards, but they had brought alphabets, electricity, water free of parasites . . . and opportunity.

Shirin's father had been born in a tent. Now he had a luxurious apartment in Moscow, another apartment in Tashkent that was his official residence, a third apartment Shirin had never seen on the outskirts of Tashkent where he kept his mistress, and an estate with a private game preserve and irrigated gardens and orchards near Samarkand, where once their ancestors had pitched their yurts.

Shirin had freedom.

She had the freedom to break free of the chains the preening men of her race still laid upon women foolish enough to submit. Oddly, Uzbek men had a whispered reputation among Russian women as potent lovers. But Shirin wasn't having any of it.

She groaned, swallowing the sound so as not to wake the fool beside her. She raised her hips toward the ceiling, meeting a lover who wasn't there, wanting. At age twenty-two, after four years in Moscow, she had gone through a succession of lovers, some better than others, none of them capable of exhausting her desires. She turned her head into the pillow, fantasizing about the artist who had tossed the painting at her. At least that one wasn't afraid of his own shadow. She imagined how he would be, holding herself open with one hand, stroking herself with the other.

With a smile she thought that perhaps the older ones had been right, that the knife cutting away the girl child's pleasure was merciful. There were times when her body frightened her.

Her mother had been horrified when she had come in unexpectedly one day to discover that Shirin had stopped shaving between her legs. She covered her ears when Shirin tried to explain that it was a desert practice, a throwback to days when there was no water with which to wash. Her mother had scurried from the room, shaking her head in shame.

I'll never go back, Shirin thought.

Her body shuddered, and she groaned like a man. But the boy at her side was oblivious of her.

I'm never going back, she swore. But she did not know where she was going to, either. She studied foreign languages at the university because languages meant freedom and opportunity, and she had a knack for them. But she did not know what she would do, where life would take her.

She only knew that she was getting out of this child's bedroom. Good in the dark, she gathered up her gold necklace with the scorpion pendant, then dried herself again with the sheet. Her clothing was littered about, but she patiently and quietly found each piece, grateful that the sleeping boy did not miss her and that she would not have to endure any more of his pleading for love and recognition.

He was a fool.

And she had been a fool for sharing his bed.

The artist was going to be much better, she was sure of it.

Rachel could not sleep. As always, when the darkness failed to find a hiding place for her, she thought of Sasha Leskov. She loved him. She loved him with all of her heart, without reservation or criticism, and she had promised herself two things. First, she would never tell him of her love. Second, she would never do anything to embarrass him.

Her body hurt. It was bad enough to be one of God's errors when you walked down the street, but it seemed unfair that there should be physical pain in addition to the emotional pain that never, ever, went away. No matter how she turned, her twisted back ached and brought tears to her eyes. Lying to her parents about it, she had stopped going for her treatments. All language and no medicine, the doctors could not really help her at all.

Poor Sasha. He had been so hurt tonight. He had not realized himself how badly hurt he was. That stupid Englishman. A fool, a fool, a fool. And then Genia . . .

She wept a little, unsure how much of it was the familiar misery in her spine and how much was her hopeless love. He was such a beautiful man. She never imagined for an instant that anything that hinted at love might pass between them, and she told herself that she was content just to see him, to speak with him when he had a moment for her.

But it seemed so unfair. Her single vanity was that she understood him better than any of the others. Perhaps the others understood what he wanted physically, but when she looked at his paintings, it was as though he were the other half of her soul. He saw the world with her eyes. When the collectives of young and not-so-young artists were straining to outdo each other in wildness, in ugliness, in rejection and topicality, Sasha painted a gray and brown back street and gave the buildings souls. He painted a landscape any other artist would have ignored, laid in a single brushstroke of unexpected color, and shattered you. Without ever sinking into prettiness, without ever making a false move, he painted a world that was unspeakably beautiful and true. Even his most abstract works had an internal harmony that no theory would ever explain. He painted away from the times, caring neither for the men in power or the artists in vogue. He painted what he saw. And what he saw was what she saw: on the worst of days, the world was ecstatically beautiful.

If only she had been born beautiful. Not like his endless succession of shopgirls and secretaries, but truly beautiful. Like the Central Asian girl Genia had said such awful things to. Exquisitely, exotically beautiful, so that she might rightfully take her place by Sasha's side. So that she could love him and rest by him. So that she might share all of his days instead of waiting nervously for a chance to spend a few public minutes with him discussing the relationship between technical neutrality and alienation in the transitional works of Larionov.

There were times when she wished she could pass her hand over his hair, to tell him that everything was all right. She understood the terrible sorrow that accompanied a true appreciation of beauty. And she wished she could help him. She hoped the women privileged to touch him gave him some comfort. She hoped they were good to him. Whenever she heard the stories of what a bastard he had been to one girl or another, she excused him. He was just frightened, she realized. Lost and frightened in a world of ferocious mortal beauty.

She had stopped thinking about sex with him. It was too hard, and in any case, her body did not function well enough. Things she had tried to do by herself only hurt her, sending tremors of agony up her spine. Now she only thought about his welfare, ever wondering how she might be able to help him, to love him in the only way she could, without ever shaming him with the thought that anyone so dismally ugly would think of loving a man so empowered with beauty.

Anyway, sex did not matter. Nor did the trail of women whose quick scents led him forever away. She would be content to speak mockingly of Glazunov and to wait for the day when she might help him just a little.

She loved him. Lying in her bed in her dark room crowded with friends' paintings, with prints and art books purchased at the expense of a thousand missed dinners, she would unhesitatingly have given her life for him, expecting nothing whatsoever in return. The world was such a beautiful place. If she could not be beautiful, perhaps she could do something beautiful someday. To make her contribution. To help him.

At last the pain exhausted her to the point where she began to sleep, thinking to the last about her faith in a higher, better form of human love.

7

THE KGB COLONEL LOOKED OUT OVER THE FACES OF the students. A superior had once written of him that he had the gift of seeing things clearly, and now he tried to see beyond the bored, unexpectant faces of the officers assembled before him, to get a sense of his audience and of these men whose lot it would soon be to stand for the rule of law in a country where the law had too long been abused, where the law had often meant only what his own kind said it meant. The colonel believed in the law, even in poor laws, because, with his clear blue eyes, he had glimpsed the phenomenal power of human evil that only the battered fortress walls of the law held at bay.

On the days when he saw especially clearly, he was not a hopeful man. He saw the forces of evil gathering strength, exercising themselves in one regional hip-pocket apocalypse after another. He suspected that, in an earlier age, he might have been a priest, holding up a cross against the demons of the night or the wild horsemen from the Asian steppes. Now his hand held only a remote control for the Western-made slide projector he had brought with him to the lecture.

He looked out over the faces of the students and saw dull fear, apathy, resentment, resignation, physical weariness. Still uncomfortable behind their new interior troops facings, these officers comprised yet another contingent of former regulars deleted from the rolls of the Ministry of Defense and transferred to the reeling Ministry of Internal Affairs. Educated for war against foreign aggressors of mythic dimensions, they were being hastily retrained to serve for—and against—their own countrymen. The faces were predominantly Slavic, with the shining black hair and southern eyes of the most troubled republics notably absent.

The KGB colonel looked out over the faces of the students, saw their futures, and did not envy them. They were going to work for an institution as sick as the country itself, a force for order that was itself in chronic disorder. The troops of the Ministry of Internal Affairs had always received the lowest priority for quality recruits, for quality equipment, for quality leadership. Now these mustered-out tank officers and missile men were supposed to increase the organization's efficiency overnight—in a country where there was more and more hatred, where there were more and more illegal weapons, where there was less and less time, and where the great and humble alike still sought to drug themselves with speech. The future of these officers was less than promising, and their faces told the colonel that many of them already realized it, if only intuitively. Overall, there was only a single face in which he would have placed any real trust, and that belonged to a senior captain with the credit of a Hero of the Soviet Union on his breast. The captain sat very still, eyes on the lecturer, waiting—and smoldering in some inarticulate shame. That was good. The country needed more men who were genuinely ashamed.

The KGB colonel, too, had plenty of which to be ashamed. But he never let the past control him—that was a fatal Russian malady. He kept his eyes, his clear, pale blue eyes, on the future.

Someday, he believed against all the force of his ability to reason, all of the promises would be kept, and men would live decently.

For now, he promised himself he would give these officers whose lives had been rerouted the best two hours he could possibly give them. As a decorated KGB colonel, he could dispense with the ritual formulations behind which other, less secure men concealed their real beliefs. And he had come to speak the hard truth. Normally, the KGB and MVD were bitter rivals. But the Ministry of Internal Affairs had grown so desperate that they were holding out both hands for assistance. Time after time, the internal security structures had collapsed under the first real pressure—in the Caucasus, in sudden hot spots east of the Urals, in the Baltics, Moldavia, the Don basin. Now the MVD's Higher Command School had opened its training schedule to include a guest lecturer from the KGB who was at liberty to say things the internal troops officers still hesitated to whisper.

The colonel allowed the students to settle in, giving them time to take stock of him, to grow slightly restless at his delay in calling for their attention. Their postures, diligent, lax, or indecisive, outlined their likely fates.

The colonel nodded to an assistant at the back of the steeply banked lecture hall and the man clicked off the lights. Let he who would sleep please himself.

The colonel pressed the tiny gray button on the remote and the first slide filled the screen:

Five blackened corpses in the tense, shriveled postures a gasoline fire left behind.

The colonel said nothing.

Next slide:

A child with both forearms hacked off at the elbows. Alive and sentient.

No comment. Next slide:

A street of burning houses, with brown men loitering, equipped with edged weapons crafted from tools, with clubs, with a single hunter's shotgun. The colonel recognized the expressions on their faces as those of men at least briefly sated and drained by the horrors they had just inflicted on others: the remorse and even tenderness of the rapist after the deed, the murderer considering the slightness of a child's corpse.

The colonel waited in silence, lips tight as a closed book.

The next slide showed a hospital ward jammed with bloodied women and children in the feverish colors of southern dress.

Then came a picture of a wheeled armored personnel carrier set ablaze. The MVD markings were still visible through the flames and smoke.

The audience began to murmur.

The colonel chased after a response with a quick series of slides showing smashed faces, gutted homes, women frozen in midscream, dead men wrapped in blankets, dead men naked in the street, wild-faced men waving Kalashnikovs . . . The final slide showed two MVD soldiers dragging a dead officer away from a riot.

On cue, the lights came back up. No one was caught sleeping.

The colonel looked into their faces again, registering changes. Then he began to speak, dispensing with all formalities:

"Sumgait. Baku. Nagorno-Karabakh. Nakhichevan. Tbilisi. Abkhazia. Some of the other slides were from quiet little local affairs that didn't merit a mention in the news. Comrades—or should I simply say 'brother officers'—this isn't a history lesson. This is the present. This is your future, your country . . ."

For the remainder of the two hours allotted to him, the colonel spoke as clearly and as honestly as he could about the situation in each of the Soviet Union's republics, in the autonomous republics and regions, in the ethnic concentrations unrecognized or divided by administrative boundaries, in the great cities. The picture he painted was unrelievedly dark. He bluntly explained how Stalin had redrawn internal borders in such a way that only a strong central authority could guarantee them, just as Stalin's foreign policy had sought to make Poland dependent upon the USSR for the retention of territories that had once belonged to Germany. He cited casualty and property-destruction figures greater than any the students had previously heard, exceeding even rumor. He spoke of economic desolation, of ecological ruin, of ethnic and religious resurgences, of radical movements and the charisma of charlatans . . . and of systemic inertia, willful blindness, bureaucratic incompetence, and corruption. None of the new-wave dissident journals or muckraking newspapers could have outdone his critique of the current situation.

"And so, brother officers," he said, "you'll receive varied assignments, with orders written in opaque language. You'll be directed to protect state property, to guarantee the safety of transport means, to reduce tensions by your presence—although your presence will more often than not inflame the situation. And in the end, you'll find that your duty comes down to one very simple mission: to stop your countrymen from butchering each other. Out of gratitude, not a few of your countrymen will do their best to butcher you. You'll receive an order to roll into some backwater where the local hooligans want to pull down the statue of Lenin in the town square, and before you know it, the heavens will be raining fire. You'll routinely be in the middle, drawing fire from both sides. You and your men will be lightning rods, drawing nature's destructive power down on you." The colonel looked around the room. "And a year from now at least a few of you will be dead."

Faces of fear, of disbelief and skepticism, of overconfidence, of anger.

"If any of you have any questions of me," the colonel said, "we still have a few minutes remaining."

Usually, there were no questions. Conditioned by the Soviet military training system, the officers listened with their mouths shut and accepted what was offered. Still, times were changing, and the colonel personally knew all too well what it was like to live with unanswered questions burning in the soul.

The Hero of the Soviet Union raised his hand.

Samsonov had listened hungrily to the KGB officer, feeling for the first time during the course that someone was offering him something of value. This colonel was a kindred spirit, another man determined to believe in his country, no matter what. And he seemed oddly familiar, calling up positive associations that wafted across the back of the brain. Samsonov was certain that he had never met the colonel before. Yet there was a resemblance to someone whom he could not quite place.

When the KGB man surprised him by asking for questions, Samsonov found himself raising his hand even before he had finished formulating his query. He wanted to establish contact with this man, not for the sake of any professional connections but simply because he sensed the possibility, however slight, of brotherhood with him.

When the colonel acknowledged him, Samsonov rose to his

feet. At the last moment, he tamed his question, exorcising it of the worst of his personal devils.

"Comrade Colonel, I would like to ask your opinion of the threat posed to the stability of the Union by the Central Asian republics."

The KGB colonel looked at him with no change of expression, then nodded to himself. For a moment, his eyes lost the officer-students and looked inward. Then he ran a hand back over his thinning hair.

"I've already addressed the local ethnic issues," he began. "But your question goes a bit further." He straightened, as if he had just made his decision on what to say. "I can only offer you a personal and subjective view. Not one based in the dialectic, I'm afraid. Short term, the problems will remain localized—sharp, perhaps bloody, but occasional and temporary. Long term, however, I see the block of Central Asian republics as perhaps the greatest threat to the integrity of the state. Unless, of course, the Ukraine were to break away, or the Russian Republic itself were to break up—but I think we can all agree that that's unthinkable." He smiled slightly.

"It's tempting to evaluate Central Asia as a collective entity," he went on. "To the unschooled man, it appears all of a piece. But there are many internal dissimilarities, even contradictions. In Uzbekistan, for instance, the level of discontent and dissidence varies remarkably from subregion to subregion, from city to city. Khiva and Bukhara are calm and relatively religious. The local religious leaders—at least those who are officially recognized—render unto Caesar, as they say. Samarkand . . . is a bit more questionable. And the situation in Tashkent is already a problem. The city's divided into distinct ethnic quarters. And there are areas where too white a face had best not go." He took a deep breath. "But what I see for the immediate future is just a continuation of the pattern of local disturbances, quick fires that use up their fuel and sputter out. Nasty, violent confrontations here and there. But we'll keep them more or less in check. I don't expect anything like the situation in the Caucasus for some time to come. There simply is not a sufficiently unified consciousness with sufficiently galvanizing grievances. The culture is somewhat passive. Islamic fundamentalism in its more menacing forms has not yet taken deep root. In fact, I see economic and even ecological problems as more immediately threatening. But, of course, one cause can lead to another." He looked at Samsonov. "I'm just repeating myself. I can't really offer you anything beyond what I've already said: Central Asia is a near-term discomfort, but it will be a serious problem in the long term." Their eyes met through the dead indoor air. "Of course, an officer could get himself killed there, if he put his mind to it."

The audience began to murmur, partly in black amusement at the last remark, partly because the scheduled time for the lecture had come to an end.

"Well, I see my time's up," the colonel said. "Thank you for your attention."

The officers got to their feet. Behind Samsonov, one student told another, "That's all a bunch of shit. Just give the blackasses a good boot in the behind and they'll come around."

Instead of following his classmates out into the corridor, Samsonov made his way forward to the podium. The KGB colonel looked up from gathering his lecture materials.

"Comrade Colonel," Samsonov began, still struggling to get the words right, "Comrade Colonel, I have a problem." He had no one to talk to on a serious level and he had made a decision to try this man, come what may.

Samsonov caught the colonel's eye dropping to the decorations on his breast then quickly coming back up.

"Afghanistan?" the colonel asked, sure of himself.

Samsonov nodded. "Comrade Colonel . . . it has to do with Afghanistan, actually. I want to be a good officer, to do the best I can. If I can't serve in the army, I'll serve here. But . . . I'm afraid . . ."

The colonel raised his eyebrows.

Samsonov waved away the misunderstanding with his left hand. "I don't mean of the things on the slides. Nothing like that. It's just that . . . in Afghanistan I saw a great many things. Perhaps too many things. I can't look at a Tadzhik or an Uzbek or an Azerbaijani, without feeling—"

"Automatic hatred." The colonel completed the sentence and the thought for him. "You feel hatred, and you can't make it stop, and you're afraid you'll do something foolish, something wrong."

The clarity of the man's understanding startled Samsonov.

He wished he could sit down with him and talk, to open his heart. He had been holding so much inside.

"Yes. I'm afraid I might do something terribly wrong."

The colonel glanced at his watch. "I've got to go. I've got a very important meeting. But listen to me." He took Samsonov by the upper arm, gripping him firmly, and looked him in the eyes. The colonel had light blue eyes that did not allow anyone inside but penetrated very deeply. "The very fact that you're worried about it means you'll do all right. I can tell about men. It's my job. And you'll do fine."

Samsonov nodded dumbly, wondering how he could establish real contact with this man.

"Trust me," the colonel said, shaking Samsonov's arm to break his reverie. "You'll do your duty, and you'll do it well."

Then, too quickly, he slipped his last papers into a briefcase and headed up toward the exit with swift, very military steps. He paused in the doorway just long enough to turn his head and call:

"And good luck, Captain."

Disappointed, Samsonov stood in the empty lecture hall, budged out of the flow of time for a few minutes. He could not think whom the colonel had reminded him of. And he wondered what his future would hold.

Finally, he roused himself. It was time to move on to the next class, which involved three hours of Leninist theory on the reactionary nature of proto-nationalism.

"Colonel Leskov," the secretary cried in a voice of alarm and reproof, "General Kerbitsky's waiting in your office. He's been waiting for half an hour."

The KGB colonel tossed his hat onto a chair in the anteroom and peeled off his woolen greatcoat without missing a step.

"Subway's a madhouse," he said.

"You should order a service car, like everyone—"

He yanked open the door of his office and went inside.

KGB lieutenant general G. V. Kerbitsky sat lump-bellied on the old leather sofa by the window, smoking a cigar. He had already filled the room with smoke.

At the sight of Leskov, the general smiled.

"I really should come to see you more often, Pavel Ivanovich. It always gives me time to think."

"Comrade General, my apologies, I—"

The general canceled the speech with the stub of his cigar. "I know, I know. Nina Mikhailovna told me you've been overeducating our brothers in the MVD again. She defends you like a lioness."

"Yes, Comrade General."

"I'd take her to be my own secretary. But she'd fight it tooth and nail."

"I'm lucky to have her."

The general nodded agreement, exhaling a magnificent cloud of blue smoke. "Anyway, she's too old for me. One of the privileges of being a general officer is having an attractive young secretary." He rumpled the corner of his mouth. "Shame they can never type worth a damn. How did it go with the MVD boys?"

Leskov shook his head. "I feel like I'm teaching blind men to drive."

Kerbitsky rolled the butt of his cigar between his fingers. "Sorry bastards." He puffed again. "So. Sit down and talk to me, Pavel Ivanovich." The cigar rode his lips like a rowboat rising and falling with the sea.

Leskov dropped into place beside the general, feeling the sofa's uneven springs nudging his rump.

"Tell me," the general said, "what's going on with our friend Ali Talala."

Leskov grimaced. "He's definitely the one. He killed Losov, his wife, his kids, even the mistress. Plus the two militiamen Losov had guarding his treasure house. And Losov's driver."

"Losov was scum," the general said. "Talala seems to have saved us a trial and a great deal of public embarrassment."

Leskov nodded, in partial agreement. But it was finally about the rule of law. It was always about the rule of law. The ten years' difference in age between the two men on the sofa encompassed a generational change in attitudes. Kerbitsky had begun his service during Stalin's twilight. He was interested in results, not process.

"The state prosecutor was ready to issue the arrest order

on Losov. We had as close to a perfect case as I've ever seen. He could've served as an example to others."

The general shrugged. "Policemen are corrupt. Always have been. The militia isn't good for a damned thing except directing traffic." He dropped his cigar stub on the tile floor and ground it out with his foot. "Can you prove it was Talala?"

"Yes."

"Beyond any doubt."

"Yes."

The general sank back into the old green leather, thinking.

"There are plenty of people who saw them together in the restaurant," Leskov went on. "Talala was flaunting the whole business. He thinks he's untouchable. And we've got an informer inside his organization. We can—"

"Talala's a people's deputy now. He's got immunity as long as he's in the legislature."

"That can be lifted. If the crime's serious enough."

"It would be an ordeal."

"The man murdered a militia colonel and his entire family. Whether Losov was corrupt or not doesn't make a difference."

"It would be an ordeal. And we might lose."

"We've got witnesses, evidence."

"We might lose. Or we might not even get beyond the first few steps. Talala may not be untouchable. But he's close to it. People's deputy. Friends in high places. A tremendous support base back home in Uzbekistan. We could lose and have riots on our hands for our trouble. I have to be honest with you, Pavel Ivanovich. Losov just wasn't important enough to our mutual superiors."

"I want that bastard," Leskov said abruptly, unable to stop the words.

"I know you do," Kerbitsky said calmly. "So do I. But we're going to have to get him on something bigger. Something that matters to the people who ultimately make the decisions."

"He's an outlaw. He killed eight people in cold blood."

The general touched his fingers to his lips, puffing on the ghost of a cigar. "Let's be honest, my friend. In this country, today, eight people don't matter so much. Oh, I agree it's a heinous crime. And I want to see that brown bastard brought to justice just as badly as you do. But you have to accept that it's going to take a while. He's just the wrong man at the wrong time." Kerbitsky smiled. "In the old days, of course, it would have all been a lot easier. Talala could have disappeared from the face of the earth and everyone simply would have pretended he never existed. Not all of the changes you and I have seen have been for the better, Pavel Ivanovich."

"I accept the rule of law. I cherish it."

"But first we have to create it." The general sighed. "Everything's just so damned in-between. Sometimes I can be optimistic. But it never lasts very long. Most of the time I see another period of troubles coming relentlessly toward us, the way you watch a thunderstorm coming across the steppes and slowly filling up the horizon." He looked off into an imaginary distance for a moment. "Listen to me. Build the case against Talala. Make it so big and so concrete that the men in the curtained limousines won't be able to close their eyes to it. Take your time. Implicate so many people above him that they'll be relieved to sacrifice him in order to appease us. And in the meantime, don't talk too much or too loudly about the rule of law around here. There are undercurrents even clever, well-placed young colonels may not notice until they find themselves swimming for all they're worth to keep their heads above water."

Leskov did not even hear the warning. He was focused entirely on Ali Talala, raging inside that a man who committed such an act, on top of countless other illegal activities, should travel freely through the streets, an honored and privileged citizen.

"And if we do build the 'big case'? If we can find out exactly whom he answers to?" Leskov asked. "Will our mutual superiors support going after them, too? Or is the new justice going to be as selective as the old?"

Leskov looked at the general. Spreading nose, old man's tufts of hair in his ears. He had worked for Kerbitsky on and off for years and trusted him. Although their philosophies might sometimes diverge, Leskov was convinced that the general, too, had come to believe in justice, in a society whose order did not rely entirely on caprice and fear. He had seen the old man take courageous decisions, even before the new winds had begun to blow. But Kerbitsky was aging, slowing down.

"First," the old man said, "let's get Talala. Let's be methodical and smart and create a position so strong it's unassailable. Let's get Talala and then, after we've taken care of him, we can start working our way up. We'll get them, Pavel Ivanovich. But it's better to wait till the wolf strays so you can kill him separately instead of taking on the whole pack at once."

"I'll build the case. I'll build a case that'll stink to the heavens if they try to cover it up."

Kerbitsky nodded, reaching into his uniform blouse for another cigar. "That's the spirit." He felt for matches.

Leskov rose and retrieved a lighter from atop his desk. Working in private, he smoked cigarettes. But he rarely smoked in front of anyone else.

"Thank you," Kerbitsky said, bending forward over the spread of his belly to accept the light.

Leskov replaced the lighter and sat back down. The general blew a fresh stream of smoke into the lingering haze.

"You know," Kerbitsky said, "we made Talala. He's as much a product of this system as you or I. More so. The new Soviet man. Between two worlds, and milking them both for all he's worth. You can even count on men like him to be patriotic, in their selfish way. He'd never want Uzbekistan to seek its independence. That would mean the end of the milk cow. We've addicted him to the opportunities for corruption only a greater entity can offer." The general savored his cigar, a Havana and one of the last benefits of the dream of world revolution.

"He's a bloody man," Leskov said.

"In the best Central Asian tradition."

"I'd like to put him in a cell today. He's got blood all over him."

Kerbitsky took a great deal of pleasure in his cigars. It was one of the last pleasures. Leskov knew the old man's home life had been going badly for years, that both his daughters had miserable marriages behind them.

"Back home in Uzbekistan, of course, he wouldn't be counted a murderer or a thief," the general said. "Just a good provider. I understand he's very popular. Providing things that the state itself has failed to provide. I never have believed that these 'mafias' spring up because all men are inherently bad. Objectively seen, they simply fill in the blanks left by the system. All organized crime exploits the inefficiencies and deficiencies of government. And finally, Talala's just a modern extension of the old Central Asian tradition of emirs and sultans, the source of plenty, the focus of duty, the giver of laws. When he profits from us, when he makes fools of us, his people can only admire him."

"A murderer is a murderer."

The general shook his head in mock wonder. "All right. Have it your way, my friend." He smiled. "You always make me think of how the original Bolsheviks must have been, the men with the fire in their eyes and the hunger in their bellies, the true believers—"

"The men we killed."

The general shrugged. "Stalin killed them. We didn't. Anyway, there are some who will tell you that you've always got to get rid of the true believers, after they've served their purpose." He smiled again.

Leskov smiled, too. "Let's just hope they wait until I've served my purpose."

After the general had gone, Leskov opened the window to let the smoke out into the winter sky. For a moment he stared idly down at the gray, darkening Moscow streets. Chased by weak headlamps and the cold, pedestrians hurried across the churned slush, faces covered against the wind. Even in the best of weather there was always a grace note of sorrow in the Moscow air. In the winter it became a symphony. Moscow was always such a sad city, a city of survivors, and he loved it very much.

He took his seat behind his desk, relishing the fresh draft. His secretary had laid the Talala file neatly in the center of the ordered stacks of books, correspondence, and information papers. She was fierce and dutiful and plain, with heavy knitted stockings and graying hair drawn into a bun. She, too, was Moscow, as were the girls still young enough to smile, necking with their boyfriends on the endless escalators in the subway stations.

He opened the cardboard file. It was thick, with paper fixed to the insides of both covers, and it flopped open heavily. There were new photos. Talala himself, small and clean, with an expression that said nothing whatsoever. Family members in Uzbek silks. All the children, the little boy looking ill. Children were the Central Asian's ultimate wealth. And Talala was poor in sons. Then there was the girl.

Leskov had been startled the first time he saw a snapshot of her. Shirin Talala. Her story was not unusual. Central Asian girl, born to privilege, comes to Moscow and goes a little wild. But this one's beauty set her apart. Even in a clandestinely shot black-and-white photo her appeal was spectacularly clear, demanding a man's attention.

Abruptly, Leskov shut the file, deciding to work on it later. He had other cases, other problems, and he had been neglecting them. He would save the Talala case for last tonight. But for long minutes, he could not shake himself free of the memory of the girl's beauty. After more than twenty years with the KGB's domestic investigative division, he could not remember more than a few cases involving such a beautiful woman even on the periphery. But each of those few cases and few women had one thing in common. They invariably ended badly.

Too much beauty for this world, Leskov thought calmly, sadly. It was a matter of physics, of chemistry. He glanced at another photo, one of a few that he kept framed on his desk. It was old, a bit faded, showing two boys, obviously brothers, the elder in long pants, the younger in baggy shorts, posed against the backdrop of an apple tree and a broken fence.

He shook his head and bent to his work.

8

THE PLANE LANDED IN SAMARKAND IN THE FIRST WEAK light of the winter's day. Ali Talala and his family and bodyguards were escorted off first, followed by the herding passengers with their oversize packages and bundles. Three large black sedans waited along the apron, engines running. A small group of airport personnel had gathered, despite the cold, to show their respect. A tiny Uzbek girl, face almost invisible in the layers and folds of traditional winter dress, held a bouquet of red hothouse carnations in front of her like a soldier presenting a weapon. At a word from a man with a knife scar that stretched from his temple to the corner of his mouth, she ran forward. Welcome home.

Talala breathed deeply. Beyond the smell of jet fuel and exhaust, he imagined he could already smell the desert. He felt a child's longing to put the airport behind him, to hurry along the modernized boulevards of Samarkand, to drive out past the insecticide-poisoned fields to the hills where his ancestors had ruled their world on horseback. But he controlled his stride, revealed nothing by his facial expression. Ritual was important. He opened his arms to the flowers and the running girl.

After a welter of greetings, Talala got into the back of the first car and it sped off, leaving the remainder of his family behind. The other two automobiles would take them directly to the great house out in the hills. But Talala had an established ritual for his arrivals home, and it was as vital for him to follow it as it might have been for a long-dead emir or khan.

He shared the backseat of the car with a powerfully handsome man in his midthirties. Exceptionally large and muscular for an Uzbek, Mustafa Gogandaev had the features of a prince from an oriental fairy tale. He combined an aura of ready physical strength with an elegance of gesture that no Russian could ever have equaled. As a younger man, Mustafa Gogandaev had earned a great renown as a destroyer of women's reputations, and his history sizzled with the failed violence of fathers, husbands, brothers, lovers. Despite his ability to defend himself, he would have been killed early on had he not been a member of the great Talala clan. His blood had saved him, time and again.

Still, Talala noted, there was a terrible justice in the world. Gogandaev had married—apparently for love. He chose as his wife a relatively poor girl from a family of no standing. But she possessed a startling beauty, boyish and slight, hardly of this earth. Gogandaev had revolted against his family, against tradition, against common sense to marry her. Groomed for a great future amid the families that actually governed Uzbekistan, he failed to consolidate his position by making a marriage that extended his clan's kinship into another family of power. Damning heaven and earth, he married his mortal angel, lavishing her with gifts. Only to find her in his bed in broad daylight with an auto mechanic sprawled over her. Gogandaev killed them both with his bare hands. And he never touched another woman, so far as anyone knew. Instead, he became a formidable and ruthless representative of his family's interests, eventually upsetting the authority of age to become Talala's deputy in all practical matters, the man who made decisions in the master's absence.

"I didn't see Shirin," Gogandaev remarked casually as the automobile sped toward the gray-black cloud of pollution that marked the real boundary of Samarkand.

"She has her studies," Talala said, examining the first hillside slum through the car window. "She couldn't come home."

"But she's well?"

"Oh, yes. She takes the Russians in stride. And her studies are easy for her."

"Everyone else looks well."

"Yes. Thanks be to God." Talala found himself using the old phrase more and more often. Historically, the Talala clan had experienced its share of problems with religion, including accusations of heresy, even sorcery. In the eighteenth century, the emir of Bukhara had levied a death sentence against any Talala kinsman caught on his territory, and even Samarkand, to which the Talalas more or less faithfully paid tribute, had not always looked kindly upon the independent spirit of the wild men from the hills. Under the Soviets there had been decades when any religious expression, any God-flavored turn of speech, no matter how casual, meant embarrassment or worse. But the sands were moving again, and he found his own people wanted more and more of the verbal soothing the old figures of speech offered. Above all, a man had to have a sense of the times.

In the distance, under the gray, draping sky, Talala saw the huge dome of the Bibi-Khanym mosque and the bulk of the surrounding ruins. Everything was wreathed in scaffolding, and an inert crane poked the sky. Neglected for centuries, the great mosque was finally, haltingly, being restored. Talala had been instrumental in allocating funds for the project. That, too, matched the tenor of the times.

The sedan swerved around packed yellow buses trailing huge plumes of exhaust. The vehicles were so crowded that the windows had steamed over, showing the passengers only as colored smudges pressed against the glass. Private automobiles and taxis shivered on their undersized wheels, while blue half-broken trucks moved the city's food and fuel. Even with the windows tightly closed, the interior of the sedan stank of cheap gas.

"Tell me, my brother," Talala said, "what's this problem down on the border?" He had slept only briefly and badly on the flight, but some matters could not wait until he had rested.

Gogandaev had only been waiting for a sign that Talala was ready for business.

"We lost an entire shipment. Two of our people were arrested."

Talala lifted an eyebrow. "Have they . . . talked?"

"No. They died early in their imprisonment."

Talala looked sharply at the younger man.

"We had to do it," Gogandaev said quickly. "I wasn't certain they could be trusted."

The two men rode in silence. A bundled boy struck his donkey with a switch, hurrying the overloaded animal along the side of the highway.

"The border troops have a new commander. He hasn't asked for any money yet. And he personally led the patrol that ambushed our shipment."

The traffic thickened around them, chaotic and familiar.

"Perhaps," Talala said, "he's trying to drive up the price."

"He's already put half a dozen of his own people under arrest. Every one of them had been cooperating with us." Gogandaev's face went cold. "We didn't even receive any warning about his appointment. It looks as though the KGB might finally be serious about closing the border."

Talala watched a bundled woman leading her bundled children along the first stretch of sidewalk. Single-story houses of cinder block and badly molded concrete perched on the side of a ravine. Black smoke rose from an oil drum.

"It goes in cycles," Talala said. "I've seen this three, perhaps four times in my life. It only hurts everyone. And in the end, the trade goes on. The Russians want to draw a border against the currents of history. But history—and trade—are stronger than the Russians." He smiled, almost pityingly. "The Russians want to shape the world to their liking. While a wise man accepts the shape of his world and profits from it."

"I believe," Gogandaev said, "that this new man is going to be a special problem."

Talala sighed. The matter was spoiling the tone of his arrival.

"We will look into this problem, my son," he promised the younger man. "But it's clear we cannot allow the Russians to overstep their bounds. And I will not seek to appease them."

"This new commander likes to go on patrol with his men. To waste himself doing a lieutenant's work."

"Perhaps," Talala said, "he's showing the lieutenants how it's done?"

"Perhaps he could meet a lieutenant's fate? The desert hills are still wild."

Talala nodded. "We will think on these things." Then he sighed. "A shame they ended their war. It was all so much easier then." During the later, most intense years of the war in Afghanistan, Talala and his kinsmen and their kinsmen had run an elaborate and beautiful operation out of Bagram airbase. Soviet soldiers had been dying of contagious diseases in the back country of Afghanistan, where typhus, plague, and cholera were as much a part of the changing seasons as sun, wind, and snow, and the bodies were shipped home in hermetically sealed caskets. The entry point had been Samarkand, where an elaborate decontamination station had been established. At first, Talala's people had merely loaded bags of heroin and blocks of hashish in with the corpses, but later they had refined the system to the point where the corpses remained behind in Afghanistan and only a body weight of narcotics arrived in the Soviet Union, destined to still the appetites of young veterans who had become addicted during their term of service to the motherland and who now patrolled the streets of Moscow or Kiev in rags, searching anxiously for a day's worth of the precious white powder or simply on the lookout for a few chips of hashish to help them forget the disdain with which their society viewed them.

"We will overcome this difficulty," Talala said in a tone of finality.

Gogandaev waited out a red light, then he said, "I hear there was a problem in Moscow, father of fathers."

"A minor matter. Another Russian obsessed with his own grandeur. Even his own people were glad to be rid of him." Talala smiled. "Like all Russians, he was dishonest even with his own kind. He stole from the hand that shielded his life. It is the most foolish thing a man can ever do."

"Indeed."

"Anyway, I expect some difficulty with the Ukrainians now. They're running so much liquor in from Poland that they may try to sell cheaply. I hope a conflict can be avoided. I would like to reach an honorable agreement with them. But they're all Slavs. Ukrainians, Russians, there's no difference. They cannot see beyond the next little scrap of advantage."

"We can deal with the Ukrainians," Gogandaev said. "If it comes to that."

"Yes. The Ukrainians still hesitate to pull a trigger. They're still afraid of the law."

"And they'll always lose to those who are not afraid."

"There is no reason to fear."

"Fear is for dogs, courage is for men."

This time Talala paused slightly before answering:

"Reason is also for men. We will think on these things."

The sedan turned the corner by the great flat box of the national museum and pulled up in front of the Registan, parking illegally. This was the first stage of the ritual.

Talala got out of the car unassisted, drinking in the cold, acrid air. His tightened eyes focused on the grand beauty of the monuments before him, empty of tourists in this bad season. He had once overheard a guide telling a group of cow-faced Russian tourists that the architectural style of the complex of mosques, madrasahs, and minarets had been excessively influenced by Persian design, that it could not be regarded as pure. For Talala, that was nonsense. He knew of no greater purity than this except the desert itself. These massive, delicately tiled glories were the heart of the city of Timur the Lame. Even after fifty years of life, Talala still felt wonder each time he stood before the monuments. In the worst light, on the worst of days, the Registan was sublime. On the good days, when the sun caught the tiles, it was a picture of heaven. The great archways offered up man's perfected skills to remark God's bounty to his chosen people. It was a mark of faith that transcended the irreligiosity of this hard age. And when you took the time to sit and really look, you sank into seas of blue and green, into dazzling golden suns, then soared to the moon on the back of a lion striped like a tiger. But the value for Talala lay beyond the visual splendor in the affirmation of his people's greatness, a greatness that would endure beyond the condescensions of soul-sick foreigners with their intemperance and lies. Sitting before the great facades, he could not understand the young people who called for independence from the Soviet Union. It seemed so clear to him that the Russians had become slaves without even realizing it. And Ali Talala did not want to free his slaves.

He sat alone for a while on a cold wooden bench erected for the tourists. In the good weather he enjoyed watching the stumbling, openmouthed foreigners, marvelous in their lack of understanding. They read to each other from guidebooks, surrounded by a world where everything of import happened behind closed doors, and prided themselves on their knowledge.

Gogandaev kept his usual respectful distance. The sheer sight of him always impressed Talala. Had he but had a son such as this. Gogandaev was a father's dream. Yet, Talala was convinced, had Shirin been born a man, she would have been even stronger, more capable. Shirin, who was his son except for a peculiar accident of flesh. Shirin, a woman with a man's soul. Of all his children, only Shirin's eyes had the depth, the range of passions, of a man's eyes. He loved her so much that he was willing to break every rule for her. He would have chained another daughter in a pit for showing half of Shirin's independence. But he knew her strength could not be broken in such a manner. She reminded him of the fabled warrior queens from a time when history existed only as remembered poetry or song. He knew in his heart she was far from an ideal daughter, but he had elected not to examine the matter too closely. He knew he could not live with certain discoveries he might make. So he let Shirin go her own way, aware of the wildness gnawing at her soul. It was as though, of all his children, only she had received his blood. He did not know what would become of her. But even now, in the embrace of his homeland, he suspected that his daughter might be better off if she remained forever among his enemies. His world had no place for such a woman. He doubted that any man would ever succeed in binding her to him for a lifetime.

He looked over to where Gogandaev waited. Not even a man such as this. Shirin was stronger than any of them. And a father could only hope for the best, ignoring the bite of whispers.

"Let's go," Talala said.

Gogandaev did not move as the older man approached. "We need to talk," he told his master. "Here, away from the driver."

Talala swept away the last shards of reverie.

"What's wrong?"

"It's Shamil," Gogandaev said.

"Karali's son?"

Gogandaev nodded. "The boy's been selling heroin. To our own people."

"Where?"

"In Tashkent. You know how things are in Tashkent now. Far worse than here."

"It's the Russians. And the other mongrels. Tashkent's their city now."

"Except for the bazaar."

"Yes."

"Anyway, I thought you should know."

"And you're certain?" Talala asked sadly. "No mistake?"

"No mistake. A boy died."

"One of ours?"

"Yes."

Talala went into a separate silence. Becoming the giver of laws. Then he looked into the younger man's hard eyes.

"Shamil always struck me as a good boy. Full of promise."

Gogandaev moved his head in solemn agreement. "What do you want done?"

"Kill him," Talala said without further hesitation.

"They're going to kill him," the woman declared. She wept. Half-buried in the winter clothes in which she had waited three days for her audience, she sat bent with humility before the desk of the man she believed held the power of life and death over her son. "The other soldiers beat him. They steal his money. He's not big and strong. They're going to kill him."

Talala considered the woman. She had come without her husband, who would have been far too proud to admit his son's defenselessness, and the traditional Uzbek in Talala revolted against such a show of independence on the part of a wife. On the other hand, she was a mother. In despair. And thanks to the dictates of Soviet power, women had votes—which were becoming newly important. Talala knew that the network of communications among the outwardly silent women of his homeland was at least as efficient as satellite communications. The man who showed charity to a desperate mother under such circumstances could only expand the base of his personal power.

There were, however, considerable problems with the case.

"Little mother," Talala said, "this is a very grave problem. It's clear that your son is being wronged. Grievously wronged. You are not the first mother to come to me with such a complaint. The nature of military service has always been harsh, and the Soviet Army is a law unto itself. It would be dishonest of me to pretend I could clap my hands and bring your son home."

"But . . . Comrade Talala . . . ," the woman began again. She had initially addressed him with the Uzbek word for *lord*, but he had quickly corrected her. "Comrade Talala, I'm so afraid. He's such a sensitive boy. He could never even abide the killing of animals."

The boy in question did not sound very sympathetic to Talala. But after all, he was a fellow countryman serving in the army of the Slavs. And at least this one was still alive. Many of the mothers of service members who came to him wanted investigations into the deaths of their sons—and they wanted justice, revenge. These were not good times to be a Central Asian drafted into Moscow's white-skinned army. Uzbeks, Tadzhiks, Kirghiz, Turkomans, and Kazhaks received only the most rudimentary military training and were assigned the most degrading jobs. On top of that, they were abused. Some committed suicide. Others died mysteriously "in the line of duty." And even a man as well connected as Talala found it nearly impossible to get straight answers out of the Ministry of Defense.

"Little mother," Talala said, "I promise you I will do all I can to help your son. I will personally look into this matter. I only hope your son recognizes God's blessing in the love of such a mother, a mother for whom no sacrifice is too great." A shame, he thought, that the boy hadn't been called up for the troops of the Ministry of Internal Affairs. That would have been easy to fix. "We must all do our best for such a fine boy. And for the precious mothers of Uzbekistan."

Talala sighed and sat back in the vinyl chair of an important bureaucrat, vaguely aware that, from Vilnius to Vladivostok, other bureaucrats were sitting in identical chairs in identical offices, listening to similar complaints. In the provinces, a man's political power was not determined by his stand on great issues, but by his ability to deliver personal help to his people.

"It's a great and terrible thing to be a mother," Talala went on. Then he carefully quoted a traditional Uzbek poet: " 'To be a mother is to see God's splendor with one eye and to see the darkness of hell with the other.' "

The woman understood that her allotted time had come to an end and she rose meekly, bowing nervously and clutching about her for her bags—an ancient carpet satchel and a plastic bag emblazoned with the image of a Western pop singer.

"Please be sure that Comrade Gogandaev has all the details about your son before you leave. You may trust him. He's like a son to me."

And she was gone, replaced by the director of a collective farm who could not get repair parts for his fleet of tractors. Next came a young man distantly related to the Talalas who wanted help securing an apartment in Tashkent. Another mother sought help in acquiring the Western medicine prescribed by a doctor who had read of its effects but could not produce any of it for her ailing daughter. A shaking, dark-faced father complained that a neighbor's boy had stolen his daughter's honor and that now the neighbor's family disavowed all responsibility. This was a very tricky matter for Talala, since it would be easy to make mortal enemies of one extended family, the other, or both. Compared to adjudicating such wrongs, even dealing with the KGB was a simple matter. Then a delegation appeared from an outlying village, humble as medieval peasants in the presence of a great ruler. Their spokesman begged Talala to facilitate the granting of a permit for the construction of a local mosque and for help in securing building materials. Five years earlier, Talala would have dismissed the plea, since granting it would have been a terrible breach of Party etiquette. Now he made notes to himself and promises to the villagers.

The parade of supplicants lasted long into the afternoon. Talala was travel weary and he longed for his home out in the hills, where his wife would be awaiting him with hot mint tea, golden bread, and freshly slaughtered lamb. His servants would have erected his yurt back in the hills, out of sight of all Russian civilization. The deep red horse carpet that had belonged to his father would be lying on his Arabian's dappled back. The cold, sweet air would come down from the mountains.

But first came duty.

The final visitor introduced himself as Mamun Ersari. The family name was very common over in western Uzbekistan where there was a large Turkoman population. The man wore a dark suit with a plain white shirt buttoned at the throat and a squared-off, embroidered cap that sat on the back of his head in the traditional manner. He looked intelligent, educated, and his hands had not been scarred by manual labor. He carried himself with a quiet insolence that only a man of good family would dare affect, and his eyes met Talala's as though the two men were equals. Talala should have known the face of such a man. He had a very good memory for faces and names, a habit ingrained in a people who had lived so long without the ability to write things down. But this man was a stranger.

"God's blessing be upon you, Ali Talala," the man said, gesturing lightly with his hand.

So that was it. Of course. Talala drew the proper cloak over his personality.

"And on you, my friend. What problem brings you to my door?"

"There is no problem. There is only the will of God."

"May His will be served."

"You are a great man, Ali Talala."

"God has been generous."

"The people follow your every move."

"I serve the people."

"They watch you and they know that a thing is right in its time."

"May God grant me the wisdom to see that which is right."

Sufi Brotherhood, Talala decided. Hard to say which splinter group. But it hardly mattered, since none of them were his friends. To these men, whose only interest was the reestablishment of the dominion of Islam, he was no better than a Russian. Perhaps worse. Once he would have thrown this man out into the street.

"Whenever the great Ali Talala graces us by returning to Samarkand," the visitor continued, "he shows respect before his people and his forefathers by halting at the Registan."

"A man must never forget the well where he first tasted the water of life."

"Ali Talala shows respect before history. But not before the One True God."

"God judges a man by what is in his heart, not by where he waters his horse."

"But Ali Talala is not merely a man. And his horse is not merely a horse. The people follow his lead. If Ali Talala were to go instead to the shrine of Shah-i-Zindah, the people would see not only that he respects his forebears but also that he is humble before God."

Talala understood. He had known the day would come when these men would try to reach him, when they would feel themselves strong enough to make the first soft threats. But even had he so desired, he could not accede directly to the man's wishes. It would have been too great a show of weakness. And the visitor knew it.

The time was still not right for a secular people's deputy and Party official to bend his knees and touch his forehead to the tiles in the old tombs upon the hill. Perhaps the day would come, and perhaps it was not too far in the future. But it had not yet arrived. Anyway, Talala had never felt drawn to the dark, lonely mausoleums with their close air and piety that stank of surrender and ignorance. He preferred the open spaces and heroic proportions of the Registan, the celebration of power, of life itself. The sight of those inlaid towers glinting in the sun quickened him with the pulse of glory. *His* people had built the Registan when the Russians were living in wooden huts in the swamps, terrified of witches and the great world beyond the trees. Samarkand had been a center of civilization when the Moscow Kremlin had been a wooden stockade. Even today, the Kremlin had nothing to equal the nearly animate magnificence of the Shir Dor. In old Samarkand, Ulugh Beg had tamed the stars with mathematics in an age when the highest expression of Russian culture had been fornication in the mud.

No. He would not give up his visits to the Registan so easily. But there was no reason to avoid all compromise. He could make a gift of his generosity itself.

"It is my habit to go to the Registan," Talala told the

stranger, "because that place sings to me of the living greatness of our people. My heart leads me there, and a man must follow his heart in such matters. But it's curious that you should come to me in just such an hour. You see, I've been planning a quiet visit to the tombs of Shah-i-Zindah for some time. It has merely been a matter of scheduling. I've made time on the last day of my stay here in the bosom of our people. I shall stop on my way to the airport. It's my duty to inspect the restoration efforts."

The visitor sat back, checked, watching Talala without a smile.

"Ali Talala," he said slowly, "reads the hearts of the people."

"It is only my duty, in such a position, in such times."

"Indeed. In such times."

Talala had changed his tone to indicate that the interview was at an end. But the stranger made no move to leave. Instead, he leaned slowly forward.

"There is," he said, "a far greater issue."

"If I may be of service to my people . . ." Talala covered his annoyance with a voice of dark honey.

"There is the matter of introducing Arabic script into the schools of Uzbekistan."

Talala smiled lightly. "That is a matter for men far greater than this humble servant of the people. And, you know, Party First Secretary Karimov does not fully support this initiative at this time."

"Then he must be moved. By men he trusts."

Talala smiled again. A mask. Karimov had bigger things on his mind at the moment, Talala knew. These were, indeed, troubled times. In any case factions had been shifting and Talala was not certain to what extent he really was trusted in Tashkent these days. Valued, certainly. But perhaps not trusted.

"The question of the Arabic script is vital to the Uzbek people," the visitor insisted.

"So are the questions of the economy, of the environment, of autonomy."

The visitor waved all that away. "Nothing is as important as the will of God. Our people must be weaned away from these bastard alphabets."

"The beginning has already been made," Talala said. "Certain of our schools already offer courses in the Arabic script for those students who have an interest."

"Such a course of action only preys upon the weakness of will the Russians have engendered in our people. The study of the script of the Holy Koran must be mandatory. For all."

"Yet there are those who would say a Turkic script is more suitable to the traditions of the Uzbek people. After all—"

"There is no question. That is only Satan throwing sand in the eyes of God's children. The script of the Holy Book is the only script."

Talala had believed that he was handling the interview well. But he had not allowed for such pigheaded fanaticism. He had made a mistake. And now it was out of control. This Ersari—and Talala had determined to find out a great deal more about him—was leaving no room for compromise, allowing no chance of a mutually beneficial understanding. He broke the rules of bargaining and the rules of etiquette. It was obvious that the man wanted a confrontation and was trying to push him beyond the calculated limits. The situation infuriated Talala, who was not used to such treatment, and he found himself longing for the old days when he had no need to listen to the ravings of such lunatics.

Overall, he disliked and distrusted the hard-core Islamic fundamentalists, who, unlike the traditional mullahs of Central Asia, rarely let themselves be exploited and who were far more interested in usurping power than in sharing it. To Talala the lessons of Persia to the south were clear.

Reluctantly, Talala began to speak. He had no choice but to display strength. Any show of weakness now would be the beginning of the end.

"I sympathize with all men who desire a better future for my people. But I will force no man to act against his own conscience. Those who wish to study the Arabic script are welcome to do so. But I will *never* be a party to anything that lessens the freedom of my people. I personally do not read the Arabic script, and I have no intention of learning it. If a child of mine wished to study it, I would not stand in the way. But I will not trade one set of oppressors for another, one set of secret policemen for another."

The visitor had gone pale. But at the close of Talala's

speech, the color rushed back into his face and the veins stood out from the hairline on his temples.

"I fear I have taken up too much of your time, Ali Talala. So great a man has many matters to which to attend. I am sorry that you cannot see the Way."

"The way," Talala said, "is never as clear as men think it to be."

"The Way of God shines above all doubt."

"May my eyes be opened," Talala said curtly.

The visitor moved his head slightly, as though indicating the physical presence of the true path.

"Indeed. May your eyes be opened, Ali Talala."

"As God wills."

"As God wills."

The stranger abruptly turned his back and went, leaving Talala in shocked, speechless anger. It occurred to him that he was really very tired. He was always tired, and he was tired of being tired. He needed time to rest, time with Ashi, time for poetry. He buzzed for Gogandaev.

A moment later the brilliantly handsome aide stepped into the office.

"The one who just left," Talala said. "I want to know everything about him."

Gogandaev looked surprised. "A problem?"

"Just get me the information. No matter what it takes."

A look of bewilderment charged Gogandaev's face. "He . . . just said he wanted to speak with you. About a place for his daughter in the university."

Talala looked at the younger man with unaccustomed sharpness. Gogandaev was a loyal lieutenant who tried to make everything run as smoothly as possible, and he was normally very good at it. But the admission of this man Ersari had been a serious mistake.

"Call down for the car," Talala said. "I'm tired. And we've got a long drive ahead of us."

"Oh," Gogandaev said, "I forgot. With your permission . . . I thought I'd follow you out first thing in the morning. I've made appointments for tonight. Minor things I didn't want to add to your list of burdens."

Talala nodded his assent. So be it. He decided Gogandaev was disappointed that Shirin had not come home. Lately, he had been showing more and more interest in her, the first interest this heroic-featured man had shown in any woman in years. Talala neither encouraged nor discouraged him. Certainly, Gogandaev would have been a son-in-law after his own heart. But Talala was far from certain that a man who could not hold a semiliterate wife from the edge of the slums would ever hold Shirin, no matter how handsome, rich, and powerful that man might be.

"We'll miss you at dinner," Talala said politely.

"I can cancel the appointments, if you wish."

"No. No, you know your duty. I won't interfere." He looked around the office. Lenin on one wall, Gorbachev and Karimov on the other. "I'm just so tired. It's time to go home."

Mustafa Gogandaev sat in silence, listening to the quiet debate. The men in traditional Uzbek dress spoke with the most confidence, assuring their listeners of the bounteous love of God even as their voices rasped with hatred. The men in Western-style suits and white shirts listened attentively, only occasionally raising a question. The exception was Mamun Ersari, the man who had confronted Ali Talala that afternoon. Seated on the carpeted floor beside Gogandaev, Ersari dipped into the stream of words whenever he sensed it veering too far from its intended course. When he spoke, Ersari's voice had a measured confidence that could easily be mistaken for broad wisdom. But Gogandaev knew better. Ersari's voice knew only a single narrow wisdom: the wisdom of hatred. Ersari spoke with the well-digested, considered variety of hatred that transcended anger to reach the cold conviction that many human lives were not worth saving, and that great sacrifices were nothing compared to great ends. It was a voice that, reciting the mercies of God, showed no mercy toward men. It was a tone of voice Gogandaev not only understood but with which he identified. Many, many lives were not worth saving.

Several of the men in traditional garments wore the headdress of religious leaders in place of the common Uzbek caps. One of those men rocked on his haunches and began, half-whispering, half-singing, to answer a question with a recitation from the Koran. The majority of the men present either did not understand the language of Muhammad or still did not understand it to a sufficient degree to follow the niceties of scripture, but it did not matter. They drank in the rhythms and the music, imagining an understanding for themselves. At the end of the little speech, all of the present voices united in the words:

"God is great."

"And do not let yourself be deceived," the mullah went on, "by false prophets, by earthly leaders who believe that compromise will clear the way for our people. Faith does not compromise. Be strong in your faith, and let no man lead you astray, even should he be your brother, even should he be your father. Only the Brethren know the true path."

"God is great," Mustafa Gogandaev said.

Ersari spoke up, and the mullah deferred. "Our brother, Mustafa Gogandaev, revealed to me the truth of these words. Today, in the lair of Satan, eye to eye with one of his servants, I saw the impossibility of redeeming a soul that is truly lost. He who traffics with the infidels makes himself lower than the lowest of women. And when the day comes, such men must be dealt with as sharply as you would deal with a woman of your blood who prostituted herself to the Russians. When the time is right, the damned must meet their fate, and the dogs of the Russians must have nowhere to turn but to their devil masters. The mightier the betrayer of the Faith, the less mercy he will receive." Ersari looked around the room with burning eyes. "The list grows longer, my brothers. When the day comes, when the fire of God descends, Ali Talala must die."

The mullah who had recited at length from the Koran woke from a mild doze at the sound of Talala's name. "The Talala clan have always been infidels posing as men of faith. They have been a speck of sand in the eye of the Prophet far too long."

"And they must die," another mullah completed the thought. "They must be removed from the face of the earth as surely as the Russian must be removed from our land."

"God is great," a lay student of the mullah said. "All such men must die."

"And the earth shall again be pure."

"Ali Talala," Ersari said, "is a blasphemer and a traitor. He would sell the infidels the bones of the Prophet Himself.

Indeed, he must die. Along with all of the males of his immediate blood."

"And his whore of a daughter," Gogandaev said suddenly. "Shirin Talala must pay for the shame she brings upon us all."

"God is great," the old mullah repeated.

9

SHIRIN STOOD IN THE SPARSE, ILL-LIT SHELTER OF AN apartment-block doorway, watching the entrance of one of the facing buildings. She had already changed her vantage point once, when a drunk became too aggressive to manage, and she had to strain to see. It was very cold, but she would not risk stepping inside to get warm. She had to be certain she saw the girl leaving.

It was very cold, with the special dreary cold that always settled over Moscow after the holidays. It was the heavy sort of cold that made all men appear identical as they drew their jaws deep into their scarves and stooped against the wind. Women who had reached a smileless age hobbled along under great mountains of clothing, trailing bags stuffed with whatever the day had offered. Steaming like antique engines, the residents of the building where Shirin had positioned herself bustled past, anxious to reach the warmth of the foyer, tramping in over the rags that served for doormats until the old linoleum floor was hidden under a black crust. Steam heat and human breath cottoned the inside of the heavy glass doors behind her, and even from outside, Shirin could *hear* the building. The structure was alive, its deep pipes groaning and the faulty elevator screaming as it halted at the foyer. There were voices, too. Shouting voices, hurling anger across tiny rooms, slapping each other with the day's frustrations. Breaking marriages in a broken building. Shirin knew with iron certainty that such a life would never be for her. She would rather die.

It was very cold. She felt the winter clawing its way up through the soles of her boots, sliding its fingers up her legs. But she stood very still, not even moving to pull her hat down lower over her ears. The slopping cold of Moscow was miserable enough. But it never cut into her the way the razor-sharp desert winds came slashing at the eyes, shocking her lungs. She willed herself to disdain this Moscow cold. As a child, on special family holidays, she had slept between a horse's belly and her father's padded cloak, under a winter sky so white with stars her pony could have plunged and galloped across heaven itself as if it were just another snowfield.

A short woman lugging two plastic bags approached the building from the direction of the subway station. Even the layers of winter clothing could not hide the woman's withered form. She walked quickly, marching on short legs like a soldier in an old film. Her bags barely cleared the sidewalk.

The woman had almost reached the safety of the doors when she pivoted and pushed up to Shirin. In the weak light, Shirin could just make out locks of chemical-colored hair beneath a fur cap fit for the rubbish bin. Small eyes hunted out of skin that looked loose and dead even in the cold.

Shirin recognized the type immediately. Old Communist. The sort who gave their love to the Party and never quite figured out what their cunts were for.

"What do *you* want here?" the woman demanded.

Shirin looked down at the human wreck.

"I'm waiting."

"Wait somewhere else. You have no business here."

"Piss off, you old bitch."

The woman recoiled. Like a snake that had been kicked but not really injured. She immediately recovered and thrust her face back toward Shirin.

"Clear off, you little tart. This is a decent building. We don't need your kind around here." Her breath enveloped them both.

Shirin turned away, deciding to ignore her.

But the woman was ablaze with the remembered sacrifices of a lifetime, with the dignity she had earned.

"I'll call the militia, you Asian slut."

Shirin shrugged. "Call the Central Committee, you old bag of shit. Nobody cares."

"I'm going to call the militia," the woman repeated. She was raging, gloved fists clutching her bags as though squeezing blood out of the plastic straps.

Shirin moved off haughtily, as if she had just smelled something unspeakable.

"Black slut," the woman spit after her.

In her annoyance, Shirin almost missed the event for which she had been waiting. The door of the building she had been watching opened and a woman came out. The feeble lamp by the entranceway showed a glint of blond hair trailing out from under the woman's scarf. It was enough. Shirin knew it was her.

She watched her rival's back recede down the street. Then she headed for the building from which the woman had just emerged, walking as swiftly as the icy, uncleared sidewalks allowed. She had done everything she could to make certain she would have the artist all to herself.

The vestibule of Sasha Leskov's building was a mirror image of all the others. The paint had lost its potency of color and the walls were mottled and scarred with graffiti. A torn poster demanded the attention of the building's residents, and sopping rags caught at Shirin's boots. The place stank of ammonia and cabbage.

The elevator in this building did not work at all and Shirin went up the stairs, feeling her way in the darkness, with broken glass crunching underfoot. Something moved independently, but Shirin ignored it, sensing the other creature's fear as readily as she could sense cowardice in men. The passage did not take long. The artist's apartment, according to the directions given by her friend, was on the second floor.

This hallway still had lights and the smell was less ferocious. The residents of the corridor made an effort to keep their sliver of paradise clean, and some of the doors had been painted over in an effort to brighten things up. Other doors had been covered with black vinyl padding in an effort to keep the world as fully at bay as possible.

The artist's flat was at the end, behind a plain door with a neatly lettered card fixed below the peephole.

Shirin was too proud and confident of herself to bother fussing with her clothing or hair. She simply ran a finger across the bottom of her nose, catching the wetness, and pushed the doorbell.

"Very pretty girl," Samsonov said, eyes lingering on the threshold of the artist's kitchen.

Sasha bent over the stove. Broad shoulders, small waist, a swimmer's body.

"Really," Samsonov went on, anxious to compliment the painter any way he could, "she's a true Russian beauty."

"Vera's all right. More tea?"

"Please. If you're having some."

Sasha brought the kettle to the table, gray cat on his heels.

"I'm not disturbing you?" Samsonov asked earnestly. "I'm not keeping you from painting?"

The artist laughed. "I'm not as industrious as all that. I'm just surprised you showed up. Sugar?"

Samsonov picked out two little white bricks with his fingers. "I've been thinking about it since I got to Moscow. But I didn't want to bother you."

"Until you got so deathly bored—"

"*No,*" Samsonov said quickly. "It wasn't like that at all." He leaned over the table, on the verge of reaching out to physically assure his host of his sincerity.

The artist sat beneath a painting of a desolate interior: a row of phone booths with doors left open and receivers dangling, leading to an open window with a blue-gray sky that looked eternal.

"Anyway," Sasha said, "I'm glad you came. Gives me a chance to redeem myself. After the murals in Potsdam." He nudged a plate of colorfully wrapped sweets toward Samsonov. "So how have you been?"

Samsonov gave the polite, common answer. Nothing special. But the truth was that he had not been well. He had not been in Moscow for several years and the deterioration shocked him. Everything seemed to be coming apart. The shops had never been so empty, the shopgirls never so rude. Punks mocked his uniform on the streets, and if you had no

Western cigarettes or hard currency to wave, the taxis skittered by without slowing or, at best, announced that they were already booked. The city was cold and gray and black, with ice everywhere on the broken sidewalks. But the weather seemed far warmer than the hearts. The men looked past you, the women looked right through you. He had been afraid to phone the painter or to drop by, afraid Sasha would turn out to be just as dismissive and unwelcoming as the rest of the city.

Samsonov simply could not believe what was happening. He lingered in the pedestrian underpasses, listening to orators of unthinkable causes as they hawked their visions and badly mimeographed news-sheets. Everything was under verbal siege, and to hear the bearded zealots tell it, all of the country's achievements were hollow or stuffed with lies.

There were beggars now: on the streets, in the doorways, in the subway stations, in the underground passages at Pushkin Square or beneath Marx Prospect. Ancient women stooped over canes with their dirty hands extended, Gypsies flocked and grabbed, and men of all ages squatted behind scribbled cardboard signs proclaiming their failed histories. On his way to the military department store Samsonov met the worst beggar of all. It was in the passage under the boulevard off the end of the Arbat, where shivering young men and women with sketch pads tried to persuade any foreign-looking passerby to have his or her portrait done in pastels. Samsonov almost missed the man, only noticing him because the top of an army field service cap caught his eye. It was the sort of cap soldiers had worn in Afghanistan.

Samsonov pushed through the crowd, angry that a beggar would wear a piece of military uniform but already half-sick at what he feared he might find.

The man sat on the wet grime against the wall, wearing a combination of military kit, sweaters, and rags. A half-running woman tossed a few kopecks into his tin soup pot and disappeared.

The man's outer shell was decked with *Afghansi* badges and decorations. His eyes were dead and swollen with yellow pus.

Samsonov had never had a weak stomach. He had weathered the worst the war had to offer. But now he felt like vomiting.

He stood over the man.

"Where were you, brother?"

The useless eyes lifted toward Samsonov in a memory of sight. The beggar's single remaining insignia of rank made him a senior sergeant.

"Salang."

Yes. The Salang pass. A casualty factory on the logistics lifeline. Once the Dushmani blew the tunnel with a convoy inside. Hundreds of men burned to death or suffocated.

Samsonov tried to see around the scarves and rags.

"Engineer?"

"Sapper," the beggar said, smiling. He had a single upper tooth remaining when he smiled. "Mine detail. You?"

Down the passageway a young man in a prerevolutionary costume began to cry out that Russia would not be saved until a new czar was crowned.

"I moved around," Samsonov said. "Kandahar, Gardez. The Panshir a couple of times."

The sightless face nodded knowingly. "Paratrooper. And an officer, too."

"Why an officer?" Samsonov asked, surprised.

"It's your voice." The beggar smiled again, black gums with one brown tooth. "You can't help it," he said good-naturedly. "We're all scum to you. And then there's your shoes and the way you walk. I knew you were an officer when you first come up."

"I'm not a real officer anymore," Samsonov said matter-of-factly. "I'm with the interior troops now."

The beggar laughed. It occurred to Samsonov that the man might be a bit mad, as well.

"Going to arrest me?"

"No," Samsonov said. "I'm not going to arrest you."

"Give me some money, then. Help out an old comrade."

Samsonov nodded to the man who could not see. He took out his billfold and selected a ten-ruble note with which he had planned to buy books. He reached it down into the beggar's hand.

As soon as the beggar felt the note dust his skin he snatched it quick as a crab, laughing madly. He drew the bill back and forth under his nose.

"It's ten rubles."

"I know. I can smell it." The beggar smiled. "I can smell everything. I can smell the women going by."

The beggar's face turned utterly lunatic.

"Listen, I'm sorry about your eyes." Samsonov wanted to run away like a frightened child.

The beggar snorted. "Don't be. It's all shit anyway. There's nothing I want to see." He laughed, nearly howling. Passersby began to stare. "Do you know how you smell?"

Samsonov began to back away, just slightly.

"You smell afraid, Comrade Officer." The beggar laughed again. "I can almost smell the shit."

Samsonov turned his back and fled. It was peak hour and the underpass was very crowded. The beggar's laughter didn't carry very far at all. In a few minutes, Samsonov was in the warm shelter of the military department store, but the clerks did not have any of the things he needed.

The next day the officers in Samsonov's transition course received their assignments. The course had been programmed to last another three weeks, but the situation in the Caucasus had taken a turn for the worse and there was an urgent call for officer augmentees and replacements. The school's deputy director called them together first thing in the morning. He read a list of names: officers to leave within twenty-four hours for Tbilisi and Abkhazia. A second list identified officers who were to leave for Baku, Sumgait, Kuba, and other Caucasian garrisons within seventy-two hours. Samsonov's name was not called. Then the deputy director read a third and final list, detailing students to posts spread across the vastness of the Soviet Union, from Moldavia to Magadan. Their travel arrangements would be handled through normal channels.

Samsonov listened anxiously in the glazed silence. The jokes were over now and the officers sat like criminals being sentenced. Each occasional effort to smile looked pathetic and weak.

Samsonov's name was never called.

After the deputy director had finished, ending with a few polished words of encouragement, the officers drifted out into the hallway. They spoke very slowly with one another, like students learning a foreign language. Samsonov slipped by the little groups and caught up with the deputy director at the bottom of a stairwell.

"Comrade Colonel?"

The man turned. He had tired, salmon-shaded eyes and a look of ill health that had not been evident from a distance.

"My name is Samsonov, Mikhail Nikolaievich. You didn't read my—"

"Yes. Samsonov. Our Hero of the Soviet Union and all that. Would've been bad blood, sending them all off to the shit farm and keeping you here in Moscow. . . ."

"Moscow?"

The colonel smiled. "You're the perfect choice, my boy, absolutely perfect. We're training up a few elite riot-control units for the capital, reaction-force sort of business. They'll need to shine."

"But you need good officers in the Caucasus."

"Anybody can do that. Bunch of blackasses. Shoot in the air and they hide under the bed." He held out his hand to Samsonov. "Congratulations. You'll have your own company. And your own battalion before you know it."

And then he was gone.

To any other man the assignment would have been an incredible stroke of luck. Everyone wanted to remain in Moscow. It was an honor, a privilege. Instead of facing down armed thugs in the middle of nowhere and dodging firebombs thrown by men he no longer trusted himself to regard as human, he would spend his time ensuring that his men marched properly and rendered ostentatious military courtesies. At worst, he would be called upon to block off a street from protesters whose blood he shared and whose psychology he understood. It was an assignment for which men begged and bribed. It shamed Samsonov that it had fallen to him.

In the student buffet his comrades complained to each other about the collapse of law and order out in the fringe republics and the social indiscipline in the streets of Moscow. They spoke as though it were all someone else's responsibility. In the faces and voices Samsonov could read fear, self-doubt, frustration. He sat alone, drinking his tea and eating biscuits, glad that he had made no close friends and that no one came by to inquire about his assignment.

Unexpectedly, an officer at the next table began to weep. He was being sent to a torn-open district on the Iranian border. He was a major, already overweight and broken to a lost routine. What, he wanted to know, would become of his wife, his children? The major did not even attempt to make a pretense of courage in front of his peers, and in a minute it was evident that the man was suffering a nervous collapse in front of them all. No one moved to help him, not even Samsonov. It was as though a greater force had frozen them in their chairs, forcing them to watch. Or perhaps it was fear of contagion. In any case, his brother officers left the man there, sobbing with his head down on the table. Samsonov quietly finished his tea and went down the hall to borrow the use of a telephone.

He had decided to call Sasha Leskov. At least, he thought, he could summon up that much bravery. He had frequently thought of the artist, remembering the good conversation on a bad night, the cold streets and the spark that had somehow arisen between the two of them. It had been the last time he had really been able to talk to someone, to feel as though his words were heard and weighed in the soul, despite all the personal newness and the inadequacies of language. Samsonov felt as though they had almost reached one another, as though, despite all their dissimilarities, they shared something rare in the way they viewed the world. Or perhaps it was all in his imagination, a result of loneliness and too much drink. Then there was the worry about how the artist would remember their exchange. After all, he had insulted the man's work.

The painter answered the phone himself and immediately invited Samsonov to come by. And Samsonov had gone, anxiously, wearing his uniform because the few civilian clothes he owned were rags and he did not even possess a warm coat other than his duty overcoat. While his brother officers had exploited their assignments to the German Democratic Republic to equip themselves with stylish jackets, with cassette recorders and videotapes, Samsonov had not bought or sold a thing on the black market. His sole acquisitions had been Russian classics bought from the German-Soviet friendship bookstores. The books had been expensive when purchased with East German marks converted from rubles. But the books had not been available back in the Soviet Union. All of the best things were marked for export, and it was far easier to find a copy of Tolstoy or Garshin in Leipzig than in Leningrad. As a gift for the painter Samsonov took along his copy of the collected poems of Akhmatova, expensive when bought and impossible to get in Moscow now. The small blue book was precious to him, but he had purposely selected a gift that would hurt him to lose. Giving away one of his books—this book—was like giving up a part of himself. And in this case, it did not even matter if the artist did not care for poetry. The giving was important.

The painter greeted him with a smile and a strong handshake, took the volume of Akhmatova, and laid it atop a row of art books without looking at it. It did not matter. The man's words were warm and quick, and he seemed genuinely pleased that Samsonov had come.

Had Samsonov been an envious man, the painter would have given him much to envy. He had an apartment all to himself, with a kitchen, bath, bedroom, and a central room that served as his studio and storage area for his work. He had his own telephone. And he had a lovely Russian girl beside him, with blond hair that could light the darkness and eyes full of love.

And the paintings were wonderful. With the cold and grime shut outside, Samsonov found himself in a world of glory. The artist's works lay casually stacked against the walls, dozens deep, with only a few current favorites hanging. Samsonov was afraid to touch the canvases at first, but the painter handled them as if they were of little consequence to him. Finally, Samsonov got up the nerve to flip through the stacks on his own.

The girl, Vera, made tea, but Samsonov let his cup go cold. There was always another painting to be held up to the light. He knew he did not have the vocabulary to explain why he liked the work, why it was good. But the paintings reached down into him, filling him with a gorgeous sorrow.

A simple Moscow street scene stopped him for several minutes. Recent, it was winter gray, with dirtying snow and buildings that seemed to shiver. On a barely visible roadway between two apartment blocks, a knot of hard-colored automobiles, seen in fragments, gave the painting its only real color, saving it from relentless gloom and bringing it to wonderful life. Without a single human figure, with only a modicum of color and fixed lines, the work somehow filled Samsonov with a sense of the soul's predicament, practical and sublime at once. The painting *was* Moscow, absolutely honest, yet redeemed. It was the Moscow he himself was too blind to see, yet it was the Moscow he felt in his heart. He had never seen anything like this before.

"You like that?" the artist asked with surprising timidity in his voice.

"I don't have the words."

"Sasha just painted that last month," the girl said.

"It's brilliant."

"Sasha just finished painting my portrait," the girl told him.

Samsonov looked at the artist.

"Show it to him," the girl begged. "Please, Sasha. I'm so proud of it."

With a reluctance Samsonov did not understand, the artist disappeared into the bedroom, followed by his cat. He rummaged audibly, then reappeared with a raw-framed canvas taller than wide. Not quite life-size, it showed the girl sitting in an old-fashioned dress with a bit of lace around the collar. The rose-brown of the dress paid an unexpected compliment to the girl's blond hair, and her face shimmered with peach and vanilla tones. The lips were faded mauve and the eyes shone with a readiness to love that made Samsonov feel lonelier than the presence of any flesh-and-blood woman could have done. Vera, the girl, was pretty. The girl in the portrait was beautiful. Yet it was exactly the same girl. The artist had understood the ways in which she was beautiful, letting them onto the canvas. It was classic, perfect. It might have been painted yesterday or a hundred years before. Samsonov could not imagine a finer gift from a man to a woman. And yet. The portrait, with its autumn tones, was somehow colder than the winter scene of Moscow.

When Samsonov turned, the artist held up a canvas splashed with color. From just the right distance, a landscape emerged, fire hot.

"I did this one when I was in Samarkand," the artist said. "There's a whole series."

Samsonov tensed. As if he had seen a snake in the corner. He did not want to look at these pictures. But the artist held up another, this one as sharp as a photo. A half-ruined house under the stars. Samsonov could smell the death, he heard small-arms fire and saw the backs of his running soldiers as they hurried for the shelter of the kishlak.

"Is something wrong?" the artist asked.

"No. No, it's just that I wasn't done looking at the Moscow pictures. I'm slow. I need time."

He felt as though, if he turned his back, the paintings of Central Asia might come slithering toward him. It was all of a piece. Deserts and death. Howling in the silence. He thought of the major who had broken down in the student buffet and went ice-cold inside. Wondering how much madness might be brewing in his own soul.

"Sasha," Samsonov began, searching for words that would not be melodramatic, "I have to tell you honestly . . . I have a bit of a problem with anything Asian right now. It's childish. But Afghanistan is still a little closer than I let on. It's no big deal." He smiled, trying to warm it into a joke. "It's just that I feel like I never want to see Central Asia or any of that stuff ever again."

The artist looked wounded. But he recovered quickly.

"There's some stuff I did in Poland over here," he said. "Ever been to Poland? It's got a different soul, it's hard to . . ."

They looked at the pictures of Poland, of seductively abstracted rural landscapes, of color studies that tricked you with depth of field and pleased the eye in a way that Samsonov could not explain. Then Samsonov looked again at paintings that had stayed with him through all of the others. He smiled and shook his head, asking again and again if Sasha minded his taking up so much of his evening. The girl disappeared into the kitchen, reemerging to invite them for more tea and a snack. She seemed relatively uninterested in the paintings, but after all, Samsonov reasoned, she'd seen them many times.

There were only two chairs at the table in the sparsely furnished kitchen. Samsonov sat on one, while Sasha took the other, with the girl perched on his thigh and the cat at his ankle. The sight made Samsonov smile, thinking that every living thing was attracted to this gifted man.

"Sorry I can't offer you a drink," Sasha said. "I don't keep any alcohol around."

Samsonov dismissed the issue with a wave. He had been forcing himself to drink less. The dreams were not much worse for his sobriety. Anyway, he didn't need much sleep. He read. Or walked.

"You told me you were in some kind of course?"

"Finished it," Samsonov said. "Today. Monday I report to my unit."

The artist's eyes flickered briefly. Disappointment? Samsonov wondered. But that was silly. Sasha had no need of him.

"Where are they sending you?" the girl asked.

"Nowhere. I'm staying here. In Moscow."

"That's wonderful," the girl said with a smile that seemed genuine. "How nice for you."

"Congratulations," Sasha said. "I figured they'd be shipping you off to Yerevan or someplace like that."

"Luck of the draw."

"Now I'm really sorry we don't have any vodka. I'd drink a toast to you."

"We'd all drink a toast," the girl said.

"I go where I'm assigned," Samsonov said quietly.

"Well," the girl said emphatically, "I think you're lucky. All those southern people are so dirty. And you can't trust them." Then she glanced at the wall clock and sprang from the artist's thigh. "I've got to go. I'm going to be late."

Sasha curled the corner of his mouth. "Vera's off to church. Evening service and prayers for my soul. Then back to Mom and Dad for the weekend. The dutiful daughter on the last train out."

"You're glad when I go away," the girl said reproachfully with a pouted smile.

"They get a weekend, I get a weekend. Fair's fair."

Samsonov smiled good-naturedly, feeling vast and desolate inside. It was always like this. It wasn't the displays of grand passion that slammed you with loneliness, but the overheard tone of mundane intimacy, the observed gesture that had become a custom of love between two others.

Sasha and his girl went through the ritual of small agreements attendant on a departure, then, with the last items tucked in her bag and her scarf wrapped twice around her, the girl left Samsonov's line of sight. A moment later the hallway door closed and the artist came back into the kitchen.

Samsonov drained the bitter dregs of his tea and glanced one last time toward the shadows where the vivid girl had been moments before.

"Very pretty girl," he said.

The sidewalks between the last subway station and the Donskoy Monastery had not been cleared of ice. Throughout the city, routine services were breaking down, but this was different. Not the slightest effort had been made to clear a path to the monastery for pedestrians. It was the small revenge of small bureaucrats. You were free to attend religious services. But there was no need to make it easy on you. Vera stepped carefully through a night so cold the air tried to hold her in place, dreaming of God and her lover.

She passed several ancient women who had come to a full stop, perching over canes to catch their breath. Other grandmothers lugged bags of food for the priests and monks, flowing slowly but steadily over the ice, accustomed to far greater obstacles than this. Vera did not offer to help anyone. The old women did not want help tonight. They relished each small suffering on their approach to God.

Vera began to pray even before she passed through the great brick portal. Please, Lord. Please, let me have him to keep. Please let him love me.

Inside the compound the pathways had been cleared by the faithful. She went quickly, anxious to throw herself into the shelter of the church. She climbed the outer steps, entered through the massive door, then slowed her pace in respect as she climbed the cold, cold inner stairs, spirit already rising at the sound of chanting and the delicious smell of incense. Inside the upper chamber she found a place among the believers, standing between old women wrapped in dark scarves, cripples, mothers with children, a sad, stocky army colonel, and a scrawny young man whose clothing flapped hugely around him, his face pale and spotted. Together, the congregation stood in silence before the candlelit wall of icons. Brass and beaten-gold gleamed, and the priest and a small male choir took turns praising Christ the Redeemer.

Vera begged God to help her, begging Him with all the purity her heart could muster, knowing all the while that she would cheat and lie and injure others to hold Sasha. She was ready to do anything. Anything at all. There was no limit to her desire to possess this man. For eternity.

Please, Lord.

She promised a lifetime of devotion, of good works, of mortal reverence. The deep, big, peaceful voice of the priest stroked her, the velvet choir cradled her in hope. Above the parted crowd, the eyes of the saints burned darkly in the remembrance of martyrdom and miracles. The pale young man twitched and began to rock back and forth until an old woman steadied him and began to pet him like a dog.

Old women piled jars of preserves, apples, bread, and money on the side altars. The powerful male voices never ceased caressing them. Some had come to give, others to take. God had a place for them all.

Vera purchased three candles from the kiosk in the foyer.

Please, Lord.

More than anything else, the portrait had given her hope. When she and Sasha had first become acquainted, he had casually mentioned that he would like to paint her portrait, and she had been scratched by the fear that he meant he wanted to paint her unclothed, the way all artists did, and she would have been too ashamed, even though she could not tell him that outright, afraid to lose him.

Then one evening he said to her, "That dress . . . it's perfect. I want to paint you like that." He had gotten tickets to the theater, through friends. She did not understand the play. But she had triumphed in her choice of clothing, her best dress, her only good dress, with the high collar and a froth of lace.

And he had painted her. Lovingly. Startling her with her beauty, even though she did think he had made the chin a bit too heavy. Then he made love to her with the dress pushed up around her waist. And she knew that he loved her, even though he could not bring himself to say the words.

She lit her last candle. Things were looking up. God was merciful. The arrival of the officer earlier in the evening had been a good omen. Sasha was beginning to change. Now he had officers for friends. Soon he would be finished with the vagabonds and Jews who devoured his time.

She relaxed into her favorite reverie, imagining herself with Sasha by her side, standing before a gold-robed priest, with the wedding crowns held above their heads. The vision was especially sharp and clear tonight. She would have him, she would have him. He had already taken the first irrevocable steps toward her.

She swelled with the confidence that Sasha wanted to marry the girl in the painting, that he only needed time to realize it. Time, and loving encouragement.

She crossed herself.

Thank you a thousand times, O Lord.

The artist opened the door just as the buzzer sounded a second time. He was not quite as tall as Shirin remembered him, nor quite as freshly handsome. She changed her estimate of his age from late twenties to early thirties. But he looked firm and clear-eyed, with good skin and none of the signs of the liquor sickness that routinely ate into male Russian flesh.

He was quick, too. He remembered her almost instantly, she could see that in the intelligence of his green eyes.

"My name is Shirin. You gave me a torn picture last week."

"Sasha Leskov," the artist answered, taking the offered hand. He was very warm after her wait in the winter night, and his hand was sinewy and alive, as though he really felt the things he touched. "My God, you're cold. Come in please."

He smiled. But with none of the stupid presumption she might have expected in another man. Neither was there the least trace of the confrontational attitude he had shown the night of the exhibition. He seemed to be in the best of spirits.

"I wanted to see more of your paintings," Shirin told him. "I was able to get your address, but not your phone number."

"Let me take your coat."

"I hope I haven't disturbed you." She felt the warmth of his apartment stroking her face, reaching down under the layers of clothing to enliven her skin.

" 'Shirin.' That's Persian, isn't it?"

"Yes," she said, surprised.

"But you're . . . Uzbek by nationality?"

He had good eyes. An artist's eyes. And he wasn't stupid.

"My family's Uzbek. But we're unusual. There's a Tadzhik influence. Anyway, Persian names are common. Uzbeks believe they fall beautifully into the ear."

The artist smiled. "As opposed to Russian names?"

Shirin smiled, too. She looked into his eyes, and nothing about him retreated at her directness.

"As opposed to Russian names," she agreed.

The artist laughed.

Shirin jumped, raising her hand to strike. Something had brushed heavily against her boot. Recalling the stairwell, she instinctively feared a rat.

Looking down, she saw a cat staring up at her with a quizzical look on its face.

"That's Vrubel. Not afraid of cats, are you?"

Shirin looked the artist in the eye again, trying to regain her inner balance.

"He just startled me. I'm not afraid of much."

"Vrubel's a friendly little bugger." The artist squatted, soothing back the animal's fur. "Probably too friendly for his own good."

"He yours?"

The artist nodded. "Come on in and have a cup of tea."

Shirin was glad the cat did not belong to the Russian girl.

At the threshold of the kitchen, she got another surprise. An officer in an Interior Ministry uniform was sitting at the table. She had assumed she would be alone with the artist. And she knew enough about her father to be uncomfortable around anyone who had any connection with the MVD.

The officer stood up, laboring with his facial muscles until they approximated a smile.

"Shirin," the artist said, "this is a friend of mine, Misha Samsonov. Misha, this is Shirin—sorry, I didn't catch your family name."

"Just Shirin."

The artist shrugged.

"I just came by to see the paintings," she said, considerably less at ease now. Things were not going well.

"Really?" the officer said flatly. "That's why I'm here." His voice had the forced sound of a machine.

"Sit down," the artist said. "It'll just be a minute." He

fiddled with the narrow range by the doorway. Shirin sat feeling the officer's eyes tracking her. Something about him gave her the chills. He was young, and good-looking enough in a dull Russian way. But there was something wrong with him. She avoided his eyes.

From what she could see, the apartment was nothing much. But at least it was clean. She had expected something of a sty from a Russian man—even one whose girlfriend practically lived with him. She looked at the artist. His motions as he prepared the tea were definite and economical, as if his hands always knew exactly how to touch an object, shaping themselves to its form with a precision other men lacked. Shirin wondered how he would touch her.

"So," the officer said, dead-voiced. "You're a fan of Sasha's, too?"

"You could say that."

The officer brushed his day's growth of beard across the collar of his uniform, and it hit Shirin with a little shock that he was far more ill at ease around her than she was with him. It baffled her.

The officer seemed to be struggling with himself about something.

"I've never met anyone who paints like Sasha," he said. "It's . . . revolutionary."

The artist laughed and reached for a cabinet.

" 'Revolutionary' is hardly a compliment these days."

"He has a gift," Shirin said, watching as the artist pried open a tin of tea with his fingertips.

It was sad, really, Shirin thought. How people lived. Whether this man was talented or not, he certainly didn't have very much to show for it. It was a blessing that he had his own flat, of course. From a practical standpoint. But it seemed a remarkably spare place. Of course, that was better than the horrible clutter the Russians loved. Trinkets, colored glass, and dust. The Russians were a tasteless people, as though they had exterminated their sense of beauty. This one . . . more than anything else the rooms he lived in had a feel of transience, as though he had never really settled in here any more than he might settle into a hotel room.

The cat stared at her. As a girl, she had owned a beautiful white cat. Two of her cousins had nailed its paws to a fence to tease her, and her father had had to kill it to end its misery. She bent down and held out her fingers.

The cat turned away and meandered over to a bowl of mashed food, stooping over it then settling, making a hump of its spine.

"What is it," the officer asked slowly, "that appeals to you about Sasha's work?"

Shirin turned on the stupid man with his stupid questions. "The violence."

The officer sat back, more confused than ever.

The artist turned from clattering in the sink. He was smiling. He was always smiling or laughing.

"She's kidding," he said. "It's a joke. There was this argument at an exhibition . . ."

Shirin could feel the warmth of the room all over her now. She had been very cold. Colder than she was willing to admit to herself. But it was all right now. And she was starting to get the smell of the artist, of his rooms, his life. He prattled to the officer, trying to explain their first meeting. But Shirin knew that some things could never be explained, and this was one of them. The thought of this man had infected her, spreading over her like a powerful sickness. With each day she had thought of him more often, with greater intensity. She had never experienced such a lack of self-control before. And she had only just realized that she had spent over an hour standing in the cold for a man she didn't even know.

That wasn't true. She knew him.

He was the one.

The artist set two cups of tea down on the table and drew the sugar bowl closer to Shirin. She could smell the day's wear on him, the maleness. Then she noticed that the teacups, which did not match, were both cracked.

She smiled, thinking, I will bring him teacups he will cherish until the day he dies.

Samsonov did not believe in premonitions or visions or anything at all that ranged between fortune-telling and religious revelation. Yet something he could not understand happened when the Asian girl entered the room. She was remarkably beautiful, by any standards. Neither in Samarkand nor in Kabul had he seen anyone who approached the vividness of her presence. Frozen through, she still moved with a grace that put the cat to shame. But immediately behind her, he saw corpses. He heard the screams of his wounded. Saw their body parts strewn along the convoy road in mockery. Beneath her perfume the kitchen had begun to stink of sulfur. Cordite. Death.

Death.

Death.

Please stop, he begged himself. Please. Let me be sane. Sane men don't react to beautiful women as though a ghost had just walked in. Please. Let me be civil and sane.

As the rockets impacted for the thousandth time, corpses sailed into the air. Old corpses, new corpses. Bone, blood, a porridge of guts. A dead hand brushed his cheek. Corpses piled on top of him so that he could not breathe.

Please let me be sane.

They all went into the room the artist used as a studio. The girl stood in the center of the room as Sasha showed her one canvas after another. She smiled, offering flat compliments. Samsonov sensed that she did not understand a single brushstroke, either intellectually or emotionally. She stood and paid for Sasha's performance with words acquired but not felt. And the artist seemed blind to her ignorance.

She was such a beautiful woman. Beautiful the way Samsonov had once imagined the women of Central Asia to be, before he had gone there. Before he had smelled death rubbed right into his nostrils.

The woman was death.

She only came to life when the impromptu exhibition reached the stack of paintings the artist had done in Central Asia. Here she at least recognized the subjects.

"I've been there," she said with childish pride.

"And there.

"And *there.*"

Samsonov could not bear to look at the paintings. He busied himself by hunting out the Moscow winter scene that had so moved him. But he could not make his eyes see it now. He was sick with loneliness. Only a sick, lonely man could react so crazily, he told himself. Only a man who had forgotten how to live.

He would have to find a girl. Even a less than perfect girl.

The prospect of returning to the dormitory for single-officer students seemed as empty as the black reaches of space.

I need to talk, he thought. To be with people more often. He had come to this apartment to talk. To discuss his failures, his nation, the soulless times. And death walked in.

No. That was all wrong. A beautiful girl, a beautiful woman had walked in.

I am walking through a graveyard.

And it is very dark.

Please let me be a sane, good man.

"How much?" the woman asked. She had chosen an oil of the Registan in Samarkand. She said it would be a gift for her father.

Samsonov watched the artist. For the first time since the drunken party in Potsdam he could see blunt calculation on the other man's face.

"Eight hundred rubles," the artist said finally. It sounded impossibly high to Samsonov, given his salary. But at the same time, he realized it probably wasn't high at all.

The girl drew out a roll of ruble notes of all sizes. It was more money than any sensible woman—or man—would have carried through the streets of Moscow.

She counted out the sum and handed it to the surprised artist. The roll of bills looked as large as it had before.

Death, Samsonov thought.

Shirin had grown bored with the ceaseless display of paintings and sketches. She watched the artist himself, inspecting the athleticism in his movements, watching the strain of muscles against his jeans as he bent and stooped and turned. Even under the loose shirt, she could gauge the strength of his back, a lean, capable strength waiting to be applied. She needed to get closer, to speak softly until she could dispense with the ritual of speech. But there was no end to the stacked canvases and piled charcoals and watercolors. And all the while the other one behaved like a typical policeman, watching her and pretending not to watch her, lurking clumsily behind her as though only waiting for her to touch the artist so he could bring out the handcuffs.

She worried that the artist had forgotten *her* in the thrall of his vanity. He held up one identical canvas after another.

It was as though men would cease to exist if they ever stopped *doing,* as though there were no cores to their beings at all. As though they were forever splashing in their terrified efforts not to drown.

It was a great relief to Shirin when Leskov suddenly drew out a series of paintings done in the lands where she had been raised. It even occurred to her that, if she bought something, she might be able to put an end to all this nonsense.

She looked at the paintings with renewed interest, trying to find one worth carrying home. She supposed that they were good enough, in their way. But it seemed so silly that a man could ever imagine he could capture *that* sky on a little piece of cloth or confine the beauty of that landscape on a scrap of paper in which a wiser man would have wrapped his lunch.

Shirin knew the smell of that air. And it did not smell like oil paints.

"It's marvelous," Shirin said, touching the artist's outstretched arm. "My father would love it. It's his favorite place in the world."

The artist glowed, then shied away his eyes to the wooden floor.

"How much?" she asked.

In the afternoon he had gone to the indoor swimming pool, timing his visit, as always, for off-hours. He had been able to disappear into the pool, into its heavy silence, without the lunchtime or evening crush and clutter of bodies. The water was sharp with chlorine, biting into him with an intensity that would redden his eyes despite his swimming goggles. He did not care. He turned and reached and pulled through the water, thrusting himself forward, turning and thrusting again, stretching each muscle before coming up for air, up into the sudden cavernous echo of the hall. He sought to weary those muscles, to purge them of sloth. He loved to swim, and he loved water. That, too, was a gift from his grandmother.

Even now, as the unhealthy fat of a Muscovite bloated across his lane, swimming reminded him of Jurmala and the lonely stretches of coastline to the north, where he had swum as a boy under his grandmother's approving eye. Latvian men, she said, were athletic and clean. Every time she said that Latvian men were this or that, she meant that Russian men were exactly the opposite. She insisted that Latvian men were honest, hardworking, and good to their wives. Even as a child he had realized that his grandmother's generalizations did not apply across the board. A walk down Riga's streets soon turned up plenty of local men who fell far short of the heroic. But these were not the men of whom the grandmother spoke. She spoke and dreamed of the beaux of her youth, of educated young men with English manners and mathematically precise parts in their hair, men who took their girls and their friends on outings in big German motorcars back in the days when Latvia still clutched its tiny independence and beauty did not have to be justified in terms of its benefit to the masses. He swam in the cold Baltic waters, a slim boy's arms stroking parallel to a tan beach, a green shore. With the sun forever stopped at summer noon. He was always happy on the coast.

The fiercely chlorinated Moscow waters scraped over his shoulders like pumice and a whistle blew, forcing a line of undernourished children into the water for a swimming lesson.

He had come home, scalp freezing, to find Vera already there, seated at the kitchen table, telling her fortune with a deck of cards as a meal slowly ripened on the stove.

She was a good girl, and totally wrong. He still did not know how to tell her.

She looked up from the cards.

"Look," she said, pointing. "See that. Today's your lucky day."

He laughed and kissed her, sticking his nose in the pot, growling playfully and stooping to pet Vrubel, who was ever starved for his touch.

Five minutes later the phone rang. It was Bilinsky, the cigarette-lunged old thief from the Artists' Union. The Union had gotten a call from the Department of Historical and Defense Arts at the Ministry of Defense. Requesting Sasha by name. Again . . . No, Bilinsky didn't know the details. Just drop by next week and see what's his name. . . . No. Really. No idea where they want you to go this time. Didn't say. Talk to what's his name. They love you over there.

"Okay," Sasha said. "So when do I get a real exhibition?"

"I thought we'd settled that, dear boy."

"We didn't settle anything."

"You know how confused things are at the moment. But

we'll talk about it, we'll talk about it. You know, it's a marvel how you get on with those military types, an absolute marvel. Damn. Sasha, I've got somebody on the other line. Do you mind?"

Maybe it *was* luck. His homecoming had been such a disappointment. He already felt he needed time away from Vera. To wean her off him. The poor girl. A good girl, really. Who wanted a solid husband. And no surprises. The entire drab nightmare.

Then Samsonov phoned. As soon as Sasha placed him, he was glad to hear his voice. There was something there. Worth pursuing. More than met the eye.

And now, with Vera just out the door, this girl, Shirin, had turned up to buy a painting at a price he would hardly have asked of a Westerner. And she was interesting. If she fucked half as good as she looked. Wonder if she scratches? With nails like that. Don't like scratchers. And the telltale marks. Had to be careful.

Probably bites, too.

Sasha wrapped the painting in brown paper, securing it with twine. Then he fashioned a handle of twine and rag so the package would be easy to carry. He knew how to tie knots effectively and economically. It was the sole useful legacy of his days as a Young Pioneer.

She was so obviously bored with his paintings he had had to struggle to keep from laughing out loud. He had enjoyed inundating her with his work, punishing her for her lie. She had not come to look at paintings any more than he went round to a girl's place to borrow a book.

She was a tough one. Probably incapable of love beyond the sweating and groaning part of it.

Despite her crimped eyes and the distant deserts ghosting all around her, it struck Sasha that they were probably two of a kind.

Rachel Traum hurried up out of the subway station. She was always afraid after dark. She did not fear rape, as did other women. She did not flatter herself so much. But she had to bear so much physical pain in her life that she feared the addition of the least bit more. She feared violence. Because she was a Jew. Because her spine had never straightened, despite the agonizing treatments her mother had forced her to undergo. Because she was small. And because the world seemed designed to hurt exactly those people who grasped what a beautiful place it really was.

She worried that the world would hurt Sasha Leskov. He was such a good man, an innocent. He was a better man than he realized. Pushing out through the heavy glass and wood doors, Rachel pulled her coat in tightly against her, bending into the sudden wind and clutching her purse against her belly. She had wanted to come earlier, straight from her work at the gallery, but she had needed to go home first to take her medicine. And to eat something. She did not want to go to Sasha's flat hungry. She did not want to take his food away from him. She did not want to take anything away from him. She only wanted to give.

And at last she had something tangible to offer. She was very proud, very happy. Her father had kept her tethered on this of all nights, insisting with a smile of vanity and love that she proofread an article he had just completed for a Western journal. Rachel was always the first to see his articles, and her father waited impatiently, childlike, for her praise. It was a family ritual, kindness and ego, and Rachel cherished the closeness of it. But tonight had been the wrong night. She had wanted to hide from her father's careful longhand, to run back out of the apartment door as though she had not heard him. And now she wanted to run again. To enter Sasha's life for a little while and make him a gift. But there was ice on the pavement. And she feared breaking a bone. There was pain enough, pain enough.

It was such a stroke of luck that it had happened today, on this particular Friday. Vera wouldn't be there. So they could talk. Sasha would make her a cup of tea. And the cat would spring into her lap. And Sasha would say the same thing he always said:

"Vrubel really likes you. He never jumps up on anybody's lap but mine. Not even Vera's."

Or Natasha's. Or Kira's. Or Liza's. Or Svetlana's. Rachel had outlasted them all.

It was sad that Vera didn't like her. It was difficult for Rachel to understand. Surely, Vera realized that she was no threat. How could she be jealous?

Rachel accepted them all. The Veras and Ludas and Tanyas. Without resentment. Because, if there was a God, jealousy was one thing he would not tolerate. Rachel could feel that truth in her cracker-thin bones.

She felt no jealousy. That part of her had gone missing. So it always surprised her how unready the other women were to share Sasha with her for a little while. For a cup of tea. And a discussion about painting.

Once, after Sasha had spoken to her at length about Latvian painting at the turn of the century, she had saved her money until she was able to go to Riga for a short vacation. She stayed with friends of friends and spent every day in the art museum, trying to see with his eyes. To comprehend the details that were so important to him. He had been happy, even moved, when she returned and surprised him with what she had done. They had spoken for hours about Lielausis and Valters, Egle and Ubans, until the girl of the moment had begun banging things about so loudly in the bedroom that Sasha had to laugh.

This was a glorious day, a glorious night. A Friday when no one would have to be unhappy.

Rachel scuttled down the sidewalk, angling her twisted child's body against the wind. Wouldn't it be wonderful, she thought, if no one ever had to be unhappy again?

All she wanted, Shirin told herself, was a man she would not have to despise. Oh, they were all such great lords, pawing and pushing at your body, so pleased with themselves when you let them in, all puffed up, drooling words they never meant, and then, without ever understanding the least thing, with a slight loss of fluid and a groan as if they had moved the foundations of the world, they became spineless, mewling things, expecting to be adored and petted, while inside you the fire had only just begun to take hold. The lonesome indignity of touching yourself to the rhythm of a man's snores, imagining you were somewhere else, with someone else, with other fingers teasing at the brilliant smallness—all of that just so you could go to sleep. And even when they had the sense to touch you, their fingers were as heavy and dead as sausages, and you always had to help them not to do it so clumsily, and you could tell that they really only wanted you to finish, to ease their consciences. Those were the best men. The worst were as unspeakable and stupid as they were quick.

And sex was only a part of it. Somewhere there had to be a man who would not get down on his knees for the sheer joy of submission. Uzbek men, Russian men, Georgians . . . you didn't need to sleep with them to know they were all the same: bellowing, two-fisted tyrants with their underlings, dogs, and women—and cowering sops in the presence of the slightest figure of authority. They were so afraid. The men she saw in the street, the boys in the university, even the thugs huddling around her father—they were always so afraid. Shirin could not understand their fear. At the very worst, you died. Where was the terror in that?

She had never made love to a foreigner. But she thought she would, given the right chance and the right man. She had no desire to emigrate. Hers was a life of privilege, and in any case, material well-being had never been as important to her as what was going on inside her. She took less than she could have, and wanted for nothing. Except a man who had not been born to live on all fours. She wondered if foreigners might not know something more about what women needed. About what *she* needed.

During her years at the university she had slept with a variety of lovers. Armed with French birth control pills from a doctor whose quiet private practice included many of the daughters of the elite, she tasted her way through Moscow's men, always disappointed, moving on unstained, almost untouched. None of them could reach her. Panting on top of her, they might have been in another room. She took what little pleasure they had to give and dismissed them, wishing only that one or the other had been a bit more capable, a bit stronger or more tender, a bit bolder, a bit cleaner. When you tried to speak with them, they were so consumed with themselves that they valued your views only to the extent they echoed their own. They wanted a sex-child who opened her legs without expectation, who would clean up their waste without complaint, who would bear their blows and bastards without nagging them about responsibilities.

The male animal.

She took pains to ensure her father did not know. For she loved and respected him, of all the men on earth. And although he had raised her in place of the son she should have been, she knew he would not be able to accept such sonlike behavior from her. A son who slept his way through Moscow might have amused him. Not so a daughter. And the great difference lay in a meager body part as unreliable as it was vulnerable.

She was stronger than men. She could feel it. She could bear things they could never shoulder.

No wonder my ancestors were accused of heresy, Shirin thought. If they were like me.

Her family had never been given over to the slavish side of religion. Up in the hills, before the Slavs arrived to decree that this hill lay in Tajikistan and that valley in Uzbekistan, the women of her tribe had ridden horses with the skill of men, and they had looked down on their settled, submissive sisters from the low deserts and plains, from the cloistered cities and harems. The women of the Talala clan were women with knives. And they preferred turning those knives on themselves to being dragged off as slaves to Bukhara. There was freedom and wildness in the hills, and her people had been far wilder than the rest, untamable. While the veiled or hooded women of the cities scurried down filth-strewn alleys to avoid even the smell of a man, her people had lived where the air was clean and the sun shone on men and women alike. The women of her tribe had been subordinate to their men. But they had never been reduced to the status of animals.

One family legend told of another Shirin, whose man had spent days raping a captive Russian woman during the wars of subjugation. Rather than endure such a humiliation, Shirin's ancestor had cut her husband's throat the night of his return.

There was humiliation tonight, too. But the competition was no empty-headed Russian countess who had strayed too far from the white-coats' garrison on her picnic. Shirin's unexpected rival was a crippled Jewess, undersized and equipped with soul-deep eyes that would have stood her in good stead as a beggar outside a mosque. The woman, whose name was Rachel, struck Shirin at once as impossibly good, selfless, and unassailable. She was the sort Shirin would have been ready to like and delighted to pity under other circumstances. But at the moment the sting went too deep as she watched the artist come to life at this Rachel's appearance. It was almost as if he had forgotten the others in the room.

He loves that woman, Shirin thought.

Oh, it wasn't a threatening kind of love. There were no beds and promises in it. And she doubted the artist even realized it. It was the sort of love men took for granted, the way you could see he loved his cat. Yes, that was it. As if he were petting the little woman with words. She did not threaten to steal what Shirin wanted from this man and never would. But Shirin could imagine that the women who shared the artist's sexual life found Rachel's presence intolerable without really understanding why.

But he will talk to me, Shirin thought. I'm more of a threat to her than she could ever be to me. She looked at the little creature, a child-woman who almost cried when she smiled, and who could not stop smiling in the artist's presence. Yes, Shirin thought. She'll have reason to hate me. She will watch as I take away everything she has to live for. And I can't stop. Won't stop.

But all this knowledge could not immediately heal the wound to her pride. Watching the artist relax so fully with another female animal. And Rachel had spoiled the effect of her purchase of one of the artist's paintings. The Jewess had sold one of the artist's paintings to Westerners visiting the gallery where she worked.

"And they want to see more," Rachel said. "They *loved* the painting. I think they really understood it. And it was the only one they took from the entire shop. They're going to call next time they're in Moscow."

"That's great," the artist said with a look more of contentment than excitement. "You always take care of me, Rachel."

Shirin felt the slightest of razor cuts.

The tiny woman blushed. She had amateurishly chopped black hair that would not stay in place, an overly wide mouth with the teeth placed a little wrong, and a noticeable mustache. Only her eyes and her cheeks falsely colored by the cold had any appearance of health.

The artist asked her if she had heard anything from a mutual friend who had left for America, and she replied that it was far too soon for any news. Then Rachel lifted her bad shoulder and a look of alarm swept her face.

"I almost forgot," she cried. "Sasha, I've already got the money for you. Mrs. Kestovich made an exception. I told her you needed it. She let me do all the paperwork." She plowed a tiny hand into a big vinyl shoulder bag. "I've got it somewhere here."

"Rachel, for God's sake. Relax."

Shirin noticed the cat curling itself happily around the cripple's ankles.

Rachel found the roll of bills, but in drawing it out, her bag got away from her and then she lost control of everything. The notes scattered over the floor, along with the jumbled contents of the bag.

The woman almost fell trying to grasp everything.

But the artist caught her.

Collecting herself, the woman got down on her knees. Shirin could almost feel the pain in the mechanical difficulties of the act. Rachel reached out a hand to the cat, who had shied away at the fuss.

"Oh, Vrubel. Did I scare you? I'm sorry."

Shirin bent down, squatting on her haunches, to help collect the woman's spilled things. And it was as if the cripple really saw her for the first time. Her features took on an incalculable sadness.

"What a beautiful girl," Rachel said in a voice of wonder. "Are you going to paint her, Sasha?"

Four people stood awkwardly in a room in Moscow. Three of them were unhappy. Rachel was unhappy because her surprise had been botched, because she would not be able to sit alone with her beloved, embracing him with language, and because, for the first time, she had encountered a woman with enough beauty to deserve Sasha and enough presence, perhaps, to hold him. Samsonov was unhappy because he knew it was past time for him to leave, and in place of the longed-for communion between friends, he faced hours of walking the frozen streets until he had worn himself to exhaustion. Shirin was unhappy because the world had not bent to her will.

Each of these three dreaded the solitude of their beds.

Rachel feared the physical pain that had already begun to squeeze her spine. Samsonov feared his dreams. And Shirin feared loneliness, although she would never have used that word, with its implication of weakness and failure.

Of the four only Sasha was happy. He felt no terror at the thought of being alone in the darkness. He was happy because Westerners had bought one of his paintings, happy more out of vanity and a feeling of confirmation than because of the money. He was happy because he liked each of the people who had fallen into his evening. He was happy because he knew what he was going to paint the next morning and because travel was on offer. And he was happy because the girl, Shirin, had a transparent interest in him.

He was not really disappointed when, impatient and proud, she announced:

"I have to go."

He knew she would come back. Sooner or later. He only had to wait. The worst thing to do with her would be to appear too anxious. And she would be a challenge, in any case. He would have to judge each step with her the way he intuited color tones as a painting progressed. She would require great skill and above all, control.

"It's dangerous around here at night," he told the disappointed beauty. "You have to be careful."

Sasha suspected she could take care of herself. But Samsonov spoke up, in a voice that unaccountably mixed reluctance and anxiety.

"I've got to be going, too. I would be glad to escort you as far as the metro."

Samsonov was hopeless with women, Sasha decided. He was stiff as a character who had tumbled down out of the last century, behaving as though it were an unpleasant duty, as though the last thing on earth he wanted to do was to walk Shirin to the subway.

Shirin offered Samsonov a queenly expression, indicating that it was a matter of little import whether or not he chose to walk by her side.

Sasha turned to Rachel. "You ought to go with them," he said, breaking her heart entirely. "It's just not safe for you to be running around by yourself at all hours of the night."

"Yes. Of course. That's a good idea," Rachel said, aching

to stay, to cover him with words as though they were a thousand kisses, thinking that it would be an ordeal trying to keep up with the healthy strides of the officer and this beautiful, beautiful girl.

Sasha almost laughed at his last sight of the three of them. They were visually impossible together, packing down the hallway in their winter armor, a human combination as absurd as the country itself.

Then they were gone, and there was silence behind the closed door. Sasha picked up his cat with both hands, lifting the animal like a baby. Vrubel looked at him with an expression that said:

"Things just are."

He let the cat down onto the floor and the two of them went back into the studio room to turn out the spot lamp.

Shirin had left behind the painting she had bought.

He picked it up, ready to run after her. Then he checked himself, grinning in recognition.

He looked down at the cat.

"She'll be back," he told the animal.

The three new acquaintances went down between the canyon walls of the apartment buildings, bitten by the wind. They were alone in the darkness. It was even too cold for drunks. Samsonov set the pace, careful not to stretch the crippled woman's abilities. He thought of what a terrible thing it must be to go through life like that, and he began to suspect he was far too ready to indulge in self-pity over a bit of insomnia and a few bad dreams.

The other one was a different story, though. Beautiful. Yes. Beautiful. But she didn't belong here. He had offered to escort her to the subway because that was his duty. But he could not bear to look at her. He felt as though he should warn Sasha Leskov.

But it was nonsense. All nonsense. Bad dreams. He was being weak.

He was crippled, too. But in a different way.

Sometimes he dreamed that he was lost in one of the labyrinthine Afghan hill settlements, running, crawling for his life. But the alleys took him nowhere. There was no way out. Only laughter. And eyes in the shadows. A dead end.

Eyes in the shadows. In Moscow, too. As the trio skated down the sidewalk toward the oversize *M* that marked their destination, Samsonov noticed a lone man sitting in a car across the boulevard. The car was not running, and it was very cold, and no man would sit in such a car at such a time unless he had a very good reason.

From the canted silhouette of the man's skull, Samsonov could tell they were being watched. His recent training had alerted him to how terrorists and the like operated and how criminals did surveillance. The car was positioned perfectly to monitor the subway entrance and the bus stand in front of it.

Abruptly, he dismissed the notion, waving a gloved hand as if in conversation with himself. There was nothing worth observing out here. Only tired buildings full of tired people. The man in the car probably had nowhere else to go.

Samsonov caught the crippled woman just as she slipped on the ice. He steadied her, then released his grip.

"Thank you," she said, flustered. Even her breath was slight in the winter air. "I'm so clumsy."

Under his grasp her arm possessed no more substance than that of a starved child, despite the layers of heavy clothing. He wondered if she got enough to eat. He knew it was becoming harder and harder to find decent nourishment if you didn't have connections. He was lucky enough to have the student cafeteria, rats and all. But how did the people manage? He knew so little about the land he had blithely pledged his life to defend. Sasha had been right back in Potsdam. He had been living in a cocoon.

He dreamed about his country and forgot about the man watching them from the parked car. It was just as well, since Samsonov didn't matter to him. The half-frozen observer's sole interest was in Shirin Talala.

10

Ali Talala used magic to watch the line of border troops move through the darkness. The magic had been purchased from Afghan smugglers who were also members of the *mujahedeen*. Originally it had helped kill Russians in the steep Afghan valleys. Now the American-made night-vision device would help kill them on the other side of the Amu Darya.

The border troops moved well enough, led by local Tadzhik scouts well acquainted with this stretch of country. Talala counted twenty-seven men. It was an unusually large patrol and a very high number of troops to kill. Talala's men had never done such a thing before and he knew that some of them were afraid. The KGB, which stood behind the border troops, remained one of the few functioning mechanisms in the land, and even as the overall Soviet hold on Central Asia decayed, the KGB refused to give up. They had even sent in this prancing new colonel, who reportedly had years of experience training the Afghan secret police. The man had dramatically intensified the pressure along the border, closing down smuggling routes that had carried trade through countless generations and arresting men who had paid their bribes dutifully over the years. Some of Talala's distant subordinates had even been shot. It was an intolerable situation.

The Russians were breaking the agreement. They would have to pay.

The border had long been a place where wise men knew when to avert their eyes. But a man had to know when to keep his eyes open as well. Ali Talala's eyes were fixed to the magical lenses that transformed the night, turning men into illuminated ghosts with fiery green limbs. It was impossible to tell which of the figures was the new colonel. But Talala knew he was there. The operation had been planned carefully to entice him, to flatter his vanity with the promise of a great success. He accompanied his men on far lesser raids and ambushes. He would be with them tonight.

The colonel would be a very clear example to the men in the Moscow offices. The border is very far away. It has its own laws.

Twenty-seven men. It was a lot of death. And there was always the risk that the action would have a contrary effect, bringing down legions of border troops and interior troops. Perhaps Moscow would not back down. But Talala's instincts promised him otherwise. The Russians had created problems for themselves far closer to home. Their heartlands were collapsing into anarchy. Talala believed that the deaths of these men—and especially of this colonel—would make the men in Moscow see that the old ways were the best ways. Live and let live. They could patrol this border with their dogs and automatic weapons as long as they liked. As long as they abided by the rules.

He did not believe that many other colonels, even KGB men, would be anxious to replace the colonel who was about to die.

The bright forms inside the magical device broke from a long single file into small clusters. Then the clusters divided again as men moved off in twos and threes, searching among the rocks for good ambush positions.

The Russians were always predictable.

The action had begun with a tale leaked to a known informant trusted by the border authorities, offering an irresistible target: a smuggling party with drugs and weapons. The planned route was hinted in a whisper, along with the date and time. All of the details had been woven together to bind the border troops' choices, to force them into one predictable ambush position.

Here they were, before his eyes, behaving as expected.

The twenty-seven border soldiers took their positions with middling discipline, certain they were alone in the darkness. But a force of almost a hundred Tadzhiks and Afghans lay surrounding the patrol in perfect silence. The men Talala had recruited for this work came from tribes and villages that had never recognized this border, whose livelihoods depended on the old ways, and whose allegiances were far closer to home than were the loyalties of the Tadzhik or Uzbek border troops with their Slavic officers. Many of these men had fought against the Russians in the war south of the river. Others would fight anyone who entered their valleys for the wrong reasons. Sometimes they fought each other. But tonight they were all united by a common enemy—and by Talala's authority and money.

The night settled into stillness again. The border troops waited for their quarry. Talala could feel the anticipation in his enemy, the anxiousness for the smuggling party to appear, the small discomforts of lying in the rocky cold. The tale had done its work well.

And the Russians were fools. They imagined themselves to be geniuses at deception. They had not brought any of their dogs, fearing that the dogs would alert and warn off the smugglers. But only the dogs could have saved them by detecting the ambush positioned around the ambush.

The night was clear and very cold. Talala preferred the cold at times such as this because he understood it and could wear it like a garment. When he moved, the cold moved with him. He did not fight it but accepted its reality. And when it was this cold, you did not have to be careful of the snakes that laced the rocky hills by moonlight.

Talala peered down the hillside at the shining bodies of his enemies. Foreign men who had strayed too far from home. Some of the junior personnel were of his own people, of course. But nothing could be done to save them. They did the Russians' bidding and now they would pay the price.

Everything was fine as long as the Russians contented themselves with floating atop the desert sea, ignoring its depths. Why did they have to disturb the waters?

In the end, Ali Talala did not like this business of killing so many men at once. But the Russians had tied his hands.

"Shall I give the signal?" Gogandaev whispered by his side.

Talala thought for a moment, then whispered, "No. Not yet."

Let them think of home and warm beds for a bit. Let them regret this. Let them feel their smallness under the multitude of stars. Let them wonder at the earth for a few last minutes.

These were bad times. If a man could choose the times in which he lived, Ali Talala would not have chosen these bothered years. There were suddenly so many difficulties. Here. In Moscow. The Ukrainians were being piggish. They were greedy and unwilling to share. They, too, wished to take that which was not their own. The situation was worrisome because the Ukrainians had so many natural advantages—the border with the Poles, the port of Odessa. They were shipping more and more drugs through Odessa. And the liquor they swept in through the border came cheaper and cheaper. Talala did not want a war with the Ukrainians. Too much energy, too many lives would be wasted. But they were bad men, men without honor, without understanding. They clutched and clutched. Talala feared for the future.

The closest border troops lay barely a hundred meters away. Talala heard the sudden metal rasp of a round being chambered. Instantly a Russian voice called out an order for silence, the words loaded with the threat of grave punishment. The voice sounded enormous through the special clarity of the desert hills.

Soon his enemies would begin to grow nervous. There would be no sign of the smugglers. The colonel would begin to doubt his information, to doubt himself.

The informer who had passed the message to the authorities already slept in a ditch outside Termez with his tongue, nose, ears, and eyes peeled from his body.

Surprise was everything.

A man coughed. Then the low hills were still again. It was a cold, clear, beautiful night, filled with celestial glory.

Talala slipped his hand out from under the optics and touched Gogandaev's sleeve.

"Give the signal."

Ruptured night. The hills caught fire and time accelerated.

Command-detonated mines lifted the darkness off the earth then dropped it again. Hand grenades flashed as though dozens of photographers were at work, and streaks of light criss-crossed and faded before the eye could fix on them, then spilled down across the landscape at a slightly different angle. The noise echoed hugely, surely loud enough to be heard all the way to Moscow. Human voices, weaker than the tools in men's hands, struggled to be heard: Russian voices, full of fear, confusion, desperation. Other voices sang to one another from perches along the ridge, familiar, ecstatic.

Caught up in the spectacular display, Talala forgot about the foreign device in his hands. In Samarkand, Intourist offered a sound-and-light display at the Registan in the first cool dark of the evening. An amplified voice, speaking for the desert and the city, regaled tourists with Moscow-blessed tales, while colored spotlights dazzled over the miracles of tile. All of it was false. This was the true voice and vision of his native land: the sound of vengeance, the sight of purging fire.

The splendor of explosions and automatic-weapons fire lessened. Perhaps a half dozen men still fired and the occasional grenade lit scuttling forms as Talala's men scrambled down over the bodies of the dead and dying border troops. Only one pocket of resistance held out, and Talala savored the desperation of the men about to die, tasting their terrible knowledge. The bullets poured from their weapons with a special shriek of fear. Then the bursts of fire became single rounds as ammunition ran low.

It was a shame, Talala thought, that you couldn't cut that fear out of them the way you could cut off an ear or a nose. So that you might send that fear back to their comrades, to make them understand how these hills replied to those who disturbed their silence.

A sudden rain of hand grenades exploded over the nest of resistance, scrubbing the earth with white fire. Then the hills were silent.

But the silence was a relative thing. After a few moments Talala's ringing ears tuned down to the sounds of men moving over loose rock and the occasional clatter of a weapon against the stone. Then came the low voices of men searching.

He had ordered them to find the colonel. And to make sure that the radioman was dead.

A lone shot echoed across the continent. After a minute or so, another man fired once, twice. Finishing off the wounded.

"Let's go," Talala said to his aide, handing him the night-vision device. "I want to see his face." And if the colonel was still alive, to take his soul from him.

The two men made their way down the rocky slope. Born in such hills, Talala moved easily across the scree. But Gogandaev was of a generation that knew this desert only from the windows of an automobile or from an old man's addled tales. The bigger, younger man slipped noisily. Across the hillside the beams of pocket lamps flicked on and off, demons blinking their eyes. Talala heard the sound of a knife ripping through cloth.

Just as the two men reached the trail along which the border troops had set their ambush, a dark form, solid against the old blue of the night, slipped up to Talala. It was the headman of a local village, feet and eyes mated to this darkness.

"We've found him," the man said in a Tadzhik dialect. "He's still alive."

"Show me."

Talala followed the man. His shoulders shadowed hugely with layers of winter dress, waist cinched in. He respectfully slowed his pace for Talala, but even so, Gogandaev lagged behind.

Two of the local warriors stood sentinel against a barricade of boulders. At their feet, a man groaned intermittently.

"I want to see him," Talala said. "I want to see his face."

Obediently, a pocket lamp flicked on, revealing a sandy-haired man in his forties. He wore a camouflage jacket that was very wet. His face, too, was wet with blood and partially disfigured where grenade splinters and chips of stone had caught him. One eye was ruined. It looked as though a raw egg had been broken into the pocket of meat and bone. But the other eye was alive. Alert.

The man's lips moved. It was impossible to tell whether he was trying to make words or simply shaking with fear and pain.

Let it be fear, Talala thought. Let him know fear beyond all words.

He was suddenly gripped by a cold rage that could have seared through heaven. Why had the Russians forced him to do this? Why couldn't the filthy beasts remain in their own stalls, licking their own sores? Why did they have to drive things this far? He felt murderous and ill with a presentiment that nothing had been finished here, that it was, after all, only beginning. What was it in men that drove them so implacably to trample another man's garden?

He bent down over the wounded man just as Gogandaev came up beside him. The KGB colonel tried to move his arm, as if to strike out. But the gesture failed utterly. The arm barely rose before the man's fingers trailed back down over the camouflage material of his tunic.

Talala's head briefly shadowed the man's face. He shifted to the side so that the light shone again over the bloody white skin.

"Don't worry," he told the Russian. "We would never send you into the next world alone. Before morning, your wife and child will die at least as miserably as you." It was not true. There would be no attempt on this man's family. But Talala wanted to crush his soul before it vanished into the night.

"And all of your work," Talala went on. "It was worthless. You see? Your own people sold you out."

This, too, was untrue. But Talala was determined to leave his enemy nothing.

With the same graceful speed with which he had once been able to leap onto a horse, Talala drew a knife from his pocket, flicked it open, and carved a deep smile into the Russian's throat.

"You'll die very soon now," Talala told him. "You're far less interesting than your wife will be." Then he stood up and walked off without a backward glance.

Gogandaev stumbled along beside him.

"We have to hurry," the younger man said. "They might have had time to radio in. And with helicopters—"

Talala closed a silencing hand over Gogandaev's forearm, feeling the heavy muscles in the darkness.

A lone shot rang out. And a man laughed.

"Let them finish their work," Talala said calmly. "I know the Russians. We have time."

The two men went down the hillside in a private silence, surrounded by the whispers of men rifling pockets and feeling over dead fingers for rings.

Shirin screamed. She was soaking wet. Inside and out. The artist's flesh skidded over her, belly sliding, pressing down on her breasts with his chest. All the while he was at her with his wonderful, wonderful fingers. It was the end of one world and the beginning of another.

It was hot in the room. The uncontrollable steam heat cooked them, and their physical desperation made it immeasurably, gloriously worse. It might have been midsummer. Under a tremendous sun. Under her sun. She closed her eyes and this time the fire came over her all the way, consuming her entirely, and the sun plunged right down into her eyes and exploded. She felt all the strength and life go out of her with a last scream that hurt the inside of her throat. Then the artist shut his mouth over hers, drinking in the scream, stealing her last breath before she died. The enormous destroying sun had gone all buttery soft in her and over her. He pushed his tongue into her mouth and she was helpless to do anything about it. He did not stop moving his fingers on her, did not stop pushing into her. Electrically, suddenly, his fingers were too much. The inexplicable sensitivity came over her and she discovered just enough life left in her to recoil from the brilliant agony under his fingertips. But he followed her. She raised a hand, the reflex of a corpse, and pushed his hand away, pulling out from under his mouth just long enough to mutter:

"No. Oh, please, no."

Then the fingertips were gone, leaving only a gorgeous ghost haunting her flesh. But he did not stop pushing himself into her. And that was good. It was so very, very good that she had no words for it. She never wanted it to stop. She closed her eyes again. And the sun was gone, leaving in its place a darkness where the soul could finally rest.

She expected him to finish. He groaned slightly, reaching down into her as though he wanted to go deeper than it was possible to go. She moaned, soul still resting, body ready to receive him. She knew he would finish now. She imagined more than felt him swelling in her, ready to pulse. But he kept on. She laid her hands flat on his back, feeling the lean muscles rolling like snakes in a velvet bag. She gave up. He could ruin her, kill her. She didn't care anymore.

Her body began to respond again.

He slowed. He breathed beside her ear and she could feel the sweet weariness in him, with everything about him exhausted except the peculiar strength between his legs. Between her own legs. She closed him in with her calves, opening herself for him to reach down into her as far as he wanted.

He rolled his hips up against her, rolling and rolling. Slowly. Not too slowly. With a quick stab he reached down into her until he had crushed himself against the delicate pulp, wet hair twining with wet hair. She could feel the end of him now. Hurting her a little. And in between the tip and the beginning there was a vast, unaccountably empty space where she couldn't really feel at all, and she could never understand that, how you could feel a man and not feel him, but it was always that way.

It was always that way. But it was never like this. This was the end of the world.

He drew himself almost all the way out of her, lifting himself off her on straightened arms. Then he fell onto her, into her, smothering her. And her body came alive again, small hips rising automatically to meet him, wanting him, daring him.

"Don't you want me?" she asked. "Don't you want me?"

He lifted her against him, changing the angle.

"Legs higher," he told her.

She obeyed. And she arched in pain, jerking as though a nerve had been cut.

"No."

He had struck something deep in her and it hurt. Then he did it again and she tried to cower, twitching.

"No. Please. No."

But he had already stopped. He had wanted to hurt her a little. Just a little. And she understood that. She felt as though she understood everything he did, even though she could not anticipate any of it.

He knew. He knew everything about her. How could he know those things? No one had ever known those things.

He shut his hand over the smallness of a buttock and pulled her against him. Touching her at the only spot that finally mattered. Astonished, she found herself blooming again. Each time he brushed her a small thrilling shock of life shot right into her soul.

He went very slowly now, resting himself. The sweat fell from his forehead onto her face, into her hair.

"Do you want me . . . to do something for you?" she asked. His mouth was so close. She could smell herself on his lips, greased over his cheeks, his chin. When she had returned, ringing his doorbell in the early-morning hours, he had tasted only of the sourness of sleep. Now he tasted of her.

He did not answer her question. He never answered. She raised her head slightly and licked his cheek.

He wrestled his lips back over hers.

He shifted his fingers slightly so that the tips just touched her anus. And she wanted to tell him to stop. Because she knew that the next step would be a finger inside her. And she hated that. She hated the thought of any part of a man entering her there, associating it with the most despicable aspects of the men of her race and religion, the men who never really wanted to face a woman when they took her, who did not want to be reminded by breasts and a voice and a woman's vacancies that it was a woman under them after all. She ached to tell him to stop, not to spoil it all. But his mouth was fixed to hers, and he was strong, even stronger than he looked, and his lips would not let her go.

He didn't disturb her. He moved his hand away, the left hand, saving the right hand clean to touch her with brilliance.

He freed her mouth, turned her slightly to the side, then wet his fingertips with his spit.

He touched her.

She was not ready. She was convinced that she was not ready. But she could not find the words to tell him, and within seconds, the last resistance went out of her and conscious thought floated away. He dusted her with two fingers, two little legs running over her again and again. Then he began to make soft circles. She had not known that she was big enough there to feel such enormous circles. He dipped his fingers down to the wettest part of her, then focused them again. He rolled the vast little bit of flesh over and over, and she imagined herself becoming enormous, as big as him. Her voice made unplanned sounds. Her voice belonged to someone else. The center of the universe was under his fingers. Underneath a single finger. The universe was going to explode again, it would not be long. And the world would end again. The cycle was endless.

With him.

Time lost its imposed validity. He touched so lightly. Always, she had needed to tell them to touch her lightly. But they never understood, never really felt her. But this one knew. He knew everything.

She arched slightly and gave a little cry. Her body was the only reality now, yet it was oddly removed, too. Not her property. It was all somehow beyond the body, though she had no idea how such a thing could be.

He briefly lifted his fingers away, just long enough to wet them in his mouth again. It all began again, on a higher plane. She pressed herself up against him, aching to be closer. She did not know or care whether or not he was in her. The fingers had become everything. The dancing fingers. There was only the dance.

She felt the first hot wave. Another man might have stopped, assuming that was all there was. And in her pride, she would have let him. But the artist kept at her.

She tensed again. This time the wave came farther up the beach, threatening her, warning her what might happen if he didn't stop immediately, and the only thing in the world that mattered was that he must not stop.

He wet his fingers again and touched her very quickly, lightly, racing over her.

She groaned, sinking deep down into the mattress. The wave retreated. But it was already getting ready to come again, curling up, pulling her down, down, down with its undertow.

"My God, you're wet," he said. "You're so wet inside. You're all over me."

His words only half made sense. But they were beautiful. It was all so beautiful.

Without warning, she tensed fiercely. Her body took over and she shoved her belly up against him. The wave rose and rose. It was going to smash down on the beach and destroy everything, it was going to flood the world. She ached for it to come down. *Now*.

The ending world, the ending world.

She arched and screamed. This time he took his fingers away quickly and gathered her stray limbs, closing her against him.

"*Hold me*," he said. "Hold me tight with your legs."

She had no strength left. The great wave had shattered everything, with the aftershocks still wrenching her insides. But she obeyed him. On their own, her legs closed over him.

"Higher," he commanded. "Take me deeper."

This time he was ready. This time she could feel it. She had not felt him in her at all while his fingers were working. But now he was filling her. She imagined that he was made out of bone, of steel. He was lunging so wildly that he almost slipped out. And she wanted him. She wanted to know that he was truly inside her, even though there was never much physical feeling that way for her.

The body didn't matter anymore. The body was dead.

"Now."

He reared his head away from her, shoving himself against her one last time as though trying to drive his entire body through her. She felt a pulse of flesh, but nothing else, nothing else. Yet it was a wonderful thing. The knowledge.

He collapsed onto her with a kiss. Shaking. He moaned and kissed her again. He would not stop kissing her. And she could not stop kissing him back in the long minutes as he lay softening inside her, with the buttery wet seeping down the crevice of her backside, over the tops of her thighs.

He was drowning now, too. They were both drowning, already drowned, and it was so sweet to hold him in her arms.

The lovers kissed, unwilling to let it be over between them. They kissed, clutching wearily, growing inevitably separate. The room was already gray with the first morning paleness. Their kisses grew shallower, less committed. They kissed and forgot everything they had just told themselves about the wonder of the world.

They kissed one last time, each thinking of trivial matters their togetherness had covered for a while, then lay in each other's arms, distant-minded.

The artist fell asleep.

As the new man in her life breathed steadily beside her, Shirin rested her face on the flat flame of a hand. She was very tired, but she could not sleep. She wondered if there would be a way not to hate this man.

Something moved. It was the cat. The animal had stayed away during their lovemaking. Now it hopped onto the mattress and flopped down against the artist's calf. It was light enough for Shirin to see the animal's expressionless eyes aimed at her.

She laid a hand on her lover's shoulder. The cat watched the gesture, then fixed its eyes on her again. The room reeked of sex, turpentine, and heavy paints.

The artist was sleeping deeply. She could feel it. Under the smooth rise and fall of muscle. She looked at him. He looked younger as he slept, impossibly innocent.

Shirin suddenly felt what a cruel, hopeless, and lonely place the world was, and for the first time in years, she began to cry.

THE JUNIOR SERGEANT HANDED HIM THE NEXT KALASHnikov. Samsonov primed the weapon, inspecting its bowels. Dirty. Not oiled. He held it higher to catch the light from the overhead bulb. At least this rifle wasn't rusty. Many of the weapons in the arms room were in such a poor state that Samsonov would have been afraid to fire them. Some were so bad they would likely have to be scrapped.

Samsonov shook his head in disgust and passed the weapon to the warrant officer standing between him and the door. The warrant officer accepted the weapon without a word, without the least change in expression. He was different now. Upon Samsonov's arrival the warrant officer had greeted him with a smile that insisted it was a joyous thing to welcome your new company commander, with a smile that declared today a great day in a great country. But the man's eyes had been winter-cold all the while.

His name was Kuzba, and he looked to be in his early thirties. Too intelligent for the smile. Too clever by half. The warrant officer had the sort of shabby good looks that appealed to women who drank, and a voice that, even at its most obsequious, was rich with self-love.

Kuzba was not smiling anymore. And that suited Samsonov just fine.

The junior sergeant, nominally responsible for the arms room, handed Samsonov another weapon. As he took the automatic rifle in his hands, Samsonov caught the young sergeant looking at Kuzba for reassurance. Wondering what in the hell was going on.

Rust coated the weapon. But at least the serial number matched the registry book this time. Samsonov tossed it to Kuzba. The warrant officer caught it and slapped it into a wall rack.

"That's the last one, Comrade Captain," the warrant officer said.

Samsonov looked at the man, letting his own eyes cool down below freezing.

"Then we're three weapons short."

"The guards have two signed out."

"I've allowed for those."

"Well," Kuzba said, lightening his voice, determined that the new commander should not take all this too seriously, "there must be some mistake. I'm sure they're around somewhere."

"Where?"

Kuzba turned on the young sergeant, voice sharpened. "Peskov. Where are the missing weapons?"

The boy looked confused. Just a draftee with a bit of extra training that gave him the title of sergeant. Samsonov had already decided that the boy was not to blame for the missing weapons.

"I don't know, Comrade Warrant Officer," the sergeant said nervously.

Samsonov could feel the boy struggling, trying to understand this new situation.

"Could be," Kuzba suggested, "they're in one of the other company arms rooms."

The sergeant jumped at the idea. Nodding his head in exaggerated agreement. "Yes, Comrade Warrant Officer. That could be."

It was nonsense. And Samsonov knew it. But he let them continue with the fantasy, curious as to what Kuzba would do next. He had already decided that the warrant officer would have to go. He could never be trusted. And he would not fit in with the new company Samsonov was going to build on the ruins of the old.

During his welcome interview, the regimental commander had assured Samsonov that he had been assigned to the best regiment in the interior troops. A second welcome interview, this time with his battalion commander, resulted in the warning that this was not an airborne unit and that it was Samsonov's responsibility to fit in. Samsonov finally arrived in his company area to find a single gangling, inarticulate lieutenant—a lost soul if ever there was one—and Warrant Officer Second Class Kuzba as the sum of his leadership cadre. The lieutenant was in the motor pool now, figuring out how to repair the four automotively inert wheeled personnel carriers of the ten total assigned to the company. After they repaired the automotive assemblies, they could begin fixing the inoperative machine-gun turrets, the broken gun mounts, and the ruined optics.

The lieutenant was afraid of his new commander. But that was all right. It meant that he might be salvageable. Kuzba, on the other hand, was not afraid. The warrant officer was merely annoyed. His routine had been disturbed, his domain had been threatened.

The company clearly had been Kuzba's kingdom. The unit had not had a captain as company commander for more than a year. All of the officers who were marginally worth their pay had been drawn off to serve in the dozens of areas of crisis or near-crisis around the country, leaving Regiment 148 of the Moscow District understrength and neglected. No one cared very much. In a crisis, the KGB troops would take over the critical functions in the capital. The interior troops would be auxiliaries. Fit to herd prisoners or regulate traffic. So Kuzba had run the company, with a washrag of a lieutenant to stand in front of the troops when the battalion held a formation.

That was going to change. Priorities were changing, the world was changing.

Samsonov closed his notebook. They had worked right through the midday meal. He had done that on purpose. He wanted to make it very clear to Kuzba that priorities were changing.

"I want to see the billets."

"The soldiers are at training."

"Good. I just want to see the billets. I don't need anybody standing at attention while I'm looking at a latrine."

"Perhaps you'd like to have something to eat first, Comrade Captain? I'm sure we could—"

"Just show me where my soldiers live."

Kuzba led the way down the basement corridor. The ceiling was low and cluttered with dented pipes. There was little light and no clean air in the passageway. The smell of standard-issue disinfectant could not cover the tang of urine where soldiers had been too lazy to leave a work detail. A succession of other company arms rooms slept behind heavy metal grates, and Samsonov wondered if they were all in the same pathetic condition as his own.

The two men turned the corner into the stairwell. A vivid poster showed a proud, strong soldier on guard duty. The caption declared EVER ALERT TO DEFEND THE MOTHERLAND.

Samsonov had not seen a single soldier who remotely reflected the poster image during his seven or so hours in the regimental area.

An older poster, going ragged, proclaimed the imminent victory of communism. Lenin, upright and visionary, stretched out his arm toward a brilliant future. On the surrounding field someone had penciled in that Lenin was a syphilitic Jew.

"Find a more current poster," Samsonov said. "And take that one down."

"Yes, Comrade Captain."

By rights, Samsonov should have been addressed as "comrade commander." Kuzba was making a purposeful distinction. Samsonov let it go. Other things mattered more at the moment.

"Where are we billeted?"

"Third floor. All the way up."

Samsonov climbed the stairs at a purposeful pace, glancing into the other company corridors as he went. Dirty. Nothing that would be tolerated in the lowliest motorized rifle unit.

His company hallway was dank. All but one of the dangling overhead bulbs had burned out or been knocked out, and the light from the windows at either end of the corridor was subdued by the plywood and cardboard used to replace broken panes. The smell was different now. The soldiers were all gone. But they had left pungent ghosts behind in the powerful odors of unwashed bedding and clothing. The rotten sweetness of ailing feet came strongest of all. Samsonov could imagine the stink when all of the men crowded into the platoon bays at the end of the duty day.

He walked into the first big room. It was lighter here, with high windows. The barracks were very old, dating to the days of the czarist military, and solidly built. But they had been neglected. The walls were so in need of paint that the mottling might have been an intentional camouflage pattern. The smell of feet was overpowering now. Yet the bay was not as bad as Samsonov had feared. The bunks were aligned neatly enough, their bedding tightly tucked. Still, Samsonov knew that this was not necessarily an indicator of healthy discipline. Neat platoon bays might simply mean that the "grandfather" system was at work. Under the age-old regime, the newest draftees were little better than slaves to the senior men. The newcomers made the beds, did the cleaning, even polished their "grandfathers' " boots. It was a military tradition, widespread in all the services, and many of Samsonov's fellow officers ignored it, since it did keep a particular kind of order in the barracks when no officers were around. But Samsonov had also known the system to result in the beating deaths of recruits who would not turn over their meager pay to their seniors or who just couldn't adjust to the endless demands.

The washroom was the worst. The sewage smell was almost a paste in the air. Nothing was clean. Broken sinks, broken mirrors. Pools of blackening water on the floor. A dried-out mop that might have been a museum display stood in one corner.

"How's our sick rate?" Samsonov asked, thinking of Afghanistan, of soldiers writhing in agony at the end of the twentieth century as plague boils swelled in their armpits and groins.

"Our what?"

"The sick rate."

Kuzba shrugged. "Same as everybody else's."

"What does that mean?"

"Comrade Captain," Kuzba said in exasperation, "some

soldiers get sick, some don't. The way it's always been. You can't order a man not to get sick."

"Where do you live?"

"Me?"

Samsonov nodded. You.

"I live down the street."

"Where down the street?"

"In the apartment block reserved for military families. Of course, it's not all mil—"

"Wife?"

"Me? Oh, no. I'm not that stupid."

"Then how did you rate an apartment of your own?"

"One was available."

"Officers' families are living in tents. In abandoned rail-cars."

"Not in the interior troops. We take care of our own."

"If I remember correctly, an unmarried warrant officer doesn't rate his own apartment in any service."

"I've been in the regiment a long time. An apartment was available."

"In Moscow?"

"They're reserved apartments."

"I want you to move into the barracks. Until the situation in the company improves."

Suddenly, the warrant officer lost his carefully affected control. He turned on Samsonov hard and said:

"Listen, Captain. If you think you can come in here and just steal a man's apartment, you've got a lot—"

Samsonov looked at the man calmly. And the warrant officer caught himself. Just in time.

"Anyway," Samsonov said, "I don't want your apartment. I'm going to move into my office downstairs. At least until things turn around." He opened a tap. The water ran brown. "This is no way to live."

"They're draftees. It toughens them up."

Samsonov looked down into the clotted slime of a bowl.

The warrant officer was clearly anxious now. All of his studied cool was gone.

"Comrade Commander," Kuzba said, "you've got to understand. This isn't an airborne outfit. And it isn't Afghanistan."

Samsonov thought of his long walks through Moscow. He thought of the beggars. And of the hungry peasant families sleeping on the floor of the Kiev train station. Of the huge rats, the like of which he had never before seen in Moscow. Of the crazy speeches in the underground passageways and along the Arbat. Of the emptiness of the shops, emptier than he had ever seen them. Of the unspeakable hopelessness of the country he loved with all his heart.

"This isn't Afghanistan," Kuzba repeated.

"No. It's worse."

"What?"

"In Afghanistan, I knew who the enemy was."

Samsonov sat in his office, in bad light, reviewing the company's expenditure records. The files had been kept ineptly, probably on purpose, but one thing was immediately evident: the company had consumed an impossible amount of fuel over the preceding months. Especially considering that half of the vehicles were broken-down.

Somebody was black-marketing gasoline.

"Lieutenant Bedny," Samsonov called through the open door. It was late. But a moment later the lieutenant's earnest, pimply face appeared. He had been sitting at his own desk, making a show of trying to reconcile parts consumption and repair records. Most of the required paperwork just was not there.

"Comrade Commander?"

"Looking at these fuel requisitions . . . it looks as though we road-marched our vehicles across Siberia and back. How many times did we actually deploy on exercises last year?"

The lieutenant thought for a moment. He was tall, with wide shoulders, but he was so thin that the effect was of a gallows hung with cloth.

"Comrade Commander, I don't think we went on any exercises last year. At least not since I got here."

Samsonov shook his head in wonder. "Driver training?"

"Oh, yes. We do a lot of driver training. Most of the draftees have never even driven a car, let alone—"

"Parades?"

"Yes. We sent a platoon to a parade."

"Range firing?"

"Well . . . we fired small arms. Not the heavy weapons, though. We went out to the range in the battalion trucks. It's way out past—"

"How long have those four personnel carriers been undrivable?"

The lieutenant looked as though he had been slapped. "I don't know, Comrade Commander."

"But you're responsible for knowing that."

"Well, Kuzba said—"

"Yes. Tell me what Kuzba said."

"Kuzba said he'd take care of it. He takes care of everything."

"And what do you do?"

"Sometimes I take the troops to a museum. A squad at a time, so I can keep them under control. And I give all the company political briefings. That's a lot of work."

"There's a battalion political officer for that."

"Yes, but . . ."

"But?"

"He's always busy."

"Doing what?"

"I don't know. Kuzba just said it would be better if I gave the classes. So we wouldn't get in trouble for missing political training. I've been very conscientious. I've done a lot of research. It's hard making up new classes all the time."

"And how often do you hold these classes?"

"Three times a week."

"For how long?"

"A couple of hours. Sometimes all afternoon. If I show a film."

"When does this unit *train?*"

"Well, we do calisthenics every day."

"What about mission training? Riot control? Light-infantry tactics? Control in an urban environment? Sniper suppression? Terrain navigation?"

"Well, we do that. Some of it. Sometimes. But we're really busy."

"With political training?"

"There's other stuff, too."

"Such as?"

"Like building the house."

"House?"

"For the regimental commander. And then we built one for somebody else. I'm not sure who that one was for."

"This isn't a construction unit," Samsonov said in astonishment.

"I know, Comrade Commander. It took us a long time. And the regimental commander still isn't happy with the workmanship."

"Lieutenant Bedny, are you aware that three weapons are missing from the arms room?"

"No." He looked like a sheep.

"Are you aware that somebody has been stealing government gasoline? In large quantities?"

"No, Comrade Commander."

The worst of it was that he believed the boy. It was a classic example of what happened when you turn a junior lieutenant loose without adult supervision. Of course, it wasn't so bad here. In Afghanistan it had meant that soldiers died.

"Comrade Lieutenant, are you married?"

The boy brightened. "Yes, Comrade Commander."

"Children?"

"A little girl."

"You have an apartment of your own?"

"Yes, Comrade Commander. Warrant Officer Kuzba found us a flat just down the road. Really, he's all right. He even gives me a ride to and from work when the weather's bad."

Samsonov perked up. "He has his own automobile?" Not many warrant officers had their own cars. Not many captains did. Samsonov thought briefly of his own life packed into two vinyl suitcases and a duffel bag. Except for several crates of books held in storage, that was the sum of his twenty-nine years of life.

"It's a Lada. He got it when he was stationed in Poland."

"I don't imagine he has much trouble getting gas for it," Samsonov said. Then he regretted the display of sarcasm.

The lieutenant looked at him like a dog that has been severely beaten without the least understanding of why.

Samsonov sighed. "Go home, Lieutenant. If it's within walking distance. Your friend Kuzba's going to be here awhile."

"I can stay. If you need help."

Samsonov was tired. And irritable. It had been a long, bad day.

"I *know* you can stay. I don't *want* you to stay. Go home to your wife. You've got plenty of late nights ahead of you."

The lieutenant saluted, hand shadowing his dreadful complexion.

Could he ever become a real officer? Samsonov wondered. "Oh, Lieutenant. Do you know where I can get some lumber? To build bookshelves for my office? Legally, I mean."

"Yes, Comrade Commander, I—"

"Comrade Commander," a new voice entered the conversation, "we can build bookshelves for you. As many as you want. Have them done tomorrow."

It was Kuzba.

"I'll build them myself," Samsonov said.

Entering the office with resurgent confidence, the warrant officer put on a whatever-you-want-boss face.

"Lieutenant Bedny, you can go," Samsonov said.

Bedny almost stumbled over the warrant officer as he left the room. When they were alone, Samsonov and Kuzba sized each other up anew.

"I hear you've got quite a talent for building things," Samsonov said.

"You have to make yourself useful in this life."

"I hear you even built a house for the regimental commander."

Kuzba smiled. Smug. "*House* is an exaggeration. Just a little dacha. You have to help out your friends, Comrade Commander."

Well, Samsonov thought, at least the "comrade commander" seems to be sticking now.

"The regimental commander's a friend of yours?"

"This is a close-knit regiment."

"And you built another house—or was that a dacha, too?"

Kuzba nodded. "A dacha."

"For another friend?"

"For a friend of the regimental commander. The district representative to the Moscow City Council."

"Any more houses scheduled to be built in the near future? Or can we begin training the company for its assigned mission?"

"Comrade Commander, we can train all you want. But you really should give yourself a little time to look around before you judge everything. There is no mission. None. We hardly even pull ceremonial duty. Sometimes we escort prisoners. Once, in all my years here, we sent some people to bust up a prison riot. But anything that really matters around Moscow—they yell for the KGB. You know how many KGB divisions there are in the Moscow region?" Kuzba let the question hang in the air, the brief silence telling Samsonov he could find out for himself, if he didn't already know. "We're just here because the Interior Ministry is jealous of the KGB. Everybody has to have a private army. And it goes back to the Stalin days. When nobody trusted anybody. The only interior troops who see any action are out in the Armenian shitholes. And all this stuff . . . all this stuff about forming special units. I'll believe it when I see it."

"Training starts tomorrow," Samsonov said.

Kuzba looked at him with a mix of condescension and hatred in his eyes. But the warrant officer's mouth wore its artificial smile again.

"Anyway," Kuzba said, "I didn't come here to talk about that. I've got good news. We found the three missing weapons."

Samsonov's eyebrows went up. He hoped it was true. He had assumed that the weapons had been sold on the black market long before, that they were probably somewhere in the Caucasus by now. Or in the hands of the local mafia.

"Good. That's very good. Show me."

Still smiling, the warrant officer led Samsonov down the hallway, then down the short stairs to the basement. It struck Samsonov as a dungeon where a man might be tortured. Or murdered. It was a miserable place, reminding him of his fleeting contacts with the Afghan secret police.

The junior sergeant stood behind his dilapidated desk, smiling proudly over three Kalashnikov assault rifles. Samsonov went closer.

The rifles were brand-new, not even the same model as the rusting assault pieces in the wall racks.

Samsonov understood. But he went through the entire process.

"Let me see the records."

The sergeant lost his smile. He scuffled through the desk drawers, drawing out the dog-eared folders. He paged through them, then handed Samsonov a smudged list of serial numbers.

Samsonov took his time. In order to be absolutely certain. He would not risk even the most unlikely mistake. But it was clear—there was no trace of the serial numbers of the new weapons in the company records.

Samsonov straightened his back and looked at the warrant officer.

"These aren't our weapons. The numbers are wrong."

"Serial numbers get mixed up," Kuzba said in a small, cold voice.

"And they're the wrong models."

"We drew those to replace unserviceable weapons."

"Even the ammunition caliber's different."

Kuzba shrugged. "That's bureaucracy for you."

The warrant officer would not show his feelings. But Samsonov read the man clearly and understood the situation: Kuzba had just given him one last chance.

Samsonov's first week in the regiment ended as badly as it had begun. It had started in the regimental commander's office, and it ended in the regimental commander's office. Samsonov surprised the colonel in the afternoon twilight. The office lights had been extinguished and the commander stood over his desk wrapped in his greatcoat, ready to go home. He looked nakedly impatient and annoyed at the sight of Samsonov, but he did invite his subordinate inside.

"How's it going down in your company, Comrade Captain?"

"There are problems."

The colonel laid his parade cap on the corner of his desk. "That's why you're here. To fix problems."

"Comrade Commander, I'll be direct. There is strong evidence—very strong—of black market activities in the company."

The colonel smiled. But it was a smile Samsonov could not penetrate. "Oh, come now, Samsonov. Surely you're not so naive. A few enterprising soldiers will always sell off their mates' caps or belts, perhaps even a few liters of gasoline. As long as it doesn't get out of control . . ."

"It *is* out of control. It's not a few liters of gasoline. It's thousands of liters. And weapons, too."

"Now just a minute—"

"Comrade Commander, I believe I have evidence incriminating Warrant Officer Second Class Kuzba. I request that the investigative division be called in."

The colonel paled. His breath became audible in the drowsing headquarters building. At an hour on Friday afternoon when a real unit would be pulsing with activity. Samsonov could not help remembering his lost, better world.

He noticed the slow clenching of the regimental commander's fists. But the man mastered himself and unclenched them again. The blood returned to his face, turning his winter-white complexion a dangerous red. His voice was less theatrically generous now.

"That's impossible. There is no such activity in this regiment. And Kuzba's the best warrant officer we've got. He gets things done."

"The evidence stands, Comrade Commander. He's involved in illegal activities. Deeply involved, I think. And the company's a disgrace."

"You listen to me," the colonel said, his voice swelling. "You're new here. And I don't care how many medals you grabbed before you got your ass booted out of Afghanistan with your snotnose paratroopers. You're in the internal troops now, and if you want to keep wearing the uniform, you're going to have to learn our way of doing business. You can't just come in here—into the best regiment in the interior troops—and start tearing things down." The colonel tried to gather himself in. But there was fury in his eyes. "If you want to work on improving training, that's fine. If you want to scrub shitholes, that's fine, too. But I don't need another army castoff telling me how to administer this regiment. And another thing. Warrant Officer Kuzba is a proven asset. You're not. So far, Comrade Captain, you're all talk. Kuzba gets things done."

Samsonov decided to play his last card:

"Like building dachas for ranking officers?"

Surprisingly, the colonel just laughed. It was not a kindly

laugh, and its unexpectedness unsettled Samsonov. He had expected a different reaction entirely.

"Yes," the colonel said. "Like building dachas for ranking officers. And if you knew the MVD regulations, you'd find that a regimental commander is entitled to certain living arrangements, and that, when the regiment is garrisoned independently, the provisions are expanded to take into account his increased social responsibilities." The man laughed again. "And you failed to mention the dacha constructed for our district representative, a man who has performed miracles in taking care of our officers and men. Without him, families would be out on the street. All in all, Comrade Captain, I'd trade a dozen ex-army officers for one more Kuzba."

"And the black-marketeering?" Samsonov knew now that he had no chance of winning. He felt humiliated, outmaneuvered. But he was not willing to surrender.

"I doubt you can prove a thing. Now, if the paperwork has been handled poorly, that's something else. I'm sure you can get that under control. But let's not blame a warrant officer for doing his best in the absence of experienced line officers. Why, Kuzba had to handle everything himself. After all, you've met Lieutenant Bedny. And you certainly wouldn't expect . . ." The colonel held up his opened palms, supporting the gray twilight.

"Comrade Commander, I am convinced that Kuzba's involved in black market activities to an extent that profoundly disgraces this regiment and the Interior Ministry. I repeat my request for a formal investigation."

The colonel opened his mouth to speak. But it took him a moment. He shook his head. "You don't listen. Do you, Samsonov? Well, let me tell you what I'm going to do. I'm going to transfer Kuzba to another company. There are plenty of company commanders who'll jump at the chance to have a man like that working for them. And you can try to run your company on your own. But let me warn you. Kuzba has friends. And you don't. The soldiers like him. He looks out for them." The colonel shook his head, more dramatically this time. "You're off to a bad start, Samsonov."

"Comrade—"

"Just be quiet. I'm not finished. Are you a member of the Party?"

"Yes."

"Then why did you order that a poster of Lenin be removed from the barracks?"

Samsonov was surprised at how much the regimental commander knew. And at how much he was willing to reveal he knew.

"It had been defaced," Samsonov said. "With anticommunist and anti-Semitic inscriptions."

The colonel raised an eyebrow. "You automatically associate anti-Semitism with anticommunism?"

"I—"

"You need to be very careful, Samsonov. Very careful, indeed. I would advise you to make certain that your company records are kept impeccably." But the colonel relaxed now that he was back in his accustomed position of control. "I'll be delighted if you can train your company up to higher standards. We've been so busy around here that some things have, in fact, been neglected. The truth is that I'd love to see you set a better example for some of my other company commanders." He looked Samsonov in the eyes. And the colonel's eyes were those of a wolf who had survived a very long time. "Just be very, very careful."

12

Vera had been standing in line for two hours. She expected to stand in line for at least an hour more. Snowflakes fell lazily, and the cold reached into her kidneys, making her sorry that she had drunk so much tea at lunchtime. But she would not risk her place in the queue. The shop doors had finally been unlocked and the block-long line had begun to inch forward.

Vera worked as a secretary at the Moscow City Council and the job had many advantages. One of the most important was access to information. When shipments of hard-to-get items were about to be delivered, some open ear in the Council building would catch a whisper. Today there were winter boots from Hungary and they were said to be very fine.

Vera and a dozen other secretaries took turns covering for each other. There was never that much work, really. It was easy enough for a few of them to disappear for a morning or an afternoon with a list of purchases to attempt on behalf of the group. Today it was Vera's turn to stand in line. And she was glad. Despite the cold. She truly needed a new pair of winter boots. The pair on her feet had been repaired so many times that every seam leaked. The mock-fur lining had long since worn away.

She hoped they would have a pair in her size. Although a

size larger would be all right. She didn't mind that. She only hated it when she had to squeeze her feet into shoes or boots that were too tight. Then she would begin to regret that her feet were not smaller and more elegant, that her blood was of the Russian peasantry and perhaps not fine enough for Sasha.

The boots. She would try to persuade the shopgirl to produce a pair in her size. Then she would buy as many pair as they would sell her for the others. The sizes did not matter. Someone would need them.

The cold chewed into the small of her back and her loins. It was a day when little things went wrong, when the world did not feel quite right. She worried about Sasha. His behavior toward her had not changed. Not exactly. Not in any way for which she could find words. Yet there was something different about him. He was the kind of man who always held something back, who always had a suitcase packed behind the door. Yet now there was an even greater feeling of space around him than usual. Like an icon that you could not approach too closely.

He kissed her. He filled her body. Even now she imagined she could feel him glued inside her from the evening before, from the hastened lovemaking that let her catch the late train to her parents' house north of the city. She had told him it was safe, that it was a good time and that it was all right. Lying. Wanting to feel him growing inside her. To finally gain some advantage over him.

To love him. To be loved by him. To marry. To bind him to her forever.

She wasn't a complete fool. She knew there would be other women in his life now and then, that he was not the sort of man to settle down completely. But she promised herself that she would be able to tolerate that. As long as the other women were not serious. As long as he did not love them. Anyway, she would find ways to punish him when he was bad.

The line shifted. Vera picked up her plastic just-in-case bag and shuffled forward. The bag was already laden with fresh eggs and jarred tomatoes, with homemade cheese and sausages smuggled down from her parents' larder. She had always despised rural life; as a girl she had longed for Moscow, a short train ride and a world away. She hated school but forced herself to study so that she could get a Moscow job. Away from the farm, with its stupid, rough-handed boys. A City Council official with whom she had slept passed her on to a district representative, who found a place for her in the central office. The representative had eventually found another mistress, thanks to the grace of God, but by that time Vera was entrenched in her job—in Moscow. And life had seemed very good indeed.

It was only very recently that she had begun to appreciate the advantages of her parents' lives. As the Moscow shops emptied and even the City Council cafeteria began to run short on food, the meals at her parents' table became ever more important. Then she met Sasha. And she was able to feed him, too. Left to himself, she believed, he would have starved. In this city, with its useless, thoughtless women.

There were no eggs in the grocery shops, but there were always eggs in the chicken coop built onto the back of her parents' house. There was always fresh milk or cheese from their cow. And there was always something extra from the common harvest, a few kilos of this or that which the central authorities would never miss. If things really became as bad as people said they would, she and Sasha could always move in with her parents. Her parents wouldn't understand Sasha. But she convinced herself they would like him. Because they would see how much the two of them were in love. And Sasha, her husband, would always have fresh eggs.

The line shortened until Vera could see the entrance doors to the shoe store up ahead. The line had formed to the right of the double doors, and to the left a disorderly mound of empty cardboard boxes had grown up on the sidewalk where lucky customers had discarded the unnecessary packing in order to stuff the boots into string bags or precious plastic bags with Western logos.

A woman left the shop, cursing at the top of her lungs. Vera's heart beat faster. Perhaps the supply had already run out.

No. Other customers continued to emerge with shoeboxes bound together with string, which they carefully unraveled and saved as they added their emptied cartons to the cardboard mountain in front of the shop window. From a distance the boots looked like real leather, not plastic, and the style was not bad at all. Thinking about the boots made Vera's feet colder and colder, and the pressure in her kidneys continued to build.

The empty-handed woman shrieked on. Gutter obscenities. Perhaps she was drunk. Two militiamen stood on the near corner, but they carefully kept their eyes on the Smolenskaya subway station across the boulevard. The police did not want problems. Her first lover at the City Council had laughed every time he saw a militiaman, remarking that the government pretended to pay the police and in turn, the police pretended to do their jobs.

A man in an enormous fur cap stepped out of line and said something to the woman. She turned on him, raising a finger like a knife. But she lowered her voice until Vera could barely hear her over the sound of automobile tires sizzling through the slush in the street. She only caught the words "Stalin" and "order."

The line moved again. Vera judged that she had perhaps fifteen more minutes to wait. The snowflakes thickened and she dusted the accumulation from her shoulders, hurriedly shook off her cap and settled it back over her gathered hair. Officers began to stream by, smart in their tailored overcoats and peaked caps, heading for the subway after a day at one of the nearby military academies or offices. They made Vera think of the officer who had visited Sasha. She wondered why he had not come back. She had liked him so much more than any of the other trash Sasha accepted as friends. She wished they would all go to America like that dirty Birman. Sasha needed prodding sometimes. She decided to ask him about the officer.

She wondered how Sasha's day had gone. He had an appointment to discuss another commission. Which meant he would be going away, perhaps soon. She wondered how long he would be gone this time. She did not think much about the places he went. Personally, she had no wish to travel, no interest in seeing foreign countries. She was happy with the thought of a married life in Moscow. With Sasha.

It was odd. When he was gone, she did not miss him so much. As long as she knew he was coming back. When sex came to mind, she forced herself to think about other things. The only thing that disturbed her about Sasha's trips to do his soldier paintings was the possibility that he might meet a woman he would find more appealing.

Vera hoisted her bag of foodstuffs and shuffled forward. She was going to make Sasha a lovely dinner. She only had to go back to the office to drop off any extra pairs of boots she managed to buy for the others. Then she could catch the subway and have plenty of time to—

The people at the head of the line began to shout and press forward. Vera saw a raised fist, heard it thump against the doors. She took up her bag and pushed forward with the others, past the desolate shop-windows.

"Stand back," someone cried. "Get back."

A spurt of customers shot from the doorway. This group did not pause to discard anything. The lucky ones hurried off with their purchases as the crowd packed in more and more tightly around the entrance.

"What is it?" Vera asked nobody in particular.

But she already knew. Even before the word telegraphed down the line. The supply of boots had run out. The shop was closed.

The crowd's outburst of anger soon subsided. It was the way things were. The men and women who had waited so long simply turned and went their way. Vera was disappointed, feet colder than ever in her old boots. But there was nothing to be done.

A bedraggled-looking girl in a clerk's blouse dropped the blinds, shutting off the pedestrian's view of the interior of the shop. The last thing Vera saw was a pair of brand-new boots on the shopgirl.

Sasha knelt in the dirty snow, sketching the church in charcoal. He had cut away the fingers from the knit glove on his right hand, and the cold slowed his action, muddling his intent. The sketches would be no works of art in themselves. But that was all right. They were studies. For a painting. For a painting that would be a good-bye gift to Vera.

He knew that she understood nothing of art, that she did not care for his painting or anyone else's. But he thought she might like a painting of an old Russian church for her wall. And he had intended to get around to painting this particular scene for years. Since it first caught his eye on the way back from the Tretyakov Gallery to the subway station. Back before the Tretyakov had been closed indefinitely.

He missed the gallery, where so many of the paintings were like old friends. And he missed the gorgeous summer weather when this church, this angle, with its backdrop of failed modernity and warm sky, had captured him. He missed Moscow—the other Moscow of green and blue June days when the world was so penetratingly beautiful that you could not help feeling that all things would soon be better. A world in which a mother's impatient voice calling after a child convinced you that love was boundless. He missed the sun on his skin in the park and the cool shadows behind the apartment blocks. He missed the delicious illusion of freedom that summer brought. In winter, every man was a prisoner and knew it.

A truck loaded with ash grunted by, tires dropping a curtain of slush across the sidewalk. Women hopped out of the way with little cries, some cursing, one laughing. A few small, heavy pats reached Sasha, dabbing his jacket and wetting his cheek. His current sketch was blotched. But it did not matter. He only needed the sketch to remind him. Of the precise shape of the world.

It was only the hard, fixed lines he needed help to recall. He had a perfect memory for color and light. Above the gray street, behind the crumbling shopfronts and the scarred domes of the church, above the boxes of boxes where families crowded together, the winter sky had a pale beauty he knew he would not forget. The snow had stopped and the clouds had moved aside to reveal a washed-out heaven of weak orange, lemon, smoky gray, and pink. Sometimes the winter twilight was as quick as loveless sex. But on the rare good days such as this, you were made a long present of this innocent, motionless gloaming, as though the world had stopped turning and life on its surface was slowly coming to a halt. It was a light in which the common browns and grays of winter took on rich, unexpected shadings, a light under which living things seemed fragile and men remembered not lovers but childhood. It was hard for Sasha to understand how everyone could simply hurry past, eyes fixed to the pavement, immune to the delicate splendor that would never come again in exactly this way. The neglected street seemed impossibly beautiful to him, the hurrying women and workless men tragically human. He wished he could show them how beautiful it all was. He clasped the bit of charcoal more tightly in his shivering fingers.

He needed all the beauty he could get at the moment. He needed to avoid thinking for a while. To calm down. Bilinsky had been a dirty, fucking, double-dealing son of a bitch. Again. Except that this time it was worse than ever before. The interview with Zarkov at the Ministry of Defense had been a shock, leaving him speechless. The new assignment made him sick. And Bilinsky had known all along, a typical Artists' Union prick.

They wanted him to go to Riga. To paint new and better murals on the walls of the downtown officers' club. To remind the officers of the Soviet Army of their historic internationalist role in the liberation of Latvia.

He had always managed to avoid working in Latvia, since other artists were delighted to go—the Riga shops were fuller than those in the interior of the country and there was plenty of alcohol. Sasha had been willing to accept commissions that took him to the most godforsaken outposts, to the Far East or the extremes of Turkmenistan. He had gone with a good heart where others dreaded to be sent. So he had never been forced to glorify the Red Army's feats in the city where his grandmother had been raped and the men in her life kidnapped or murdered.

He had never been troubled by his work for the military. The paintings and portraits meant nothing to him. They were the work of a craftsman, not of an artist. Technically correct, they were soulless. He might have been selling the military potatoes or boots. It was just work.

But there were always borders in life. He had always sworn that he would not do such work on his grandmother's earth.

She had wanted him to be a serious painter. She had wanted him to be a serious man.

Immediately after the interview with Zarkov, he had stopped by the Artists' Union, furious.

"You *knew* I never wanted to work in Latvia," he told Bilinsky.

The bureaucrat made a gently amused face. "Why not? Why ever does it matter so much?"

"It's personal."

Bilinsky rolled his eyes up into his head, gesturing exaggeratedly. These artists, these artists. Whatever am I going to do with them? He was a prosperous-looking man, not ill-natured, who had long since given up the stress of painting out his little talent for the joys of power.

"Sasha, please. You have to understand. They requested you by name. You're the only one they'll accept. You know how the military mind is. They get obsessed."

"I can't do it."

"But you've *got* to do it, dear boy. Come on. Wouldn't you like to spend a little time in Riga? Didn't you tell me you grew up there or something? And I could give you an address . . ."

Sasha hung his head. "Boris Borisovich, I'm asking you. Please. Find me another assignment. Anywhere. I'll take anything. But tell them I can't go to Riga."

"But they *want* you."

"Tell them I'm sick."

Bilinsky looked at him with fatherly reproof stretched over swollen features.

"Tell them you have a better man for the job," Sasha suggested.

"But, dear boy, the fact is I *don't* have a better man for the job. And it's so important for us to keep the military happy. Especially in times like these. After all, who knows what tomorrow may bring."

"And if I refuse?"

Bilinsky's face never lost its expression of parental concern. "Then you'll never work for the military again. And we'd have to reconsider your entitlement to an Artists' Union flat, of course." His smile was heavy with kindness. "The permit for the Union's shops would be revoked. Of necessity. In concern for legality. And it goes without saying that you'd never get an official exhibition."

Sasha did not know what to do. But he already suspected that he would break this last remaining rule of decency. That he would, indeed, go to Riga. He had whored away the best of his life for these people. Why not this last act of self-abasement?

"Anyway, dear boy, you don't have to leave immediately.

You've got a few weeks to work yourself into the proper frame of mind." Bilinsky came around from behind the desk and dropped a fat hand on Sasha's shoulder. "Really, you should be honored. Proud. You've gained a remarkable reputation for someone so young. Why, if you'd only take it all a bit more seriously, you could have everything." He tapped Sasha with big fingers that had long since forgotten the feel of a brush chasing over canvas. "Everything."

Sasha nodded dully, appalled at his own weakness. Anxious to get away and hide behind his sketchpad. He even welcomed the small penance of working in the cold.

It seemed as though everything had started to come apart. The business with Vera would have to be settled. And then there was Shirin.

He had not seen her since their single shared morning. She had left no address, no number. And he was too proud to hunt after her. But whenever he thought of her, a novel hunger struck him. As though he had known her long enough to be on the verge of addiction. He remembered her body and its actions with wounding clarity, and he ached with the hope that she would be standing in his doorway soon.

Riga would spoil that, too. He imagined her returning to find him absent, then forgetting him.

He had to see her again. At least once more.

Riga. Vera. Shirin. And who in the hell was going to look after the cat?

He briefly considered postponing the break with Vera until after the Riga trip, just so Vrubel would have someone to look after him. But he dismissed it as too despicable. Even for a man who would defile his grandmother's grave.

He left Bilinsky's office with the feeling that everything was collapsing around him.

Bilinsky called after him:

"Stop by our grocery shop before you leave. Tell Nina Alexandrovna I sent you. She has lamb chops of the first quality."

But he did not need lamb chops. Vera would bring the customary little treasures from her parents' larder. Vera, the woman he was about to purge from his life. He was being unfair. She was a good person, an innocent. But was life fair? Should a man keep on pretending to feel affection for someone out of convenience? When the girl dreamed of marriage and the man had no intentions?

His grandmother had wanted him to be a good, serious man. And it was all such shit.

He had hurried back to his apartment to gather his materials, with the subway car slowly emptying as the train clattered away from the center of the city, plunging up into the daylight then descending again. He had not even taken time for a swim, sensing that today even the temporary tomb of water would not be enough to annihilate his cares. When it got this bad, there was only the blank sheet of paper or stretch of canvas waiting to help him reduce the world to a manageable size. To get control of it. To copy it down. Then to put it away.

Now the light, the beautiful, soothing light, was failing. Soon it would be too dark to pirate the street's details. Soon the world would disappear. And it would be all right to slink homeward in the dark nonworld, pretending that something worthwhile had been achieved.

He told himself he could not go to Riga. But he knew all the while that he would go. He was a coward.

His spirits rose only once on the way home, and then only briefly. Passing by a hairdressing salon, he thought he saw Shirin. But the girl turned more toward him and he saw that she was plain and that he had been ridiculously mistaken.

"Why?"

"It's for your own good," Sasha said. Vera was crying and he could not look at her. He looked at the cat, who had curled himself against the base of the small white stove, worshiping its fading heat.

Vera did not hear him. Or she chose not to hear.

"Why? But *why?* For God's sake, why?"

"Vera . . . you're a beautiful woman. You deserve someone who'll really take care of you, someone who—"

"But I don't *want* anyone else." She wept.

"Vera, we've had a beautiful time together. I just don't want to spoil it by dragging it on too long. You don't understand. You just don't know me. I'm a real shit. I'm horrible to be around. You just haven't seen it yet. My God, I'd be the worst husband in the world, and you need—"

"But I *love* you."

"You can't love me. I'm not worth loving. You need to find someone else."

"I *love* you." She raised her tear-burned eyes, begging him to look at her. "I *love* you. Don't you understand? I *love* you."

He had not been prepared for this. He had endured the words dozens of times. There had been plenty of women. Some of them had even been sincere. But this one was different. She retained no pride. He could not meet her stare.

The cat yawned and dreamed, pushing the air with its paws.

"I love you," Vera said. "Please. Just tell me what I did wrong. I'll never do it again."

"You didn't do anything wrong."

"I'll change. Just tell me how you want me to be. I'll change."

"I don't want you to change."

"I can be any way you want me to be. Please." Her face deepened with a look of pathetic determination and she straightened a little. "I'll stop going to church. If that bothers you. I'll give up God for you."

The doorbell rang. Sasha leapt from his chair. He would not be able to let the visitor in. But whoever it was, he was grateful to him for this little interruption, for the chance to leave the kitchen and the girl for at least the time it would take to go down the short hallway, open the door, and make his excuses.

"Please don't let anybody in," Vera called after him, voice immature with pain.

Without bothering to look through the peephole, Sasha undid the locks and opened the door.

It was Shirin.

"May I come in?" she asked.

It had begun to snow again and the wetness in her hair looked like random diamonds. Sasha had never seen a woman he wanted more.

"Shirin," he began in a low voice, "this is really bad timing. I'm sorry . . . you'll have to excuse me."

He wished he could speak freely. He wanted to beg her to return. His body took her scent through all the layers of winter clothing.

She had worn an almost-smile. Now it faded.

"One of your many conquests, Comrade Leskov? Or are you just too busy for me?"

Sasha did not know what to do. He wanted to hush her. But he did not want to appear cowardly in her eyes. He did not want to do or say anything that would drive this woman away forever.

He just needed time. Just a little time.

"It's a personal matter," he said. "Something I'm settling."

Shirin nodded coldly. And he sensed that, however long a relationship with her might last, hatred would always be close to the surface. It had been there when they first touched, immediately. For the first time in his life he felt the possibility and risk of really loving a woman. The enormity of it shocked him.

"I suppose I'd better be going then," Shirin said. Her tone of voice declared that it made no difference to her whatsoever.

"No," a small, iron-hard voice declared from behind Sasha's back. "You can come in. I was just on my way out."

Samsonov had just left the warmth and light of the subway station when he saw the girl. Coming at a run, with her hat awry and the snow catching in her hair. He recognized her at once and moved to greet her. But she went by him without seeing, eyes glittering like ice, tears frozen to her cheeks. Pushing through a crowd of joking boys, she disappeared into the station.

On an impulse, he followed her. Back into the clack of turnstiles and the steaming air. She stood in front of a change machine, fumbling in her purse.

"Vera Petrovna," he called, closing on her. Her nose was red and her eyes were swollen. "Vera Petrovna, it's me, Misha Samsonov. Are you all right?"

The girl looked at him with eyes that began to see.

"We met at Sasha's. Remember?"

She nodded. And she began to cry again.

"Can I help you? What's wrong?"

An old woman steered a broom around their feet, redistributing the grit that covered the floor. Jostling citizens hurried by to nowhere. The crying blonde struck Samsonov as the ideal of a Russian woman. Pale and beautiful. Overflowing with emotion. When last he had seen her, she had been on her way to church. She seemed lovely and hurt and pure, with the cloying warmth of the station melting the snow in her hair.

"What is it?" he asked.

"That bitch," Vera said, eyes catching fire. "That whore."

They rode the trains together through the depths of Moscow. There was nowhere else to go. There was no decent place to sit and talk, no safe, warm cove where a man might offer comfort and a glass of tea to a woman adrift. For the first time, Samsonov found himself wishing he were a foreigner with a pocketful of dollars or marks so he could invite her to a clean, pleasant place. The country he had pledged his life to defend offered no such refuge to its own kind or holders of its own currency. The luxuries that could be shaved from the city went to foreigners or to the Soviet citizens who preyed on them. It had never much troubled him before. Material well-being was unimportant. He had needed only uniforms, food, and books. But tonight the world looked different. And all he could do was to sit helplessly beside the girl in the hurtling car, listening as a mechanically distorted voice warned of upcoming stations. She wept, then wept less. She cursed the artist, then adored him again. She spoke of the other one, the Uzbek girl, in language that would have surprised him in a soldier's latrine. And she asked him—asking the city above the tunnels and the sky above the city—what she was going to do. Whatever was she going to do?

Samsonov wondered if any woman would ever love him with so much determination. Certainly not one as beautiful as this one. Like luxury, he had not thought much about it, disciplining himself away from disappointment. Living first for the army then for a dream of a country that he was being forced to admit existed only in his dreams. He looked down at her hand clutching an empty glove and wished he might take her fingers in his own, telling her that everything would be all right. But he knew that this was not a world in which everything would be all right, and he was afraid that she would suspect his motives in touching her and that she would be right.

In the great stations in the heart of the city, crowds of people waited on the platforms, refugees from work going home late or young people reinventing culture. At Dzerzhinskaya Station, a gang of teenagers boarded the train. Their heads were shaved except for wild greased spikes of hair, and they wore thug jackets decorated with tin fan buttons. One boy carried a guitar in a sack. They spoke in drawls and slurs, using new words from a fractured new world. Samsonov could not understand their conversation, but he recognized the sharp reek of hashish on them, familiar from the soldiers who had traded hand grenades or stolen side arms for a few nuggets of forgetfulness in the Kabul bazaar.

As the punks were exiting the car a few stops later, one with a swastika earring looked back over his shoulder and spit at Samsonov's feet, saying:

"Fuckstick."

Then they were gone, and the train accelerated in the direction of the outlying stations, and the girl said that she was never going to love again.

Eventually, they changed lines and caught the ring route back to Komsomolskaya. The girl had decided to go home to her parents, who lived in a village just north of the city, and she needed to catch the last commuter train. She was never, ever, going back to Leskov. *Never.* She began to weep again.

Samsonov gave her the number of his battalion headquarters. She could leave a message. If she ever needed him. She absently took the piece of paper he had torn from his pocket log and put it in her purse, doing it with such unconcern that Samsonov knew the number would get lost.

But that was all right, he told himself. He had nothing to offer her. And she would find her way back to the artist. It never occurred to Samsonov that his friend might not want such a woman back. She would find her way back to her artist and perhaps they would run across each other again when next he came to steal a few minutes of Sasha's time. He'd been on his way to visit his friend when he intercepted the girl. He'd had a tough, bad few weeks, without time to read or even properly arrange the books hastily unpacked onto the new shelves in his office. This was the first night he had felt justified in breaking free for a bit of personal time. He had so much wanted to look at his friend's paintings again, to remind himself of the Moscow he could no longer find in the city streets or in the little prison of the barracks. He needed to see his country through the other man's better eyes. And then to drink a glass of tea in the peace of the artist's kitchen and to talk.

The railway station had the look of wartime. Families from the far, poor provinces, crowding into Moscow illegally in hope of a better life, slept on blankets spread over the dirty floor. Rats nudged through the shadows, and the great hall stank. There were lines before the last open ticket windows, with all of the automats broken down. A fixer hustled a little group of Western tourists through the human debris, hurrying them toward their train. The foreigners crowded together, avoiding contagion. A child with a grotesquely swollen head and a few strands of carrot hair howled in pain, real or imagined.

Vera had a regular pass and they went through the hall as directly as they could, stepping over stray legs and islands of trash. A militiaman leaned against a pillar, smoking a cigarette, and paid Samsonov's uniform no mind. It was all crumbling. At any moment, the ceiling would collapse, followed by the sky. And nobody cared.

On the platform, the girl surprised him. Without a word, she hugged him, holding tight to him, unexpectedly strong. She tucked her face against his coat, and after his initial alarm, he rested his chin lightly on her thick blond hair, savoring its damp smell. The shock of the woman against him aroused him physically, but if she sensed anything, she paid it no mind. She just held to him, on the verge of weeping again, fighting it. Then she let go of him as suddenly as she had come to him, and he felt the loss with a force that seemed to knock the air out of his lungs.

"Thank you," she said, "for your kindness."

And she boarded her train.

As he watched the last railway car disappear into the night, Samsonov felt unusually weary. He did not understand everything that was happening inside him. But then he had not understood his feelings for a long time. He went back through the sprawled, snoring masses in the waiting hall. In a corner, two drunks slapped at each other. Samsonov caught just enough of the exchange to grasp that one man had stolen the other's cigarettes. The militiaman was nowhere to be seen, and the fighters slowly, clumsily bloodied one another. Moscow had become a city where men killed each other over such trifles.

Samsonov went back into the subway. He could not bear the heart of the city tonight. It was all falling down, collapsing under the weight of error and misery. How had it all gone wrong?

He drowsed in an empty car and mused over the girl. Vera. So lovely. He still held the fragrance of her in his nostrils.

When he returned to his office, where he slept on a camp bed, he switched on the light and found the floor covered with destroyed books. Tolstoy, Lermontov, Garshin, Pushkin, Chekhov. Dostoevsky. The books, collected over more than a decade, had been torn and cut, their pages ripped and crumpled or shredded. Then someone had urinated over them. Samsonov fell to his knees, reaching for a single volume that appeared intact. But it was only an empty shell. Someone had been very methodical.

At least they got this right, Samsonov thought.

There were tears in his eyes. He gathered a few stray pages together and held them against his breast the way a girl might cradle a torn picture of her beloved. He was not angry. He simply felt that the very last of the little he had possessed had been taken from him. He did not understand this world anymore. He did not, could not, understand the sheer viciousness. He felt like a fool.

He laughed. It had occurred to him that it was easier for him to understand how men killed other men than to grasp how they could do this to his books, and he wondered if he had not grown as sick as the world around him. After all, what did these scraps matter? Mayakovsky had been such a fool. And Tolstoy—what possible message could Tolstoy offer a world such as this? It was all nothing but words.

With great delicacy, with patience and love, Samsonov began sorting through the casualties.

13

CIGAR SMOKE CLOUDED THE GENERAL'S EYES. LESKOV had always enjoyed visiting Kerbitsky in the old man's office, despite the bad air. The big room was like a museum, filled with souvenirs of the general's long career abroad before he had changed directorates. There was a stone Buddha from the years in Hanoi, a wooden face with empty eyes from Ethiopia, and hammered brass from Central Asia. Daggers in enamel sheaths crossed primitive battle-axes on the walls. Few KGB generals were as ready to display their careers as Kerbitsky. The secrecy was deeply ingrained. But Kerbitsky had always been different, and it was his openness that had drawn Pavel Leskov to him years before. Leskov had always believed in the older man, trusting him. But now the faith was weakening.

"Comrade General," Leskov tried again, "there is no doubt in my mind that Talala was behind the massacre."

"I know, I know," the general said, not quite meeting Leskov's eyes. "But we have no proof. No hard evidence. In fact, all the indications point toward local smugglers, probably from the Afghan side of the border."

"Talala has long arms and money. He can buy Afghans. Comrade General, first the man assassinates a militia colonel—"

"A very corrupt militia colonel," Kerbitsky put in.

"—and now he murders a KGB colonel on duty with the border troops, along with an entire platoon of his men. God knows what he'll try next. The man's out of control."

"Let's not overdramatize the situation, Pavel Ivanovich." Kerbitsky strained at his cigar, the smoke more important to him than oxygen.

"You know what he's up to. With the Ukrainian dealings and the alcohol and drugs. No accommodation between them is going to last. The streets of Moscow are going to look like . . . like Chicago. With gangsters gunning each other down."

"I always wanted to see this Chicago," Kerbitsky said. "I like the old American films. Anyway, perhaps we should just let them kill each other. After all, it could save us a lot of trouble."

"And we look weak. Powerless. Comrade General, walk the streets of this city." Leskov gestured out through windows that had not been opened in a very long time. "Everything's breaking down. There's no respect for law and order, for authority."

Kerbitsky smiled. "You sound like an old Stalinist."

Leskov paused, taking the comment seriously. "No. No. I don't mean that kind of order. I mean law. The rule of law. Laws that men can respect, under which they can live decently and without fear."

Kerbitsky shook his head. "Pavel Ivanovich, you're certainly not the only one who wants law and order. But be sensible. We can't arrest a man of Talala's stature without ironclad proof. We've discussed this."

"There's going to be blood."

Kerbitsky shrugged. Then he laid the stub of his cigar on the rim of his ashtray and grew more serious. "These are times . . . when it is best to move slowly." His voice was uncharacteristically low, almost cautious. "In times such as these . . . we may not want to call too much attention to ourselves."

Leskov was horrified to hear these words from a man he had always deemed courageous, a voice for reform.

"We have to do our duty," Leskov said in a shaken voice.

"Our first duty is to survive. To get through all this. Pavel Ivanovich, every day, every single day, I hear friends and colleagues changing their tunes. Everyone's scared again. A few years ago, even last year, everyone with a brain was for change. We, of all people, knew the folly couldn't go on. *We* had the accurate statistics. *We* knew how swiftly the West was moving ahead of us. *We* wanted to modernize, to change, to cast off the deadwood. But not one of us realized the enormity of the task. Not one of us had an inkling of how sick the country was. Not just the economy, but the whole pile of shit. It's funny. We, of all people, failed to realize the degree to which only fear was holding us all together. We took away the fear. And now look. We opened the floodgates a little way, and the whole mechanism collapsed. And now we're drowning and everyone's trying to rescue himself." The old general shook his head. "Pavel Ivanovich, I'm still for reform. Because I see no real choice. But far more powerful men than me are losing their nerve. No one expected the breakdown. And everyone's looking for scapegoats." He rubbed the wet dead end of his cigar across his lips. "We haven't even hit bottom yet. It's going to get worse. Much worse. I don't trust anyone anymore, not us, not the army . . ."

"The army could never rule," Leskov said. "And they know it. They have no program. And you can't run a modern economy with bayonets and tanks."

"*If* you've got a modern economy to run," Kerbitsky said. "Anyway, you're thinking rationally. And men are not rational. Far from it. If this century has taught us anything, it's exactly that. We're born half-mad." The old man stared at the African mask on his wall, as if talking to it and not to Leskov. "There comes a point when men simply feel the need to act. To *do* something. Anything. Whether or not they have a program. Whether or not they have any real hope. Oh, I think such an outbreak is still a long way off. A year, perhaps two. But one year ago I would have judged it to be unthinkable." The old man looked very tired, the veins yellow and purple under the meat of his cheeks. He patted the humidor on his desk, as if soothing a good animal. "I wonder how long my friends in the Cuban security services will keep sending me these."

"If things are so bad," Leskov said, "then it's our duty to do all we can to improve the situation. Really going after Talala, doing it now, would be a first step."

"Talala's a speck of dust in a whirlwind."

Kerbitsky had never before been so blunt about his feelings. Leskov was grateful for the honesty, at least. But he felt as though something had broken inside him. He had known that Talala was powerful, that he had mighty protectors. But he had imagined that, with the law on his side . . .

"So," he said to the man who had almost been a friend, "I've been wasting my time on this."

Kerbitsky swiveled straight forward in his chair and made a hard face.

"*No.* No, you haven't been wasting your time, goddamnit. Don't you understand? We just can't do it alone. I need you to catch that bastard in the middle of something so big and obvious that no one can deny it or cover it up. Not something down on the Amu Darya. Here. Right here in Moscow. Where some of those glasnost journalist sons of bitches can latch onto it and smear it all over the headlines until Talala becomes such a liability that even his friends in the—that none of his friends can save him. Make them *want* to get rid of him, to cut their losses."

Leskov nodded. He was disappointed that the old man had not been this honest with him earlier in the game. But he felt sorry for Kerbitsky, too. It struck him that it must be a very hard thing to work all your life to become a general officer in the security services only to find that you did not have the power to arrest a flagrant criminal. A hard thing to find out what kind of country you really lived in. Yes, it must be a very hard thing to be a general under such circumstances. It was hard enough being a colonel.

Leskov looked down at the old Turkoman rug with the burn holes. "All right. Thank you. It was important for me to understand."

"Don't despair. Don't give up. We'll get him. He'll make a mistake."

Leskov nodded, picturing the sort of mistake it would require. How many more corpses? In this land of the rule of law.

"Yes," Leskov agreed. "We'll get him."

And that was all. He saluted and left, glad of the relatively fresh air in the secretaries' antechamber, out in the green corridors. It was a bad day. But he was determined not to give up. The country had enough men who had already given up. Someone had to fight back, to make a start. Even if it made no difference in the end.

One of his field agents was waiting for him in his office. The man was tough and honest, and he knew the Moscow underworld in remarkable detail. Leskov valued him and was always glad to see him. They had been working together on the Talala case for a long time now.

When the office door closed behind them, the agent looked unusually ill at ease. He fidgeted about in his oversize jacket as though he had been shot full of amphetamines. It turned out he had nothing of significance to report on Talala himself. But there was something new on the girl, the looker.

The man seemed to be having trouble speaking.

"Well, what the hell's the matter?" Leskov asked, growing impatient. It had been such a bad day. A bad year. "You look like you expect to get the firing squad."

The man looked up. Earnest. With no trace of the street-tough manner he affected when working. He had known Leskov for years, knowing him the way only a really good security man can know his superior, and Leskov had always accepted the situation. Nonetheless, he was startled when the man finally got the words out:

"Your brother's involved."

He loved the smell of her. As they neared each other, on the edge of the first sex of fingers and tongues, he hunted his nose over her hair, catching the scent, moving on to the warmer fragrance that rose off her shoulders and the axis of her arms. He kissed over her, smelling more than tasting, with the smallish breasts oddly scentless and wanting to be bitten ever so lightly, just threateningly, but with the full force of sexual gravity pulling him lower all the while. Her belly was hot and damp from their mingled sweat, from spillage. Running his lips, his tongue, over that intoxicating flatness, he began to get the full ripeness of her, wanting to soak in it, wondering briefly how you could ever paint a smell that tore at your muscles and bones. Then he had the first slicked hairs under his chin, and the raw perfume of her filled him. He brushed his face over her, that dark gravity still drawing him down, sweeping her with his lips, his nose, chewing into the soft, soft meat where her thighs ended, arrhythmic to her moans. The magnet in her pulled his tongue into the wet, and he felt positively drunk with her smell. Almonds and butter just starting to go bad. Graceless, he rubbed his lips, his lower face, into her, wanting to coat himself. Appalled at the power she had over him, he never hinted at it in words. But he thought she must know it, sense it, feel it, in his surrender. She called out raw sounds, deep and intense, muscles tightening.

He touched her up high with the tip of his tongue, searching over her, hunting through the marvelous complexity of those folds of flesh, of shying hair and speckles of foam. She shuddered as he kissed her and lifted her legs a little higher, a little wider. He began to make circles, sinking deeper and deeper into the smell of her, remembering not to crush her, not to use too much force, even as he wanted to grind himself viciously against her.

"*There,*" she said.

The rise and fall of her lower body came as steadily as the sea. A sea of flesh and smells and wet that would not stop. He had always been amazed at the differences in women, how some did not smell bad yet inexplicably put you off, how some reeked almost unbearably yet made you want them, how their perfumes ran from pickle sour to this opiate mélange of browned butter and nuts. He never understood it when men, and women, too, assumed that all females looked the same below the waist when it wasn't true at all. Beyond the obvious differences in color or thickness of hair waited the complexity of shapes, of lines and depths and shallows, of prominent bones and puckered flesh, of whites and tans, purples and reds, grays and browns. Some of them were aesthetically perfect, while others seemed crammed together or tucked up as an afterthought, too small or too big, from perfect to crazily awry, deeply secret or swelling out of themselves as if they couldn't wait to get at you. For years he had sketched them from memory, trying to understand the wonder of it. You had to do it by recall. Because it was a rare woman who would lie there with her legs open while you took charcoal or lead to cold paper. They all wanted their portraits done, and they loved the light eroticism of allowing their breasts to be transferred to canvas, tolerating even a dark shadow where their long thighs kissed together. But he had never met a woman who was not ashamed somehow of the blunt physical reality of that part of her, even when it gave her the most intense pleasure of her life. He had never met such a woman. Until now. Shirin took no more notice than if he were inspecting her shoulder. Unless he touched her. Then she laughed and everything started again.

Neither had he ever before wanted a woman to be less clean. So often, especially with the country girls, they hadn't even a proper sense of *how* to wash. You couldn't get lips or tongue near them, even if you wanted to. Anyway, the very thought of oral sex either shocked or horrified half of them. Then there were the clean girls with bad luck, forever plagued by small infections and Russian ignorance. Once a painfully clean, good-mannered girl had left him with a stubborn white rash in his mouth. But Shirin's cleanliness riled him. Every time she rose to wash he resented it, that washing away of him, even more so the suppression of her gorgeous smell. He wanted simply to hold her down on the bed. For days. Until the bedclothes, the entire room, the world, was soaking with her. He smelled her and wanted sex. Even when he had just finished. Even when his body had nothing left to offer. He smelled her and his soul got into the act, urging him to pull her to him again and again.

Shirin gave a little cry that was different from the others and he lifted himself abruptly, gliding up over belly and breasts, dropping his wet mouth onto hers as he slid into her. He let her taste herself. She kissed back anxiously, starved for him, for the *we* that he brought into her mouth, into her belly. He pushed all the way up into her, as far as he could go, until bone braked against bone in a crush of hair. She was so small, almost tiny. Frail boned. But with a depth that took all of him easily. With muscles that only came to life in bed.

He rubbed his wet cheeks over her face, smelling her again. He kept trying to find some end to her, to bury himself in her. The practiced distance with which he made love had disappeared entirely and he felt like an excited, inexperienced boy, just aching to get at her, to get closer, deeper, to find her, to move her.

She fought. Not against him, but with him, against the world. The room was torrid with the uncontrollable heating, and they ran sweat as though they had been oiled. The almond body smell of her rose and made him feel as though he were going crazy. He slammed himself into her. But she only moaned, rolled her face to the side, and accepted him. He sensed that she would not tell him to stop even if he were damaging her. Even if he were killing her.

He rolled them onto their sides, going at her from a different angle. She adjusted as though there were no bones in her body, only a giving elasticity made for sex. She molded to him, eyes closed, lips open. And he kissed her and clutched her, grateful that she was one of the women who liked being kissed during sex.

They were all so different, so different. It was a miracle.

And Shirin was the miracle of miracles. She kept him forever on the verge of release, he could barely hold back. Yet he managed to wait, to push her to the edge, too. He rolled back atop her, pushing at her with absolute fury, but she only made that same giving sound and raised her knees again. At times she looked at him with open, thinking eyes, even as her body seemed on the verge of madness. He chewed into her shoulder, feeling the bone under the veneer of muscle and skin. He wanted to bite her very hard, to draw blood, and he had to call himself back.

"Fingers," she said, asking, begging. "I want your fingertips."

That was how it was with her. She loved sex, the pure, unadorned act. But to reach fulfillment she needed to be touched. Sometimes she could have a row of light orgasms simply by taking him in her mouth. But vaginal sex brought her only so far. She had told him how she had had to do it with other men, unashamed, rubbing the flaccid remains of them against her with her own hand because they could never sense how to reach her. Their fingers were heavy and unguided, stupid to her responses. So all she could do was to let them finish, then, when their sensitivity had passed, stroke herself with them. But the best orgasms had been under her own fingers.

Then he had touched her. He had gotten that one thing right in his life. He could not understand why other men could not get it, could not sense the beauty under their fingers. To him, making love to a woman meant trying to hear past all the acquired noise, to seek out her original melody, the song of her body, to hear it and respond in harmony. Shirin was so natural and easy to him that he found himself wondering if there were not something beyond the flesh, some natural pairing beyond the limits of consciousness. It seemed to him as though Shirin had been made for him, for his tastes, his desires, for his sense of beauty. But he never allowed himself to think such things for very long.

Because it was all just bullshit, after all.

Under his fingers, she tightened. He had to move himself up on her to avoid being expelled from her body. She closed her eyes hard and began to rise toward the first small glory. He sensed her so well he could even tease her a little. He rewet his fingertips in his mouth, quickly, then slicked them back over her. She convulsed lightly and fell back. He felt a warm wet soaking over him, pulsing out of her. Women were different that way, too. Some never gave you this gift at all. But with Shirin, as she began to sink into rapture, it came as a series of floods, welcoming you, asking for more. He began the finger dance again. And she climbed, losing herself in a swell of ecstasy then calming and beginning again at a higher stage.

"Give me your breast," he said.

Obediently, she cupped her left breast in her hand, pushing it up, making it as full as her slight body allowed, and he curled down to suck and chew at her.

She shivered. Two of his fingers played with her and she tightened so much that he slipped out of her belly after all. She was so far gone she did not notice. She tightened and tightened, hurting his hand between her thighs, forcing it into a painful angle, one of her hands riling the breast into his mouth, the other on the back of his head, drawing him in. He could feel the greater waves rising now, the kind that came just before she exploded.

She groaned. Like an animal. Kicking a little. Her steeled belly climbed up on him, tormenting the hand that needed to stay with her. He pushed it all the way down and began to stroke her with the meat of his thumb.

She shook. He had to hold to her. She shook and tensed and made an out-of-breath sound that rose from oblivion. She jerked as if touched with electricity and groaned hugely, almost breaking into a scream. In a panic of sensitivity, she knocked his hand away and gasped in wonder.

Roughly, he pushed himself back inside her. She had ripened with wetness and she responded to him with a readiness that shocked him a little after the intensity of her orgasm. She was always, always ready for him, the first woman who had not, at some point, told him she could not go on. Tiny Shirin. Who never gave up.

"Do you want me?" he asked.

"Oh, yes."

Her eyes were closed and she was so far gone that he could hardly believe she had answered him. He wanted to *reach* her. He gripped the flesh under her hips, locking her against him, and drove into her with a ferocity that had to hurt her.

"Do you *want* me?"

"Yes. *Yes.*"

"Then *take* me. *Deep* inside." With a free hand, he nursed her legs up behind him. "*Hold me.*"

With all of the strength in his body, with all of the swimmer's muscles and weight of bone, he plunged down into her, letting go. She held on to him with her thin, strong arms, with her fine, lean legs. He ground himself against her, even now wanting to go deeper, to reach her, *to reach her.*

Later, as they lay wordless in each other's arms, the artist realized he was afraid. Afraid that he might break apart and love this woman, and even more afraid that it would be for all the wrong reasons. He was afraid she would prove dishonest, unreliable, empty of even the minimal virtues she would need to bring to a love to make it endure. He was afraid of the loss of self-control, afraid that only now, at age thirty-five, had he discovered something with a meaning so intense that he might never be able to give it up. For the first time in his life he wondered how he would manage when a specific woman turned away from him, and he could not laugh away his fears. He knew already that he would love her, thinking that perhaps he would love her for a long, long time. He wanted to speak to her, to try to open her with words. But all of the possible constructions sounded trite and flat. He wanted to say, "Now that I've found you, I'm never going to let you go." But instead of speaking, he simply drew a palm down over her hair and onto the velvet damp of her back.

He was terribly afraid and he longed for his body to reawaken so that he could tell her how he felt in the only way that seemed real, the only way he could trust and believe in. He wished he could make love to her without ever stopping, so that they might always be together that way, at least. He held her in his arms, a small girl-woman of muscle and bone the sum of which was so much greater than the parts. He held her tighter, terrified of losing her before their relationship could fill itself out. It seemed to him that no man could ever have been so afraid of losing a woman.

He did not understand, of course, how he had shaken the girl. He understood her body and that gave him the illusion of understanding much more of her than he really did. Above all, he did not understand how alike the two of them were in their loneliness and in their uncompromising, destructive abilities to love.

Thaw. As you hurried along the icy walks your boots picked up the slush and the clinging wet worked in between the soles and the uppers. In Moscow, so far from the sea, the air had a raw tang, almost a saltiness, and you imagined it to be warmer than it was and you had to be very sensible not to undo your jacket. It was not the beginning of spring. Not yet. This was a false thaw, a false hope, yet it carried the promise that, in a few more weeks or a month, the earth would loosen itself enough to drink down the melt and countless small quakings would slowly paint the vacant lots green. In the middle of the workday, three laborers squatted by a rubbish fire at a construction site and a bareheaded man passed a bottle. The sky rolled with clouds bound to storm elsewhere, and in the line before the small grocery shop that serviced the ranks of apartments, a young woman closed her eyes and lifted her face as though the summer sun were already pouring down over them all.

Sasha walked quickly. His hair was still damp from his swim. He had not taken enough time to dry it, anxious to return to his empty apartment with its hungover smell of Shirin so he could try to paint her from memory, to steal this gray light and rub it into his palette, to try to get a grip on her, to fix her under his brushes. The brisk wet air reminded him of the sea winds that came graying in over Riga, and he thought over how he would have to go and do that unwelcome work, how he had never wanted this and how it was so much harder now because he did not want to leave Shirin. He worried that she would simply wander off into other beds during the weeks of his absence. Accustomed to supreme self-confidence regarding women, he found himself worrying that another man would prove more appealing to her, more capable of reaching her, of shaking her awake to life. Somewhere a man was waiting who would offer her more or the illusion of more. While he painted lies in Riga.

Today's swim had not brought him the accustomed peace. He had been tired and the muscle work had been nothing but a labor. He had tried ringing Bilinsky one last time, pleading with him for a briefer, nearer assignment. But they wanted him in Riga. Where the wind blew in off the great bay, following the river until it found its way into the curling streets of the old town, howling down the centuries, creaking the old heavy signs, and ripping at roofs and gables. He had only good, loving memories of Riga. Now he felt as though he were being sent to shit in its streets.

And they were taking him away from Shirin, from warm, dark, golden, southern Shirin. It was such an overgrown, crazy, senseless country, fouled with imposed Russianness, with the triumph of the mediocre, from cities where the horses of the Teutonic knights had sparked their hooves on the cobblestones to deserts where wild, gaudy horsemen had swarmed down over caravans of silk-laden camels. It was all too big, too big, too big for any one man, any one life, any one government.

A ghost of rain tickled his face just as he ducked into the shelter of his apartment building. The vestibule was filthy with the residue of winter, and a grandmother with a mop argued with an old man with frayed ribbons on his jacket. Sasha ignored them, dashing up the stairs, boots crunching over bits of slimed glass. He had learned to live right past all this, not to let it touch him. Even with a Russian family name and a Russian's internal passport, he could still never quite think of himself as one of *them.* With their big fists and their little souls that they sought to magnify with liquor and weeping.

When Bilinsky had sentenced him to the job in Riga, it had unleashed the other torrent of blood in Sasha's veins, the blood of the Latvian son of a Latvian mother, whose own mother had never accepted the coming of the Russians. Not even when they knocked her down in an alley and fucked her by turns.

How on earth was he going to paint the glorious triumph of the Red Army on the walls of Riga? In Germany or Georgia, it was all just a fantasy, fairy tales with guns. She'll never forgive me, he thought, as though his grandmother were still alive. It struck him that, since his grandmother's death, Shirin was the first human being he had even come close to loving —loving in the sense that you could not bear the thought of the loss of the other. He had never really loved his mother that way, not with a big, overwhelming love. His childhood need of her had evolved into pity and affection, nothing more. She had been too small somehow, forever cringing in the shadow of the officer to whom she had given herself, while his father's face thickened and reddened and his temper shortened. Sasha always thought of his father as he had been just before his death. It was impossible to see in that corpulent bully any trace of the strong, smart lieutenant who had charmed a Latvian girl away from her family, her country, and her senses.

Sasha opened the door to his apartment, relocked it behind him, drew off his scarf, and just barely saw the uniform trouser legs under his kitchen table.

Hurling his jacket into his studio, Sasha stalked into the kitchen.

His brother sat peacefully on the far side of the table, smoking a cigarette. He looked clean and very well-groomed, still handsome, but in a way that was a little too neat and orderly to attract a really interesting woman. Sasha noted that the uniformed man's hair had grown much thinner since the last time they had met. He looked at Sasha with calm, intelligent eyes, petting the cat, who lay on his lap in a tight-eyed swoon.

"I was admiring your paintings," the KGB colonel said. "You just get better and better. It's a gift."

"Get down, Vrubel." Sasha shooed the cat roughly and the

startled animal dashed off for one of its hiding places in another room.

"Bad day?" the intruder asked.

"What do you want?"

His brother snubbed out his cigarette on a cracked saucer. "Can't we talk? Can't I visit you?"

"We don't have anything to say to one another," Sasha said. This is how my father would have looked, he thought, if he had taken care of himself. If he hadn't been such a stupid drunken pig. "Anyway, you never come to see me without a reason."

"That's your choice. Not mine."

"And you've got no right breaking into my apartment. I'm not a criminal. I have a right to be left alone."

"Can't we talk?"

"I have nothing to say to you."

His brother nodded. Slowly. "Maybe I have something to say to you?"

"Then say it and get out."

"Not even a cup of tea, Sasha?" He gestured toward a pair of fine oriental tea bowls Shirin had left behind.

"Tea's hard to come by these days. I don't get everything free from the KGB."

"Couldn't you please just sit down so that we could talk like two adults? If not like brothers?"

"Do I have a choice? Or do I get carted off to prison if I refuse?"

"Don't be asinine."

Face and heart locked, Sasha took the remaining chair.

"So talk."

"Sasha, I'm worried about you."

"I get by."

"That's not what I mean. I know the painting's going well and all that. I was wrong about that and I'm sorry. I'm very proud of you. Your work is really very good. When you're painting what you want to paint." Sasha could feel his brother trying to capture his eyes. "The rest of it is, of course, just a technical exercise."

Sasha felt a surge of anger. Pasha had always been like this. Always the wiser, always judging, lecturing.

"I didn't know you were an art critic."

Pavel shrugged and leaned back from the table. "I'm not. But . . . it's my life's work to recognize what's genuine and what's not."

Sasha smirked at him. "And that's why you're here? To lecture me about authenticity in the arts?"

Pavel tipped his head a little, a gesture of thought, of weighing words. "Well, in a sense, it's also a matter of what's genuine and what's not. You've been seeing a girl. Shirin Talala. How much do you really know about her, Sasha?"

Sasha went cold. It took him a moment to form an answer.

"I know," he lied, "all I need to know about her. Anyway, the women in my life are none of your business."

Pavel nodded in agreement. "Normally, that's true. And I've never interfered in your private life."

"Horseshit."

"No. No, all that was different. I just . . . I was simply afraid that an artist's life, that somehow . . ."

"And now you want to tell me who I should and shouldn't screw."

A change came over Pavel. It was slight enough so that only a brother or the subject of a long interrogation would have noticed it. His face wore a look of renewed determination, gone very serious.

"Yes. This time, yes."

"Shouldn't you be out tracking down criminals? Or spying on foreign tourists?"

"Sasha, please. Listen to me. This isn't a joke. Do you know anything at all about Shirin Talala's father?"

Sasha put on a snide, street-punk demeanor he had not worn in years.

"He's some big deal from Uzbekistan. Party pig and all that."

"Listen to me, Sasha. Ali Talala isn't just another Party hack. The man's a killer. He's as corrupt, as evil, as any man in this country. And it could be damned dangerous for you if he decides he doesn't like his little angel sleeping around with some Russian artist who has a reputation for swinging his cock all over Moscow." Pavel twisted the flesh of his nose. "This place even smells like a whorehouse."

With the force of revelation, it all clicked into place for Sasha. He understood his brother now.

"You turd. What you really mean to say is that you don't want the KGB to find out that the brother of their shining star is having an affair with a gangster's daughter. All you're thinking about is your fucking career."

Pavel ran a hand heavily over his temple, lower lip dangling. "Oh, for the love of God, Sasha. That's twisted. There's always a possibility he could be trying to get at me through you. But *you*'re the one I'm worried about. You live in your little world of paints—you don't know what it's like out there. I've been working the Talala file for two years, and if there's any one thing that marks these people, it's a taste for revenge. They never forget and they never forgive."

Sasha didn't believe a word of it. "If this guy's such a cold-blooded murderer and all that, why isn't he sitting in prison? Why don't you just arrest him and protect us all?"

"That's another story."

"Shirin's not a gangster," Sasha said flatly, definitively.

"I never said she was. At least we have no proof that she's directly involved in anything. No, Shirin Talala's a very bright young student of foreign languages who's extraordinarily stupid when it comes to choosing men."

Sasha winced. Despite himself.

"Shirin's free to do what she wants."

Pavel nodded. "Sasha, she's bad business. The whole family's bad business. Evil."

"Shirin's not evil." Sasha was sure of that one thing. Even if everything else his brother said happened to be true, Shirin was not evil. Lost, perhaps. The way he knew now that he was lost himself and had always been lost. But not evil.

Pavel shrugged, lifting his shoulder boards. He looked very tired. "Maybe not. Maybe she's just a mixed-up kid. But her father's a bloody monster. For God's sake, *think,* Sasha. The son of a bitch could hurt you, kill you. It wouldn't even spoil his lunch. I mean, with all of the other women out there . . ."

Sasha looked at the brother who could never really be his brother. "I choose my own sleeping partners. And, it seems to me, I've got a better track record than you when it comes to choosing."

Pavel sat back again. So tired. And hurt now, too. But Sasha wanted him to hurt. To pay him back.

"My boys," Pavel said quietly, "would like to see you again. You don't have to take it out on them. You're still their uncle."

"Are you so sure you're their father?"

Pavel refused to become excited. "Oh, I think so," he said softly. Then he smiled. "But who really knows anything in this life? The important thing is that they're good boys."

"The last time I saw them, they didn't even look like you."

"They look like their mother." Pavel's voice remained quiet, almost fond. With no trace of bitterness. "Little Sasha draws, you know."

"Maybe you should get married again," Sasha said, teasing his brother as cruelly as he knew how. Pavel would never marry again.

"No," Pavel said seriously. "I'm not cut out to be a husband. Perhaps not even a father. Maybe I'm too much like our old man. Anyway, I've got my work."

"Be honest. That's what it's all about, isn't it? Your holy work? We don't want to embarrass the record of the up-and-coming colonel, do we?"

"*No.*" Pavel leaned forward, and for an instant, Sasha thought his brother was going to reach across the table and grab him. "Can't you just get it through that cunt-drunk skull of yours that I'm worried about you? These are bad times, Sasha. *Very* bad times. And you're brushing up against very bad men. It's a lousy combination."

"I can take care of myself," Sasha said. But his insides were already churning with concerns.

Shirin.

"No, you *can't,*" Pavel said. "That's just it. You *can't* take care of yourself when you're dealing with these people."

"So I should take the advice of the KGB . . ."

"You should take a brother's advice. This one time."

"I don't have a brother."

"Don't be childish."

"I don't have a brother."

Pavel reached out and seized Sasha's wrist. He had a very strong grip. "This skin," he said, shaking his brother's forearm, "the blood, all of it. It's the *same.* Can't you understand that? We're all that's left. We're brothers, whether it suits your self-inflated sense of whatever the hell you think you are or not. We're *brothers*. And I don't want bad things to happen to my brother."

"We stopped being brothers the day you put on that uniform."

Pavel released his hand. He sighed and sat back, shaking his head. "Why do you have to be so high and mighty?"

Sasha leaned in to attack. "And you? That uniform's the last thing our grandfather saw. Before one of your thugs put a bullet in his skull. And your ribbons. What the hell are they for? *You* never fought in a war." Sasha stood up, reaching across the table toward Pavel's chest, but his brother knocked his hand away. "Maybe that one's for raping some terrified little girl in a cellar. Or maybe it just commemorates the anniversary of old rapes. And that one. What's it for? Burning books? Or just for shooting the authors? I guess the one on the end's just for toadying, for sucking Russian ass till you're so soaked in shit you'll never be clean again." Sasha ran out of words, out of breath, out of anger.

Pavel rose. He looked sick with sorrow. It occurred to Sasha that he had placed himself entirely in the wrong, that Pavel was as honest as you could expect a man to be and that he was doing his best. He was an unlucky man, in so many ways.

But Sasha could not relent. It was impossible to admit to this graying man in the well-tailored uniform that he just might be right about some things, some of the time.

Pavel drew on his overcoat, jouncing it over his shoulders to settle it properly. He looked indescribably sad.

Sasha looked away.

"Please," Pavel said. "Be careful." And he let himself out of the apartment.

Sasha sat. He noticed that it was raining steadily beyond the faded curtains. The thaw would not last. The rain would turn to ice. Then the snow would come again, making the footing treacherous. It had only been a false thaw and spring was still far off.

Vrubel padded in from the next room and sprang up onto Sasha's lap. He stroked the cat without thinking, staring out at the closed sky. He no longer felt the urge to paint. The afternoon was a blasted thing.

The cat began to purr.

"You're a whore, too," Sasha told the animal.

PART TWO

The Far Country

14

IF YOU LEAVE THE UZBEK CAPITAL OF TASHKENT BY ONE of the major roads, along which the clean, uncrowded buses reserved for foreign tourists groan through their gears, you emerge suddenly from a new, tolerably green city and climb into spare hills where horsemen still survey their herds of sheep from the ridges. If, however, you are driving alone at night and the ill-placed road signs simply confuse your tired eyes and heart, you might stray into a web of worsening streets where the startled faces in your headlamps make it clear how unexpected you are, perhaps even how unwelcome. If it is only evening, you might still see the off-angles and livid patches where homes not destroyed by the last earthquake have been spackled back to habitability. Some of these neighborhoods are for the ethnic Slavs, who live ever more apart from the other residents of this city, and if you have not been in this country within a country for very long, you might be jarred to see a young blond woman in jeans bathing her child in an open sewer. But most of these neighborhoods, which are home to those without influence or ambition or enough luck, belong to the Uzbeks and a weave of Tadzhik and Kirghiz families spun down from their lonesome hills. If the last light of evening reveals your white skin, or if you stop at the wrong corner or turn into a blind alley, the faces that stare at you will show a curiosity that is not at all a manifestation of traditional Uzbek hospitality. It is very important to establish as soon as possible that you are American or German or English or French or Argentinian—anything so that you are not taken for a Russian in the gathering darkness, when all of the midday proclamations of brotherhood are laid to rest. If there is still enough light, your clothing or your good white teeth alone might rescue you from an uncomfortable time, heralding you as foreign and therefore wonderful, but if the night is too heavy to show off your health and finery in those dirt or half-paved lanes, you must speak quickly in your own language, willfully laying aside those carefully memorized words and phrases in Russian. Nothing will happen to you that way, and eventually, you will emerge back into the city of earthquake-proof, white high rises and broad, unbusy avenues, and you will find the road you missed, coming away with nothing worse than a slight loss of time and a heightened sense of adventure. All this, of course, is only if you do not know the way.

For those who know the way there is another road. It leads beyond the shanties with their fruit trees and old broken machines, past the old villages digested by the city's expanding girth, until the narrow paved track edges along a walled park. There are no signs on the wall, no heroic slogans, and it is in remarkably good repair. Only rarely do the old bricks show through the stucco. There is a double iron gate, but you might easily miss it, perhaps distracted by a man sitting sideways on a donkey as its hooves chop homeward. The wall is high enough so that a man cannot see over it, and a thick plantation of trees grows just behind it. Behind the trees lies a mansion with well-kept outbuildings. Built in the last peaceful years of a Russia that was formally Imperial, before the great war came and the rhetoric changed, this was a country retreat for aristocratic officials sentenced to a tour of duty far from St. Petersburg. Today everything is very different, and a local citizen passing by, even if he or she did not know the details, would realize that the wall and the trees and the quietly watched gate protect the leisure of weary representatives of the People, men exhausted by the never-ending work of building a better future. Such a retreat would not be open to just any People's tribune, of course, but only to those who gave most fully of themselves, whose achievements outshone those of the plodding rank and file of bureaucrats. A man or woman privileged to know the exact purpose of the old mansion that had survived revolution, civil war, and earthquake might smile knowingly, even sharing a joke with a companion he trusted. But no passerby would look too hard if a black limousine suddenly emerged from that dark, recessed gateway. There are, in the end, things better left alone.

In the mansion in the park behind the wall there are numerous apartments, all serviced by a discreet staff. Important men, who might well socialize with one another in their homes or in Tashkent's government restaurants, usually spend their hours in this mansion studiedly apart from their colleagues, although, on occasion, there have been celebrations of historic dimensions. These get-togethers are similar in that some of the participants invariably live to regret them. They are also similar in that no outsider is ever invited, and certainly no Slav.

In one of the apartments lived a young woman with a worsening limp. She had two companions. The first was an old burlesque of a woman whose face bore the scars of a lapse between the onset of illness and the beginning of medical treatment. The old woman sought to reduce the visibility of her scars with bright makeup that no respectable Uzbek woman would ever wear. The other companion was a muscular man of indeterminate age. He had been chosen to be the young woman's companion because he was brutal and homosexual. He was very grateful to hold this position because it offered him a degree of protection in his vices, although he never brought any manifestation of those weaknesses back with him when he returned from his weekly trips into the city. Both the old woman with the marks of ill luck on her face and the man with the brawl-ruptured hands received good salaries to serve as companions to the young woman with the limp and to guard her. They had to make certain that no outsider, nor any visitor or other resident of the mansion, had any contact with her whatsoever. And they had to ensure that she did not disappear one day into the alleys of Tashkent or back into the hills from whence her family had sold her off for a very high price as soon as it became apparent that their handsome thirteen-year-old daughter had the good fortune to suffer from a degenerative hip disease. The old woman and the shadow of a man understood that, if anything happened to the young woman, they would pay with their lives.

The young woman's name was Ashi and she had already lived in the house for more than ten years. When the great man could not be with her, she was happiest in the spring or autumn, when it was neither too hot nor too cold and it was pleasant to sit in the garden. She and the old woman would sit on a bench under a tree, keeping apart from the other women who lived in the house and who were often friends with one another, and the old woman would help her learn the poetry that the great man loved. The words always sounded beautiful, even when she did not entirely understand the meaning, and she tried hard to get them by heart because it made the great man so very happy. She sat in her silks with the garden soft around her, imagining that the poems were about her and the great man. The old woman knew a remarkable number of poems without resort to books, and she taught them to Ashi with the passing years. Ashi felt a certain affection toward the old woman with the ravaged face, although the old woman gave no sign of affection in return. There were only poems to be learned, old stories that had to be gotten word for word, or songs, although Ashi had not been blessed with a good singing voice to complement the luck of her disease. Earlier, the old woman had taught her other things, as well, but Ashi knew them all without further tutoring now.

Her disease went slowly, but each autumn when they returned to the garden after the burning summer, it was a little harder to walk. She was not allowed to use a cane or crutch, since that would have detracted from the effect.

"Be thankful unto God," the old woman told her. "He has made your fortune."

Sometimes the great man did not come to her for months at a time. Then he might be with her every night for a week. She was happiest when he was with her. She loved to please him. She lived for his kind words. But above all, she lived for the midnights when he would temporarily put to rest the burning inside her.

Sometimes she thought she would go mad. Her body was

such a curious, curious thing. She had no power over it, really, and she knew that it was a good thing to be locked away so that she could save herself for the great man. She did not know how she could possibly remain decent and clean in a world full of men with her body craving every one of them. It was far, far better to be locked away.

But it was terribly difficult at times. Sometimes at night—or unexpectedly in the middle of the afternoon—her body would begin to move without her willing it, burning and burning until she could smell herself smoldering through her silks. She was always glad when the old woman began to fuss over her again, making her as pretty as art allowed, in preparation for the arrival of the great man.

"Be thankful unto God," the old woman told her. "Had this man not taken you for himself, your father might have given you to some filthy pimp who would have sold you in an alley behind the bazaar. And then your blessing would have been your curse."

Ali Talala was tired and his mood was foul. All of Ashi's skills could not raise his spirits. Akanayev had summoned him to Party headquarters in Tashkent, interrupting Talala's stay with his family in the hills below Samarkand, disrupting the schedule that would have brought him back to Moscow to meet with the Ukrainians, but worst of all, underlining the very real limits of Talala's power.

Akanayev had been shameless. Instead of inviting him for a glass of tea and speaking with him as an old comrade, Akanayev had left him standing before his desk like a schoolboy.

"Are you *mad?*" Akanayev had asked, his voice displaying a barely controlled rage. "What century do you think you're living in? You can't behave like one of your smear-assed bandit grandfathers." Akanayev pushed himself back into his chair in theatrical disgust, framing himself under the portrait of Lenin with the accentuated Asiatic features. "Who do you think you are? *Who* do you think you are, Ali Talala?" He drew himself back to the desk and leaned forward. "What you do in Moscow, in the Russian's house, is one thing. But it takes a very foolish man to soil his own home."

"The Russians need to be taught the limits of—"

"Shut your mouth and listen." Talala winced as if cut with a whip. It was unthinkable that Akanayev should talk to him this way. "This escapade . . . was unforgivable. You owe an unpayable debt to us all. For your folly." Akanayev shook his head. "What on earth possessed you? To kill a KGB colonel? And to butcher, my God, how many was it? Never mind. One would have been too many. Do you really want to give the Russians an excuse to sweep us all aside and rule with tanks?"

"The Russians have their hands full."

"Never underestimate the Russian capability for brutality. You foolish, foolish man. This is a time for going delicately. None of us knows what the future may hold."

Talala could not remember a single instance in his life when he had felt so humiliated. Had another man spoken to him in such a manner, he would have killed him. But Akanayev spoke for the handful of men who ruled the whole of Central Asia, not just one city or valley or region or clan. And Talala understood the gravity of the message.

"Is that all you have to say to me?"

Akanayev crossed his arms over his chest, leaning back again. "Yes. As long as you understand. Do your dirty work elsewhere. Not where your brothers must bear the responsibility."

"Is that all?"

"Yes. Leave my sight."

It was too hard, too shameless.

Talala had just reached the door when Akanayev called him back.

"Listen. I want to tell you something else. Unofficially. As an old friend. Keep an eye on young Gogandaev."

Talala stiffened. "Mustafa Gogandaev is a son to me."

Akanayev nodded. "Watch him, my friend, watch him."

And that was the cruelest trick of all. Talala saw through it. The hardest punishment a man could receive was to have doubt sown between him and his kith and kin. He understood instantly why Akanayev had warned him: to make him fear his own. To ruin his sleep with false cares. It was a cruelty Talala had not expected from Akanayev. Or even from Akanayev's superiors.

Talala had not even bothered to stop off at his city apartment for a change of clothing. He ordered his driver to take him directly to his beloved.

Smiling with a joy that was nearly physical rapture, Ashi had limped toward him. The old whore and the twisted bodyguard discreetly disappeared, leaving the lovers alone. He could feel Ashi's flames even when they were not touching. He could feel her want, the same way his father and grandfather before him had felt that enriched desire in their mistresses. In the tradition of Persian princes, the Talala chiefs kept concubines with diseased hips, women who flared with eroticism as their bones rotted away. Only those in the last stages of tuberculosis approached this sexual intensity, with their half-mad lust at the edge of death. And to find such a woman who also possessed Ashi's select beauty was to feel the touch of the finger of God. The whoremaster lucky enough to find such a one as Ashi had his fortune made. Men would travel far for a night, an hour with her. But Ashi was Talala's alone. His beloved. His treasure. His jewel.

The last man to touch her other than Talala had been the doctor who inspected her and purged the worms out of her before her master first embraced her. She had been irresistible even as a half-child. Now, as she slowly continued to sicken, she had become a miracle. Often it took all of his self-discipline not to board a plane and come to her. To taste her mortal glory yet again.

Yet, today, all of her attentions, the pourings of mint tea and offerings of fruit, barely interested him. He reclined on the carpets, elbow stabbed into a great embroidered pillow, and mulled over the day's events as Ashi recited to him in her evening voice. He knew her: she could feel that he was still far away, and that would make her deliciously afraid. He knew how badly she wanted him. How she needed him. Every woman had a whore's soul. And Ashi's soul was crumbling with her bones.

" 'Come that I may touch you—reach me your hand,' " she recited, " 'nevermore to leave you—reach me your hand! Oh, see the darkness that lies over the earth, in the dark—' "

The blow cut her off. Talala had rolled over, swinging his open hand, and he caught her hard on the side of the mouth. Ashi was small and the slap knocked her back over the cushions, drawing blood instantly. Talala rose to his feet, standing over her, hand poised to descend again.

"You stupid cow. You whore-daughter of a whore-mother. Can't you learn anything properly? It's '*upon* the earth,' you slut, not '*over* the earth.' I should beat you and throw you into the streets, you mindless bitch."

Ashi cowered in terror, afraid even to wipe away the blood trickling from her mouth. She knew what it could be like when the great man was angry. She knew what it was like to be beaten for the evil that was in her. She did not even dare say that she was sorry.

"Leave my sight," Talala commanded.

Ashi crawled out from under his shadow. Each time she put down a knee the jolt telegraphed pain up through her joints and along her spine. She tried to hurry, to please the great man by her obedience, but her body kept crumpling forward with the effort. In the doorway she hauled herself to her feet and bobbed into the mattress room with the walk of a camel.

Talala watched her go, feeling the first stirring of desire. He did not follow her immediately. It was important that she have time to cry, to reflect, to worry. Then the reconciliation in the darkness would be so sweet, she would become a wild creature, wild as a mountain torrent during the melting of the high snows. He would bind her in his arms and assure her of his devotion. She would weep for joy.

He reclined on the big pillow, choosing an orange from a nearby display of fruit. Everything would be all right. If the emirs of Bukhara had not bowed the heads of the Talalas, these bureaucrats would never bring it off. His thoughts moved from the old glories of his family to the upcoming business in Moscow. The Ukrainians could not be trusted, of course, but perhaps he could show them that their self-interest and the interests of Ali Talala were one and the same. At least for the moment.

Nothing lasted forever. Not even love and beauty. You had to sweep it up and lay it across your saddle in the hour of opportunity. No chance ever came twice.

He thought briefly of Shirin, hoping that she would somehow find her happiness and fate as he had found his own.

Poor Shirin. Born to be a son, mocked with a daughter's carcass.

Feeling much better, Ali Talala rose and traced the path of his beloved.

The great cities of Uzbekistan have personalities as distinct as those of great men. Tashkent is aggressively new, a Soviet monument, a socialist phoenix re-arisen after a ferocious earthquake. It is also the formal seat of Central Asian religious authority and home to officially sanctioned Koran schools. Yet it is the most superficial of the Uzbek cities, and despite the towering hotels and apartment blocks, the palaces of culture and sport, and the clean promenades with cafés that appear European if you do not look too closely, it is somehow the most ephemeral, a city born and reborn by decree and not because the power of a holy shrine or a bend in a river drew men to it early in history and enduringly. It is a city that governs, and what it cannot govern, it dreams of governing. If you stay on the great boulevards it seems a Russian city. But behind the cement facades, the city has another heart. Below the new bazaar pavilion and its concrete ramparts, the old alleys steam with discarded offal, and shabby teahouses cater to farmers and herdsmen come into town to sell their wares and buy a few shoddy manufactured goods to take back to the hills. The spice market, vivid with color and scent, offers flavors for the cookpot and other for the soul, although you must first be trusted before the old folk remedies appear from a pocket or a sack behind a sack. Descend the stairs that separate the new bazaar where all are welcome from the dilapidated shanties where the Slavs go only in groups and a country boy smiles and proudly thrusts a dripping sheep's heart in your face, sending flies to brush your hair and cheeks. Tashkent is a city that does not bear close examination. It is the city of the future, and it lives day to day.

Samarkand is very old and very beautiful, as long as you do not expect beauty to be easy. There is the old Tadzhik city, the nineteenth-century Russian imperial quarter, and a modern, Soviet Samarkand, as well. But the pull of the old is very strong. After a little while, all the new construction becomes virtually invisible and the imperial houses hide under the shade of the trees. In the end you see only the towering bulb of the Bibi Hanum mosque, forever waiting to collapse again, or the perfect and majestic Registan, or the antique mausoleums on a barren hill surrounded with more recent dead. This is a city of souls. But they are unhappy souls, the sort who haunt out their discontent. Samarkand is a place of pilgrimage. But it is not a holy city. Its monuments ultimately speak more of power than of piety, its adornments too lavish for any self-respecting God. Very old and built upon layers of death, Samarkand has the most pungent feeling of life of any of these cities.

For death you go to Bukhara. Bukhara is a very holy city; it has remained fetidly holy despite the best efforts and intentions of our century, and like all holy cities, it stinks of cruelty and oblivion. Never eradicated, the city's Koran schools are growing in number, and although the mullahs by and large take care to render unto Caesar, the air here is redolent of patience, not of submission. Bukhara has survived massacre and near-total destruction, time and again, and by local standards, the invading Russians were amateurs, fussing with treaties where stronger conquerors simply killed all living things. Noted for their cruelty and wealth, the emirs of Bukhara built cruel, wealthy citadels and mosques, madrasahs and minarets. All the while they were sick. The water supply of Bukhara, based on great cisterns, was infected with parasitic disease. The people washed themselves for God and took into their bodies a worm that grew and wandered, shocking them with pain until it finally emerged through the skin of a thigh or shoulder. The worm then needed to be trained around a stick, carefully, so that it did not die before leaving the body completely. Otherwise, it rotted away inside the victim. Red doctors, full of fervor, virtually eradicated the disease in the twenties, attacking it with hygiene, discipline, and rudimentary drugs. But there was another worm, too, that had embedded itself in the hearts of the people. The worm of faith drowsed, but never died. And as the stresses of modernity became too much for the old Islamic orders to bear, and cultures that could no longer compete chose instead to revel in their backwardness, Islamic fundamentalism began to spread throughout the Middle East and North Africa. Despite the Soviet-enforced cordon sanitaire, the Central Asian republics gradually, quietly, proudly, and hopefully began to surrender to the past. More than any other city in Uzbekistan, Bukhara, so long drenched in blood and ignorance, was ready for God's Word.

"God is great," Mamun Ersari said.

"God is great," the others echoed automatically. The acoustics within the old Koran school had a light ring, muted by the woodwork of the intricate false ceiling and the cheap modern rugs upon which the company sat. Candlelight threw deep shadows and caught the gilt of the painted heaven above their heads. The men were five in all. Ersari, robed, looked more Persian than the others, while Mustafa Gogandaev's business suit stood out at the other extreme. The man beside Gogandaev was called Baxram, and he had devoted his life to restoring old mosques and madrasahs. He wore a shapeless blue workman's coat and a square Uzbek cap whose embroidery shone. As a Sufi brother, Baxram knew that God's eyes saw beyond a man's finery and did not mind the honest garments of labor. The remaining two men were dressed alike in Uzbek winter robes, the same clothes they wore to help their students enter the world of the Book. One was very old, and the pull of age on his face made him look Chinese. His mouth hung eternally open and his chin shone wet around a sparse white goatee. The man beside him was younger, with a brown mustache and eyes that always focused beyond the target of his speech.

"And you see the wisdom?" Ersari asked. He held his right hand up before him as though holding an invisible cigarette.

"Yes," the young man with the distant eyes answered. "This much is clear."

"There can be no question," Baxram said impatiently. Capable of spending hours lovingly fitting a single aquamarine tile into the dome of a mausoleum, he could rarely bear the torpor of other men's irresolution.

"There is no question," the young man assured him.

"It is a thing that must be done."

"Yes. It must be done."

"It is only," the old Chinese-looking man interrupted, "that there shall be so much blood. And the blood of children . . ."

"We must not think of the matter in such a light," Ersari said firmly, his voice as cold as the night beyond the old wooden doors. "It is foul blood, the blood of a damned line, heretical, cancerous. The children must be saved from the devils budding within them."

The old man nodded, and the younger man with the faraway eyes said quickly, "My father has no doubts. But the teaching requires the question. Only God is never questioned. It is through questions that we learn."

"And now," Gogandaev said, "the time for questions is past."

"God is great," Baxram replied. The light of a dozen candles reflected in his eyes.

"God is great. Truly, He is great."

"And it is very important," Gogandaev went on, "that none escape. There can be no witnesses. It must be plausibly represented as the work of the Ukrainians."

"It is clear."

"And it must happen very quickly, once the word is passed to you. Everything will depend on that."

"It will happen quickly."

"The guards will let us in. But they, too, must be killed. They're all infected with his sickness, his greed."

"The guards, too, will be killed."

"As God wills."

"As God wills."

A silence came over the men as each meditated on the future. Gogandaev sat quietly, in outward reverence. But in the end, religion was not so important to him. He appreciated its disciplinary functions, its moral force to impose a modicum of honesty on men and modesty on women. But he resembled the city from which he came in that power would always be more important to him than sanctity. He was a child of Samarkand.

Baxram broke the pall of meditation. His voice said that something had occurred to him suddenly:

"What of his whore? The one he keeps in the Sin House in Tashkent? Shouldn't she be killed, too?"

Gogandaev smiled. "Oh, no. Not her. Talala loves his limping slut more than any other creature on the earth. Except for his whore of a daughter. No, I have something special in mind for his concubine."

"Remember," Ersari said, "she is not of his blood. And she has given him no children. She was bought as a child. To harm her—"

"She has born his weight, she bears his guilt," Gogandaev said. Then he softened his voice, desiring no quarrel with Ersari. "But she will be spared. From death. The price she will pay . . . will be different. To plague Talala's soul in hell."

"And the eldest daughter?" Baxram asked feverishly.

"She dies."

Later, as he lay in his bed in the tourists hotel that towered so oddly above Bukhara, Gogandaev considered how perfectly all of it had been devised. Of course, Talala had written his own fate. In the old days, when a man could simply carry his family back into the hills, the Talalas had been able to risk alienating all sides. But today the world had grown too small for such independence. Each pillar depended on the other to support the dome of heaven. Well, Talala, once dead, would be more famous and would do more for his people than he had ever done while alive.

Gogandaev thought of Ersari and Baxram and the others and laughed to himself. A little religion was a very good thing. Too much blinded a man. Oh, they would all get what they wanted. For a few flashing moments. But Mustafa Gogandaev was not such a fool as to believe that Central Asia was ripe for government by Islamic fundamentalists. No, that was years away. But fanatics were always impatient, and these men had persuaded themselves that the millennium was already at hand. You had to go carefully with such people. And you had to be certain you could get rid of them once they had served their purposes.

In the morning he would fly back to Tashkent. To meet Talala before the old fool flew to Moscow. Then he would make an appointment with Akanayev to bring him up to date. The leadership of the Communist Party of Uzbekistan, already looking beyond the days when there would still be sense in calling themselves Communists, had to remain informed if they were to force Moscow to behave as desired. When things started to happen, they would happen quickly. It would be important to maintain control of events and the reactions they inspired.

It had been a long day and Gogandaev was tired. But he was never a man to let opportunity pass him by. He turned onto his side, reawakening the boy who lay sweet-breathed beside him, and kissed him deeply.

15

LESKOV LAID THE OPENED BOOK DOWN ON HIS CHEST and rested his eyes. The ceiling light made an orange-red horizon behind his eyelids. Fitting color, he thought.

One of the very few perks of which he took advantage as a KGB colonel was access to books. All kinds of books. At present he was reading the first volume of *The Gulag Archipelago*.

He believed what was written on those pages. Although he was too young to have firsthand knowledge of the really bad days, he had experience enough of his people—not just the KGB, but the Russian people as a whole—to understand how all of it had happened.

The statistics that wanted to drip zeros off the page and the anecdotal histories of a suffering too vast to comprehend neither shamed nor angered him. It all simply saddened him to the point where he had to lay the book down over his heart and pause.

It seemed as though his people were forever condemned to make the worst possible mess with the best of intentions. The early Bolsheviks—many of them, anyway—had truly wanted to build a better world, to create a new order of justice and decency, of dignity and freedom from want. But they had relied on a blueprint created by an intellectual who knew philosophy but not his fellow man, refined by others who had despised the laborers they idealized. Oh, the words sounded so lovely, even today. But the reality was a catastrophe.

It had been a fatal error to assume that all men were inherently virtuous and selfless, that they only needed to be freed from the old regime. It had been folly to assume away greed and jealousy, hatred and simple misunderstandings. In retrospect, it seemed to Leskov that any system that relied solely on man's innate goodness was fated to reinforce the very opposite tendencies in the human character. Then there was the legalistic paradox: only law and honest policemen allowed the citizen to explore his potential goodness. Freedom was a very powerful drug, and too much of it could be fatal.

He felt the weight of that mortality in the streets. Delighted to cast off old, repressive strictures, his fellow citizens were running blindly over the edge of the abyss of freedom. It was in the blood, in the blood. Where the Westerners had centuries of compromise genetically programmed into them, his own kind knew only extremes. Either freedom that collapsed into anarchy, or a world of camps and human ciphers.

What is to be done? he thought mockingly. What is to be done?

For his part, he had determined to be as honest as he could be, to work hard, and to cultivate a higher level of patience than the boorish apathy to which his countrymen were prone between their intoxicating stabs at revolution.

He opened his eyes. On the wall opposite the foot of the bed hung a painting of Yalta. A vacant street curved down from a hill, water running silver in its gutter. The sky was a dark blue that almost stormed, and the curtains of the nearest house swept out of an opened window, reaching toward the invisible sea, toward the observer. It was a rich, quiet painting, and it had cost him much of his savings when he bought it from the tiny woman with the crimped back. She had told him that the painter, one Alexander Ivanovich Leskov, would someday be recognized as a great artist, one of the greatest of his generation, and the buyer should treasure his purchase and protect it. The tiny woman spoke with such unrestrained joy and affection that it was clear to Leskov that she knew his brother and that she understood and valued his work on a level that Leskov himself could not. He could only say he liked it, without the words to explain why.

Well, his brother had always had quite an effect on women. On all shapes and sizes of them. Leskov wondered if his brother even realized that the crippled woman was in love with him. Well, sometimes it was better not to have trained eyes and ears, not to be conditioned to alert at the scent of human weakness. In the crowded art shop among the staring Soviet citizens and money-heavy tourists, he had wanted to reach out to the tiny saleswoman, to lay a hand on her unlucky shoulder and tell her to forget Sasha, that he would only hurt her. But it would have spoiled everything, and besides, Sasha was right. It was none of his business.

Perhaps Sasha *was* right. Floating from one woman to another. Without investing his soul. Perhaps it would even save him from the Talala girl.

God only knew what a mistake he himself had made, with his notions of loving.

But then there were the boys to think of. You couldn't count them as a mistake.

It was astonishing how you could love with all your heart and mind and soul without exciting or sustaining love in the object of your affections. Amazing that so much feeling could have no effect at all. It seemed to Leskov that the only true happiness was to love and be loved in return. And those lucky enough to experience that—how little they seemed to grasp the rarity of their good fortune: to love and be loved.

Could you honestly say you loved your work? No. Perhaps you found it fulfilling, even became addicted to it. But that was not love.

Work. Leskov lay in his sparsely furnished room in the KGB dormitory for bachelor officers and transient officials, staring at a painting he no longer saw. Down the hall a roil of masculine laughter marked the point in the evening, in any evening, when lonely men came together to share a drink and a joke, anything not to remain imprisoned in their rooms any longer. His people, his kind. Whether security officers or dissidents, Party hacks or hairdressers, they could not stand to be alone. And yet, he was often alone. By choice. The mother's blood, he thought. You can't escape it. Any more than Sasha can stop being his father's son.

Leskov hoisted the book back to the light, but soon laid it down again. We're all prisoners of so much, he thought. It's a wonder we can make up our minds to cross the street.

The afternoon meeting had been typical. No one had made a decision. If only the bearded zealot who had compiled this book could have seen us, Leskov thought. The mighty KGB. Unable to make a decision to make a recommendation so that higher-ups could make a decision to make a recommendation so that the highest and mightiest could decide to decide.

The issue was nuclear weapons. At the height of the Cold War, the military and security services had jointly devised a program to disperse nuclear weapons storage sites throughout the Soviet Union, often to remote spots, to ensure that some of them would survive a first strike by the Americans. Today, some of those storage facilities lay in increasingly unruly republics. Guarded by KGB units, the nuclear weapons were safe enough for the time being, and most nuclear weapons were in fact of no use to a gang of street thugs or even terrorists, unless they happened to have a lot of know-how plus missiles or jets or heavy artillery to deliver the warheads. But with the distant republics talking about independence and threatening to establish their own armed forces, the situation was growing ever more troubled. While much of the rhetoric from the republics was simply hot air, events in the Caucasus had shown that some men, at least, were willing to back their words with blood. From the Baltics to the Chinese border, the formerly docile were becoming dogmatically anti-Soviet and anti-Russian.

A bright staffer in the Kremlin had raised the issue of nuclear weapons security, and now the Kremlin wanted an answer. One by one, KGB experts offered their in-house assessments of the threat level in the various republics and autonomous regions. The views tended to fall into two main camps. There were those who did not want to acknowledge the potential problem at all, since they believed it would reflect negatively on the KGB's competence and abilities if the weapons were to be withdrawn precipitously. Prestige was critical in times such as these. Ultimately, the matter could be "handled." The best policy, according to the adherents of this school, would be to exercise tighter control in the outlying regions, to clamp down now before things got out of hand. The remainder of the experts believed the weapons should be evacuated. Bring them all back to Mother Russia, and do it immediately. Before some incident occurred to embarrass the security services and perhaps create a very real danger. None of the officers present offered an objective analysis. True to their training, they considered the political implications first—especially the implications for their own organization.

Leskov tried to give a sober assessment. First of all there was no threat from organized crime in this regard. And the level of unrest in Central Asia remained much lower than in other real and potential trouble spots. He projected two types of localized disturbances over the next two to three years. There would be violence based on old ethnic rivalries within the region. Then there would be protests based on regional ill-feeling toward the Slavs, who were currently decried as exploiters and nothing more. But all of the disturbances would be local in nature. Without a unifying factor, no region-wide or even republic-wide unrest would occur. Finally, while a threat to nuclear storage sites could not be fully discounted, should it occur it would come from a fringe group. The central authorities remained by and large dependent on Moscow, although they were distancing themselves wherever they could. Any threat to the storage sites would be because of their symbolic nature, not because any of the weak radical factions in Central Asia really expected to seize and employ nuclear weapons.

"So, Pavel Ivanovich," a thick-lipped general had said, "you're in favor of leaving the weapons where they are? In the specific case of Central Asia?"

"Yes," Leskov said. "Certainly, there's a potential for problems. But I think it would be too hard to keep the withdrawal a secret. It would be perceived as a vote of no confidence in the local authorities, just when we should be bolstering them. And it would be perceived as an admission of weakness. My recommendation would be to proceed with the withdrawals of the tactical warheads from the Caucasus and to see how that goes. If the program runs smoothly, we may decide to proceed with withdrawals from Central Asia under the guise of fulfilling disarmament treaties. Anyway, if we don't calculate Kazakhstan into the problem, there aren't that many storage sites down there."

"So you see no real threat?" the thick-lipped general pursued him.

"Comrade General, rioting could break out tomorrow over some minor issue and it could spread all across the map. I can't guarantee anything. But I see no sense in prodding a sleeping tiger."

"Noted," the general said. "Pavel Ivanovich believes the weapons should stay put. Who's next?"

In the end, they had all agreed to put off the resolution for more study. Everyone was afraid. That it was all coming apart. This issue was only one among many.

He had returned to his office to find one of his assistants waiting with a message from an informant in Tashkent. Leskov listened, and something inside of him went sick. The timing was too bitter, it had the feel of fate.

"There aren't many details," his assistant said. "But our man claims that one of the Sufi fundamentalist groups is cooking up trouble, some sort of disturbance. And Talala's involved somehow."

"But," Leskov said, exasperated, "it just doesn't make any sense. Talala's always kept the religious crowd at arm's length. He doesn't trust them worth a damn. Besides, public disturbances aren't what he's about. He's a dead-of-night operator. And there's no profit in stirring things up. His line of work wants peace and quiet at home."

"But . . . if you still believe he was responsible for the death of Colonel—"

"Yes," Leskov snapped, "I know. I *know*. Damn it, I wish I could think clearly for once." He pushed off from his desk with both hands, banging his roller chair into the old iron radiator. "What the hell would he get out of it? Why on earth get involved with the fundamentalists? It's asking for trouble."

"Well," the assistant said, "maybe he's not involved in a positive sense. Our man didn't really know much. All he said was that Talala's name came up when the fundamentalist thing was being discussed."

Leskov wiped a hand over his forehead, pushing back his thinning hair. "I've just got to think. Talala. Fundamentalists.

Public disorder." He shook his head. "Where the hell's the tie-in?"

His assistant sat thoughtfully. He was a good man, a thinker who just didn't have the knuckles to get ahead in the organization. Leskov had taken him under his protection, for what that was worth.

"Get in touch with our man," Leskov said. "Tell him his information's not good enough. Tell him we need details, facts."

"I already have, Comrade Colonel."

"Listen, Arkady Petrovich, you're a smart bugger. What do you really make of all this?"

The assistant shrugged. "I really don't know. But I'll say this—I don't like the smell of it. My gut feeling is that our man isn't just picking this up. I think it's being fed to him. I think somebody's giving him just enough information to tantalize us. To prepare us for something, to steer us in a desired direction."

"And which direction is that?"

"I don't know."

"Well, that makes two of us. But . . . that's an interesting proposition. I need to think about that." He loosened his tie and undid his top button. "Maybe they'll throw us another bone or two. Where's Talala today?"

"Flying back to Moscow. There were other rumors, not connected, about some kind of dust-up down in Tashkent. Apparently the Party boys locked his heels and explained the nature of the universe to him."

Leskov nodded. "Probably over the border incident. I can imagine the reaction that got in Tashkent. Talala's going out of control, and it's not the way those boys like to do business."

"You'd almost think," his assistant said idly, "that Talala's getting to be more trouble than he's worth."

Lying on his bed in his undershirt, listening to his comrades laughing down at the end of the hall while he plodded through a book by a man who despised him although they had never met, with his thoughts drifting tiredly from a beloved brother who would not be loved to the unbelievably hard-souled woman who was the mother of his two sons and on to nuclear weapons sleeping in the far country, Colonel Pavel Ivanovich Leskov suddenly realized that he was a fool.

An absolute fool.

He sat up in bed, paying no attention to the book as it slid down over the bedclothes and thumped onto the floor. It was all so clear. As clear as such a matter could ever be.

Talala had not established any sort of alliance with the religious fanatics. On the contrary. He was going to be their victim. Perhaps in the course of some sort of staged disturbances. Oh, there were a thousand details to be worked out, but Leskov's instincts were fully aroused. Without a single shred of proof, he knew with utter certainty that Talala's own people were going to kill him. Leskov did not know when or how or where or why. But he knew in his soul it was coming.

The question was whether or not it should be prevented.

Samsonov stood in the battalion headquarters, sweat clotting inside his exercise uniform. The synthetic fabric clung and itched, and the legs of the track pants were always too short after washing. He could not help feeling at a disadvantage across from the perfectly uniformed operations officer.

"He's not here this morning," the ops officer said.

"Where is he? How can I reach him?"

The ops officer smiled as though they might share a manly secret between them.

"The battalion commander . . . doesn't always feel obliged to report his whereabouts."

"I need to talk to him."

"Oh, come on, Mikhail Nikolaievich. It can't be all that important. Maybe I can take care of it for you?"

Samsonov looked him in the eyes. "All right. It was your tasking, anyway."

The ops officer smiled as though he had known all along what was coming.

"How on earth," Samsonov continued, "do you expect me to train my men when you keep siphoning them off for bogus details?"

The ops officer glanced around the crowded room and closed a hand over Samsonov's biceps. "Come into the commander's office."

A moment later they were alone behind a closed door.

"No need for the rank and file to hear all this," the ops officer commented.

"Comrade Major, you knew well in advance that today was an important training day for my company. It's been scheduled for weeks."

"Yes. Urban assault, suppression of snipers, that sort of thing. Very useful." The man's voice implied that he was talking to a bright child, but to a child, nonetheless.

"Correct. We've got permission to use an army training site for one day. And I've got transport laid on, special equipment, field rations, pyrotechnics . . ."

"But what's the problem? No one would dream of interfering with your training. In fact, we all find it very ambitious. Admirable."

"But you've pulled seventeen of my soldiers."

The ops officer tightened his eyebrows in recollection. "That's another matter. Every company has to contribute to the accomplishment of the mission."

"What mission? I'm trying my damnedest to train my men to do their jobs. To accomplish their mission, as I understand it. What mission is it that takes away seventeen of my men?"

"Missions are diverse."

"These kids haven't done shit for the past year. They couldn't even guard their own bunks, let alone contain public disorder. Half of them have never fired their assigned weapons. They're just a pack of disorganized thugs."

"Now, now. Surely it isn't all that bad. They did extremely well on the last unit inspection."

The office was very hot. The dead air plastered the exercise uniform to Samsonov's back and thighs.

"You and I both know what it takes to do well on those inspections."

"Standards are standards," the major said.

"But why? Why today? And why seventeen? You know damned well they need the training."

The major leaned back onto the edge of the commander's desk, making himself comfortable for as long an argument as Samsonov wanted. Every minute spent arguing was a minute lost from the planned training.

"Why? Because those men were requested by name. Your company just happens to have the best carpenters in the battalion. If not in the entire regiment."

"They're not in uniform to be carpenters. And who requested them by name?"

"Warrant Officer Kuzba."

"That cake of shit. The regimental commander moved him out of my company. And you still let him take my soldiers."

"The battalion commander," the ops officer said, "has great faith in Warrant Officer Kuzba. The man gets things done."

Samsonov balled his fists, perching them on his hips. Then he dropped them away again in disgust.

"And what happens," he asked, "if one day we're actually expected to perform in an official capacity? What happens if there are riots, a natural disaster, prison revolts—any of the things we're supposed to prepare for?"

The ops officer smiled indulgently. "I admire your conscientiousness, Samsonov. I really do. But let me ask you something. This regiment has carried this number and been in these barracks for twenty-seven years. Do you know how many times we've been called upon to respond to a serious problem in those twenty-seven years?"

"Things are changing. The times—"

"We parade," the ops officer said, spreading out empty hands. "We answer the roll call. Sometimes we escort prisoners, although there aren't so many of them these days. We supplement the detention-center guard forces during holidays. We build the occasional dacha or maybe a new sports hall. And we allow the high and mighty to sleep well at night, knowing that we're available if anybody turns out to be foolish enough to disturb their rest on a scale the KGB can't handle." He smiled. "Although everybody knows they'd call out the army before they'd call on us. We're the ultimate auxiliary troops, my friend. An afterthought to an afterthought. Blessedly forgotten." He slapped his hands onto the thighs of his perfect trousers. "Oh, I understand your discontent. I really do. Paratrooper. Well, *ex*-paratrooper, anyway. And a Hero of the Soviet Union. Cast down into this trough. Of course, you want to make an impression. To do great things. But sooner or later you're going to have to face the facts, Mikhail Nikolaievich: there are no great things to be done here."

For a moment, the major personified everything Samsonov

despised in his countrymen, especially in the millions of bureaucrats, in or out of uniform.

"You're talking about the past," Samsonov said in a carefully controlled voice. "Things are different, things are happening. Sooner or later we'll all be called upon. Look at Sumgait, at Nakhichevan . . ."

"We're not in the Caucasus. We're in Moscow. Count your blessings."

Yes, Samsonov thought. And that's that. He knew he was wasting time. By now his soldiers would be in their duty uniforms with their side arms issued. Waiting for him.

"Thank you, Comrade Major, for your generous consideration."

The ops officer lazily returned Samsonov's salute. "Don't be a hardhead. There's no future in it."

Samsonov marched out through the office with its sleepy complement of clerks—boys either sharp enough to manage the endless paperwork the officers did not want to do themselves or sufficiently well-connected to merit a soft, safe position. Samsonov wished he could train them for a few weeks. Just to give them a taste of a real soldier's life.

A thin boy with a fouled complexion and the shoulder boards of a junior sergeant flagged Samsonov down.

"Comrade Captain? I have a message for you." He bent down over the mess of papers on his desk.

Samsonov paused, mind idling. In the distance he could hear the out-of-tune growl of trucks. Waiting to transport his soldiers to the training site.

"Here it is," the junior sergeant said. He held out a scrap of paper: a phone number, and the words, "Call me at work, please. Vera Petrovna."

"When did she call?" Samsonov asked.

"Oh, a couple of days ago. I guess I forgot about it. Until I saw you, Comrade Captain."

Samsonov jogged off to join his company. He wanted to search out a phone that instant, to hear her voice. He could see her so clearly. Crying on the subway. She probably only wanted to talk about Leskov, to ask for some kind of help. But that was all right. He would accept any excuse to see her again. It took all of his self-discipline to go straight to his barracks block and his duty.

The training went better than expected. Lieutenant Bedny had done a good job of rounding up the necessary ropes and gear—overall, the lieutenant seemed to be trying hard to make up for past derelictions. Even the weather cooperated. A thaw had drawn the ice from the ledges and roofs of the abandoned buildings the army used as an urban-combat training site, and the day's dark clouds rolled by in silence, holding their bladders. At first the troops were sluggish and reluctant, with a few of them clearly afraid of the tasks before them. But as soon as Samsonov had lured a few of the company's roughnecks into rappelling down the side of a building, more and more of the others wanted to get in on the action. Samsonov showed them how to tie safe knots, how to lob grappling hooks, how to enter a window properly, and how to clear a building floor by floor, room by room, from the top down. He split them into teams and let them play against one another, with Lieutenant Bedny and him serving as umpires. All the while, he watched to see which of the troops had the most agility or the most sheer guts, judging which of them were liable to take foolish risks and which others would never have found the courage to throw themselves off the roof of a five-story building on a thin rope without the prodding of peers. During a brief lunch break, Samsonov trotted outside the facility to a public phone by a bus stop, dreaming of Vera, only to be disappointed upon finding that the receiver had been torn away from the body of the instrument.

He ended the day's training with a personal demonstration of more complex methods of rappelling, showing the men how to run a rope without a knot so you could retrieve it behind you, and how to run face earthward down the side of a building or cliff, firing as you went. Finally, he threw himself wide off the roof, sailing through the gray air on a single rope, and stopped himself within one meter of striking the ground. A number of the men applauded and yelled their approval, which was a far cry from the usual response Samsonov got as he tried to work them toward the minimum standards of soldierly effectiveness.

He could not think of them as anything but soldiers. And he feared the day when they would be called upon to do a soldier's duty. He had seen what happened to the slovenly draftees shipped randomly to the line units in Afghanistan, how their lack of capabilities, of basic awareness, had killed them or their comrades, and he had resolved to do his best to get these boys ready for whatever might come.

And he felt in his heart and soul that something terrible was coming.

"Next time," he told his men, "you're all going to do what I just did."

Back in garrison, he stood by patiently as his men cleaned their weapons and turned them in to the arms room. Only when the last automatic rifle was inspected and stowed did he allow himself to break away and walk—swiftly—to the nearest subway station, where he knew there was a bank of phones.

He almost missed her. Another secretary called her back from the hallway. As soon as she answered, the moment he heard her voice, he began:

"Vera Petrovna, I apologize. I only received your message today, and I—"

The woman laughed. Not forcefully, not with any real sense of humor. It was a laugh of instant forgiveness and perhaps even of relief.

"I'm so glad you called," she said. "I was beginning to think you didn't want to be bothered."

"Honestly. I only received the message today."

"I believe you, Mikhail Nikolaievich."

"Call me Misha. If you want to. Please."

"I'm glad you called, Misha. I thought perhaps . . . we could get together and talk again. I need someone to talk to."

"Of course." He had spent the whole day thinking over where they might meet. "Listen. Perhaps we could meet tomorrow afternoon. People don't know it, but the main military bookstore on Spasskaya has a little cafeteria upstairs. It's quiet. And they always have pastries and biscuits and—"

"I thought perhaps, if you aren't too busy, we could meet tonight. I can take a later train home."

"Tonight? Yes, of course. It's only that the bookstore closes—"

"There's a buffet in the station. It's . . . at least you can sit where it's warm."

"Wonderful. I'll see you there. I just need some time—"

"I'll be waiting for you, Misha."

Samsonov hurried back to the barracks to wash and put on a presentable uniform. He warned himself that it was important not to expect too much, to remember that this woman was in love with another man, and with a friend, at that. But he could not help thinking of her in a way that utterly ignored the situation.

For the first time in weeks he entered the cubicle where he worked and lived without feeling a pang at the sight of the half-empty bookshelves with their torn, twine-bound texts. He quickly changed into an exercise suit and gathered his toilet articles for the trip upstairs to the showers. The soldiers were at dinner and the building was very quiet. If he moved sharply, he would have a few minutes alone to get ready.

When he opened his office door, he was surprised to find that someone had switched off the hallway lights. Or perhaps it was just another problem with the electrical system.

He was even more surprised when his first step out into the darkness brought him a blow to the head that erased everything else.

Vera waited. She spent minutes then hours fending off reptilian drunks and the occasional militiaman. There were only two other women in the buffet and they disappeared intermittently, each time with a different man. Her tea went sour and cold. Every time an officer's cap appeared above the half-curtained doors, she alerted. But Samsonov never came.

She had hoped that he might be able to tell her something about Sasha, who would not even speak to her on the phone except to say that, although he was sorry, everything was over between them. She hoped Samsonov would visit him, as her spy. She wanted to know what was happening in Sasha's life, whether or not he had begun a serious relationship with the Asian girl.

It had all gone so terribly wrong. It was laughable. After all the months of lying to Sasha as she tried her best to get pregnant, she had finally succeeded. It was unmistakable. And now everything had gone wrong. More than anything else in her life, she regretted the fit of pique and pride that had led her to walk out of Sasha's door, leaving him alone with that little black bitch. She had been a fool to simply go, giving him what he wanted so easily. Had she stayed, she might have prevented anything irrevocable from happening, she could have persuaded Sasha to keep on loving her. But she had walked out of her own free will.

She wondered which of her sins she was being punished for. Perhaps simply for lying. But how could you live and not lie? God was so hard. Where was His mercy, His forgiveness? Had she really deserved this?

She imagined that she could feel the child growing inside her, although she knew it was too early. And she thought of the time before when she had needed to go to *that* clinic. It had been so horrible. She did not want to suffer that again.

Maybe that was why God was punishing her. For killing the other child. But what choice had she had? What choice was there ever? Or perhaps she was being punished because she had not been honest with Sasha about that. Perhaps she should have told him, confessing all. But she already knew enough men to know that their capacity for forgiveness was considerably more meager than God's.

The waiter eyed her with a mix of lust and impatience. God only knew what he was thinking.

If God wanted us to be so good, how could he make us like we are? What was the sense of it?

She looked at her chipped cup. Why did everything have to be so dirty? The world was so dirty that you could not help getting the dirt inside you.

A man entered the buffet in an officer's uniform. But the color of the fabric was wrong, and the man was too old, too heavy.

He had said he would come. He had told her to call him Misha. Why would he be so mean? He had seemed so nice. He had seemed . . . reliable. A reliable man. She grimaced, thinking that she should have known by now that there was no such thing.

The first thing that Samsonov realized was that he was still alive. The second thing was that not-quite-identifiable parts of his body hurt him. Someone was speaking, although at a very great remove. Someone was touching him.

"Comrade Commander? Comrade Commander, are you all right?"

"I'm all right," Samsonov said, surprising himself. He had no idea whether or not he was all right, how badly he was hurt. But it was automatic. Of course he was all right. He was always all right. He always survived.

"*The helicopters,*" Samsonov said urgently. "Can they get the helicopters in?"

"What?"

"Goddamnit, can they get the helicopters in? Tell them we can't hold out any longer."

"Comrade Commander—"

"Do as I *say,* man."

You had to move fast. You had to get it exactly right. One mistake and they would kill you and all of your men.

There was no firing. That was good. They had stopped firing. Maybe they were low on ammunition, too.

Maybe they were gone.

In a sudden panic, Samsonov opened his eyes.

"*Cover the rear approaches,*" he shouted. "*The bastards are in behind us.*"

Then he saw the poster on the wall. Lenin. What on earth? Was he in a hospital? Oh, not again. He never wanted to go through that again.

"It's all right, Comrade Commander," Lieutenant Bedny told him.

Yes. Samsonov tried to shake the hurt out of his head. He'd been dreaming again. What was going on?

His head ached terribly. His body hurt. He did not want to be wounded again, did not want—

He realized where he was. How foolish. How very foolish.

"I'm all right," he said.

"Can you sit up?"

He tried to rise. But his muscles did not reach far enough.

Bedny helped him, cradling Samsonov's big shoulders against a bony arm.

"Who did this?" the lieutenant asked. "What happened?"

Samsonov tried to smile. His face hurt and those muscles did not want to function, either.

"Don't know," he mumbled.

"Can you sit up alone? I'm going to call the duty officer."

"*No,*" Samsonov said. "My own fault. Foolish."

"You look like . . . I don't know what you look like."

"I've looked worse. I can promise you, I've looked worse."

He remembered now. They must not have hit him hard enough. Or he would not have remembered so easily. The darkness. A sudden explosion of lights. Yes. And then, when he was down, they had beaten him, kicked him. He raised a hand to feel if all of his teeth were still there.

His teeth were sound. He was glad. He had kept his teeth through countless parachute jumps and a bad war. It would have shamed him to lose them in Moscow, in his own barracks.

He moved his legs. Okay. And his crotch didn't hurt. He'd been through worse. Much worse.

His own men? Kuzba? Why? He was only trying to keep them alive. They just didn't know what it was like.

"I think," Samsonov told the lieutenant, "I'd like to wash the blood off my snout."

He could see the lieutenant's face clearly now. Very pale. Shocked. Just wait, Samsonov thought. Wait until you see a man laughing like crazy with his legs blown off below the knees. Wait. Until you see what an absolute mess a man is when his insides are on the outside. The chaos waiting to explode out of our guts. The way the blood covers everything.

With a twitch, Samsonov remembered something else.

"What time is it?" he demanded.

The lieutenant glanced at his watch. "Quarter after ten. I just got back from turning in—"

"Oh, shit."

Samsonov and Vera finally met. On a Saturday afternoon he waited for her under a small arcade on the Arbat. He was early, and she was late. Killing time, he smoked a cigarette and listened to a hate-spitting orator dressed in a mock-czarist officer's uniform. A woman, similarly dressed, collected donations and hawked mimeographed pamphlets. Most passersby paused only briefly by the last filthy banks of snow, milling in the cindered wet, listening for a few minutes then moving on. But a dedicated band of listeners functioned as a chorus, agreeing grumpily with the man's pitch.

Samsonov listened with a growing sense of shame, realizing that not so long ago he might have taken the man's arguments half-seriously. He was struggling to be a good man, to overcome his prejudices—even those against Central Asians. He refused to be a prisoner of his nightmares. He sought to master himself, to forge his soul into a tool of humane honesty, and he believed he was making progress. Even if he could not love every one of his fellow men, perhaps he could mature into patience and respect for them. It wasn't just idealism, he told himself, but a practical matter, as well. The country's situation was becoming so desperate that everyone would have to work together in the rescue effort. He was convinced now that he and his countrymen would never progress until they began to take responsibility for their own actions and failures.

It was astonishing, really, how a man could change, how he could come to view his former self with such disdain.

What a fool he had been. In so many ways.

"And who stole the Revolution?" the orator demanded of the raw city air. "The *Jews* stole the Revolution. Who plotted against the peasants and stole their land? *The Jews.* Who starved the peasants, the soul of the Ukraine and Mother Russia, to a miserable death?"

"The Jews," a spectator answered.

Heads nodded, a besotted voice concurred.

"Who is working secretly among us now to destroy the economy? Who's behind the shortages in the shops? Who's getting rich on the black market? Who does this cooperative movement benefit?"

The Jews.

The speaker took off his old-style cloth cap and waved it above his head. He looked mad to Samsonov, who could not fathom the level of serious interest the man seemed to excite.

"There is an unbroken Zionist conspiratorial tradition that seeks to keep the Russian people and all other Slavic peoples in eternal slavery. Jews and Freemasons in the streets of Moscow are working night and day to hold the Third Rome in bondage. Many of them have carefully interbred with unsuspecting Christian women to produce children who cannot be detected on sight. They take Russian names . . ." He made a fist around his cap and raised it heavenward again. "But their day is coming. Oh, their day is coming. We'll flush them out of the sewers. And the Third Rome will rise again . . ."

Vera took Samsonov by the arm, startling him. It took him

a long moment to transition to the full reality of the lovely blond woman at his side.

"Listen to that filth," he told her, tossing his cigarette butt to the ground. "Can you believe it? Is this what freedom brings us?"

He saw her looking at the bruises retiring from his face.

"It was the Jews who killed the czar," the orator shrieked. "He paid with his life because he had the wisdom to see through the Jew plots and schemes. God bless him a thousand times, Nicholas Romanov only wanted to keep Russia for the Russians, to prevent the Jews from squeezing the last kopeck from the Russian people . . ."

"He's crazy," Samsonov told the woman. He felt genuinely angry now, enraged by the memory of his own stupidity in years past, although he had never believed anything this extreme. "Nicholas the Second was an utter fool who threw away armies and his crown. Have you ever heard such garbage?"

Vera shrugged, squeezing his arm a little. "Oh, I don't know. It kind of makes sense, in a way."

He looked at her, surprised. "You can't really believe that? It's pure anti-Semitic claptrap."

Vera looked slightly wounded. "I'm *not* anti-Semitic. I just don't like Jews."

The orator began to sing. Male voices from the crowd began to sing along with him, although most of them stumbled over the words.

" 'God save the czar.' "

To Samsonov, this was pathetic, debilitating indulgence. The perversion of history as an excuse for failure. His countrymen always had a ready excuse for their failures, when what they really needed was to roll up their sleeves and go to work. He was about to give Vera a serious lecture when she suddenly collapsed against him in tears.

"Sasha's gone to Latvia," she said. "And I'm pregnant."

16

IT RAINED INTERMITTENTLY, WITH SQUALLS BLOWING IN off the Baltic, and Sasha turned up the collar of his leather jacket. Instead of taking advantage of the lunches in the officers' club where he worked, he wandered through the old town, remembering. How his grandmother had led him by the hand, and how it had been possible to feel every bone in her fingers. The old cast-iron cats on the roofs made him think of Vrubel, and he hoped his well-paid neighbor was taking adequate care of the animal. Then he went down the cobblestone alleys to the stolid German cathedral, recalling not the bitter history imparted by an aging widow but rather, his own past, where it was always golden summer and a child ate sweet cakes topped with strawberries while his grandmother dismissed the Russian language with a lavender wave, explaining that a Latvian gentleman needed to speak his own language, then German and of course, French, although English was not entirely without utility. She dismissed Russian literature as "the immaculate posturing of barbarians."

Now the Latvian people dismissed the Russians with graffiti splashed on the walls of medieval houses: RUSSIAN OCCUPIERS, GET OUT!

Nonetheless, his grandmother had spoken Russian with him as she patiently arranged the leaves of sound behind which meaning lay concealed, slowly bringing his Latvian verbs to blossom. He had not learned until much later how ill she was. Suffering from the effects of syphilis acquired from one or more of the men who had held her down in the passageway behind her home. In the first years after the war there had been no medicine. Later, there had been means to help but not heal her. The sickness had burrowed into her bones. Her face remained untouched, arrogant, hawklike, while her body crumbled. She stood erectly at great pain to herself, leading the child who was her last hope for meaning in life, telling him love-soaked tales of the country to which she so desperately wanted him to belong.

Now the boy was a man, with the first creases around his eyes, painting lies on the walls of the dusty officers' club on Merkel Street. During a recent demonstration, students had splattered the facade of the club with red paint, but inside all was quiet order and unwillingness, as the officers assured one another that they were merely biding their time. Revolution spiced the air, but the Soviet officer corps contented itself by hiring someone to paint the evidence of their glory on the walls of a seldom-used upstairs hallway. It was a joke, if a poor one.

Sasha strolled down his grandmother's street in the early twilight, eager to see the high curved window behind which she had lived and died. But it was all too hard in the end. Returning to his hotel, he went by way of the grubby street behind the brilliant art nouveau apartment buildings, where the servants had groused in wooden shanties in the days before even wooden shanties had become rare and desirable housing. It was a lonely, lonely city now, where a dead, disappointed woman roamed, and the man who had so let her down tormented himself with the imagined faithlessness of another woman who was far away.

Sasha had brought a new ghost to Riga. Shirin had never been there, never been exposed to the raw Nordic wet that had such a spare truthfulness about it. But Sasha's thoughts adorned the city with her. When it was dark, the old town grew heavy with monuments and mists, and the occasional brightness of a streetlamp reminded him of the unexpected fire that had only just come into his life. It seemed impossible, intolerable to him that Shirin was not by his side. So that he could kiss her fine lips and regale her with memories. Crossing the park where once the city walls had stood, the sight of meandering lovers made him slow his pace as their joy reinforced the weight of his loneliness. In the new town, the broad avenues and side streets with their celebrant turn-of-the-century facades filled his eyes but not his heart. He had always loved traveling, relishing the separateness, the freedom. He had never before missed a woman left behind with anything more than intermittent sexual nostalgia.

But he missed Shirin. For the first time in his life, he plagued himself with thoughts of what a woman might be doing in his absence. He recalled the snot who had been with her at their first encounter, and he could not bear the notion that she might be clutching such a creature against her breasts and belly. It was all so difficult. He understood so much about her, yet knew her hardly at all. And she had not even offered him a telephone number, miffed that he was leaving.

He worked dutifully on the mural project, anxious to finish. His task was to depict the long, noble struggle of the Communists to defeat reactionary, nationalist forces in Riga. The Latvian Rifles had to be worked in somehow, bristling with sacrifice. Then a panel had to show the fraternal deployment of the Red Army to defend Latvia against fascism. There would be nothing about the German advance, of course, or about the tens of thousands of Latvians who had volunteered to fight on the German side to rid themselves of Stalin's secret police. The visual narrative would simply move on by historical magic to the triumphal reentry of the Red Army into the city as the Germans were driven back. He was to end with a contemporary scene portraying the warm, binding relations between the Soviet Army and the local population.

It was a bigger project than he had been led to believe. There was at least two months' worth of work to be done. The thought sickened him.

He knew that Shirin would not wait two months for any man. She was too vital, too aflame. And she was so beautiful. She had no need to wait.

The first weeks were utterly miserable. And the tenor of the city made them worse. Riga had changed, in ways that should have thrilled him, that would have made his grandmother proud. Very few Soviet flags remained. Instead, the old Latvian colors flew. The theaters were full of *Latvian* plays, and someone had draped black crepe around the plinth of the big statue of Lenin on the boulevard. The city's museums and exhibition halls were full of *Latvian* displays. Buildings were being restored with pride. The works of forbidden painters had reappeared, and there were even plans to mount a major Vidbergs retrospective in the Fine Arts Museum. There were stunning exhibitions of Latvian design from the interwar years: graphics, chairs, ceramics, and fashions, displayed below old theater posters and handbills. Silent Latvian films had been resurrected for special showing. By any standards, it was remarkable what the tiny nation had produced in the brief years of its independence.

There were other exhibitions, too. In the history museum two large rooms had been rededicated to the victims of Soviet rule. The displays were agonizing to look at: glass cases filled with prisoners' gloves, broken eyeglasses, despairing, loving letters, lists of victims—and photographs, photographs, photographs. A young husband. An accomplished actress. A balding politician and a braced military officer. Doctors, writers, lawyers, hoteliers, policemen, shoemakers, carpenters. Black-and-white miniatures of life, captioned:

Shot.

Missing.

Died in the camps.

Died of unknown causes.

Shot.

Shot for antiproletarian activities.

Sentenced to fifteen years.

Died in the camps.

Shot.

Shot.

Shot.

The men and women who had designed splendid radio cabinets or tried to govern, who had made a nation laugh or sought to heal its illnesses, who had drilled with hunting rifles on the weekends and tended dairy herds on the green, green land:

Shot.

The photographs, the eyes, the smiles anticipating no harm, the hair carefully groomed for the camera—all this struck

Sasha with a force that no written words could have transmitted, that not even his grandmother's stories had managed to convey.

On leaving the museum, he tried to strike up a conversation with two women attendants in the foyer. His Latvian was grammatical and in his view, not at all bad, although he clearly had an accent. But the women were not interested in talking to him, and when he finally gave up his attempt to assert his Latvianness and walked away, one of the two women followed him with a stage whisper:

"Russian scum."

In the stores the clerks would not sell him anything worth having. He did not have a residence card, therefore he was not entitled to shop in Riga. Immediately upon hearing his Russian accent, the shopgirls became ruder than the lazy little bitches in Moscow, who set a very high standard. He walked out onto a city bridge, leaning on the railing, watching the hydrofoils separate from the dock and refeeling the antique skyline of the old town. He held an unread handbill in his chilled fingers. The poorly printed headline cried, "Freedom!" There were rumors that the Republic of Latvia would formally declare its independence from the Soviet Union in May. But Leskov was a Russian name . . .

The old hotel where he was quartered had no hot water and no really clean sheets, but it did serve good Latvian beer, if you were willing to wait forever for a waiter's attention. The lobby was spacious and warm, but smoky, with the electric lights weak as though they had lost a little more energy each year since the hotel's heyday between the wars. He always envisioned how elegant it must once have been, all nut wood, leather, and brass. When his unkempt room became too lonely, he sometimes came down and sat in one of the great bruised chairs and read. The desk clerks had no interest in him since he was not one of the odd Western tourists who strayed in when the newer Intourist hotel was overbooked, but that was all for the best. He was content to sit and read and dream, although one night he did sketch the lobby, populating it with figures from his grandmother's youth.

He was not wanted elsewhere. He was just tolerated at a disco where, after paying an outrageous cover charge, he was allowed to sit amid drunken Iraqi military officers who interrupted their pilot training each evening to pursue enormous Russian whores with boxes of cheap candy. It was the kind of place where the militiaman took his bribe right over the counter and the waitresses only perked up at the sight of hard currency. The bored bandleader pocketed a tip and dedicated yet another rendition of "Lambada" from Mustafa to Natasha with love. Sasha went back to his room early and sketched Shirin's portrait from memory, tearing up sheet after sheet of paper when she simply would not come right.

It was a bitterly lonely city. He traced out the cartoons of the murals, trying not to think too much, doing it all mechanically. But now and then a sketched face would begin to bear an uncanny resemblance to one of the photographs in the history museum, and he would have to begin again to ensure that his subjects all wore the bland, unscathed features prescribed for Soviet heroic painting.

He realized that he had been a fool. He had imagined that Riga would welcome him with open arms, as one of her own. He had thought that he would always have a home, that Riga wanted him. But only his grandmother had wanted him. He had not earned his way, but had simply assumed that all this was his by birthright. Thinking like a Russian, he told himself sourly.

A few weeks into his stay the early-spring showers thickened into a storm. Although it was only a few blocks from the officers' club to his hotel, he was soaked through by the time he pushed in through the oversize doors. He tried to shake off some of the water before penetrating the heart of the lobby, but it was hopeless. He would have loved a warm bath, but he had been informed there would be no hot water again this week due to ongoing repairs.

Miserable, he went to the desk for his key.

The dull-eyed clerk drew out the room key, accompanying it with a small white envelope. He handed both items to Sasha with an air of doing the guest a very great favor.

Sasha tried to dry his hands on his clothing, but it only made them wetter. On the way to the stairs, he opened the envelope, holding it away from his body to keep the contents dry.

There was a door pass for the hard-currency hotel by the

Lenin monument. And there was a note with a room number.
It was from Shirin.

He feared someone might try to stop him. But the doorman readily acknowledged his pass, and the slope-shouldered militiaman in the lobby merely gave him a tired look. A girl behind a trinket stand glanced at his clothing and shoes, then went back to her reading. Sasha waited by the elevator, but no matter how many times he pushed the button, the device did not make a sound. Finally, a passing waiter said:

"Under repair."

He went up the stairs, past the garish sign promising an authentic Parisian revue in the hotel's nightclub, past the shut hard-currency shop, heading for the seventh floor. His wet shoes slipped on the stairs. Outside the dirty windows the near rooftops began to spread out and the wet streets gleamed under headlamps. The rain had gone dreary, but the storm threatened to lash back at any moment.

The hotel sought to appear as Western as possible, so the floor attendants were kept out of sight. Instead of sitting barricaded behind desks in the hallways and scouring visitors with their eyes, they hid in tiny cubicles, brewing tea and listening to the radio. The corridor leading to Shirin's room was vacant and pungent with disinfectant. Behind one of the doors a television played loudly.

But it was silent behind Shirin's number. He shrank with worry that she would not be there. Afraid of everything now, of all the thousand things that might still go wrong, he tapped the wood with his fist.

She opened immediately. As if she had been waiting and waiting. First he saw her eyes. Then the hair drawn back, the robe loose over her breasts. Behind her, the window showed rain streaks, a purple-black sky.

"You're wet," she said matter-of-factly. Then she was tight against him with a warmth he could feel through his sodden jacket. Her eyes shut and her mouth reached for his lips.

There was no helping any of it. He closed his wet arms over her. She tasted slightly stale, wonderfully familiar. Yes, she had been waiting. For him. He broke a little away from her body, still kissing her, and stripped off his jacket. Then she began pulling at his jeans, not caring about the shirt. Her robe opened.

"I'm bleeding," she said. "Does it matter?"

"Nothing matters."

The bed was very narrow, set lengthwise into a shelving unit. He had to pull her away every few minutes so her head would not strike the wood. It was up to him to look out for her since she did not care about anything except what he was doing to her body. She bucked against him, almost too strong, too desperate, and he dug into the mattress with his knees.

"I don't want it ever to stop," she said once, floating up almost to reality. Then she sank again.

She was so small. It was impossible to believe that she could be so small and yet so strong. She molded her thighs around his hips as if holding on to a horse without a saddle.

She was very wet, too. With an acid wetness. Wetter than the rain-wracked city. He could feel her blood running warm over his thighs. The wetness made her feel bigger and easier and he had to grasp her buttocks for purchase.

"Please," she said. "Your fingers. Touch me."

He teased her once, lightly, and she groaned as though he had been tormenting her forever. It did not take her long. Everything was compressed, intense almost to viciousness. She closed her eyes again and mounted a half-crazy smile. Her sounds rose, her body arched under his fingers. She shivered and almost squeezed him out of her. A cry tumbled down into a moan: a very deep, almost mannish noise. Then all the power evaporated from her limbs and she slapped the side of her face into the pillow.

He went at her roughly, cupping the top of her head in the palm of one hand to protect her from the headboard. Beneath him, she was two women now, one peaceful, with an angel's smile, the other with hips that never stopped churning.

Her face was so still, so perfect. He touched her with his free hand, the hand that had frisked away her devils, and it left a streak of blood on her cheek as though he had cut her with a razor. He caught the mortal scent off his hand, off the fingers where bright red mingled with dark clottings, and he surprised himself with the suddenness of his response.

"*Deep,*" he bossed.

"*Yes.*"

After a broken wave of kisses there was only the blather of a television behind the thin wall and the slap of rain blown hard against the window.

"I don't think," she said eventually, "it was ever so beautiful."

Then she ran a hand between her legs, painted the fingers broadly over his face, and laughed.

She was right. It had never been so beautiful. They lost themselves in the night, first one reawakening then the other. In the morning the storm was gone and he woke ferociously hungry, but unwilling to rise before he had reached into her again. It was too early for her. The sex pleased her, but she couldn't finish; her body woke slowly, in stages. She told him to end it without her, but he was hesitant. Out of love, out of vanity. So she took him in her mouth.

The bed was a disaster, a battlefield. Shirin's cheeks were brown with dried blood, her lips glazed with him. She kissed him, rubbing their mouths together, whiskers, blood, wet.

"When do you have to go to work?"

He had no idea what time it was. Early? Late? He looked around the room, but there was no clock. Only a litter of clothes and foreign-language books: a formal text, a Hemingway paperback, others with titles too fine to read from a distance.

"It doesn't matter. I'll go in later. Artists are eccentric. It's common knowledge." He stretched, stiff from the crowding of the single bed and glued over with the old liquids off their bodies.

"We can have breakfast together," she said.

The thought of breakfast made his stomach hurt with emptiness. He had not eaten any dinner the night before, he had simply forgotten it.

"We can have breakfast," she repeated, "and then you can go to work. And then you can come to me again."

An abrupt sadness cloaked him. "How long can you stay?"

She looked at him. And smiled. "A little while. We'll see."

"And the university?"

She sent him an expression of unconcern. It was all so easy for her.

"Later," she said. "Please. I don't want to think about it

now." She giggled like a little girl. "You've made me so full of you I can't think. There's no room for thoughts."

"We've ruined the sheets," he said, not without a childish pride.

"Oh, the floor attendant and I have already made friends. She'll understand." Shirin smiled. "Anyway, it'll give her something to gossip about."

He had so many questions for her. But she disappeared into the bathroom and turned on the water.

He decided to wait, to let her develop things as she chose. He was in love and didn't care for much else. He was in love, shamelessly happy, and only faintly troubled by the memory of his brother's words.

Who was she really? This ineffably desirable woman sitting across the breakfast table. She looked young and clean and pure in the morning light, as though she had spent the night in a virgin's sleep by her mother's side instead of contorting her body under him and pulling him greedily inside her. But the world was full of illusions. It was nearly impossible to get at the truth of things.

The truth was that he felt tired and old. Fucked out. He had hurried to the hotel without a practical thought, and now he sat unshaven amid the traffic of the breakfast hall, wondering how long he would have the energy to please her, how long it would be before the fire of youth drew her away. She looked profoundly lovely and desirable. Why on earth had she come all this way for him? And how had she managed it? His brother's warnings stirred in him again as he spooned his tea, echoing against his will.

There were three standards of breakfast service. The sprinkling of off-season Western tourists sat at the most bountiful tables, and the waiters more or less paid attention to them. The tables for the East European tourists were a distinct notch down in quality. The few Soviet citizens lucky enough to stay in the hotel came last. But it was enough. The breakfast was more than he was accustomed to eating, and he was able to stretch his belly with bread and jam.

"I'll quit early this afternoon," he said. "I can work right through lunch. I'll show you the city."

She finished chewing, then smiled at him.

"Perhaps you could visit me first? In my room?"

He smiled, too. This woman had come in answer to his dreams. They were spectacular together, and the first spring sunlight was drying the treetops in the park beyond the big windows.

Once in a lifetime, he swore to himself. It can only be like this once in a lifetime. And not in every lifetime. It made him feel mature to realize the rarity of the woman across the table. With her fine small hands tearing a piece of bread. No matter what her history might be, she was worth loving. He had decided to think of her as a jewel that had passed from owner to owner, none of them able to alter its essence and with no trace of the previous owners remaining.

He heard raised voices and music. Coming up from the street.

Automobile horns began stinging the air, then abruptly quit.

The song rang out clearly, and Sasha recognized it with a shock.

The Western tourists got up first. They hurried over to the windows and pointed, clucking away in German and in an English unlike the brittle classroom language with which Sasha was familiar.

Shirin nodded toward the foreigners. "When I look at them," she said, "I feel as though this country is nothing but one huge circus. And we're the performing animals."

Yet she, too, rose. The sound of the singing was magnetic.

Sasha followed her and they crowded in among the tourists and waiters. Everyone strained to see.

In the street below a crowd of several hundred people straggled from the parliament building, past the hotel, to the military headquarters down the street. They carried banners and placards in Latvian, Russian, and English. RUSSIANS OUT. DEMOCRACY NOW. FREE LATVIA. REMOVE SOVIET OCCUPATION ARMY. The flags of all three Baltic republics flapped and fell above their heads, maroon and white . . . red, yellow, and green . . . black, blue, and white.

"What are they singing about?" asked a tourist with a bright little pack belted into the folds of his stomach. "Does anybody know what they're singing about?"

After a moment's hesitation, a waiter said:

"They sing our national anthem."

"The *old* national anthem," a blond waitress clarified.

"We will be independent soon," the waiter said, breaking out of the armor of caution. "Perhaps even in May."

The woman by the tourist's side had been trying to take a snapshot through the smoked glass. Sasha found the richness of the fabric of her clothing fascinating.

"Isn't this exciting, Howard?" she asked her man.

And she was right. It *was* exciting. The Latvian police strolled along beside the crowd but made no move to interfere. The world was changing so fast. The unthinkable was becoming possible. Sasha was only sorry that his grandmother had not lived to see this. Despite the slights Riga had offered him over the past few weeks, he felt his heart go faster.

The crowd and the singing dwindled off down the block and traffic resumed. The spectators sat back down to finish their breakfasts.

"If I had any guts," Sasha remarked absently, "I'd be out there marching with them."

The sharpness of Shirin's reaction surprised him.

"They're asses," she said coldly. "Nothing will ever really change in this country."

She was wrong. His life had changed. As soon as he was outside, alone in the fresh, bright air, he swelled with the exuberance of love. It did not matter what slogans men hurled at one another, let them play out their chosen roles. Already cured of his momentary infatuation with politics, he felt indifferent to the crumbling of empires. He let his still-damp jacket hang open, greeting the change in the weather, the glorious turn of his life. Oh, he wished the Latvians well. Let them be free. They could even be free of him, if they wanted. He existed at a remove from all that. The desire he felt for Shirin was so strong that he was certain no external events could intrude upon it. The sun shone on the still-wet streets, the park was raw with new life, and nothing mattered but the marvelous woman whose bed he had just left. His brother was a lying son of a bitch. He'd known that much for years.

He threaded his way through the downtown crowds to his hotel, shaved, lay down on the bed to rest his eyes for a few minutes, and fell asleep for three hours. It was early afternoon before he made it to the officers' club, where two privates in ragged work uniforms were scrubbing the latest graffiti from the entranceway. He could still make out the words: RED FASCISTS.

Inside, officers from the headquarters filled the lobby, drawing out their lunch break. A colonel raged at a group of subordinates. A civilian had spit on him in the street. It was intolerable. It was high time to put the Latvians in their place. The country needed order, discipline. There was no respect anymore.

All just words. The ranting of men dislocated by the times. Everything was different now.

Except his job. He unlocked the storage closet where he kept his materials, then pressed himself back against the wall opposite his work, trying to get an overall view of the first sketches he had copied onto the plaster. It was such a joke. It could just as well have been 1950 as 1990. The shining heroic faces. The submachine guns held up like torches of liberty. The faceless German dead, heavy-booted in the rubble. It was vital not to think about any of this. It was only a job. Like driving a bus. It was none of your business which route your superiors ordered you to follow. You did your work, took your pay, and shut your mouth. He was lucky, in fact. He had so much freedom. And privileges. Everyone knew the paintings were just a joke. No harm done.

He worked until four. Determinedly industrious, unwilling to pause, he accomplished a great deal. He penciled in details and soaked in the luxurious anticipation of Shirin.

She was waiting for him. Perhaps she would always be waiting for him. The strength of his sexual response to her startled him and made him preen a little. They made love with a wildness that turned into uncalculated experiments. His body dreamed of a way to go deeper inside her than before, deeper than any other man had reached, and she rolled her head to the side, gasping, offering the occasional perfect word. They ravaged the sheets again and both had to wash before they could go to eat.

Of course her father was a mafioso. And so what? Was that any more dishonest than the work of some Party bigwig? Or his own work, for that matter? The country was built on lies and nothing but lies, and all Shirin's father's line of work meant was that she could negotiate a room in a hard-currency hotel or command a table in a restaurant. They ate in the Kavkaz, a basement nightclub where a citizen without connections or bribe money could not get through the door. It was heavy with smoke, a little unclean, and teeming with a mix of celebrating families, gangsters, whores, and privileged officials. There were no tourists in evidence and Sasha guessed the ambience was a bit too rough, too uncertain for them. But it was a marvelous place to sit across from his beloved and drink Crimean champagne.

A clanging band with an abundantly fleshy singer blasted down the hall, returning yet again to the easy rhythm of "Lambada," the rage of the season and a warm breath from the West.

Shirin asked him if he wanted to dance.

"I don't know how to do the lambada."

Shirin sniggered. "None of them do. I've seen how it's really done. But they'd arrest us here. Come on, anyway. We'll dance however you want."

So they danced, with bastard steps, Shirin teasing him along. On the close dancefloor other couples tried variations from a modified fox-trot to formless separateness. Two southern men danced together, circling, with their hands high above their heads. All of the men ogled Shirin the moment they imagined their wives or girlfriends weren't looking, and Sasha thought only of the moment when he would lay her down naked on the spotted sheets in her hotel room.

Hard currency changed hands under napkins at nearby tables, and previously unavailable bottles of Georgian cognac appeared wrapped in dish towels. The food was plentiful and spiced. Sasha ate with enthusiasm, fueling himself for the hours alone with Shirin.

After dinner, pleasantly touched by the alcohol, he led her through the park, past the art institute and the museum, heading for the street he loved most, his grandmother's street.

Even at night the old splendor was obvious. There was nothing like it anywhere else in the Soviet Union, nothing like this combination of lightness and pride. He tried to explain it to her, to share a bit of the legacy with the first woman he had ever really loved in such a way. He laughed at a remembrance and told her how, when the Red Army settled in back in 1940, the wives of the ranking officers had decided to go to the opera. They had plodded arrogantly down the aisles wearing nightgowns purchased in Riga for the occasion, imagining that they were elegant evening gowns and delighting those members of Latvian society who had not yet been deported or shot.

Shirin laughed. She had a hard, small, uncompromising laugh. He pointed out the details of the buildings, leading her by the arm. Cats darted and a drunk pissed in an entryway. Down at the end of the street the guards in front of the KGB headquarters stood drearily in a pool of light. He told her how the Riga city government was doing everything in its power to preserve and restore its heritage. He told her a little bit of the true history and even tried to describe the lascivious purity of Vidbergs's prints. He told her a little about everything except his grandmother, merely pointing out the architectural oddity of the great curving window above the trees.

They made love again. And again. In between, they stood in the darkened hotel room looking out over the city lights, past the old church spires and the insinuated line of the river, past the cankering new apartment buildings on the far bank and the big communications complex, looking off into the distance, not wanting to see too clearly. They ate sugary chocolates and drank salty mineral water and kissed until their chafed bodies hunted against each other one more time. He made love to her with no real energy remaining, softening in the process, slowing, almost sleeping, then firming again at some slight smell or touch. She was worn, too, and only the wetness he had left behind in her let them go on. Finally, she could not climax anymore. But it was still too beautiful to stop, it was as though making an end now might mean making an end forever. He had never felt such a physical desperation. Then he fell asleep, only to wake again ready for more sex. He did not even know if she returned fully to consciousness. And it did not matter. It was all a dream. His last orgasm was little more than dryness.

He dreamed of a human-headed dog. The creature tore at his stomach. He had no hands, no arms with which to fight back. The dog was orange and bloodred and it chewed agonizingly into him, and there was no one to help him and he could not run away. He woke, imagining that he was screaming, but Shirin lay dead asleep beside him, exhausted and breathing so deeply it was almost a snore. He gathered her long hair away from her neck and touched her with his face, closing her in an arm, holding to her for salvation. She was so frail, really. Asleep, muscles relaxed, she felt as though a strong child could snap her in two. He slept again, without remembered dreams.

The morning came gray, and when he awoke, Shirin had already risen. She stood in a silken wrap, staring out the window at the cupolas of what should have been a church, at the column of a statue, at the future. When he closed her in his arms from behind, he was startled to find her crying.

"What's the matter?" he asked. He had never dreamed that this woman might cry.

More diamonds fell down her cheeks.

"It's so beautiful," she said. "Do you think anything so beautiful can last?"

17

THE GUARDS AT THE GATE TO THE TALALA FAMILY COMpound outside Samarkand recognized Mustafa Gogandaev immediately and allowed the two carloads of men to pass. Their interest only awakened when the second car stopped just inside the gate and two men emerged from the rear seat. By then it was already too late.

The lead car with Gogandaev halted directly in front of the main house.

"Remember," Gogandaev told the other occupants packed into the vehicle, "there's the wife, two daughters, the boy. Six servants. And two more guards."

It went very quickly. The inhabitants of the great house were so surprised they hardly thought of resisting. Only Talala's wife attempted to strike back, clawing at her attacker's eyes. But the bullets were much quicker and more powerful than her fingers.

Gogandaev's companions killed the two old male servants first. There was no hurry with the women. When Gogandaev entered the children's quarters, the girls and the little boy, all herded together, gave shrieks of relief still shaded with fear.

"Uncle Mustafa!"

But Gogandaev merely turned to the life-beaten faces of the men around him and said:

"Recall the sacred injunction. No female should die a virgin."

Then he grabbed the little boy by the upper arm and dragged him into another room. When he was done, he left the boy broken-necked on a carpet and came back out to watch the men with the girls. They were already too badly off to scream anymore. But they made interesting sounds. It was a shame, of course, that the whore Shirin wasn't here. But she had disappeared. No one could find her in Moscow or anywhere else. Whores had a devilish instinct for self-preservation.

"Enough," Gogandaev commanded, finally impatient.

A knife appeared.

"No," Gogandaev said. "This has to look like the work of Slavs. Beat them a little more then shoot them."

The sixteen-year-old stopped screaming. She looked at Gogandaev with eyes that were far too old and knowing for her age.

"Kill that one first," Gogandaev said. And he went to inspect the work of the other members of his party.

"My children, too?" Ali Talala asked in disbelief.

"Wife, children, servants . . . all that could be found," Gogandaev's heavy voice reported through the telephone.

"My wife killed, too?" Talala demanded, utterly unable to accept the words already spoken.

"As I have said," Gogandaev told him, his voice softening.

"All my pretty ones? Did you say all?"

"You must seek to bear it as a man."

"I must also feel it as a man," Talala said in a suddenly icy voice. Then, dropping the receiver into his lap and curling over it, he began to wail as though someone were methodically breaking his bones, one after the other. He could not help himself. He was no longer a man. Tears staggered down his cheeks. "Did heaven look on . . . ?" he begged the empty room around him. "Did heaven look on . . . and not . . . ?"

Gogandaev's voice, made tiny, sounded from the fallen phone. At last, Talala brought the warmed plastic back to his ear.

"My eyes," he said, "my eyes are a woman's eyes."

"You must . . ." Gogandaev said slowly, "bear it as a man."

Talala shook his head. How could such a burden be shouldered? How could the stars look down without taking part in the defense of his family?

"Who?" he begged the distant voice. "Who has done such a thing?"

Gogandaev hesitated. "It's unclear . . . but the way it happened . . . the things that were done . . ."

"Mustafa, son of my heart . . . what do you believe?"

Gogandaev paused, then sighed and spoke:

"I believe . . . it was the Ukrainians. They have betrayed you. They have betrayed us all."

"But how? How could they do this? It's not an hour since I spoke to Balenko. He . . . offered me a consignment of Scotch whiskey."

"All Slavs are dogs. They lie. They have no honor. And . . . if you could see . . . if you could see the way they did these things . . ."

"Tell me."

"I cannot."

"Tell me."

"No. With all the respect my heart feels for you . . . I cannot obey."

"Please. Tell me. How they—"

"It's over. You must go on."

"The girls. My little chicks. Did they—"

It sounded to Talala as though Gogandaev, too, had begun to weep. "I have taken care of everything," the distant voice said. "It will not be known . . . the details . . ."

Talala nodded in gratitude. The shame, added to this agony, would be too much.

He had already thought of Shirin. She had been almost his first thought after the reality of the tragedy had struck him. He had not heard from her in days. But that was not unusual. She was such an independent girl, the girl who should have been a son. Perhaps she was unharmed. He decided to say nothing to Gogandaev about her. He did not want to trouble the younger man's heart further, certain that Gogandaev, his right hand, had special feelings for Shirin. Of course Gogandaev concealed them. Out of humility, nobility. In a world where there was so little honor.

"Mustafa, son of my heart . . . there is a matter . . . I do not want to dishonor the memory of my wife . . . but you . . . you know my heart . . . the burdens . . ."

"It is all right," Gogandaev said. "I have already seen to the matter. Ashi is safe. The old one told me she was sleeping like an angel."

"An angel," Talala said slowly, grasping at the image, "an angel."

"But . . . father of my soul . . . if you will allow me—have you news of Shirin?"

Talala imagined the torment in the younger man's heart.

"She is away," Talala said, trying to be merciful. "I believe she is safe." He spoke the words with conviction, as though he could force them to be true. "Mustafa, my son . . . are you certain that *all* of them . . . ?"

"I am sorry."

"I cannot . . . believe it."

"I am sorry. I have seen them. All."

"And you believe that the Ukrainians . . . ?"

"My eyes tell me that. And my heart."

"But *why?* There would have been wealth enough for all."

"You know the Slavs. Their greed. Their treachery."

Talala closed his eyes, visualizing the horror yet again. The girls. His poor, innocent girls. How they would have suffered. He could not stop his mind from filling with pictures so lurid they bent him down, forcing him to clutch his belly.

But the boy. At least the boy would have died . . . without degradation. At least his son would have gone to God unscathed by this hard, hard world.

"How can it be?" Talala asked. He steadied the receiver against his ear.

"If you know where Shirin is," Gogandaev said, "you must tell me. Let me protect her."

"I don't know. I know nothing. I'm an old man." And for the first time in his life he felt as though it were true. He had become an old man. In minutes.

"We must find Shirin."

"Don't worry," Talala said vacantly. "Don't worry." He wanted to comfort the younger man. But it was so hard. "I will care for Shirin."

"But you will need time. To strengthen yourself."

Time? What was time? As though a man might hold it in

his hand. Or bind it to his wrist, pretending that the circling slivers of metal regulated the universe. There would never be enough time to bear this pain.

"I am strong," Talala said, wishing to believe it. "I still have you, son of my heart. Together, we will punish the devils who did this thing."

"We will punish the devils."

Talala could bear it no longer. He rested the receiver back on its cradle without a word of warning. Yes. The devils must be punished. But first he needed time. To mourn. To begin to believe.

He rose, hands astonishingly empty. He walked across the thick bed of rugs that covered the floor and opened the door to the outer chamber of his Moscow apartment.

His two bodyguards looked at him nervously. Whatever they had heard, it had been too much for them. Or perhaps they had only felt the indescribable sorrow in the air.

No, Talala remembered. He had moaned like a woman. And he feared, he was apt to do it again. He did not know how much longer he could control himself, how much longer he could remain upright.

Why had the Ukrainians done this? There would have been enough for all.

He knew why. He understood it. It was the first law of the conqueror: there had to be more conquests. There could be no peace, no contentment. When the men on horseback left their hills, there could be no going back. The Ukrainians had simply recognized the truth more quickly. And he had paid dearly for his blindness and his trust.

"Leave me," Talala told his bodyguards. There was no fear in him. Nothing mattered now.

"Revered—"

"*Go.*" His voice was the voice of a lion, as though the terrible striped beasts high above the Registan had come to life. A lion with the stripes of a tiger, a killer and a king.

The bodyguards hurried to unlock the front door. Talala knew they would merely loiter in the hallway until morning. But at least he would have a measure of privacy. In which to give way to his grief.

He turned back to the main room where his family had so often waited for him, to the chamber he had tried to turn into a dream of the tents in the hills of his childhood, rich with carpets and antique helmets, with silk and old wool burnished to the texture of velvet, with silver and brass. He had tried to bring his home with him to these northern streets. But it all had been an illusion. He had managed only to bring the evil of the north to his home.

The prayer rugs in his private life were rare and beautiful treasures that hung on the walls. For the first time, he strode over to a silken masterpiece that had come from Persia in the years before borders became such definite matters, and he tore it from its fastenings.

He laid the carpet so that it pointed away from the northern men, away from the Western delusion, and knelt upon it. He spoke no words, chanted no prayers. His mind was empty. But his body rocked and bowed like a mechanical doll gone out of control. He hammered his forehead into the fabric, grinding the skin, longing for the knotted treasure to convert itself magically into glass, nails, stone.

Suddenly, all of his strength left him and he froze with his forehead down, cradling his throbbing head between his forearms, fingers clasped behind his neck.

"God is great," he cried, as though drunk with the knowledge of heaven. "Truly, God is great."

There was so little left to him. A sick woman he loved profanely, helplessly. And a daughter scorched with a man's soul. He had known for years, perhaps forever, that Shirin would never find happiness, that she was marked by God to suffer and end badly. But he had struggled against it. He remembered how he had held her in his arms when she was a child. And how she had ridden a wild pony better than any male child might have done, with her braided hair flying.

He would try to shield her just a little longer now, to spare her every precious minute of life. His own life was nothing.

Slowly, he lifted his forearms and torso. Then he let himself fall again.

"God is great."

The love between Shirin and Sasha was bound to fail, of course. Everyone knows such passions cannot endure. Love lasts only between those ready to compromise, to settle, to surrender. Shirin burned much too brightly simply to flicker down into the mortal night of togetherness. She lived in a hard country and was sometimes destructive by circumstance, although, in fact, she wished to do good. But the desire to do good is as much the enemy of love as is time itself. Success in love may bloom from a thousand varieties of selfishness, but never from the will to effect good. Most absurdly of all, Shirin sought a lover who could take the place of God. She never realized it. But it is precisely those physically vibrant, sexually annihilating human beings who harbor within them the fiercest longings for revelation. It is no accident that the religious poetry of medieval saints gasps with imagery so sexual that we still feel their torment after so many centuries. What other human activity reeks so muskily of God as sex?

Sasha is a lesser figure than Shirin. He has better eyes, but not that great emptiness of soul. Full of the beauty of the world, he experiences bouts of self-pity, but you certainly could not call him God-bothered. For Shirin, sex was a journey to a mystical destination. For Sasha, sex is pure physical ecstasy enhanced by the opportunity to dramatize himself. At his best, Sasha has just enough of an inkling of the infinite blackness beyond the last streetlamp to intuit the futility of loving a woman such as Shirin. Not consciously, of course. But like most men, Sasha is a coward where women are concerned. Confronted by a dramatic situation, Sasha might impulsively stand up to a bullet. But he will never be brave enough to love fearlessly a woman with deserts shifting through her heart. His weakness was a shame in this case because, had he been just a little braver, he might have made Shirin truly happy. Oh, he made her happy enough for a time in the bare little room where they played out the most beautiful hours of their relationship. But had he been brave enough to love without fear, without reservation, without caring for anything or anyone but Shirin, he might have become her mortal God.

Anyway, I am going to tell you how their relationship finally came apart. It is the story of two basically well-intentioned human beings who behaved with such vanity and stupidity that I can hardly bear to write it down.

"I'm bleeding," Shirin said.

Sasha looked up from his self-satisfied drowse. Shirin sat

on the edge of the bed, inspecting herself with her thighs opened. He judged the slender back swished with her hair, a love-polished thigh.

"Again?" he asked, idly touching her spine. "I thought that was all finished."

Busy with herself, she did not turn to face him. "No, this is different. I'm torn or cut or something. It hurts."

He scratched at her golden skin. There had been so much sex. *So* much. He did not want to cause her pain, but he could not help being a little pleased that he had injured her and not the other way around. They had been together in Riga for over a week and he was chafed raw, but able to go on, if necessary. They had pushed their bodies further than the flesh alone really compelled them. And he had proven the stronger. It was a relief. He felt beautifully weary, almost hallucinatory from the lack of true rest. And he felt proud of himself.

"Put some of that cream on it. It'll be all right. It was just too much sex for you."

She closed her thighs and leaned back over his torso, catching her shoulders lightly against the wooden backing between the side of the bed and the wall. Her breasts shone pale in profile, with little coffee tips. A flat belly.

"I just didn't want it to stop," she said. "It was foolish, I suppose. I should have said something to you earlier."

"Has it been bothering you long?"

"A little while."

Sasha laid a hand on her belly. Warm. As though the sun had been resting on her.

"Have you . . . ," Sasha said carefully, "ever had so much sex before? In so short a space of time?"

Ego-quickened, he waited for her answer.

She pulled her eyebrows tight, thinking back. She was totally innocent of the sense of his question, caught unawares by his matter-of-fact, confident voice.

"I've had a lot of sex," she said honestly.

"This much?" He rose slightly, pulling his hand back from her flesh.

She shrugged. "No. No, I suppose not. Anyway, nothing this intense. It's so beautiful with you."

Had Sasha been mature or wise or grateful by nature, he

would have stopped at that, accepting his triumph. But he was none of these things.

He waited a bit, admiring her flesh and simmering with jealousy. Then he returned to the interrogation.

"I'm just curious," he said nonchalantly. "Have you ever counted up your lovers?"

Shirin touched herself and made a face as if it really did hurt.

"I don't count," she said. "It doesn't mean anything. You just wash them away when you're done."

The image jarred him, calling up an unpleasant memory from the day before. She had left the bathroom door open and he had come round the corner only to see her squatting over the toilet, douching herself by drawing up the water with her hand. He had found it unexpected and revolting, but she seemed to think it was the most natural thing in the world.

Suddenly, Shirin smiled. It wasn't a very big smile, but it was beautiful and guileless. She laid her head down on his chest and tucked her legs up onto the narrow bed.

"You're the first one," she said, "who ever really meant anything." She rubbed her face over the hair growing above his heart. "I love you so much. I can't believe it."

"Weren't you ever in love before?"

She considered the question with great seriousness. "I thought I was falling in love a few times. But it always turned out to be nothing."

"How do you know," Sasha asked slowly, "that this won't turn out to be nothing? That you won't get tired of me?"

He could feel the muscles in her cheek moving against his chest. She shifted so that a breast flattened against him.

"No. This is different."

"But you've had a lot of lovers."

Her shoulders moved. "A lot of sex. You're my first lover." And she sighed, still naive when faced with the resolute folly of the male. "I didn't even know what sex was, really. I mean sex with love. It was all . . . just gymnastics."

He cringed, picturing her with countless others. In the coilings of sex. Imagining how his predecessors might have been better than him in one way or another. It chewed into his soul.

"Approximately how many others were there? Before me."

Shirin was silent for a time. Then she asked flatly:

"You mean complete sex? Vaginal? Or anybody who—"

"The ones who were inside you."

Her small shoulders moved again. It really was unimportant to her. Then she grimaced.

"Nine or ten?" she asked, as though he might know better than she did. "A lot of times I just couldn't go through with it. You realize you've chosen badly. The smell's wrong, or the way they touch you. I don't know. A lot of times I just got up and left. Maybe there were only seven or eight."

"Or maybe more?" The spoken numbers stabbed him.

"I'd really have to think about it." She raised herself up on one elbow, small breasts jouncing. She looked baffled, starting to alert to the dishonesty in his tone. "Why is it so important?"

"It's not," he said quickly, lying as he had never before lied in his life. He had made himself a promise that if the number of her lovers was less than twenty, it wouldn't mean a thing. But now even seven or eight seemed an astronomical and cruel possibility. He could never bear the thought that so many men had shared her. "I was only curious. I just wanted to understand you, to understand how you became the woman I love."

He pulled her back to him, determined to fuck her until it caused her as much pain as her honesty had caused him.

"Sasha, please."

He snorted and manhandled her under him. Then he kissed her and nudged his knees in between her legs. On the outside she was dry, just a bit gummed with his residue. But inside she was still soaking with him, so wet it hardly gripped. She made one slight noise of protest, but offered no physical resistance beyond turning her face out from under his kiss.

"You're hurting me," she said softly, as if it were merely a remark and she had already given up all hope of persuading him to stop.

"After all the times you've spread your legs," Sasha said with mock joviality, "one more time won't make any difference."

But it did make a difference. Shirin could not understand what was happening. Sasha pushed himself into her with exaggerated roughness, and she felt the delicate flesh tearing in little white streaks of pain. It burned, all of this unimaginably removed from the rumpled ecstasy their bodies had managed not an hour before. She tried to move her legs so it would not hurt as much. But nothing helped. Finally, she gave up and lay still.

Sasha had been groaning over her, gone with desire. Now his physical passion came to an abrupt stop. He remained inside her. But he lifted his torso away from her breasts and looked down into her eyes.

"I don't fuck corpses," he said.

She was bewildered. She wished he would get to the end and go to sleep. She needed to think. And she was hurt, and the hurt was rapidly expanding beyond the physical. She had resigned herself to letting him do whatever he wanted, sensing the devils in him. But she could offer him no more.

"Maybe I don't appeal to you anymore?" he said. "Maybe it's time to move on to the next cock?"

She almost told him she loved him, almost pleaded. But in the last instant, as his words tumbled down through the air and exploded in her heart, she began to go very cold.

"You're hurting me," she said. "Get off."

And he did get off. He seated himself coldly at the foot of the bed, surveying her as if she were his mortal enemy.

She simply could not understand the change in him. She loved him. Still. She loved him so much that no amount of cruelty or stupidity would ever completely destroy that love. She loved him far beyond her ability to explain it to herself or to anyone else. She had believed they were two halves of one soul.

"Maybe," Sasha said, lips thinned, "it *is* all about my brother."

"What?"

"My brother. That's it, isn't it?"

She was astonished. "What on earth are you talking about? You never told me you have a brother."

"Don't lie to me."

She was still reeling. It was as though a totally different person were sitting before her. As if Sasha had been possessed by a spirit, by an evil, evil spirit, the way it happened in the old legends.

She drew her body together, tucking herself into the most

distant corner of the tiny bed, then covered herself with the sheet.

Sasha did not realize it, but he had just seen the naked body of the woman he loved for the last time. In the days to come he would torment himself by remembering the line of a shoulder glimpsed in the chaos of sex or the way her belly declined toward the dark tangles. He would live to have many regrets.

He was tired, of course. Exhausted to the point where sex mingled with nervousness and capability dimmed. To the point where the world became unreal, after the body's spectacular passions had begun to wilt, mute, crack. Unable to accept his happiness as surely as he was unwilling to pause for sufficient sleep, he felt his brother's warnings throb ever more strongly in his heart. And even if all that proved to be nonsense, one thing seemed clear to him: if Shirin had been so easy for him to fuck, she would obviously be just as easy for the next man. And the next. In any case, she was not to be trusted.

The fact that he loved her with disabling intensity multiplied the explosiveness of the mixture.

"I'm going," Sasha said. He waited for a moment, but when the tiny woman curled up in the corner of the bed did not respond, he stood up, limbs weary, soul scorching because the woman had not crawled to him, begging for his understanding forgiveness and love. He turned his undershorts right side out, slipped them on, then pulled on his jeans. He looked down at the dark hair, the still face turned to the wall. He felt as though she had done something unspeakably brutal to hurt him.

He tucked in his shirt and cinched his belt a notch tighter than usual. He felt like spitting on her, insulting her further. At the same time, he wanted to reverse the process of dressing, to take her in his arms and comfort her. But it would have been unthinkable to behave so weakly.

In the morning, he knew from previous experiences, it would be all right again. His anger would cool. Really, it was important to get it all out of the system. There would be a reconciliation. In the meantime, the idea of sleeping alone, of really sleeping, did not seem so bad. He only wished he did not have to walk all the way back to his own hotel.

He put on his shoes, then his jacket, eyeing the litter of her room. The books had lain untouched since the first night.

He wished she would make a gesture, give him an opening. He glanced down at her. Had only she been crying, it might have been enough of an excuse to close on her again, to change the outcome. But her face remained still, open-eyed, dry. Regarding the stained wallpaper.

He gathered the few items he had left in the bathroom, making noise so she would know he was serious.

He longed for a word from her now. The anger was already fading. And he was sorry for what he had done. He was sorrier with every moment.

He left without saying good-bye.

He did not sleep well at first. He tossed, tormenting himself with alternate visions of Shirin, until his eyes ached dully and his skin greased over with a light, stale coating of sweat. Then, toward morning, he plunged down hard into unconsciousness and finally took the sleep he had needed for days. He woke just after noon, jarred by a maid's unceremonious intrusion.

He felt near panic. Unable to believe his foolishness. He was ashamed of himself, and sorry. It all seemed so clear now. He could not understand why he had been such an absolute and unforgivable bastard. Shirin was everything. And Shirin was innocent. It was only that the quality of her innocence was so different that it required more understanding than he had been able to sustain. He felt physically sick at the thought of his words and deeds.

He washed and hurried down through the dilapidated museum-piece lobby where it was always twilight. Out in the street, the sunlight came as a physical shock. The air still had a chill to it, but it was markedly different now, full of life, invigorating. He hurried past the other pedestrians, the sole focus of his life a reconciliation with Shirin.

It was Sunday and there was little vehicular traffic. But as he turned into Lenin Street, he saw a brightly colored crowd ahead of him, surrounding the freedom monument erected between the wars in the heavy Nordic style then popular. The column towered over the still-distant Lenin with his arm outstretched toward Shirin's hotel.

Perhaps a thousand people had assembled, with more strolling in from the center of the old town, across the park, from the side streets. They held placards and banners he could not yet read, but the maroon-and-white flags and the folk costumes worn by many of the women sent an unmistakable message.

A bald man addressed the crowd with the help of a handheld megaphone. The device crackled and squeaked, sabotaging the clarity of his speech. But the inner circle of the crowd applauded, and their applause spread back to those who could not really hear, who could only intuit the message.

On any other day, Sasha might have stopped to listen, to nibble at the dream: freedom, independence, a history restored. But behind the crowd, Shirin's high-rise hotel dominated the skyline. He looked up past the trees with their first flecks of green, hoping that he might somehow pick out Shirin's window, that he might spot her looking out, waiting for him. But all of the windows looked the same.

Three girls in folk dress unintentionally blocked his way, one of them lovely, all three laughing and smelling of lilacs. He darted between them and a stubble-faced man clutching a bottle of beer.

On the far corner a knot of uniformed men in black berets watched the demonstration with hungover faces.

But all of that was another story, another picture. He jogged across the last street, digging into his pocket for the hotel pass. But it wasn't really necessary. The doorman was off his station, watching the demonstration in the company of a waiter.

Sasha ran up the stairs. On the first floor, he quickly scanned the line before the restaurant. Just a tour group, perhaps Bulgarians. There was no sign of Shirin.

He ran upward, stumbling once. The stairs bit cramps into his calves. There was nothing in the world that he wanted to accomplish beyond holding Shirin in his arms again and telling her as humbly as he could that he had been in the wrong and that he was infinitely sorry. He had never apologized seriously to a woman; it was a manner of virginity in him, and he was anxious to surrender it.

He went down the corridor with long thumping strides. He wanted to run, but would not risk making too much of a scene and attracting the attention of one of the lurking floorwomen. He passed the room where the television always played loudly and the noise was indescribably welcome, a sign that everything might still be as it had been before his plummet into folly.

He tapped out a short, sharp burst on Shirin's door. Hoping she would fling it open and fall into his arms. But the response came slowly. He knocked again heavily, deliberately.

The door opened.

A man. Obese in his undershirt, unshaven. Sasha's first notion was that Shirin had taken a degrading lover out of spite. But the man's eyes only looked baffled, perhaps a little afraid. There was no smell of Shirin.

Stammering, Sasha looked again at the number on the door. No mistake.

"Sorry," he said. "Sorry." He turned back down the hall, feeling as if a strong man had just punched him hard in the stomach. Then he ran, stumbling down the stairs. Unreasonably, he hoped to spot Shirin on each landing, amid the crowd in the lobby. But there was no sign of her, no scent, none of her fire in the dull, disinfectant-stained air.

He queued until it was his turn to talk to the lone girl working the front desk.

"Excuse me. I need to know if a woman named Shirin Talala checked out. She—"

"Are you from the police?" The clerk's eyes were small gray stones.

"No, I'm her—"

"We don't give out any information on our guests unless it's requested by the police."

"Please. There's been a silly mistake and I need to—"

The clerk muttered an obscenity that was still a shock to hear from a woman's lips then looked beyond him, smiling exaggeratedly and greeting the next man in line in English.

Sasha went out into the street and stood for a moment in the bright, chilled light, trying to clear his head with deep breaths. The crowd down Lenin Street sang an old Latvian folk song and a militia vehicle raced down the street, followed by another.

He wandered back toward the old town, numb and unable to think. Then he suddenly woke up:

The train station.

For a few minutes he had hope again, telling himself that, leaving on such short notice, she would have to take a train. He would find her at the train station, waiting for him to overtake her.

He jogged across the city, blind to everything but the series of snapshots of Shirin flashing through his mind. But she was not waiting for him at the station. Nor was a telephone call to the airport of any use. She was gone, with magical speed, as though she had only needed to sling her belongings over the neck of one of those small desert horses.

He sat on a bench by the river, astonished at his stupidity. He sniffed his fingertips, but he had thoughtlessly washed the last trace of her away. A child waved from the deck of a barge while its mother hung out clothes to dry. The churning brown water slowly took them away.

Eventually, his mouth tightened with a sick grin and he rose again, crossing back over a flat, deserted square with a bad sculpture of false heroes. He pissed in an archway then cut sharply away from the old town, crossing the green belt again, marching down a parallel boulevard to avoid the crush and gaiety of the demonstrators, following the smoky trail of a city bus route past the outer core of fin de siècle facades, past the shut shops whose windows tumbled abundance in comparison with the bare, hungry shops of Moscow. He went past young couples pushing baby carriages in the peaceful Sunday light, past new, already decomposing apartment blocks, past silent workshops and over a bridge that crossed the burnished plaid of the rail lines, through the deserted quarter of factories where it looked as though nothing had been modernized since the boom on the eve of the Great War—nothing except the huge billboards in faded primary colors shouting, Glory, glory, glory to Lenin the god, to Lenin the supergod, to Lenin the god for whom all mankind had waited down the millennia. Glory, glory, glory to Lenin, who had blessed Soviet man with new heavens and a new earth. *Glory, glory, glory!*

Beyond the poisoned creeks and soot-dusted shanties the world turned suddenly green. The spring was much more mature here, and the first full leaves tipped the branches where the sun lazed down. There were bird sounds and the occasional rush of an automobile.

He remembered the way, although his previous visits, years ago now, had been by taxicab or bus. The unmarked turnoff onto a gravel road lined with tilting utility poles had not changed. Two young deer stood in a field, as though remembered, as though they, too, had always been there. And he remembered the fence with gray paint peeling off the metal and the way the ground rose slowly to reveal the dense plantation of monuments with fading photographs of the dead held fast by marble wreaths. There were names and dates, dates and names. Fresh flowers caught the eyes, while only withered remnants lay on another grave. He remembered the path as though he had a map burned into his flesh.

Still, there was a surprise in store for him. The space around his grandmother's grave was perfectly kept, unlike so many of the other weedy, slightly unkempt memorials. It appeared as though a regular hand was at work. He did not understand it, after so many years. But his mind was on stronger stuff and he casually allowed that perhaps some admirer of the old woman was still alive, that she had enjoyed a love of which he had known nothing. Everyone had secrets.

It was pleasant to sit on the low rail around the next grave and let his sweat dry in the sun. It pleased him that someone else still remembered the old woman. Her resting place was a miniature garden waiting only for a bit more warmth and water in order to bless the eyes with color.

He had been crying for a long time before he realized it. The flesh, so recently everything, was a minor matter now. He spoke to his grandmother without words, raw emotion seeping through his flesh, toning the air, the gravel and grass, the still-cold earth. Silently, he confessed the utter mess he had made of everything.

The old woman had tried so hard. But it had done no good. He lowered his face into his hands.

In the background a few families paid their respects to their own dead. They kept their distance from Sasha, as if they knew better than to come too close. He decided he would try the hotel again when he got back to town, even though it would be of no use. It was just that a man needed something on which he could fix his hopes, something to believe in.

What had he ever believed in?

At last he spoke aloud to the marble marker before him: "What am I going to do?"

Then he rose and walked away. Without really thinking about it, he began to make the long trip back to town.

A new quarter of the cemetery had been opened along the access road, and a man in a dark blue worker's blouse swung a pick down into the earth. Sasha paused a few meters off, watching the labor until the man paused and returned the stare.

"You the caretaker?"

The man looked Sasha over. Then he wiped a dark blue forearm across his brow.

"One of them."

"Maybe you could help me?"

The man did not answer. His face was flat, neither friendly nor hostile. He had not shaved for a few days.

"It's about my grandmother. Peksnis. Charlotte Peksnis. She's buried over there." Sasha pointed across the regiment of markers.

The caretaker nodded slowly under the weight of the sky.

"Her grave's been tended," Sasha went on. "Somebody's been taking care of it."

The man's skull moved again: yes.

"Can you tell me who's been taking care of it? I'd like to thank them."

The caretaker smiled slightly, then a bit more broadly. Half of his front teeth were gone.

"Thank me, then. I take care of it."

The look on Sasha's face struck the man as comical and he laughed.

"Not for free or nothing. Nothing's for free so long as you're up here on top of the ground. I get paid for it."

"Who pays you?" It suddenly seemed very important to know who else had loved the old woman, who had done a better job of loving her than he had ever managed.

The caretaker thought for a moment. "Well, I'd really have to look at the records. It's there somewhere." He grinned, black and yellow. "I don't remember names so good unless you're dead. Anyway, the money always comes on time. In the mail. I only met the guy one time."

"Can you at least tell me what he looked like? Anything at all?"

The man shrugged, then leaned on the handle of his pick, pondering the visitor. "About your size. Losing his hair though. A little older than you." He coughed and emptied his throat onto the earth. "You know how it is. All them officers look alike. All's I can tell you is he was KGB."

On Monday morning Sasha arrived at the officers' club punctually and found a staff officer waiting for him.

"General Kondratov sends his greetings. He was looking over your sketches yesterday and he was delighted."

"Great," Sasha said. The response was automatic, official, uncontrollable.

"He just wanted me to pass on his hope . . . that the project will be finished in time for the May Day celebrations. There's going to be a dinner, quite an affair. And if you don't see a problem . . ."

"I'm anxious to finish."

"Good. Very good. The general will be pleased. And of course, if there's anything you need . . ."

"No."

"Good. Very good." The officer opened his mouth in a little oval, expressing that he had almost forgotten one little thing. "Oh, yes. The general did have one minor criticism. In the third panel. The Germans look, perhaps, just a bit too heroic. Perhaps you could do something? And the general would like a few more tanks in the background. He began his career as a tank officer, you know."

Sasha smiled. From the grave. "Easy to do."

The officer brightened. Clearly, he had feared an unruly discussion with some temperamental artist. But there was nothing temperamental about this artist at all.

"Good. Very good. The general will be so pleased. And I can definitely tell him the work will be done by the first of May?"

"I'll be gone long before then."

"*Very* good."

After the officer's departure Sasha drank a cup of tea with

the kitchen women then climbed the stairs to his world of colors and turpentine. He puttered through his materials, holding the long, polished handles of the brushes one after the other, saying good-bye. He closed his eyes repeatedly, strengthening his resolve. Then he stood back as best the narrow corridor allowed, taking one last look at his work.

The general was right. The Germans looked far too heroic. And the background obviously needed more tanks. With little red stars. More tanks. And more tanks. And more tanks.

The building in which the officers' club was quartered had been erected long before the Soviets arrived. Perhaps it had once been a czarist officers' club. It didn't really matter. All that mattered was the quality of the construction. The doors were big and heavy, and they fit perfectly into their frames.

The door to the big closet where he stored his supplies was perfect, opening from right to left. He drew it wide. Then he fit the fingers of his right hand over the lip of the frame, just above the lock, splaying them. With his left hand he gripped the door hard, as though afraid to lose control of it, as though it had a dangerous life of its own. He was sweating and his bowels felt loose. But he had made up his mind.

He took a very deep breath, closed his eyes, and slammed the door on his fingers with all of his strength.

18

SHIRIN WALKED INTO THE DARKNESS. THE LIGHT AND warmth of the subway station receded as her heels tapped along the concrete. Wisps of fog thickened the intervals of shadow between the streetlamps, dampening her face like the touch of cold, wet hands. At the end of the street the spiky mass of the university rose black against the diffused night glow of Moscow. The dormitories hid behind arcades of raw trees, and their lights floated in the mist as though the buildings were alive and lurking, preparing to make a move. But nothing really moved except Shirin and an occasional car back on the boulevard, and the soddenness of the atmosphere tamped down the sounds of the great city down across the river.

Shirin shifted her suitcase from one tired hand to another, feeling very much alone.

She had fallen asleep on the train and she had dreamed. There was a sickness inside her, deeply embedded, devouring her like a patient animal. Chewing her womb, her heart. She was dying. Yet she went about the everyday business of living and no one noticed. Even when the small sharp teeth of the disease bit suddenly, crippling her with pain, the men and women moving past her paid no heed. She woke to a middle-aged man's hand on her thigh.

She could not understand what had happened with Sasha. She felt sick and betrayed. One moment she told herself cynically that what she had gotten was a fair return for the idiocy of allowing herself to love, then, a minute later, she felt as though there could be no future for her without that same love. She knew it was over. She would never go back to him, never again share a bed with his strong, lean body. He had destroyed their chance together, and that could never be changed. But Sasha had seemed like her life's dream made flesh.

In the end it emerged that she had merely been so enraptured by the flesh that she had turned him into a dream. Never again, she told herself. *Nev*er again. There was no such thing as a great love. It was all an illusion, a mirage created by the heat of the body. Love was a lie.

She turned the corner and followed the formidable line of the buildings. They were like fortresses. But weren't all buildings fortresses? Inside which people barricaded their lives? Prisons to which men and women anxiously consigned themselves? It must have been better, she thought, when we lived in tents, when there was no choice but to feel the heat and cold and the desert winds right through the wool and felt, when there was no hiding from what you really were: a feeble, unknowing thing. The old women were right. The world was haunted by witches and jinn. And all of them were evil.

Staccato laughter sounded from a high window, falling like the clatter of dice on a backgammon board. The damp night pierced her skin. She wanted to curl up in her bed, facing the wall in the darkness so she would no longer need to worry about the face the world saw. She had been so angry. Ablaze. Furious. But that had burned out of her as the train pulsed beneath her rump. Mostly sorrow remained, the immeasurable melancholy left after the greatest hope in the world came to nothing. She was not weak. But she knew she was going to cry. It would take still more tears to wash the last of Sasha out of her.

It wasn't just that men were so vile. The worst of it was that they were ineptly vile. They could not even get the viciousness and abuse right. And all you could do when you were stupid enough to love one of them for a while was to wash him out of your system with your tears the same way you squatted and flushed the last of him out from between your legs.

The next lamp had gone bad and it was so dark she could barely see the line of pavement ahead of her. Each footstep sounded over a great hollowness, as though the crust of the earth were an empty eggshell. Dirty-cotton fog hung from the trees. She changed her suitcase from hand to hand again, flexing fingers cut by its handle.

A hand clutched her upper arm from behind. She dropped the suitcase just as another bigger, stronger hand grabbed her from the other side.

She twisted around as best she could, wanting to face her attackers, to fight. And she glimpsed shining almond eyes.

"Your father," a voice whispered in her native language, "has been looking for you."

She felt a glory of relief. Her father. Yes, he would have been worried. She had never just vanished for so long a period before. And it was so hard for him to close his eyes, she knew. But there was no choice, there was never a choice.

She breathed, filling the hollowness within her with cold, damp air. Her father wanted to see her. It was all right. Yet . . . a deep black place in her soul felt almost sorry that these strange hands were not going to punish her.

One of her new escorts released her arm and reached dutifully for her suitcase. A few seconds later, the other man let go his grip as well. It was going to be all right.

But there was something wrong, too. In the past, such men would never have dared lay a hand on her.

"You're going to Istanbul," her father told her.

She was shocked. He had not offered her a word of greeting. There was no embrace to carry her back to the gorgeous ignorance of childhood. Her father had not been this brusque with her in a long time.

"But . . . why?"

"You don't need to know why." His voice signaled a wild impatience, uncharacteristic. "It's time you began to do what your father tells you. Without questions."

They were alone in the main room of the apartment, where the floorscape of carpets and the tapestries on the walls devoured voices. The air was stale, as though the curtains had not been drawn and the windows had not been opened for days.

"Istanbul?" She was surprised, but she had nothing against such a trip. It would be a good time to go away. To go far away. To erase memories with distance. And she had never been to a country beyond the reach of socialism before. As a Young Pioneer she had gone on a youth exchange to the German Democratic Republic. And she had been on a sight-seeing and shopping tour to Prague. But Turkey would be interesting.

What if Sasha was on his way to Moscow? What if it could all be repaired? He would never be able to follow her abroad.

No. It was finished. Ruined. To compromise now would be unworthy, pathetic. All that she had felt—that she had imagined herself feeling—had been fouled beyond redemption.

"It's a special trip," her father said, gentler voiced. "It will be very good for you. Officially, you'll be a member of a state delegation negotiating a maritime agreement. You'll be an interpreter."

"But I don't speak Turkish. Uzbek is close, but it's not identical."

"It doesn't matter. It's a formality. You will be called upon only . . . in extreme circumstances. And you speak English. And French."

"But what will I do?"

Her father opened his hands. It was a small, nervous gesture. Shirin wondered what on earth was going on.

"Enjoy yourself," her father said without the least hint of a smile. He looked so tired. Older. "There must be a great deal to see in Istanbul. It will be educational for you." He drew a thick envelope from the inner pocket of his jacket. "Everything is taken care of. You will even have your own room. Here, take this."

It was money. Dollars.

A lot of dollars.

"There is an address, too. And a name. But you are only to make contact if . . . if something seems as though it isn't right. If you have some kind of trouble." Her father looked away from her as he spoke. Then, suddenly, he turned and looked deep into her eyes, as if searching for something.

"There's also a business card. For a shop in the Grand Bazaar. Where you can sell this."

He produced a necklace of elaborate gold filigree swirled about diamonds and emeralds. It was the most extravagant piece of jewelry Shirin had ever seen outside of a museum.

"Wear it. You'll be treated as a diplomat at customs. There will be no difficulties." Her father draped the piece across her collarbone, then closed it behind her neck. "Wear it under a sweater. So that no one can see."

His fingers hesitated on her neck. Trembling.

Shirin felt an explosion of panic.

"Father? What's the matter?"

Instead of answering, the old man pulled her against him. He smelled of coppery sweat and cheap scent. She shut her eyes and closed her arms around him, wanting more than anything in the world to be a child again and forever.

He held her very tightly. Without offering a word. She knew now that something was terribly wrong.

The embrace lasted a long time. Shirin hugged until her arms began to ache.

Instinctively, she sensed that the matter with Sasha had diminished in relative importance, that there were far greater dangers in the world than a broken affair.

"When do I go?" she asked, face still pressed against her father's shoulder.

"Tomorrow."

"So soon?"

"In the morning. The papers have all been prepared."

"What's wrong? Please tell me."

"Nothing. I only want you to see Istanbul."

She knew it was a lie. And she knew that he would know that, too. But it was only the spoken word, not the truth, that mattered now.

"Please tell me what's wrong."

Unexpectedly, she felt a small drop of wetness strike her forehead. Her father tightened his embrace.

"What could be wrong? When a man has such a daughter?"

"I'm a bad daughter." She was crying, too.

He raised the level of his arms so that he crushed her mouth against the fabric of his jacket, hushing her.

"God has his reasons."

"I've been so bad."

"You were meant to be my son. Life played a trick on us both."

They had never spoken this way before. And Shirin sensed that they would never speak to one another in such a fashion again. A man of her people did not speak in such a way with such a daughter. The only choices were to beat her and lock her away, or to close your eyes.

"I'm sorry," she said.

"A woman should never be cursed with the heart of a lion."

They were silent for a little while. Shirin thought that, if only it were true, if only she possessed a lion's heart, she would never have felt so much pain.

"Mother will worry," she said finally, thinking out loud. "She always worries."

Her father squeezed her. "I'll explain everything to her. And to your sisters and your brother."

"I'll have to bring back nice gifts for everybody."

"Yes."

"They'll be jealous."

"Everyone is always jealous of my Shirin."

"I'll have to phone them to say good-bye."

Her father twitched. "It's too late. They're all asleep."

"I'll call them in the morning."

"There won't be time."

The two of them stood leaning against each other for support, falling into their separate silences. Shirin felt as though the universe were shifting around her. It was an indescribably heavy, awesome thing.

"Something terrible has happened," she said suddenly. It was barely a question. The world was a place where only terrible things happened in the end. Where there could be no love or trust. Where everyone lied. "Hasn't it?"

Her father moaned and his face magically covered itself with tears, as if the drops had fallen from heaven. He released her, staggered backward, then sat down on the clutter of rugs. He looked frighteningly old.

"I'm a foolish, foolish man," he said. "I trusted the Slavs."

* * *

"I just don't trust the Uzbeks," Leskov told General Kerbitsky. He paced the rectangle of his office. "I think they're trying to manipulate us."

The general unplugged the cigar from his mouth and dusted the ashes from the breast of his uniform. He was gaining weight. Leskov knew that the old man overate when he was very nervous. Now Kerbitsky's tunic strained at the buttons as he sat. "How? To what end?"

Leskov locked his hands behind his back.

"That's just it, damn it. I don't know." He shook his head like a bothered horse, then buried his chin again. "I can't think it through. But I absolutely cannot bring myself to trust them as a source of information."

Kerbitsky's eyebrows rose, then fell. "Well, a good chekist never trusts anybody."

Leskov paced, turning at the desk just before his toes struck it. The smoke from the general's cigar was thicker than the fog that had settled over Moscow.

"A Central Asian never gives you anything for free. It's always a barter of some kind. There's always a purpose."

"You're describing mankind as a whole, Pavel Ivanovich." Kerbitsky centered the cigar between his lips and sucked in the smoke with a light snoring sound.

"At first it seemed to me that someone wanted Talala out of the way. Dead. I was absolutely convinced I had the answer. And now—"

"And now," Kerbitsky interrupted, "we're being given warnings so we can save his life. In the name of interdicting criminal activity."

"Yes," Leskov said, knee almost striking an empty chair. "Yes, exactly. Except that I don't believe anything has really changed. The pieces are all the same as before. I just can't fit them together."

Kerbitsky chuckled. He dropped the nub of his cigar onto the carpet and ground it out with his heel.

"Perhaps," he said, "I can help you out a little bit."

Leskov stopped and looked down at the swollen old man. Kerbitsky's eyes were alive with good humor.

"Please, Comrade General. I'll take all the help I can get."

"I have a bit of news. From separate channels. I think it may interest you. I know how it's been eating at you that

Talala has protectors in high places. In Tashkent. Even here in Moscow. And I know you'd like nothing better than to see him behind bars."

"There's nothing in the world I'd rather see."

The general shifted, trying to make more room in his uniform for his bulk. "Well, you can have your wish. Apparently, our friend has made the powers that be very unhappy. He's fair game."

Leskov unclasped his hands. "That's great. That's—"

"There's only one condition. You've still got to catch him doing something red-handed, something grossly illegal. We've got to be able to make it stick, to put him in prison and keep him there. With the full force of the law."

"With the full force of the law," Leskov repeated. His mind began working very quickly.

"It's apparently very important that Talala not realize he's being sold out by his former protectors. We snap him up and they'll make a great show of doing everything they can to protect him, to help him. But they won't really want him out. It'll just be a bit of theater. We've got to have an ironclad case, though. Something we can put in the newspapers so it can't be covered up. The way we planned it all along."

"They don't want him to talk," Leskov said. "They don't want him to start telling tales and naming names."

Kerbitsky shrugged. "One case at a time. The way I figure it, his protectors have plenty of other cutthroats under their wings and they don't want to lose their credibility. The KGB will have to shoulder all the villainy by itself." He smiled. "But we're used to that."

Leskov resumed his pacing. But he went more slowly now. "We've all become amazingly cynical, Comrade General."

"It's our job to be cynical."

"But . . . doesn't it bother you? That we live in a system where a man like Talala can prosper? Until the bigger fish decide to flip him out of the pond?"

"I suspect that men like Talala have always prospered. In every system. And I suspect they always end up about like this. He's simply become too much trouble. For everyone."

"I can't believe that. I can't believe there isn't a better way to live."

The general raised an eyebrow. "Careful, my friend. That's

still dangerous talk for an officer of the KGB. No matter how much things have changed."

Leskov was thinking, and he did not really note the seriousness in the general's voice.

"I have to tell you, Comrade General . . . I almost felt sorry for Talala. When I heard about the business with his family. Oh, he's a monster, all right. But he always took good care of his family. And you know how important family is to an Asian."

"Pride," Kerbitsky said. "He committed the sin of pride. May we be spared from it."

The secondhand smoke burned in Leskov's nostrils. "I've always tried to see the world through my opponent's eyes. Now I see Talala's world collapsing around him."

"And deservedly so."

Leskov ran a hand back over his thinning hair. "So he's simply become too much trouble? And that's that? And you don't believe they're playing us for fools, Comrade General?"

Kerbitsky shrugged, shifting the tight cloth over his shoulders. "Seems clear enough to me. They want him out of the way where he can't create any more embarrassments."

"So the KGB is 'allowed' to put him away."

"At long last."

"But why not just kill him? Why kill his family and not him? There's something that stinks about all this."

"Maybe it was revenge. Of a refined sort. They're a cruel people. And you told me yourself you don't believe the Ukrainians did it."

"Not a chance," Leskov said, sure of this one thing.

"But Talala wants blood?"

"Talala wants blood. It's the only way."

"So . . . if the competition didn't do it . . . that means his own people did. A revenge thing, like I said. Cut and dried."

"Well," Leskov said, "I'm convinced it was Central Asians. But that still leaves a lot of possibilities, a lot of factions to choose from. And remember that bit about the fundamentalists, the Sufi Brotherhood? They fed us that. Then the source went mum. My man in Tashkent can't come up with a single clue." He began to pace again. "I'm absolutely convinced somebody's trying to manipulate us. And I don't want to let any of those bastards make fools of us all."

The general twisted up his mouth, growing a little impatient. "I just think that they want Talala out of the way. And that's that. The word's come down the line."

"Then why not kill him? They're certainly not hesitating out of moral scruples."

The general reached into an outer pocket for his cigar case. In the old days, when his uniforms still fit him properly, he had carried his vices in an inner pocket.

"You've always told me what devils they are, Pavel Ivanovich. Now I suspect they're out for a special sort of revenge. First they kill his family. Then they help us put him away so he can live and reflect on his fate. Oriental cruelty and all that."

Leskov shook his head stubbornly, planting his feet on the carpet. "I still believe we're being manipulated."

"Don't you want to put him in prison?"

"Of course I do. I've been dreaming about it for years."

The general gnawed at the long cylinder of tobacco, then struck a match. He puffed the cigar to life.

"Then don't drive yourself crazy. One step at a time. We'll lock that son of a bitch up. And then we'll see."

Leskov ran his hand over his scalp again. The exposed flesh at the back of his head was damp with sweat. "You're right. I know. But it just eats at me. I don't want us to look like fools."

"And you personally resent the notion that some greater force might be controlling you?"

"Yes."

"Well, that makes you a very vain man. And a born atheist, by the way." The general poked his cigar at the air. "We're all controlled in one way or another. Parents, a government, a boss, a wife." He smiled. "And then . . . if there turns out to be a God after all . . ." He rearranged his backside. "We're being given a gift of Talala. And I'm all for accepting it as graciously as possible."

Leskov paused and leaned back against the edge of his desk. "I suppose you're right."

Kerbitsky nodded and drank more smoke. "I take it you'll move in on him when he tries to go for the Ukrainians?"

"Most likely," Leskov said. "Unless he gives us a decent opportunity before that."

"Remember: we want him alive."

"Or *some*body wants him alive. Even though it means he might spill his guts to us. As if that weren't a risk."

"The Asians never talk."

Leskov looked down at the general's feet. Kerbitsky always sat in the same place, and the old carpet was dotted with rust-colored burn marks.

"Anyway," Leskov said, "*I* want him alive. I want him to see that there really are laws, and that they apply to him as well as the next man."

Kerbitsky glanced up at him.

"In any case," the general said, "alive."

Leskov nodded. The density of smoke in the room was making it difficult to breathe. He wished the general would leave. Not least because some of the thinking he would have to do would be about Kerbitsky himself.

How had the dispensation to pick up Talala been passed down to the general? From Akanayev or even Karimov himself? Or from some other Party-cloaked criminal in Uzbekistan? Or had the blessing come from someone with a distinctly paler skin right here in Moscow? How did it all fit together?

He needed time to think. He did not really believe Kerbitsky was corrupt, of course. Nothing beyond the routine hunger for perks. He had witnessed the general's dedication time after time, that was the reason they had gravitated to each other. But what kind of system was this where criminals gave the highest law enforcement arm of the state permission to arrest someone? Leskov had truly believed that new possibilities had arisen with the changing times, that a clean sweep might be made, that the rule of law might ultimately triumph. But now it seemed that only the faces changed—and not all of the faces.

He looked across the soiled air at the general, wishing the old man would just clear off. There was work to do.

But Kerbitsky gave no sign of pending departure. Instead, he took the cigar out of his mouth and tapped the ashes onto the carpet.

"One more thing," he said to his subordinate. "You can relax. The . . . attachment between your brother and the

Talala girl appears to have come to an end. And no great harm done."

Sasha sat in the gray light of his kitchen, stroking his cat with his good hand. Vrubel lay sprawled across the table, as though serving himself up for dinner. Ordinarily, Sasha would never have permitted it—the tabletop was a declared cat-free zone. But it did not matter now.

The neighbor appeared to have taken good enough care of the cat, but Vrubel always hated Sasha's absences and had his way of letting Sasha know it. Upon Sasha's arrival, the cat had hurried to him, curling his head against his jeans and offering his back to be petted. But Vrubel soon mastered his excitement and pattered off to sulk over the interval of abandonment. Sasha had been sitting at the table for over an hour, going through his mail more from habit than interest and drinking tea, before the cat finally forgave him and plopped his furred guts over the litter of postcards and envelopes.

The sole letter that made an impression on Sasha was from Lev Birman, who was prospering in America. He lived in San Francisco and wrote that his paintings sold for phenomenal prices and that there was so much good food he was getting fat. There were plenty of girls, too, since all of the American men were homosexual. Lev concluded with a virtual demand that Sasha join him in America, where an artist could have a future instead of simply disappearing into the swamp of the Soviet Union.

Sasha replied to the advice with one brief, snorting laugh. He felt remarkably empty, unable to connect with the physical reality around him. The fingers of his right hand itched and ached and wanted to move inside their heavy plaster prison. The doctor in the Riga clinic had laid them over little steel rails, carefully straightening them and nudging them back into sense. She had shown him the X rays, mosaics of crushed bone. She was not hopeful. She could not promise him how much use of the hand he would regain. And she was sorry she could not offer him an anesthetic to help him through the ordeal. But supplies were short and had to be saved for truly severe cases. She was middle-aged and aging, brusque at first, with a personality that bristled like her short, wiry gray hair. Only when she read his case summary and discovered that he was an artist did she begin to soften, finally speaking to him as a mother might to a hurt child. She rolled and pressed the splintered bones, suturing and stitching the exploded meat, calling sharply to an assistant then slipping back into a mothering voice. The shock had begun to wear off and it hurt very much, but Sasha tried to be a man about it. Behind a torn room divider a little girl's snowy femur gored the air, and she managed to keep silent, even though her case, too, was not deemed sufficiently serious to merit even a local anesthetic.

"Moscow's cutting back on all our supplies," the doctor told Sasha in Latvian. "It's an attempt to show us how dependent we really are. As if the sick and injured have a nationality."

Sasha was injured and sick. With his smashed hand, and with thoughts of Shirin infecting him, poisoning his blood. Immediately upon his arrival in Moscow he had taken the subway to the Lenin Hills, so impatient to track down Shirin that he did not even go home to clean himself first. He finally located her dormitory. But there was no trace of her, no one had seen her for weeks.

Where was she? Somewhere in the depths of Central Asia? Off with another lover, consoling herself? What had he done?

It was evening when he finally made it back to his apartment, with all of Moscow under a heavy fog. The streetlamps had a peculiar detached glow, as if they were very far away, and voices carried from hidden mouths. Even inside his own chronically overheated rooms it seemed as though the vitality of the universe had been tamped down.

Each time he tore open a letter, awkward and left-handed, the sound of the separating paper stood alone, apart from all other things. It was as though the pall of fog had followed him inside, had burrowed into his soul. Confronted with the stack of mail, he had briefly thrilled with the possibility that there might be a message from Shirin. But there were only letters from Vera, which he put aside without opening, a note from Rachel, gleeful at the sale of another of his paintings, and the letter from Lev Birman, as well as a few identical notices from the Artists' Union and some postcards, including one posted from Budapest by a girl he had nearly forgotten.

He stared at the cat, touching the miracle of its life. The complexity of the mask around Vrubel's eyes, the perfect symmetry of the tiger pattern in the fur, never ceased to amaze him. Life was so beautiful, and all mankind did was spoil things.

"Hungry?" he asked the animal.

But Sasha made no move to rise and act. He continued to sit dully, ever on the verge of screaming out Shirin's name.

The phone rang.

Shirin?

It was Bilinsky from the Artists' Union.

"What's the meaning of this?" he demanded, voice raised, unwilling to waste a second on preliminaries.

"Of what?" Sasha asked flatly.

"You know what I'm talking about. Damn it. You're supposed to be in Riga."

"I broke my hand."

"Well, wasn't that convenient? You can't fool me, you arrogant son of a bitch. You told me yourself you didn't want to go in the first place."

"That's true."

"And now you conveniently break your hand."

"It's not convenient. As a matter of fact, it's extremely inconvenient."

"Don't be sarcastic with me, you shit. You get out of line with me and you'll never receive another military commission again."

"I don't want any."

"What?"

"I don't want any. The doctor wasn't sure whether or not I'll ever regain enough control of my fingers to paint again. But even if I do, I don't want any more military assignments. The glorious Soviet military can kiss my ass."

"You're crazy."

"Yes."

"You son of a bitch."

"Is that all?"

"No, that's not all, damn it. I've been getting calls for the last two days. General Kondratov's furious. He wants to know who's going to finish his murals."

"There are plenty of hacks around. It's not hard to paint that shit. You know it yourself."

"General Kondratov wants you."

"Well, he's out of luck."

"And he wants that project finished by the First of May."

"Send him somebody. The cartoons are already on the walls. It'll be easy."

"He wants *you,* you ungrateful bastard. Listen. I had an idea. I'll send Grubenko to do the actual work. But I want you to go with him. Supervise him, help him out. See that Kondratov gets what he wants."

"No."

"You can't tell me no. Listen, I can even get the honorarium raised."

"I'm not going. Not now. Not ever."

"You'll never work again. You'll *never* get an official exhibition."

"It doesn't matter."

"I'll have you thrown out of the Artists' Union."

"I resign."

"You can't behave this way. You can't talk to me like this."

"Fuck yourself," Sasha said. "And your shit Union."

"You'll lose your entitlement to your apartment. It's only yours by the grace of the Artists' Union."

"It doesn't matter."

"You'll have no place to go. Your ass'll be out on the street."

"I'll manage."

The doorbell rang. Vrubel jumped down from the table and trotted into the hallway, ears up, nose alert.

"You've betrayed a sacred trust," Bilinsky cried.

"Yes," Sasha said. "I have." He dropped the receiver back into its cradle.

The cat paused halfway to the door, waiting for Sasha. He looked up with an expression of a far more profound intelligence than Sasha had ever seen on the face of anybody in the Artists' Union building.

"They can all go fuck themselves," he told the cat, and together they went to challenge their visitor.

It was Vera.

She was wet. It must have begun raining. Even in the bad light, her eyes were very blue. So different from Shirin's eyes. Hopelessly shallow and unseeing, by comparison. Incapable of ever catching fire. Sasha's first thought was to wonder if he would ever be able to make love to another woman after Shirin.

"Can I . . . come in?" Vera's voice shook.

Sasha nodded.

But she made no move to enter. Her mouth opened, eyes fixed on the sling over Sasha's chest, on the heavy contraption peeking out from behind the cloth.

"What . . . happened to you? Your hand—"

Sasha shrugged. "An accident. It's nothing."

"But your hand . . . your painting."

"I'm going to take some time off."

She pushed past him into the hallway of the apartment.

"Are your fingers going to be all right?"

"More or less. It's no big thing." He watched as she slipped off her coat. He was unwilling to help her, unable, somehow, to touch her. As she stepped into the light, he saw that something had gone wrong with her complexion. She had tried to cover the little eruptions with makeup, but the rain had streaked it away.

"It's all right. It's normal." Then she took a theatrical breath. "I'm pregnant."

The cat, done sniffing, wandered back into the kitchen.

A month before, the news would have shocked Sasha. Now it was as if they were talking about strangers glimpsed on the street.

"You told me you were being careful."

"Accidents happen. Sometimes . . . when God wills a thing . . ."

"Vera, I told you all along—"

"Oh, I know. You don't want to marry me. I know. You told me."

"I'm not going to marry you. I'll help you, but . . ."

"I don't need any help." She said it blithely, a schoolgirl declining aid with her homework.

"Don't be silly."

"No. Really. If you won't marry me, if you don't want me anymore . . . I can manage on my own."

"How did you know I was home?"

She turned away, heading into the kitchen, her smile losing strength. "I didn't know. I've been coming every day. Waiting. To tell you the good news."

"Don't joke about it."

"I'm not joking. It *is* good news. I'm going to have a baby. Whether I have a husband or not. Whether the baby has a father or not."

"Vera, for God's sake. Think for a minute. In a country like this, in times like these . . . and you're young. You've got so many chances. But with a child . . ."

"I'm going to have the baby." She sat down at the kitchen table, eyes glancing over the litter of mail, her own unopened letters. "And I really would like a cup of tea."

"How long has it been? How many months?"

"Don't concern yourself. I told you, I'm going to have the baby."

He filled the kettle with tap water. "You can't blackmail me into marrying you, you know. It wouldn't work. It would only end in divorce, and then it would be an even bigger mess. I don't love you."

"But you *did* love me," she said suddenly. Sasha knew that her buoyancy, her flippant tone, was nothing but an act, a desperate attempt to brace up a falling sky.

"No. I never loved you. I never said those words. We had good times together. I have good memories. And I hope you do, too. But I never told you I loved you."

"You didn't have to say it."

"I never lied to you, Vera." He cleaned out the tea sock. It was beginning to tear. Then he opened the cabinet and reached automatically for the little tea bowls Shirin had given him. At the last instant, he caught himself and chose two old cracked cups.

Vera changed the subject. "Is that a letter from that Jew friend of yours?"

"Lev Birman?"

"Yes. Him."

"He wrote from San Francisco. He says it's wonderful."

Vera gave a snort of disapproval. "America's full of Jews. That's why he likes it. They like to crowd together."

"He thinks I should go to America."

"He's probably lonely. And miserable."

Sasha checked the sugar bowl for vermin. To his relief, there were a few remaining chunks of sugar, but no signs of life. "Anyway, Lev's probably better off than he was here."

"Maybe you should go to America," Vera said defiantly, pouting.

Sasha laughed, thinking to himself that, if he wanted a Russian wife, he could do no better than this woman. But he did not want a Russian wife.

The kettle made a simmering, waking noise.

"No," Sasha said, "I really can't see myself in America." He had never given it much thought. But America seemed so far away, so unreal. Not worth thinking about. In any case, he doubted the Americans would show much interest in granting a visa to an artist with broken fingers. With the Americans it was all business, business, business. He knew that much. "No, that's really not a possibility."

"Because of your little Asian whore?" Vera asked in a voice of mock sweetness. Sasha thought he had never heard so much bitterness in a woman's voice before.

"Vera—"

She exploded into sobs. "Your baby . . . your baby's in me . . . and you'd rather be with that . . . that . . ."

He almost weakened, almost took her in his arms. But he stopped himself just in time.

She lowered her face to the table, weeping into her hands, into the pile of mail.

". . . and you'd rather be with your black whore . . ."

Sasha looked down at the storm of golden hair. And he shook his head. Because she was right. If there was a single good reason for not going to America or anywhere else, it was Shirin. The faint possibility that he might spend one more night with her. That he might at least see her again.

Abruptly, Vera looked up, searching across the room with her wet blue eyes.

"Tell me . . ." she said, "at least tell me that you don't love *her*."

Sasha looked into her eyes. Their time together seemed immeasurably far away. As if he had made love to her in some distant childhood.

"*Please*," she begged, "just tell me you don't love her, either."

He told himself that it would not hurt anyone if he said the words she wanted to hear, to gentle her through her pain. She had loved him, perhaps loved him still, beyond the hunger for a husband and father for the child disrupting her beauty. He told himself that it really would be all right. But he could not get his mouth to open.

Her face took on a look of terrible fear, and she stared at him as though she had managed to look through his outer skin to see a monster lurking beneath. She began to shake her head in short jerks and her mouth opened, heavy lips trembling. Her eyes were red and shining.

"Oh, my God," she said, "oh, my God." Then she began to scream and jerk in her chair, stamping her feet on the floor.

He reached to catch her. But he was too slow. She hurled herself onto the floor, flailing with her arms and legs. The cat's hackles rose and he shot out of the room.

Sasha tried to stop her, to grasp her arms with his good hand. But she screamed as though being tortured. She kicked wildly, knocking the table away from her in stages, spilling the dregs of a bottle of milk over the floor and toppling a chair. She had no words left, only a primitive agony.

She began to make a long groaning sound. As if she were dying. As if her soul were dying. Her eyes shut and the expression on her face looked ridiculous, comical, the way certain unfortunate women looked when they reached orgasm.

He tried to work his way through the flailing limbs, but she struck him blindly in the face, very hard, and he drew back automatically, protecting his broken hand.

She began to breathe very deeply, with absurd exaggeration. She opened her eyes and said:

"Not her . . . not her . . ."

Then she curled up like an infant in the womb, an infant carrying an infant, and began to cry like a normal woman in pain.

The kettle shrilled. Sasha yanked it off the burner and switched off the stove. When he turned to face her again, Vera was sitting up against the wall. She looked at him with an empty expression, face raw.

"How can you be so cruel?" she asked. Her shins were bleeding from kicking the table and chairs.

Sasha looked down at her, then looked away.

"I don't know," he said honestly.

* * *

When Vera had gone, moving down the hallway like an old woman, Sasha found his apartment astonishingly empty. He sat cross-legged on the floor of the room he used as a studio, surrounded by his paintings, looking intermittently at an oil sketch he had been doing of Shirin before his departure for Riga. It was a bad job. He had not begun to capture the spiritual ferocity, the sexual depth and resilience, the intelligence. It was merely a painting, unfinished, of an attractive woman, beautiful as were so many others in the world.

Shirin would never come right. Not one of the pencil sketches he had attempted had pleased him. A foray into charcoal had come closest to success, the crudity oddly suited to her fineness, but that effort, too, had fallen short. He had been surprised by the limits of his talent. Women had always been the easiest subjects. But Shirin was different. She would not permit herself to be captured so easily. By a man of minor talent and less understanding.

The cat snored and dreamed against his thigh. Well, he had a big enough stock of paintings to guarantee he wouldn't starve. If worse came to worst, he could peddle them to tourists on the Arbat or in Ismailovsky Park. He smiled. He was being humbled in every possible regard.

He did not know where to go. Was there a place on this earth that would allow him to reach back into Shirin's life? He told himself that it was all purely physical, that she was nothing but a damned good fuck, an Olympic gold medal piece of ass. But he could not bully his emotions so easily. He loved her. And although he knew it was nonsense, he believed he needed her. Somehow, she had grasped what he was about, perhaps even knowing him in a way he could not know himself. She had touched him with the eternity of the stars.

He passed his hand over the cat's silken pelt. Vrubel soothed out his limbs without opening his eyes, then settled again.

"I can't go on without her," Sasha told the drowsing animal.

Then it was too much. He felt as though he were caught in the biggest and emptiest building on earth, alone in endless, echoing chambers. And he could not bear it. He stood up, waking the cat, who made a sound of annoyance then sulked off toward his food dish.

Sasha pulled on his jacket, wearing it loose over the arm that held the heavy cast. It was late, almost to the point of rudeness. But he could not bear his loneliness. He needed to talk. About Shirin. About what had happened. About what was happening inside him, about what might happen. He did not want to laugh or drink. He simply wanted to sit and speak with somebody who might at least pretend to understand.

He thought of Samsonov, who was the kind of man who might get it, who might understand loss well enough to sympathize without the stupid flabby emotionalism that puffed up the Russian heart. But he had never thought to ask Misha where his barracks lay, and there were so many barracks in Moscow.

That left Rachel. And it was probably for the best. Really, there was no one else with whom he could discuss such personal things. He had always been able to share his intimate ambitions with her, things he would never have spoken in the presence of another, not even in a lover's bed. Rachel was able to view such things objectively, as though she were assessing a work of art.

Rachel. And he had not even sent her a postcard from Riga.

He marched through the heavy wet air, taking a shortcut to the subway station that he had never revealed to any of his lovers because it would have been too dangerous for a woman at night.

The path was empty. The fog had chased everyone indoors, carrying with it old fears implanted in the genes of the race. The subway station, too, was deserted, and he shared a car with only two other people, a huge welt-faced paratrooper and his frail girlfriend. The couple stood amid the empty seats, with the paratrooper holding to an overhead strap with his left hand and clutching the girl against him with his right arm. He looked massively strong, as though he would protect her against any threat that might ever approach. The paratrooper whispered something in her ear and she glanced furtively at Sasha, smiling to show a gold front tooth.

Rachel's mother and father answered the apartment door together. Sasha smiled, hoping they would not be too annoyed by his late, unannounced appearance. The mother was solidly built, low and powerful, the man thin and of medium height.

Neither of them revealed the slightest trace of deformity, of the biological error that had distorted Rachel's body and life. Sasha knew that there was a younger sister, too, who was married and perfectly healthy.

The Traums stared at Sasha in surprise for a moment, then the mother gasped with enormous concern.

"Alexander Ivanovich, what's happened to your hand?"

They invited him inside, speaking lowly. Rachel had been ill again. She was sleeping. But Sasha needed to drink a glass of tea, at the very least. And there was a piece of torte . . .

Sasha always liked the Traums' apartment. He felt well and welcome in the cramped space between the book-lined walls. In the few spots where there were no books, paintings from an earlier generation, socialist realism of the best, rare sort, had been hung. Mementos and folk trinkets braced up aging postcards from Israel, New York, and Vienna. The tiny rooms always smelled of cooking and medicine, and they were always warm. Rachel's grandfather had been an important Bolshevik, responsible for bringing culture to the workers and peasants. He had been purged in '37, his brother in '48. But the family had survived, squeezing into ever smaller spaces, shutting their mouths, reading their books, and contenting themselves with rickety ideas.

"What's wrong with Rachel?" Sasha asked.

Her mother placed a fine old china dessert plate in front of Sasha. At his words, her hand began to quiver, chiming old silver on glass.

"You know she isn't well, Alexander Ivanovich," the father answered. "She's never truly well."

They spoke in low voices. In the corner of the multipurpose room, a folding bed had already been made up for the night. The single bedroom belonged to Rachel, it was her little world. Full of art books and sketches given to her by artists she had helped, who had always taken advantage of her, with one Leskov oil, a swirling study of a grouse in flight against a brown landscape with a single dwarf tree. She had bought the oil from her shop, without telling him, and he had been furious when he first saw it hanging there, insisting she take back the money he had received for it. But she would not take the money, saying it made her proud to buy one of his works. It hung over her bed and was, he considered, probably the only painting of his owned by someone who understood it as more than mere decoration. She expounded on his technique, his visual grasp, his influences. Then she laughingly admitted that she really liked it because the bird looked so graceful and free.

The torte was very good, alerting Sasha to how hungry he had become. He could not remember when he had last put food into his mouth.

"Your hand will be all right?" the father asked.

Sasha nodded, full-mouthed. He was surprised. Ill or not, he had expected Rachel to appear in the bedroom doorway at the sound of his voice. But the door remained closed, inert, dead.

Rachel's mother poured from the teapot: a stream of hot water.

"Anna," the father said softly, "you've forgotten to put in the tea."

"Oh, I'm sorry," the woman said. But instead of returning to the tiny kitchen, she sat down and began to sob.

"What's the matter?" Sasha asked earnestly. "Is Rachel all right?"

The mother wept on, and tears welled up in the man's eyes, as well.

"Rachel will be fine." He reached across the table and closed his hand over his wife's wrist. "Don't cry now, Anna, don't cry. You don't want to wake her up."

"Please," Sasha said, "if there's anything I can do . . ."

The old man shook his head, smiling under wet eyes. "She'll be all right. She just needs to rest. It was such a terrible thing for her."

The woman stood up and left the room, hiding in the shallows of the kitchen.

"Rachel had a bad experience," the man explained in his soft voice, a voice meant for reading old books aloud. He was a professor of philosophy. "She was beaten up. . . ."

"My God."

The man maintained his gentle smile. "It's the times, you see. They beat her up. They didn't even rob her. They just beat her and they . . ." Tears streamed down his face. "She's not strong, you know. And they beat her. And said things to her. Because . . . because she's a Jew." He looked at Sasha beseechingly. "What does that mean? What does it mean? This family hasn't been religious for seventy years. Longer. Why is she a Jew? What's a *Jew?*" He began to raise his voice slightly, looking at Sasha as though he really expected answers. "Then they took a knife—"

"Stop it, Yakov," Rachel's mother said from the kitchen doorway.

But the old man could not stop himself. "Then they took a knife and they carved a swastika into her back . . ."

"Stop it."

". . . and they urinated on her . . . while she lay there on the ground. While my daughter lay there on the ground. Because she's a Jew. Tell me, what's a Jew? And what kind of world do we live in?"

"Please, stop it," the mother begged in a broken voice.

"*What kind of a world do we live in?*" the father demanded. "Where young boys do such a thing to a crippled girl? What kind of world is this?"

The bedroom door opened. Rachel stood wrapped in an old flannel robe that reached from the swell of her bad shoulder to her ankles. She was smiling.

"Sasha," she said happily, "you've come home!"

19

SHIRIN BOUGHT A SOFT SUEDE JACKET IN THE GRAND Bazaar. It was a normal thing to do and she had given herself over to the painfully normal. The jacket was brown, with a luxurious Western cut and feel that would once have delighted her. She bought it dutifully, although she did not want it. She bought it because the universe was collapsing around her and she sensed that only a determined practice of normalcy, the doing of those same mundane things she would have done in her past life, might hold things together a bit longer.

The Turk who sold her the jacket was tall and very handsome. They spoke in English, although they found they could understand each other partially by speaking in Turkish and Uzbek, inheritors of a mutual antiquity. They spoke in English because English was the language of business, and it was a very clear, cold language in which each could limit the amount of personal revelation. She let him seduce her, after an evening squandered in a dockside fish restaurant. He was very good at the mechanics of sex, practiced on a herd of foreign women anxious to get full value from their vacations. He was very good, and Shirin watched in detachment, almost disgust, as her body caught fire beneath him.

Since she was, in his view, from his world, he wanted her from behind. Shirin made no objection, accepting the clear subjugation, even finding that the position suited her much better. She didn't have to look at him, to smell his breath, with its odor of stale cooking oil and beer. He was anonymous, his face and soul unimportant. He was a thing that worked in and out of her, calling up a response as impersonal as it was intense. He was very good, but when he tried to touch her to release the madness building up in her, she roughly pushed away his hand and did it herself. She told him in a voice startlingly disparate from her submissive posture that he was not to finish inside her, then she let go and sank into her own world, exploding under her own fingertips and lashing herself with thoughts of Sasha. She buried her face in the mattress to drown her scream and sank still further into herself as her partner finished, withdrawing obediently at the last instant to fire himself over her buttocks and the small of her back. When he tried to touch her again, she rose, wiped most of him away, and dressed. He tried to paw and persuade her at first, but she was so resolute that he finally ignored her and went to work on his accounts while she was still hunting for her purse.

She hated Sasha. Istanbul was ripe with spring. New green leaves simmered in the exhaust of traffic jams and tourists clutched their cameras in one hand while the other hand tested nervously to see if their wallets were still in place. The Turkish men leered, the women sniffed, and the boys offered to shine your shoes in the open plazas where paper refuse feathered over grass trodden thin and you sat down to rest on the wreck of centuries. Minarets lanced the sky, and by the university, female students in Western fashions brushed by others in head scarves and long mouse-colored coats. Shirin had no responsibilities at all, her position was a joke, and the closest thing she had to any official contacts were the late-night visits to her hotel door by a drunken Soviet trade official determined to share her bed. She was free to see the city, to marvel at the overflowing grocery shops in even the poorest quarters, where water still had to be lugged from a public spigot by children hardly bigger than the water cans. She was free to wonder at the brilliant festival of commerce, to visit the architectural monuments and museums. She was free to do it all, and she did it all, even though none of it reached very far inside her. All of it was finally as meaningless as the leather-goods salesman splashing himself over her backside only to be wiped away without a trace. But it was important to remain in motion. In the harem of the Topkapi Palace she almost laughed out loud, thinking how ill-suited she would have been for such a life, but the laugh withered as if strong hands had closed around her neck. She thought again of Sasha, thinking again and again of how much she hated him.

She hated him because she loved him so much. Even now. Even after his ignorance, his folly, the unforgivable extent to which he had disappointed her, betrayed her, spoiled the one good thing she had ever known with a man. She had believed in him, and that was enough to make her laugh now. Only it was a bitter laugh, the way a special breed of prisoner might laugh as he felt the muzzle of the revolver hard and cool against the nape of his neck.

She hated him because he had taught her how shallow and worthless she was, and the lesson would not cease. Her selfishness astonished her. For she spent far more of her waking hours thinking about the ruin of her love than about her lost family. She struggled to keep her mother, her sisters, her small brother, foremost in her mind, to suffer dutifully for them. But it was always Sasha who returned. Although she knew she would never return to him.

She had rarely known shame. The things that she had done in her life she had done willingly, always ready to face the consequences. But now she was ashamed. Sasha was a pig and a liar. He was a liar of the worst sort, the kind who did not need words in order to tell the worst lies imaginable.

She was homeless now. She had always thought that Moscow would be her home, far from the backwardness of Central Asia, far from the careful marriages and the obsessive mishandling of all things female, far from the schizophrenia of male vanity and distrust, far from the stupid tyrannies of mothers-in-law and the magnificent freedom, reinforced by Sovietization, to work away a lifetime to support the preening male animal. Marginally literate women worked in the cotton fields, where the insecticides ate into their hands and wombs, while their men lolled in the teahouse shade. The city women of Central Asia, educated, fierce, commanding, imagined they were free because their husbands let them go to the beauty shop and manage the family finances and worries. Shirin had always known that such a life, in such a place, was not for her. But the knowledge of what had happened, the loss of her family, nonetheless shocked her with her rootlessness. For she could not imagine herself in Moscow now, either. Her father had said his great mistake had been trusting the Slavs. And that had been her great mistake, as well. She felt as though Sasha had cut great pieces out of her body, pieces that would never grow back.

One night her drunken suitor proved particularly insistent, banging on the door of her room in the cheap hotel where the Soviet embassy contracted rooms. And Shirin let him in. He was so surprised to find himself standing before her bed that he did not know what to do at first. But she helped him. She kissed him on his fouled mouth, in response to which he discarded all politeness and pushed her down on the bed, shoving her skirt up toward her waist and fumbling at his belt. She helped him, drawing down his trousers. He smelled, and his undershorts were discolored. She slipped away from him in order to help him, removing his trousers entirely. Then she climbed back onto the bed and knelt over him. He was only semihard, fighting the alcohol in his body, and she took him in her hand, wrapping the other around his testicles. The man positioned himself more comfortably on the bed.

Shirin squeezed as hard as she could, digging in her nails and ripping at the flesh. Then she flew out of the bed with the athletic sureness with which she long ago had mounted ponies under her father's approving eyes. Her suitor was so shocked that he choked on his first scream. But now he howled, grabbing himself, curling up, and rolling back and forth on the bed. Shirin picked up his trousers. There was blood on her hands. The man slowed and grunted, eyes beginning to hunt for her. With all her strength, she punched the trousers through the closed window, shoving them through the storm of glass then releasing them into the street below. And she ran for the door.

The spring nights were cold. She had come away without either her old jacket or her new one. But it did not really matter. In a way, she welcomed the discomfort. And she felt proud of herself, as if she had vanquished an evil jinn. The blood caked on her fingers, under her nails, and men in the darkened streets made far more explicit offers than they would have made by daylight. Shirin simply ignored them. She cried for a long time. Crying and walking through the maze of streets to the boulevard where taxis swooped in toward the awning of a luxury hotel and small boys hovered behind the liveried doorman, competing to hawk polo shirts and socks with little alligators. The city was a layer cake smashed with a fist, its strata of history intermingled, confused. Behind an iron railing gravestones crowned with stone turbans clustered in a tiny niche. The soiled earth of the shrine was littered with wrappings from the McDonald's restaurant across the street. A Byzantine archway led to a Polish export shop, and a huge Mercedes blustered fumes as it waited for a donkey cart to clear the street. Shirin wandered, jostled by the night crowd of university students, tourists, and hustlers. She saw it all, the color and light and motion, but the intensity of life before her only reminded her that her own world was dead, dead, dead.

She sat down on a stone wall before the ceremonial gate of the university and lowered her face into her hands. She wished her father were present, so he could take her in his arms. He had been the only one, the only man whom it was possible to trust. All the rest of them were made up of filth, small wants, and lies. She wondered how badly she had injured the fool who had pounded so adamantly on her hotel room door, knowing all the while that she did not care. Nor would it matter to the inevitably fat wife he had left behind in Moscow, whom he inevitably beat and who inevitably betrayed him.

Why did it all have to be so *small?* Why did it have to begin with such limits, and why did men and women insist on drawing those limits around themselves even more constrictingly than necessary? Why did everyone want to become smaller and smaller? She had not wanted to be small, and they had killed her family and poisoned her insides with desires that could never be stilled, and it was all just because she had not wanted to settle for the same smallness for which the rest of humanity longed.

Mankind built its monuments on a grand scale, on an even grander scale, not to honor God but to divert his attention. So that they might disappear in the shadows of their cold creations. Becoming ever smaller and more insignificant.

Shirin raised her face to the black sky. A few stars were visible through the thick, bad air. She clenched her fists.

An old man in a cloth cap approached her slowly, as if closing on an animal that might bolt. He stepped out of the shadows into a wash of light that caught his unshaven face then released it again.

"Miss," he said in English, closing on her quickly now, reaching for her, "miss, you come home with me. I am so nice to you."

Shirin sprang to her feet in a rage beyond words. She pushed the old man's chest with a force for which he was not prepared and he stumbled backward, tripping over a broken spot in the pavement. Shirin was already running as he fell.

It never stopped, never stopped, never stopped.

Once, she remembered, she had not wanted it to stop.

She ran into the deepest shadows, into the smell of garbage and human waste. Not so far away the boulevard pulsed brightly. But she could not go back. She was never going back.

It was very cold and the heavy jewelry her father had given her seemed to coil about her neck. Nothing was safe. She had laughed at safety once. But she had not understood anything in those days. How fragile it all was. How small you became despite yourself.

"*Sasha,*" she said out loud. "*Sasha.*" She was crying hard. She did not understand how he could have failed to love her back. When she had loved so much. When there had been a chance to love so much that the world would not have mattered. How could he have thrown such a chance away? When it was her only chance, her last chance? How could he not have loved her? "I only wanted to love," she said, sinking to her knees on the wet stone. "I only wanted to love." She dropped herself flat on the ground and began to crawl, as though trying to sneak away from her life.

Two figures loomed before her. Black shadows against the distant light of the street.

"It doesn't matter," Shirin muttered in the language of her childhood. "It doesn't matter at all."

The figures took a few tentative steps closer.

"What did she say?" a young woman's voice asked.

"I don't know," another female voice replied. "She has an accent."

"Is she Turkish?"

"Perhaps she's on drugs."

"Perhaps she's a prostitute."

Shirin understood nearly everything. She had a brilliant ear for languages. It was only the men and women who spoke them that she could never understand.

"Leave me alone," Shirin said. And she surrendered to her tears as a child might have done.

"We have to help her," the first woman said. "She can't stay here."

"But if she's a prostitute?"

"It doesn't matter."

The two young women bent over her, trying to help Shirin to her feet, finally managing to lift her. She was so weak. She let them help her. It didn't matter. Nothing mattered now. They were right. She was a prostitute. A whore beyond description. Because she had not wanted to accept her smallness. Because she had wanted to live.

Shirin's senses were so far gone that it was not until the three of them made their way back into the flood of neon light that she noticed that her saviors wore head scarves and long coats.

"Can you walk now, sister?" the larger of the two young women asked her. "Do you have a place to go?"

Shirin shook her head. "I have nowhere."

And this is how Shirin found her way to God at last.

Playing God was hard work. For weeks Leskov's reinforced special section had been attempting to monitor every moment of Ali Talala's life, to become omnipresent. The mission passed down by Lieutenant General Kerbitsky was clear: catch Talala in the act. In the middle of as wicked an act as possible. And catch him publicly. It sounded good, but was, in fact, very hard to do. It required not only good, uninterrupted information, but a great deal of intuition, as well.

Leskov's intuition told him that the opportunity was coming. But as the days of little sleep turned into weeks, his powers of analysis weakened with exhaustion. He virtually lived in his office and he could feel his mind overfilling with unhelpful details, yearning to empty itself. Each day he grew a little more afraid that he would get it wrong.

He took another sip of staling tea, fighting the urge to drop his head onto his desk and shut his eyes. The more details his men unearthed on Talala's life, the harder it became to grasp the man's essence. Only the externals were clear. And it was very clear that Talala's longtime protectors, both in Moscow and back in Uzbekistan, had turned their backs on him completely. Only Talala did not seem to realize it.

Leskov still could not figure out why all of the men who pulled the great levers did not simply send an assassin after Talala, if they really wanted him out of the way. It was an easy thing to do these days, with the country overrun with out-of-work thugs of every description. Champion sportsmen down on their luck and mustered-out veterans competed for work as bodyguards, as extortionists, as triggermen. For a few rubles more than a regular job would pay. Or if the wet work was especially nasty, for hard currency. It would have been the easiest thing in the world to arrange a fatal accident for Talala. But they wanted him arrested.

It made no sense to Leskov. Given the possibility, however remote, that Talala might start gushing the names of those who had sold him out, the arrest and trial seemed lunatic. Why would the men Talala had served permit it? Leskov could not bring himself to trust the situation at all. He did not even fully trust Kerbitsky any longer. Not in the ways that really mattered. He felt that enormous wheels were turning just beyond his range of vision.

Personally, he wanted Talala alive. Alive and if possible, talking. He hoped that, by some miracle, he would tease names and dates and interrelationships out of Talala, information he could then make so public, or at least so notorious within the system, that more arrests would have to follow. So that the law might, at last, make a difference.

He rested his face in his hands, massaging his eyes with the fat of his palms. And he thought of his brother. Why on earth did Sasha have to be such a terrible fool?

Perhaps it was in the blood. The same source of unreason that made one man take on a system that had made corruption a way of life caused his brother to throw away his career over a dubious woman.

In any case, that affair was over now. With the Talala girl shipped off to Turkey and Sasha licking his wounds. Leskov wondered what would become of the girl. How would she fare when her father was locked away? Would someone feel duty bound to protect the daughter of the man who had been sacrificed? Leskov doubted it. He suspected that the girl's safety was a temporary thing at best, that she was wandering blindfolded toward the edge of the world and that neither he nor any other man would be able to do much about it.

Had Sasha truly loved that girl? Leskov could not quite believe it. Shirin Talala existed at too great a remove from all he personally valued. He could not imagine any man loving her. Wanting her, yes. She was undeniably a beauty. But love, to Pavel Leskov, took root in other soils. He suspected the whole flaming business had been just another of Sasha's sexual infatuations, seasoned with exotic spices. Surely, it had not been love.

It never occurred to him that he might be jealous of Shirin Talala, wounded by the notion that the girl could draw love so readily from his brother's heart when his own years of seeking that love had led from one failure to another. It never occurred to him how very alike he and Sasha were in their need to be loved even as they mocked the idea of enduring affections. Leskov's failed marriage, the distance he always felt between himself and the sons sentenced now and again to spend a weekend with him, the sons he loved but could not reach, the chasm between him and Sasha, his quiet terror of trying to begin again with another woman, all of his history was fastened down so tightly deep in his heart that he could no more see Shirin Talala clearly than she could see into herself. Crippled by experience, he could not credit more than a tenuous connection between sex and love. In his world, sex was a thing that drove people apart, not something that bound them together. Sex could never be trusted. It teased men and women into making promises they could never fulfill, making liars of them all. It filled you with false hope. Then, one day, you came home early, like the subject of a million jokes, and heard your wife's familiar cries, the voice that had sworn to love you forever, responding to another man's flesh.

Leskov was dozing when an assistant burst into his office.

It took the colonel a moment to rouse himself, to recall where he was and escape a dreamer's sense of loss.

"*He's making his move,*" the junior officer cried. "Talala and his gang are moving, and Maleshkov says they have enough weapons to start World War Three."

Leskov shook his head, waking himself fully. Then he jumped to his feet.

"Get the alert unit moving," he barked. *"Now."*

Ali Talala sat in the back of the limousine in the special silence of a man expecting to die. He had done his best to provide for Shirin—Gogandaev would look after her upon her return—and he had done what he could for Ashi, too. But there were times when the dead were more important than the living, when honor became more important than love, when yesterday's screams for vengeance rang more vitally than any whispers of future happiness. Only blood could wash away blood.

Yet he found that Ashi filled his heart. He pictured her amid the roses by the fountain, telling love through antique verses. He loved her in a way he had never been able to love the honest woman his father had selected to be an eldest son's wife, in a way you could never even love your own flesh and blood, not even one as dear as Shirin. He would miss Ashi and it was hard to think he would never again feel her body roiling against him.

It was going to be bad. He had waited, patiently, for the Ukrainians to assemble, waiting until he was certain they expected nothing. Tonight the hour had come. They were eating and drinking themselves sick like the snub-nosed pigs they were. Celebrating the marriage of one Slavic piece of walking scum to another.

There would be many guns, his own and those of the Ukrainians. Perhaps others, as well. Talala knew the police or some agency had been watching him. Perhaps it was even the KGB, out for a revenge of its own. He could not tell for certain. Even if a man wore the uniform of one service, his loyalties might be to another, anyway. No one could be trusted. Not ever. Perhaps the Ukrainians had bought more protection than his own kind had been able to buy. Perhaps the militia would be waiting. Or a special force from the

Interior Ministry. Or the KGB. Or mercenary thugs. Perhaps the Ukrainians had gotten wind of something after all.

It did not matter. It would happen too fast. He had enough firepower in the three automobiles to shoot his way into the restaurant where the party was in progress. Perhaps he would even be able to shoot his way back out again. But that did not really matter. What mattered was that many of the Ukrainians were going to die, along with their wives and lovers and children.

The service automobile bounced from pothole to pothole, dodging renegade taxicabs and trams and splashing waves of rainwater across the blackened street.

"Hurry, damn it," Leskov told the driver.

The man hunkered closer to the steering wheel as if he expected to feel a lash across his back.

Leskov felt in his guts that it was all going to turn out badly. The Ukrainians had gathered by the dozen in the Golden Kiev, a cooperative restaurant owned by the syndicate. A clan wedding reception was under way in the big upstairs dining room. There would also be Western tourists downstairs, as well as foreign diplomats and the sort of high government officials and Hero Artists of the Soviet Union who had access to the hard currency necessary to feed in such a place. The situation had the potential for getting dramatically out of hand.

Kerbitsky wanted to catch Talala in the act. And he might just get his wish. But Leskov had made up his mind to defy the general, if he could get to the restaurant in time, before Talala. He was going to cordon the place off. If Talala wanted to shoot it out, he could shoot it out with the KGB. Leskov was not going to stand by idly and permit a bloodbath. No matter what his superiors and their superiors wanted. There were sufficient charges piled up against Talala already. Even if he were just going to the reception to deliver flowers, they could lock him up for a long time.

The automobile struck a huge break in the road where Gorky Street met the Ring. The vehicle shook as if going to pieces. Everything was coming apart. The roads were bad, the times were bad. Men and women went with their heads bowed down again. An explosion was coming, and nobody knew who would be left standing afterward, and everybody was afraid.

Leskov grabbed the microphone of the special service radio, and glancing through the rear window to make sure the other cars were still following, he called:

"Blackbird, this is Falcon. Status report. Over."

"This is Blackbird. They're turning off the Ring."

Damn it. They were going to be too late. It was almost a certainty.

Leskov tried to radio the two-man team he had stationed in the vicinity of the restaurant to keep tabs on the Ukrainians.

"Songbird, this is Falcon. How far are you from the site? Over."

He waited for a response, and when it did not come, he called again. But there was no answering voice. The car was moving through a radio shadow. Or something had already happened.

They were so close. If Talala would only take his time, if he went carefully, they might still be able to stop him. But if he moved quickly, Leskov knew his own men would arrive in the middle of a gun battle the like of which Moscow's streets had not seen since the Revolution.

"All stations," Leskov told the microphone, "this is going to be very straightforward. The lead car goes directly to the far end of the street and blocks it. The trail vehicle remains blocking the near end. The rest of us are going to pull up right in front of that goddamned place. And nobody fires unless it's in self-defense. There'll be dozens of innocent people in that restaurant."

And I want that son of a bitch alive, Leskov thought.

The other cars acknowledged the message. Some of the voices were nervous. The times had changed dramatically since the days when a KGB uniform had been better protection against a bullet than any body armor.

"*Hurry,*" Leskov told his driver.

It was wonderful. After days and days of hotel food even drearier than the Moscow streets, Herb and Beverly Masters were finally enjoying an authentic Russian meal. Or a Ukrainian one, anyway. Same difference, as far as Herb was concerned. The important thing was that the food was edible and plentiful. Even by Topeka standards. The waiters were a little slow, but Herb blamed that on the wild wedding party upstairs. The guests were shrieking and laughing and stamping their feet so hard that the crystal chandelier shivered and chimed above Bev's head. Compared to other Soviet waiters, these guys were downright polite, even helpful. But they kept disappearing upstairs with trays of food.

Overall, the tour of the Soviet Union for which they had paid through the nose had turned out to be a pain in the butt. It was called the "Glories of Old Russia" tour, and everything might have been Russian and it damned well looked old, but there wasn't much glorious about it. Leningrad had been filthy and decrepit and there had not even been many souvenirs worth buying. The promised tickets to the Kirov ballet had never materialized, and it had rained most of every day. Moscow was proving even worse. The hotel breakfast buffet this morning had consisted of stale bread, oatmeal, some awful kind of cheese, and thin tea. There had not even been any butter or jam. In Leningrad they had at least had jam, even if it was the same brown slime day after day. And the Tretyakov Gallery was closed for repairs. Bev had been crestfallen. When their Intourist guide quietly told them that she knew of a very good cooperative restaurant where the waiters spoke English and guests could pay in dollars, Herb and Bev had been excited. The alternative would have been standing in line for an hour outside McDonald's. And they did not want to do that, especially since somebody had stolen Bev's umbrella during lunch and the damned rain had followed them down from Leningrad.

For once on this damned trip, things had turned out well. The Crimean champagne was too sweet, but you had to take some things in stride. Herb drank it as a chaser for the vodka the waiter had placed on the table without waiting to be asked, and Herb started to feel that he was beginning to understand these people, to get at their essence. It was a hell of a life. They had it rough, and it just went to show you that Harry Truman had been right about your goddamned Commies. Run every last thing into the ground. It was only a shame the kids had to pay the price. Begging for chewing gum on that street with all the artists and the lacquer boxes. Hell of a thing. You had to wonder what these people would do if you ever laid a good Kansas steak in front of them.

"It certainly sounds like those people know how to have a good time," Bev said, looking up at the ceiling.

Herb finished chewing and swallowed.

"You know, angel pie, this is more like it. This is how I expected the whole tour to be."

Bev sipped at her champagne. "I hope you tipped our girl enough."

"The guide? She's glad for anything she gets. I gave her a couple of bucks. You going to eat the rest of that pickled stuff?"

Upstairs, a bass voice shouted two syllables and a rough chorus took up the sound as a chant. The invisible guests began to stamp rhythmically on the floor, then erupted into cheers and laughter. Someone began to sing.

"Isn't this exciting?" Bev asked.

Talala's men did not kill the doorman immediately. Threatening him silently with their weapons, they pushed him aside, leaving him for the men who would remain outside on guard to beat to death. Then Talala and his men went inside, quickly and quietly. Except for Talala himself, they were armed with compact folding-stock automatic weapons of the sort carried by Soviet paratroopers or special operations forces. Not all of Talala's men were Central Asian. One was a Balt, one a half-Tartar, and two of the others were ethnic Russians. All of the non-Asians were veterans of the war in Afghanistan who had discovered in themselves a taste for killing and a loyalty to money that bespoke the times. It especially pleased Talala when he could set Slavs to killing Slavs.

Talala carried only a pistol. The automatic rifles were intended to kill as many human beings as possible as swiftly as possible, without discrimination. But Talala wanted to choose individual targets.

The men raced through the vestibule and up the stairs, ignoring the woman behind the cloak counter and a tourist returning, grim-faced, from the toilet. The first shots fired struck a waiter who was reaching under his jacket.

The shots came too late to serve as an effective warning. The dinner orchestra played on out of inertia as the first of

Talala's men smashed through the upstairs doors. Some of the younger Ukrainian men in the banquet hall reacted quickly. But their responses were not efficient, hampered by drunkenness and the presence of their wives and children. Some guests had not bothered to carry weapons to the reception, assuming it would be well guarded. No one expected an attack of such ferocity. The syndicates were building webs of interregional alliances, feasting bountifully off the decaying carcass of the state. Despite some doubts, the alliance between Ali Talala and Bogdan Chibchenko, who ran Kiev as though the city were family property, seemed to confirm the Western-style, businesslike relations between criminal empires. Chibchenko was, in fact, in the best of spirits when the gunmen burst through the door. He had flown to Moscow especially for this wedding, matching one of his key lieutenants to the daughter of a vice minister for foreign trade. And like most of the revelers, Chibchenko was drunk.

Human beings react variously when faced with their impending deaths. Some freeze like animals caught in headlights. Others dive under tables in comic desperation or hunker down behind flimsy chairs, hoping that the killer's eyes and bullets will miraculously overlook them. Others fight, flinging at their attacker the first objects that come to hand: a plate of cake, a bottle, a fork. Some stand huge-eyed, flapping their arms in a penguin imitation and asking, "What's going on? What's happening?" Some just scream. One type of man reaches to protect his loved ones, another forgets them. Women often try to move between death and their children, sometimes even between death and their man. If you have seen a lot of death—not just fighting, but *death* in its much greater range—you know that women are really much braver than men and that no creature is braver than a mother. Yet, some mothers run wailing toward imagined exits or hurl themselves through windows, thinking only of themselves. It is difficult to predict how individuals will react under such circumstances, since we are not consistent creatures. He who is transcendently brave on Friday night might be an appalling coward on Monday morning. Our lives have different values to us in different years and different moments. But perhaps the most uniform human beings are musicians, who almost invariably try to protect their precious instruments before thinking of their lives. Anyway, when you have a big room packed with human beings dying in front of one another, there is a lot of color and noise. There is no order, and afterward, no survivor can tell you what happened with much accuracy. All they can report is what they imagine might have happened, cobbling together a history from a few vivid scraps of reality collected in terror.

Two former special operations officers led the assault, followed by Talala and four more men, all of whom had killed before. Four others remained downstairs, combing the ground floor for hidden threats and providing security. Two guards remained outside, pummeling the doorman to death with the metal stocks of their weapons and their boots, while the drivers idled their cars and nervously smoked cigarettes.

The assault team members distributed their fire efficiently. The two lead figures split right and left in the hall and began to spray bullets inward from the corners of the room. The next men concentrated their fire on the middle of the room and swept outward. Talala stood calmly among them, seeking out the most important targets.

It was hard to see at first. The room was not bright, and heavy cigarette smoke had already given it the appearance of a battlefield. But Talala had good, trained eyes. His father had taught him to read the steppe, to understand the portent of a distant kick of dust or a small swooping bird, and even in the chaos of bodies pushing, running, falling, and exploding with blood, he soon spotted Chibchenko.

The Ukrainian boss was a fat man and fate had overtaken him behind the head table with an oversize napkin tied around his neck. His bodyguards stood immediately behind him, handguns out. But they could not fire through the swirling crowd for fear of hitting their own people. The hard young men stood with absurd, helpless expressions on their faces, pointing their pistols then withdrawing them again, like children playing bang-bang. Chibchenko's mouth hung open. As a young man, he had been a killer, with a survivor's reflexes. But he had lived too well for too long. He had grown soft and slow and fat. He had even stopped carrying his personal weapon because it chafed him wherever he tried to conceal it against his body. He relied solely on others for his protection now, which was something a man should never do.

Talala shot a screaming woman in the head to clear his field of fire, then he shot the bodyguard behind Chibchenko's left shoulder. He began walking forward through the bullets and falling bodies, uncaring. Chibchenko alerted to his presence, but Talala did not meet the fat old man's eyes for long. He stepped behind a beefy woman who was staggering about covered in blood like a bull being slaughtered by amateurs. Under her raised arm, Talala shot the second bodyguard in the head. Then he turned and swiftly shot a young man who had been closing on him with a knife.

The one thing that registered on Talala was that he had never heard so great a noise in his life. The half dozen automatic weapons, the odd pistols fired in response, the shrieking—all of it swelled unbearably in the hall, as though, unable to escape through the walls, the volume gained physical mass, pressing down hard on a man's skull. Yet, despite the bigness of the noise, you could still pick out astonishing details: a voice, remarkably sober, saying, "I'm shot. Look. Good heavens, I believe I've been shot." Or a woman's voice screaming itself raw with the repetition of the words, "I love you, I love you, I love you . . ."

Talala walked up to the table where Chibchenko sat over a half-finished plate. The fat man shook his head slowly, in wonder. Talala took the time to look deep into his eyes now and saw weakness, misjudgment, age. But not fear. Chibchenko was too shocked to be really afraid. He raised an empty hand above his plate as though to catch a ball Talala might throw.

"Why?" Chibchenko asked. "Why?"

Talala raised his pistol and shot the fat man point-blank in the chest, watching the body ripple and almost fall backward. The Ukrainian's mouth still formed words. But there was no longer any sound. Talala shot him again. Then he fired once more, sending the bullet into his enemy's head.

Chibchenko's weight held him upright for a few moments, even as his head whipped crazily, spitting brains out the back. The gunfire continued around the two rivals, but there was less shouting and screaming now. Then, for one bare instant, there was a convergence of silences as everyone either reloaded or searched out a new target or fought for breath.

Chibchenko's corpse slumped sideward, slowly gathering momentum until it slopped onto the floor.

Talala found himself stumbling forward against the table, as if a horse had kicked him with one of its hind legs. It was a terrible blow and he had to catch the edge of the table to hold himself upright before he realized that he had been shot.

The circus of noise began again. The odd silence had not lasted more than a second or two. But time worked differently when death was trying to kiss you on the lips, to get its arms around you. Talala saw a Ukrainian teenager on the floor behind a body. The boy was struggling to reload an old-fashioned revolver, his fingers trembling uncontrollably. Talala shot him in the top of the head and watched the boy's entire body contract then expand again like a spring toy.

When next he turned around, Talala saw that only three of his men were still on their feet. Two searched out remaining targets with their weapons ready, while the third man had fixed a short bayonet to his assault rifle and was tramping through the bodies, swinging the edged weapon low into bellies and backs with the motion of a man scooping up coal with a shovel. The expression on his face was rapturous, almost holy, and his sweat flew from side to side.

"*Let's go,*" one of his men—the Tartar—shouted at Talala.

Yes. It was enough. It was time to go.

His left side felt heavy as cement and increasingly numb. Something wet was covering his left leg.

Then Ali Talala saw a strange thing. A young woman in a blood-smeared wedding dress came walking toward him, stepping on bodies as though they were mere bumps in the carpet. Her blond hair was almost white, revealing Polish genes, and she was a pretty girl even now, with her pale hair awry and her face streaked with blood. She had a child's mouth below the eyes of a lioness, and she carried a table knife in her right hand.

Talala would have shot her as he would have shot a fine game animal, but for one thing:

She limped.

There was a little space of floor where no bodies had fallen. The bride crossed it with pained slowness, staring at Talala. Her feet cindered splinters of glass into the parquet.

Talala did not even raise his pistol. The girl was not going to hurt him. She was only reminding him of how sweet life was. The way Ashi came toward him with her burning eyes and worsening limp, hoping his mood would be such that he would fold her in his arms and stroke her hair. It was a terrible thing how life drove you onward, ever further from the things you loved. Once a man embarked upon a path such as the path he had chosen, the law applied implacably: you always had to continue to expand your power and your domain. Because the moment you ceased to expand, you began to contract. And the contraction accelerated with fatal speed. Until you imploded. This law was immutable.

There was no sacred equilibrium, no balance. That was all a fool's dream. There was only the horizon racing away from you and the bitter realization that happiness on this earth was a thing of moments, perhaps a matter of a stray hour.

The girl in the fouled wedding dress closed on him as if to embrace him. Limping, the hip turning as its socket slowly disintegrated. When he had first seen Ashi, she had been able to run a little. Not the way other children ran, but the way a hobbled lamb might try to run, out of the boundless joy of living. Even then he had sensed that she would be more than a pampering of his sexuality, more than a simple concubine. But he had never expected to love her so much, to love to the extent that he was ready to die for that love, to shake off the inborn mortal greed for the next breath.

The girl in the gown was not Ashi, of course. She limped with a wound that had spilled blood down the skirt of her wedding dress like the stain on a virgin bride's sheets. Talala felt a wave of hopelessness spreading over his body, aggravated by the numbness brooding in his side where a small-caliber bullet had entered his flesh. It was all so strange. And so hopeless. This life.

The bride fell against him, shoving the knife into his belly with all her weight. She was young and thin, but she had gathered a wonderful strength and she sent the knife in past the cloth of his shirt and the net of his underwear. It surprised him how exactly he could feel the blade going in. It felt very big. Huge. It was at least the size of the curved swords his ancestors had wielded from the backs of their desert ponies.

He stumbled backward, with the girl clinging to him. He dropped his pistol and began to stagger. Then his hired gun with the bayonet on his rifle plunged the blade into the small of the girl's back. Talala saw the surprise register in her eyes, smelling her breath, their lips close. Then the girl fell away, drawing the table knife halfway out of Talala's stomach.

He looked down, amazed at the way the bit of steel hung there. Then he instinctively pulled it the rest of the way out, groaned, and fell to his knees.

He had even forgotten Shirin, his own blood. There was only Ashi, and he hoped, he prayed, that someone would take care of her. Gogandaev, perhaps. Yes. Just so that no one abused her or hurt her. She was a jewel, a treasure, with a spirit so clear . . . so clear . . .

The thug with the bayonet was very strong. He hoisted the bride into the sky, spitted on the weapon. He laughed as though playing a child's game with her. The girl wriggled and gasped, hands and feet pummeling the air, hunting for a fastness. Then the mercenary dropped her heavily at his feet, took a deep breath of cigarette smoke and cordite, and began stabbing her in the buttocks, driving her across the floor. The girl moaned and tried to crawl away.

Talala took up the pistol he had dropped on the floor and aimed it at the back of the girl's tormentor. He fired. And he kept on firing until the weapon had emptied itself.

It was all wrong. Where were his men? They were all gone now. He couldn't see anyone. Someone was singing. But it was in a language he couldn't understand.

He had failed. In all things.

The bodies surrounding him were not really dead. They were all pretending. He could see them moving. Oh, yes. They were all moving. With their bloody hands, their bloody faces.

There was gunfire in the distance. How far away? Very far. It didn't matter.

Who was singing?

Was that Ashi singing? Was she singing for him? The old songs, silvered with centuries?

No, no. Everything was wrong.

There was never any hope, and God's greatness lay in his generous willingness to let men believe otherwise. Hope was all there could ever be, and there was no hope. It was so very clear now.

Ashi on her knees in the darkness.

Come, let me touch you! Reach me your hand!

But there were voices. Very near. At first they shouted, the men in the heavy boots. Then they grew more controlled. Perhaps his people had returned for him. Perhaps you *could* buy such loyalty. Perhaps . . . Ashi . . .

Men stood over him. He sensed it. But he could not see. There was something in his eyes, something the texture of raw egg whites.

Miraculously, his eyes opened and he saw. Someone had turned on a brighter set of lights. A man knelt down by his side. Talala recognized the uniform of the KGB.

"*Get an ambulance,*" the man on his knees commanded. His voice was mighty. *"Now."*

The man's face bent closer. Yes, it was a KGB officer. He had not even taken off his hat and it made his head appear huge. Talala could taste the man's breath and its slight sourness spoke a biography.

"You're going to live," the officer told Talala. "I'm going to make sure you live, you bloody bastard."

Leskov watched the stretcher-bearers carry Talala through the vestibule. The ambulances had lined up just outside the door. It was an indescribable mess. Among the guests had been three people's deputies, a vice minister, all of his ranking assistants and their families, and one general. One of the deputies might live, if he had better than average luck and a much better than average surgeon. The rest were gone.

Kerbitsky had wanted Talala caught in the act. And Kerbitsky had gotten what he wanted.

Leskov had never seen anything approaching the carnage in the upper room. Yet, downstairs, not a single patron of the cooperative seemed to have been touched, although several of them had been spattered with an unlucky waiter's brains. Leskov wished he could simply say good riddance. He would have preferred to believe that the dead had deserved to die. But he knew better. The law was not a matter of convenience. It applied to all, under every circumstance. Even when no one cared.

Talala and his men had spared no woman, no child.

Leskov stood in the vestibule, watching the rushing medical

teams, unsure of what to do next. The sights and smells had shocked him far more deeply than he was yet able to realize. He believed that he was in a perfectly normal state. But he could not even bring himself to go back out into the street and file a radio report with headquarters.

A quartet of medics came down the stairs with a heavy load. Their clothing was stained as if they had been working in a slaughterhouse.

So this is how it ends, Leskov thought.

He jumped. Someone had touched his sleeve.

It was a foreigner, a man in a good suit.

"Do you speak English?" the man asked. He had conspicuously healthy teeth in an otherwise middle-aged face, and Leskov assumed they must be dentures.

"A little bit."

"Are you an officer?"

"I am an officer of the KGB."

The foreigner looked startled. He backed off slightly, withdrawing his hand as if he seriously regretted ever touching Leskov's coat.

"What do you want?" Leskov continued.

"It's . . . my wife's all upset. We'd like to leave now."

"You may go. You are not necessary."

The man looked relieved. But he made no move to go. "There's a problem."

Leskov felt a surge of impatience coming over him. But he maintained his discipline.

"And what is this problem?"

"We have to pay the bill."

"What?"

"The bill. We haven't paid our bill. Our waiter's dead."

"Just go," Leskov told the tourist. "I think it does not matter now."

The man looked at Leskov with a mix of nervousness and exasperation quivering around his mouth.

"You don't understand. Beverly wouldn't stand for that. She'd never leave without paying the bill."

"So tell her that you have paid."

"But she'd know. Beverly knows me. She can always tell when I'm making something up."

Leskov turned away. It was ridiculous. He had no time for

a crazy tourist. But the man caught him by the arm. This time the grip was surprisingly strong.

Leskov was about to strike him. But he caught himself. The foreigner was crying, tears all over his cheeks.

"Could you tell her?" the man asked. "Could you tell her I paid the bill? Please?"

It was crazy. But Leskov was ready to do anything to get rid of the man now. He shook his arm free.

"And where is your wife?"

The man smiled, instantly grateful.

"She's just over there."

He led Leskov to a corner table where a well-dressed woman in her fifties sat upright with a peculiarly intense stare. At first Leskov thought she was in shock and that that was what had unsettled the tourist. But when he came closer, he saw what all of the others had missed. Underneath the little jacket she wore, just below the first fall of the tablecloth, the woman was covered in blood. And her stare seemed so intense because she never blinked.

"Tell her," the tourist pleaded, "tell her I paid the bill."

20

Samsonov married Vera on the day of the restaurant massacre. Following an abrupt civil ceremony, they went dutifully to the grave of the Unknown Soldier under the Kremlin wall and Vera laid her bouquet on the wet marble. Renegade raindrops spotted her makeup, drawing a nervous hand to her cheek. Her skin had broken out badly under the stress of pregnancy—and she so wanted to look her best on this of all days. Samsonov understood and hurried her away to the shelter of a borrowed automobile.

The church service followed. The priest's schedule was crowded and Samsonov and his bride had to share the rite with another couple whom they had never met. Samsonov was not religious, but he found the atmosphere of the church deeply satisfying. It haunted him with notions of Old Russia, of a time when, somehow, against all historical evidence, things must have been better. The low smoke of the incense and the moan of church Slavonic soothed him, convincing him that he was doing a thing both good and right.

Vera's parents had come down to Moscow for the ceremony, as had a country-faced assortment of aunts, uncles, and cousins. Samsonov was backed up only by Lieutenant Bedny and his wife, a young woman as spiteful and greedy as she was prematurely stout. Samsonov had not invited any of the other officers from his unit, since he knew they would not come. He was an unpopular man, growing more unpopular day by day.

His company had received new uniforms. With black berets. The battalion and regimental staffs had hidden away for as long as they could. But the metastasizing disturbances throughout the country's extremities had finally overcome the immune system of the Interior Ministry's barracks, motor pools, and overheated offices. The Ministry had directed that one of the battalions in Samsonov's regiment be designated as a special reaction force for civil disturbances. The regimental commander, in near shock, selected the battalion in which Samsonov served. Because only Samsonov's company, out of the entire regiment, had been training seriously. And because the regimental commander would not be unhappy to see Samsonov deployed to some distant trouble spot.

Samsonov's fellow officers in the regiment had never liked him. There was no semblance of the old, highly professional camaraderie of the airborne forces or even of the lackadaisical brotherhood of regular army units. And now his fellow MVD officers truly began to hate him. Thanks to *him,* their pleasant routine had been disrupted. Thanks to *him,* they might just be shipped off to Armenia or Azerbaijan or some other pisspot of a place where the best a man could expect would be a long separation from his family—if he didn't get a bullet in the back.

The enlisted men in Samsonov's company were divided. The wilder, more adventurous types swaggered about in their new olive uniforms, adjusting their berets for maximum effect on the opposite sex. But the rest grumbled and passively resisted every attempt Samsonov made to turn them into something resembling a military organization. He had never learned who had attacked him in the darkened hallway. He had proceeded as though the event had never taken place, demanding all that he could of his charges and cutting his losses when necessary. He could not even depend on Bedny for much. The lieutenant meant well, Samsonov was convinced, but if there had ever been any real soldier in him, his initial experiences with the internal troops and Kuzba's corruption had ruined him. All Samsonov could do was to assign

Bedny tasks within his meager capabilities. The rest Samsonov had to shoulder himself.

And there was a lot to shoulder now. It was a difficult thing to train a company whose interests rarely caught fire, working under superiors who resented and even feared him. It was difficult to be an officer with such responsibilities and problems when you also had a new wife to care for. It was especially hard if that wife happened to be expecting a child.

Samsonov had gone to see Sasha. He felt no resentment toward the artist, no jealousy. Often, he forgot that the child in Vera's womb was not his own. He loved the woman, as only a man who has been lonely for a very long time can love. He loved without reservation, without pride.

Sasha was cool to him at first. They talked about everything but Vera. Sasha had broken his hand and he simply smirked and looked away when Samsonov asked if the doctors expected it to interfere with his painting after the cast came off. Sasha's apartment had gone dirty, and for the first time, it smelled of cat. Sasha himself appeared to have aged. He was unshaven, although it was late in the day, and his left hand was smudged black and gray.

Samsonov asked to see his friend's paintings again and Sasha shrugged, leading the way into the room that served as his studio, with the cat trotting along beside him as if the animal were watching over him.

The paintings were even finer than Samsonov had remembered. It was amazing, really, that a man could see so clearly and then put it all down on canvas or drawing paper. It occurred to Samsonov that the child Vera would bring into the world would need to be given every opportunity to develop any talents inherited from its natural father.

On a table by the window lay a series of charcoal sketches. The topmost was unfinished but recognizable as the Central Asian girl Samsonov had encountered in the artist's apartment some months earlier. There was an intensity in the sketch that Samsonov could feel but could not explain. It was almost as if the artist had suffered physical pain with each sweep of the crayon.

"I remember her," Samsonov said.

"It isn't a good likeness," Sasha remarked. He stood in the

gray window light, with half of his face in shadow. "I've been trying to work with my left hand . . ."

"No. It's very good. Left-handed or not."

Sasha backed out of the light, retreating from the sight of his work.

"None of the sketches do her justice."

The aura of unhappiness and dirt around his friend suddenly made sense to Samsonov.

"She's gone?" he asked, surprised at his own matter-of-fact bluntness.

The man in the shadows nodded. "I've been trying to work from memory. And it just won't go."

Samsonov shifted the heavy rectangles of paper, revealing an entire series of portraits of the Asian girl. Desperation in the cheekbones; lips and eyes wet with white chalk.

"But . . . the sketches are very good," Samsonov said.

For a moment, Sasha seemed on the verge of speaking, of opening up. Then he failed to find the strength. Surprised at all he could intuit, Samsonov realized that, in the end, he had a far greater capacity for happiness than did the artist. The everyday appearances were the reverse of the truth. No matter how it all turned out with Vera, Samsonov knew that he would find happiness in it. Even if it was only the happiness of duty.

"You must love her very much," Samsonov said.

The shadow broke into motion. Sasha knelt before a rank of paintings propped against the wall. "Here, pick one out. I want to give you a present. If Vera doesn't want it around, you can just throw it away."

Samsonov almost began the normal round of protests. But he sensed that Sasha was beyond all that now and that the best thing he could do would be to accept the gift without making a fuss. Anyway, he wanted to own a painting by Sasha Leskov.

It was such a difficult thing to explain. He was marrying a pregnant woman his friend had treated very badly, yet he felt no resentment. More than anything, he felt gratitude. For Vera. And he was glad that someone had the eyes and hands to paint the world as he himself saw it. Lovingly, he went through the offered paintings, looking at each one twice before selecting several for a third inspection.

"This one," he said finally. "Is that all right?" It was a

painting of a Moscow church. He chose it because he thought Vera would like the theme.

The artist nodded his approval, even smiled a little. Samsonov sensed that his friend had decided not to open up and that he wanted to be left alone. But Samsonov could not help feeling a great warmth toward the man with the broken hand and the cat preening against his trouser cuffs.

"You're sure you don't mind? About Vera?"

Sasha looked surprised. "Why should *I* mind?"

"Well . . . she was your girl."

Sasha shook his head. "You're a better man than I'll ever be. And you'll be a thousand times better for Vera. God, I don't understand myself sometimes."

"And the other girl? I forget her name."

"Shirin? She's gone." Sasha looked down through the unswept floor. "It was all my fault."

"You really love her?" It seemed clear enough. Yet there remained a part of Samsonov that could not begin to grasp how a man could turn away from a woman such as Vera and squander himself on someone with a brown skin, no matter her beauty. He was trying to work through many problems in his soul, to prepare himself for possible deployments, but he still could not completely control his responses at the sight of an Asian face. His dreams had lessened in their severity. But waking reality was still something of a problem.

"I love her," Sasha said quietly, "as I never believed that I could love."

"Well, if she's gone and it's your fault, can't you just apologize? Patch things up?"

"It wouldn't be possible."

"Have you tried?"

"I can't."

"Why?"

"She's not here, for one thing. Anyway, it's hard to explain. I got everything all wrong. *Too* wrong. There are some things . . . that can't be forgiven."

"You want to marry her?"

The artist appeared surprised at the thought. "I don't know. I'm not sure it could ever have worked out." He smiled at a flickering vision. "Sometimes I think we made the best of what we had, that there wasn't any future in it. But I can't help myself. She's not here. And nothing else matters."

Sasha stooped and picked up the cat, turning it over against his sling and rubbing its belly. The cat lolled its head back toward the artist's armpit.

"I never had the faintest idea about the meaning of love," Sasha went on. He chuckled. "I always figured love was just what women felt the first time somebody threw them a decent fuck." Suddenly, he grinned. It was the grimace of a corpse. "But you don't want to hear all this. You should be happy. Celebrating. Vera's a wonderful girl. She just wasted a little time on the wrong guy."

"You'll meet somebody else."

The artist smiled down at the cat cradled against his chest. "Oh, I'll meet plenty of women. Plenty. It's the easiest thing in the world."

"And you'll fall in love again."

"No."

"You can't say that. That's something a child would say."

Sasha agreed. "But I'm childish. I don't think women ever understood that. And I can tell you, my friend, that I will love Shirin Talala until the day I die. If you want to dismiss that as nonsense or exaggeration, fine. But I know in my heart that she was . . . that we were two halves of one soul." He smiled again. "Not that I expect that to make much sense."

Samsonov lifted the painting he had selected so that he could examine it in the fall of windowlight. He wondered if Sasha really felt the rapture his brushstrokes communicated.

"It's a wonderful painting. Thank you."

"You know, Misha," the artist said, "sometimes I think there truly is justice in the world."

Samsonov looked up abruptly, face sobered. "I don't."

But if there was no justice, there were at least occasional flakes of joy that fell from heaven. After the religious ceremony, Vera's family put on a reception up on their state farm. All of the relatives and neighbors contributed food or a bottle or two and a cousin played the accordion. Samsonov adamantly refused all attempts to get him to drink alcohol—he had sworn to Vera that he would give it up—but he enjoyed the happiness dancing around him nonetheless. Vera looked golden, a Russian princess, as she accepted the congratulations of grandmothers and sullen village boys annoyed that she had married an outsider. She had covered the spoiled patches of skin with more makeup, and as Samsonov watched the succession of relatives and failed suitors dancing with his bride, he could not fathom how Sasha Leskov could have turned his back on such a beauty. He was so happy that he felt genuine sorrow at his friend's misfortunes. He would have liked Sasha to have been present to share in the joy. But that, of course, would have been impossible.

Vera never spoke of Sasha anymore, but it felt as though the love she had carried in her heart for so long had changed into a complex of emotions far meaner. Samsonov did not yet dare to tell his bride he had visited Sasha. The painting he had taken as a gift lay wrapped behind his desk in the barracks, waiting for a more appropriate time to enter their lives.

There was no place to hang the picture, anyway. There were no apartments officially available, not even an empty room, and Samsonov did not own hard currency for bribes nor could he swallow his pride and ask for help from those he despised. He signed onto the eternal waiting list, hoping against hope, and in the meantime, Vera took all of the little treasures she had been allowed to buy in the state bridal shop home to her parents. Their honeymoon consisted of a weekend in a borrowed flat in Moscow, with a promise of a possible trip to the Black Sea in the summer, if things went well.

Samsonov made love to his wife for the first time on their wedding night, undressing awkwardly in a room filled with the possessions of one of Vera's girlfriends. He went about it with great gentleness at first, not certain of how much she could bear without harm to the baby inside her. But Vera herself drove him toward an ever greater physical intensity. Until he lost control of himself, ending the act before he had truly reached her.

He lay in that bed beside his sleeping love, awake and full of worry. Would he be able to please her? Physically? Emotionally? Materially? Perhaps she needed more than such a clumsy, ill-paid man could give? Would he ever be able to create a little world in which Vera would have comfort and safety? Would they send him off to one of the country's wounded places before he could provide for her and the child?

Cradling Vera in his arms, he still feared that he might somehow lose her, just when his life had found a new purpose. He smiled at himself. If he could not save all of Russia, perhaps he could save just this one tiny piece of it.

"I love you," he told the sleeping woman, speaking into her hair and wishing he were a stronger, better man.

Shirin sat by a tomb in the green city of Bursa. The sky wanted to rain and the air was cool with the scent of earth and stone. Across the afternoon, heaven had slowly lowered itself onto the hills, obscuring the high-perched houses and the tips of the cypresses with gray wisps until you felt you could reach out and wet your fingers. The boulevards below sizzled with traffic, but in the courtyards surrounding the old Turkish mausoleums there was a bird-prickled silence that kept the auto horns from the valley far away. The fountains were dry but the stones of the pathways and the blue-green tile facades of the monuments shone polished and wet in the heavy air. Shirin imagined she could feel God's hand grazing the hair on her forearms. It was an alert, cool, warning touch that reached through the fabric of the long gray coat that covered her from neck to ankle. Then God's fingers rested lightly on the white scarf covering her hair. She closed her eyes and surrendered to the stillness.

Fatima was right. This was true freedom. All that she had once imagined freedom to be was mere libertinage. When, a bit earlier, two young men had passed by sparing her hardly a glance, she had not been the least bit disappointed. The clothing that Fatima and her friends had given her had seemed odd at first, almost ridiculous. She had always imagined that the fundamentalist women who wore such garments were hiding themselves away, afraid of life. But she had been wrong. The cloth that covered the hair and flesh freed the woman. From the desires burning in the eyes of strangers. The magic of the simple garments freed the soul, allowing the woman to define herself instead of relying on men's eyes to define her. Shirin had always thought that such clothing was a tool nervous, rancidly jealous men used to oppress women. But she had been ever so wrong. The long coat and the pure white head-covering simply freed a woman from unwanted attention, from public reduction to a mere sexual device. This was liberating armor.

It was deliciously humbling. She understood intuitively that God wanted humility from her. She had worn fine clothes. But she had not worn them so much out of love for ornament or even pride. She had worn her Western clothing casually because of its availability, without thinking much about it. No possessions had ever really mattered, no inert object had ever held lasting power over her. She had accepted those things that she found pleasant, but had not longed for them. She had longed only for love, and she had searched down the wrong path. But God understood. And He forgave.

Shirin did not realize it, of course, but all of this newfound devotion was determined by the same constellation that had driven her to sexual fury. Her stars had fitted her equally well for stringent self-denial, for an asceticism as intense as the physical rage that had burned from her belly to the tips of her limbs. But there was no middle ground. Shirin was born deprived of any talent for moderation. The world was either an overripe, pulpy, bleeding fruit, or it was cut of white marble.

She sat on the white stone of a low wall behind the tomb of a long-dead sultan, savoring the harshness, the growing ache in her buttocks. It was all so clean, so utterly clean. The rain would come and wash the earth as clean as the knowledge of God had newly washed her soul. She had pledged to God to give up everything she could think of and was dismayed only that nothing remained that truly seemed worth denying herself. She wanted to give and give, to rid her spirit of all encumbrances. Then, perhaps one day, she would be pure again.

It was good to sit still now, without the least shaming physical irritation. At first, the world had pursued her, mocking her. She had developed a sharp case of vaginitis, the first such ailment of her life, and the itching, the changed smell, and discharges had revolted her. The body was . . . ultimately . . . a foul thing, so unworthy of the tribute she had paid it. She had found a good English-speaking doctor, and you could buy all the necessary medicines in Turkey without bribes or connections, and she seemed to be well again, or nearly so. She had interpreted the ailment as punishment for her disgraceful behavior, for imagining that she might find in the arms of the male animal the love and solace that spilled only from God. It was a punishment . . . and a warning.

She heard footsteps on the gravel path, the measured tread of a woman. It was Fatima. She and two of her friends had brought Shirin to Bursa from Istanbul to see the old unprofaned treasures of a time when men had not yet blinded themselves to the presence of God. The city had waited beautifully in the pearl air, pale masonry and orange tile climbing the soft green hills as if each man strove to live closer to God than his neighbor. They had attended a meeting of students where a speaker attacked the secular structure of Turkish society, stopping just short of a call for holy war in the streets. Afterward, they ate lunch in the home of an auto industry executive whose daughter replied to her parents' avarice and luxury by covering her hair in a plain scarf. There was so much inequality and injustice. The young woman could not understand why her parents could not see it. She spoke fervently, barely pausing to accept the next course from the servants. Then they all piled into one of the family cars to carry on their pilgrimage, having saved the Muradiye mosque and tombs for last.

The solemnity of the shrine pleased Shirin beyond words.

"Am I disturbing you?" Fatima asked gently, closing the distance between them. She was a plain girl, made plainer by the simplicity of her dress.

"No, sister. Not at all," Shirin answered. Although there was plenty of space to sit on the wall, she made a gesture of shifting to the side, welcoming her new friend.

"I always find it so humbling here," Fatima said. "In the old days our people had such a sense of beauty. How have we lost it so completely?"

Shirin smiled. "You're beautiful, Fatima."

"I'm ugly." Fatima grimaced. "I know that. But I'm fortunate to be so. God is great and did not curse me with your beauty. It must be so difficult for you."

Shirin looked down at the polished stones of the pathway. "All of my difficulties . . . were my own fault. There's no one else to blame."

"You mustn't be too hard on yourself. You were among the unbelievers. There were too many temptations."

"I was blind," Shirin said. "And I was a fool."

They sat for a while in silence. The wind came up, moving the sky and chilling the flesh. Shirin thought of Sasha, moved with sadness and pity, but without a ghost of conscious desire. Sasha was so alone. He was one of the lonely men. Shirin was convinced that it was only their mutual loneliness that had bound them together. The terror of death lurking in the empty bed of the godless. Sasha was lost.

"Are you thinking of your family?" Fatima asked.

"Yes," Shirin lied.

"It must be terrible. But perhaps you will be able to help your father. To lead him back to God."

"Yes," Shirin said absently. Something was broken in her, something that Sasha had broken, and it had not yet healed. It was going to take a great deal of faith.

"And you still have no news of him?"

Shirin looked up, waking. "Who?"

"Your father."

"No. Nothing for weeks."

"I'm sure he's all right."

"Yes."

"Perhaps you should try to telephone him."

"Yes."

"You might sleep better. You need to sleep. You were crying again last night."

"Yes. I need to sleep."

"And you haven't changed your mind? About going home?"

"I must go."

"You could stay here. You would be welcome among us. You would be safe."

"God is great," Shirin said softly, the way she might have whispered to a lover. "If He wills it, I will be safe. But I must go home."

"But you will not cast off your faith? When you cast off our clothes?"

Shirin smiled gently and laid her hand on the covered forearm of her friend. "Don't worry. You've saved me. I'll never go back to Moscow. But I want to be among my own people. It's difficult to explain. I was so wrong about so many things for so long. I despised all that was good. Now I want to go home and make amends."

"Men will look at you again."

Shirin touched the kerchief on her head, straightening it. "In Uzbekistan the women have their own clothing. It's not sinful."

"But men will see your hair."

"But I won't see them." Shirin smiled again. "I'll send you a photograph of the clothes my people wear. You won't be ashamed of me."

Tears came to Fatima's eyes. "I worry so. I worry about you among the unbelievers. When we found you—"

"I'm different now," Shirin said. "Don't worry. You saved me. And I'll never go back to . . . the way I was." She stroked Fatima's forearm. "I was searching for so long. And I didn't know what I was looking for. But now I know."

Shirin felt confident. God willing, all things would turn out right. Anyway, she was genuinely unafraid of dying. She had come to understand the triviality of her life. If the men who killed her mother, her sisters, and her brother ever came for her in the night, she would be ready. They would only be coming to free her. From the body's urgency and decay. She was not afraid of any of that. Her sole fear was that she might, one day, by accident, meet Sasha Leskov again.

"You asked to see me?" Pavel Leskov said.

The man in the hospital bed looked at him with a face wiped clean of all emotion. He appeared tiny, shrunken, as though he might just be able to squeeze through the bars on the window when nobody was watching.

"Are you the chief investigator?"

"For your case," Leskov said.

The man nodded slightly without lifting his head from the pillow. His skin was the color of old, unpolished brass. Healthless. Yet he had been strong enough to survive wounds that would have killed the average man. He looked to the side, away from Leskov.

"Then I want to talk to you."

It was hard to believe that this small man fastened down with bedding had so recently held so much power in his hands, that he had caused so much death. He looked more as if he should have been hawking bruised melons in a bazaar.

"Talk," Leskov said.

A trace of anger passed over the man's features, a glint of the old conscienceless power lit his eyes. Then he mastered himself and said:

"Sit down. Please. Closer to me."

Stone-faced, Leskov drew a chair to the bedside, positioning it beside the nightstand with the phone. As a rule, prisoner-patients in the KGB hospital did not get their own telephone, but the device had been placed there on Leskov's orders. Talala was free to phone anyone he wanted. Leskov had known in advance that Talala had been cast off, that none of his old protectors would talk to him. Even if the phone had not been tapped. And he wanted Talala to find that out for himself. He was allowed to ring all the unofficial numbers and leave all the cryptic messages he wanted. No one responded.

It was a curious situation. Leskov was still trying to figure it out. Men in higher positions than that of his superior, General Kerbitsky, had made it emphatically clear that they wanted Talala's life saved. The best specialists were called in. Yet, beyond keeping him alive, no one wanted anything to do with Talala. Kerbitsky continued to insist that Talala's former protectors wanted him tried publicly. But it made no sense. Talala had the power to spout names that would embarrass top Party officials from Tashkent to Moscow. Why would those same officials want to risk trying him?

Meanwhile, there were other problems. Leskov did not believe that Talala knew about them yet, and he was gambling on the old gangster's ignorance. There were already demonstrations, however small, in the streets of Samarkand, Kokand, Tashkent, and a half a dozen minor points. They were anti-Russian in nature, responding to the news that People's Deputy Ali Talala had been arrested by the KGB. Talala's constituents, members of his extended family, his tribe, still viewed him as their champion, as a protector, and insisted that everything had been staged to discredit one of their own in order to assert Russian authority in Central Asia. The demonstrations had been controllable to date. But they made Leskov nervous.

The odd thing was they didn't seem to make the Party officials in Uzbekistan nervous. These were men whose legitimacy still rested largely on the central authority in Moscow. But they seemed to be doing nothing to maintain the security of their positions. They neither called for internal troops to suppress the demonstrations nor sought to pander to the dissidents by agreeing that Talala had been wronged. Publicly, they were doing nothing at all, although, in private, they remained adamant in calling for Talala's trial and punishment.

Leskov could not make sense of it. He knew it was all some sort of a black game, but he couldn't figure out the rules. He sensed that powerful hands were manipulating events, steering even his investigation, but he could not say to whom those hands belonged. First, he had thought they wanted Talala killed, he had been convinced of it. Now they swore they wanted him alive, in KGB custody. If it was a game, then what was the prize? What sort of jackpot was waiting at the end of all this?

One thing the demonstrations had managed to do was to revitalize the issue of removing all nuclear weapons from the non-Slavic republics. Normally calm voices whispered about civil war next year, next month, next week. There was an atmosphere of panic that, despite everything, still did not seem justified to Leskov. Far from helping to control the situation, he believed that the removal of nuclear warheads—impossible to keep fully secret—would simply inflame the situation, widening the gap between Slav and non-Slav still further, while nuclear weapons left undisturbed in their heavily guarded facilities were of no immediate threat. It made him shake his head. Even if some lunatic were to roll a nuclear warhead through the streets of Samarkand, it would pose no danger without technical preparation and a delivery system. It seemed as though the country had acquired a taste for hysteria. And the one concrete result was that forces would soon be set in motion to clear out the nuclear storage sites sleeping quietly in the steppes and deserts of Central Asia. Leskov felt deep down in his guts that it was a bad move, and he argued against it. But he lost. The special troops were going in: KGB units to move the warheads, and the poor bastards from the Interior Ministry to stand between the citizenry and the KGB. It was the wrong action at the wrong time by men in the wrong uniforms. It would take a miracle to avoid rioting or worse.

There was nothing more he could do about all that now. But he was determined to make the most of his opportunity to exploit Talala before some bigwig changed his mind and set the bastard free. His investigator's instincts told Leskov that Talala was broken. Still dangerous, perhaps. But broken. First he had lost his family. Now, as Leskov had taken discreet pains to make clear to him, he had been abandoned by his old comrades. Leskov had just given it time to sink in.

The call came, just as he had expected. Ali Talala did not want to deal with subordinates. Clinging to his last vestige of importance. A small sick man in a hospital bed in a barred room. With no hope.

"What do you want?" Leskov asked.

"You know what I want." Talala's Russian was correct, yet still accented and with the occasional lost ending.

"Tell me anyway."

"I want to strike a bargain."

"The KGB doesn't bargain."

"That's a lie."

"The KGB sometimes makes allowances, or grants rewards. But it does not bargain with criminals."

"All right. Then I want you to reward me."

"For what?"

"For what I'm going to tell you."

"First tell me."

"No. First you have to look me in the eye, you Russian scum. See if you can answer me truthfully."

Leskov stared into the hard brown eyes with the whites gone yellow and old.

"They sold me out, didn't they?" Talala asked.

"Who?"

"You make it hard. I'm trying to give you your heart's desire. You know who I mean. My people. Those whose blood stands between me and God."

"No," Leskov said. "They didn't sell you out. They simply gave you up. They didn't ask for anything in return."

"But *why?*" the old man asked. It was a surprisingly serious question. Leskov was certain that he had him then. And he was equally certain that Talala understood that he knew it and did not care any longer. "Why did they turn their backs on me?"

"Too much blood perhaps?"

Talala shook his head adamantly. "They don't care about blood. Do you believe they care about blood?"

"No."

"Then why?"

"I don't know. I thought perhaps you could tell me."

Talala looked off at the peeling paint on the wall. "I have few regrets. I don't regret any of the things a policeman would like me to regret. There's no remorse. I'm only sorry that I trusted the men I trusted. That I killed the wrong men."

"You know it wasn't the Ukrainians? Who killed your family?"

"I know it now. I was a fool. I'm amazed at my foolishness."

"You killed a lot of innocent people."

"Nobody's innocent. The Ukrainians deserved to die. I just killed them for the wrong reason."

"I don't have time to chat. If you really have something to tell me, fine. Otherwise . . . it's late."

Talala knew he was bluffing. Leskov could read the knowledge on the man's face. But it was not a matter of speaking truly now. It had to do with establishing a position of power.

"All right," Talala said bitterly, "listen to me. I want you to guarantee that no harm will ever come to my daughter. I want the 'Sword and Shield of the Party' to watch over her. They'll try to kill her. To hurt me. For that reason alone."

"That's all?"

"That's all. Promise me that and I'll tell you everything you want to know, my policeman. I'll tell you things the like of which you never dreamed. I'll tell you things that will rob your sleep for years to come."

This was it. Everything Leskov had been waiting for. He could not explain it exactly, but he knew that Talala would not lie now. That he would speak the truth. Perhaps because it was the greatest evil left to do, the last revenge. He was breaking the code of his people. But his people had broken faith with him.

"All right," Leskov said. "We'll watch over your daughter.

She'll have the best protection it's humanly possible to provide."

"But she mustn't know it. She must be free to live. I want her to think she's free."

Leskov nodded. It was such a strange and fateful world. He knew now that he had been wrong about at least one thing. Shirin Talala had not been trying to get at him through Sasha. The girl simply had slept around until she hit the random lottery number. Had Talala known of the relationship he would have imagined just the opposite, that the KGB was trying to get at him through his daughter. It was a world of infinite paranoia, where men imbued the most random events with malevolent meaning. His was a nation eternally looking over its shoulder.

"I promise you," Leskov said, "that we will do our utmost. As a reward for your services." He paused for a moment. "And that's all?"

"Yes. I want my daughter to live. As best she can. You'll see," he said softly, looking away again. "She has devils . . ."

Leskov was surprised. He had expected another very specific demand. It troubled him that he had misjudged Talala.

"Where do you want me to begin?" Talala asked in a dead voice.

"Wait. What about the woman in Tashkent? Your mistress, Ashi?"

Talala closed his eyes as if allowing himself to dream for one last moment. Then his face took on the most sorrowful expression Leskov had ever seen.

"You can't help her," the old man said, opening his eyes to look at the fool sitting beside him.

21

SAMSONOV LAY BESIDE HIS WIFE IN AN APARTMENT BORrowed for the night. Vera was crying. She had been gaining weight rapidly, and when she sobbed, her breasts shook heavily in the bad light. Samsonov stroked her hair. She had the most beautiful hair he had ever seen: golden, luxurious, a nest for the tired heart.

"I won't be gone long," he told her again. It was not exactly a lie. He honestly did not know how long the deployment would last. He suspected it would be a matter of months, at least. It was always easier to send troops than to bring them home. But he saw no point in passing on his speculations to his wife.

Vera wept. "I don't believe you." There was no anger in her voice. The words were spoken quietly, hollowed by her lack of faith.

He shifted his body against her and bound her to him with his strong arms. "These things happen. It's part of my job."

"But you could be hurt. Killed. You might never come back."

Samsonov laughed. "Verushka, Verushka . . . if Afghanistan didn't get me, a bunch of Uzbek hooligans certainly won't." He believed that. Yet he had a bad feeling about this mission. Of all the places they might have sent him and his men, Central Asia was the worst. It was too close to Afghanistan. Too close to the memories. Just when the bad dreams had begun to ease. He did not trust himself to make wise decisions if confronted by an angry brown mob. He could not help it. They would always be the people who set the mines, who sent rockets crashing into his soldiers' tents in the middle of the night, who tortured Slav prisoners before killing them. In his soul the war was far from over. *Those* people against us. Intellectually, he knew he had it all wrong, and he fought his prejudices. But the mind was ultimately weaker than the emotions. Samsonov feared he would turn out to be a bad man, a man without honor. He feared the challenge of the brown faces. He feared himself. Even more than he feared this separation from Vera.

He hoped it would not drag on too long. He wanted to be present when the child was born. She was his wife, and he had slowly begun to feel that the child was truly his, as well. Other men might laugh. He was strong enough for that. Samsonov looked forward to playing a part, however small, in bringing life into the world. Troubled though that world might be.

He had seen so much death. Blasted trenches and antique skulls in the night. Child soldiers marveling at the sight of their legs five meters away from a torso that had not yet begun to feel pain. Frightened, crying children with guns. Killing and dying. Once, down in Paktia, they had staged a party for one of the other company commanders who had served out his tour and was about to go home. They had a case of Soviet vodka bought from the Afghan bazaaris. And a missile from the surrounding hills had struck the sandbagged tent dead on, from above. Samsonov had only survived because he had staggered off to urinate. The most difficult part had been in the morning, trying to sort out which body parts belonged to which head so that the families might receive the right pieces of meat to bury. Sealed caskets had become Afghanistan's number one export to the Soviet Union.

He did not want any more death. He did not want to make mistakes. He did not want to be a bad man. But he had a sick feeling akin to the one you got when you realized you and your men were standing in the middle of a minefield.

"When do you have to go?" Vera asked in a child's voice.

"End of the week. Thursday, if we're ready." The barracks had been chaotic. No one had anticipated such an order. They should have known something was coming. But even after the redesignations and issuance of new uniforms, the battalion and regimental staffs had attempted to deny the new reality, imagining that, somehow, if they were not ready, they could not be called. Wishing the future away. Now the unit found it had no adequate upload drills, no plans, no experience. Sheepishly, the operations chief had called Samsonov to his office for help, just when Samsonov needed every moment to prepare his own men for the move. It was a shock to officers accustomed to comfortable garrison duty. It was almost going to be the way it had been in the airborne forces during special operations in the mountains in Afghanistan. Each man would take only what he could carry on his back. Then the unit discovered that it did not even have a sufficient number of rucksacks to issue to the troops.

He had stolen this night with Vera. There was so much to do. He could have worked around the clock. But he was desperately in love with his new wife, in love for the first time in his life, and the iron discipline that had structured his adulthood proved surprisingly brittle. He needed to feel Vera's flesh against him, to kiss her, to believe he was loved in return. He was ready to give her anything. If only she would love him.

Yet, after arranging the apartment for the night, he had been almost afraid to come to her. Afraid she would be angry, that she would blame him. He had gone first to see Sasha Leskov. To say good-bye.

He just caught Sasha. The artist was loading his last possessions and his cat into an old automobile. The cast on his arm was smaller now, cut down to a filthy minimum. Metal spurs protruded from his hidden fingers.

Sasha was being evicted from his apartment. He had been thrown out of the Artists' Union and the flat was Union property. Samsonov's instant thought was to wonder who would get the apartment. Then he reddened, ashamed of himself.

"Let me help you with that," he said. "Where are all the paintings?"

Sasha made a mildly disgusted face. "Here and there. Friends are storing them for me. Rachel has a bunch."

"Where will you go?"

Sasha jammed a plastic suitcase into the packed backseat of the car. "A friend's parents offered me a room for a while. Until I find something. Their son emigrated to America. And they miss having him around. It won't be so bad."

"You need to shave," Samsonov said suddenly. "And to wash. What's the matter with you?"

"I'll be all right."

"You're giving up. Quitting."

"What's to give up? What's to quit? In a country where apartments matter more than people." Sasha snorted. "Christ, the neighbors are like vultures."

Samsonov felt even more ashamed of himself. Then he said: "You loved her that much?"

Sasha stood up straight, punching his good hand into the small of his back to beat down the strain of carrying his life out into the street.

"No. I didn't love her that much. It's present tense, not past. I *love* her that much. Here and now." He spoke in a clipped voice, fighting emotion. "I'm sick to the death whenever I think of her. And I think of her all the time. All right?"

"And you still haven't gone to her?"

Sasha made a worn, sour face. He looked so much older. Then he laughed. "I still don't know where she is. I've tried to find her. I swallowed my pride. Every last drop of it. But she's gone. And nobody knows a damned thing. Or they're not telling me."

"There must be something . . . some way . . ."

"Oh, yes," Sasha said bitterly. "There's one more possibility. And I've sunk just about low enough to try it."

"Shave first. And pull yourself together."

"I don't have an officer's discipline. Or honor. *Vrubel,*" he called. The cat came bouncing over to the car like a loyal dog. "Come on, boy. Time to go."

"Good luck," Samsonov said, holding out his hand.

Abruptly, Sasha dropped his cynicism. He accepted the gesture, grasping Samsonov's fingers in his left hand. "Good luck to you, too. And be careful, Misha. You're a good man. Remarkably good. In the future you should try to choose your friends more carefully."

Sasha lowered himself onto the broken-springed seat and

began the labor of starting the car, mauling the gearshift with the cast on his hand. The cat hunkered down on the floor of the passenger's side, watching without the least concern.

"See you when you get back," the artist said, ready to pull away.

"Yes, I'll see you." But Samsonov had a cold, white feeling inside that he would never see his friend again.

"I love you," Vera whispered, closing her breasts against Samsonov's chest, warming him. "I don't want you to go."

"Do you really love me?" Samsonov asked quietly. He, too, had been unable to sleep, thinking about friends and lost comrades.

He could feel the tiny electricity of her surprise at the question.

"Of course I do," she said. "We're married, aren't we?"

Leskov waited for General Kerbitsky's coughing fit to pass before concluding. The general choked over his desk, gagging and gasping, but the heavy cigar never left the fingers of his right hand. His face reddened until the nose literally turned purple, then he spit into the wastebasket, swiveling about, with his big neck squeezing out over his fastened collar. His lungs sounded ravaged and weak. As though he were dying. But in time, the general recovered and stuck the cigar back in his mouth, stifling the last sputtering coughs.

The general's office was sour with old smoke and the smell of wet boots. Slowly, the museum feel lent by the memorabilia of Kerbitsky's career was being overwhelmed by the presence of machines: telephones, of course, but also a television and a video recorder, a computer that Leskov had never seen the old man touch, a tape recorder, a paper shredder—even a portable stereo cassette player. Electronics were the new trappings of power. The true quality and brands did not matter, so long as the devices were obviously Japanese or Western. It did not even matter whether or not the possessor knew how to turn them on. They were jewels for the well-dressed office.

"It's incredible, Comrade General," Leskov continued, gesturing toward the file folder in the center of Kerbitsky's desk. "The connections go even higher than we thought. Wider. Deeper. Talala used everybody and everybody used

Talala. Not just the old Uzbek mafia. Look at the names. The list reaches right into the Kremlin. And it's not just holdovers from the Brezhnev crew. It makes you sick."

"Our country," Kerbitsky said in his old smoker's voice, "is sick."

Leskov shook his head. "I never realized how sick."

"And you, Pavel Ivanovich, would like to cure Mother Russia of her ills."

Leskov looked up, cued by something in the tone of the general's voice.

"This is what you want," Kerbitsky went on. "This is what you've been working for, longing for . . ." He tapped his fingers over the file. "Isn't it, Pavel Ivanovich?"

"It's what *we* wanted. To get to the root of the problem, to find out how far the cancer had spread."

"And the answer . . . is not pleasant."

"No."

"The cancer, as you call it, appears to have run through the patient's entire body."

"The KGB is clean. Talala couldn't cite a single instance of a KGB officer being bribed."

The general waved away the qualification. "But you'll agree, the cancer appears to be everywhere."

"Yes."

"And you're horrified."

Leskov considered that. "Surprised might be a better way to put it. Although horrified comes close enough."

"I think you're horrified, Pavel Ivanovich. And you can't wait to take a scalpel to the patient." The general looked at the younger man through a mist of cigar smoke. "But . . . have you stopped to consider . . . that the patient might not survive such an operation?"

"Comrade General—"

"Pavel Ivanovich, I respect you. I have never had a harder-working subordinate. I have never seen you take a calculated action, angling for a promotion or whatever. You remind me of how the original chekists must have been. All afire with a vision. But just like those dead dreamers, you're sometimes blind to the practical side of life."

"You mean . . . we're not going after them?"

"Of course not." Kerbitsky hefted the packet a few inches

off his desk then dropped it for emphasis. "How could we? Who would be left to run the country?"

"This country doesn't run. It staggers. Because of corruption. And lies."

"True. Absolutely true. Tell me, how long is it that you've been working with Talala? I'm talking about these face-to-face interviews."

"He's been talking to me for the better part of two weeks now. I didn't want to brief you until I thought I had most of it down. I've been working on the report itself since late last night."

"And you've put your heart and soul into it. You've done good service."

Leskov lost control of himself for the space of one sentence: "We've *got* to go after these bastards."

Kerbitsky looked at him sympathetically. "And if you did? If we did? They'd crush us under their bootheels. Who'd sign the arrest order? Who'd carry it out? Pavel Ivanovich, sometimes we have to content ourselves with small victories. We wanted Talala. And we got him."

"Comrade General, there's still something I don't trust about all this, there's something wrong with this case."

"You've told me that before." The general patted his pockets for another cigar, then gave up and bent over to reach into his humidor. His voice strained with the effort. "But sometimes even the best officer's instincts are wrong."

"Doesn't it bother you? Don't you smell the stink on this?"

The general settled back into his chair. "I'm an old man. I've been an officer in this organization for almost forty years. And I can assure you: everything has a nasty odor. Every man and woman stinks to the stars. Everyone has something on his or her conscience. That's the first principle of the KGB." He smiled indulgently. "The Talala case is no rottener than half a dozen others I've seen. And the world has kept turning." His smile became fatherly. "Listen, we'll put Talala away. That seems like a small victory to you now, but once it would have been otherwise, you would have been celebrating. You've let your appetite run a little bit out of control. Try to put things in perspective."

"It sickens me," Leskov said calmly, "that my country is governed by men such as these."

"And do you suppose it's better elsewhere? In the West, perhaps?"

Leskov shrugged. "It must be better somewhere. I refuse to believe that the entire planet is this sick. It makes you want to vomit."

"Pavel Ivanovich, men and women are the same the world over."

"I can't believe that. I *can't* believe that there isn't . . . a possibility of decent government, of rule by law. A possibility of laws that are worth respecting."

Kerbitsky shook his head, cigar held out in space. "You're a dreamer, Pavel Ivanovich. A dreamer. It's a noble thing. But dangerous, too. Tell me—is this the only copy of your report?"

"Yes."

"And your notes? Where are they?"

"In my office. In my safe."

The general fixed his cigar between his lips and hoisted himself out of his chair. He took up Leskov's report and walked over to the shredding machine, turning it on. The machine grumbled. Calmly, Kerbitsky began feeding page after page into the jaws of the device. His face remained expressionless, a worker on an assembly line, with many years experience. When he was done, he switched off the machine and tossed the empty folder to Leskov.

"Destroy your notes," Kerbitsky said. "Keep the information in your head. It may prove useful someday. But officially, the investigation is terminated."

"And Talala? If he starts talking at the trial? We can't just let this go."

"We have to pick our battles. If it makes any difference to you, I'll admit I'm as disgusted by all this as you are. But that changes nothing. Noble gestures are out of vogue. The times want practical men. And it would not be practical to throw away both our careers—and quite possibly our lives—on this. It's futile. And that's that."

"And the trial?"

The general held up his palms. "Oh, I suspect they'll think better of a trial. It'll end up being a very quiet sort of affair, I'm sure."

"Then why all the fuss? Comrade General, there's just too

much that doesn't make sense. We're being played like puppets."

"Pavel Ivanovich, I'm recommending you for an award. You've done a magnificent job. And I think you should take a vacation. The weather's already lovely in the Crimea."

Leskov felt a wave of desperation. "*Please.* Don't you see we're being used? There's more to all this—"

"There's always more to things. That's natural."

"This is different."

"How? Give me something concrete. I see the system purging itself of a man who's outlived his usefulness, who's become a problem. I see a few small-change demonstrations out in the middle of nowhere. And I already see us overreacting, shifting nuclear weapons, sending in troops of every description. The real danger now lies in getting carried away with ourselves. We just need to let things quiet down on their own. You're just too close to the case to see that."

"Comrade General, I swear to you that something is terribly wrong."

"Get some sleep, my son. You're exhausted. You've been under a great deal of stress." The general snubbed out another cigar.

Leskov shook his head. "Something is terribly wrong," he repeated.

Loud voices sounded from the antechamber. It was an argument between a male and a female. A moment later the door swung open and one of Leskov's assistants half-stumbled in. The general's secretary followed at his shoulder, protesting the unscheduled interruption.

The younger officer's eyes were wild and he appeared out of breath. He ignored the general and spoke directly to Leskov:

"Talala's dead."

Leskov felt the jolt go through his body, settling in his knees. It wasn't an ending. It was a beginning. And something terrible was coming.

The room fell silent for a long moment, with only the clouds of cigar smoke in motion. Then Leskov asked:

"Suicide?"

The younger officer shook his head.

"No. Murder."

* * *

Colonel Leskov lay on his bunk, staring at the oil painting hung beyond the foot of his bed without seeing it, wondering what was coming next. He felt helpless. A very important prisoner had been murdered in a KGB high-security hospital and nobody had a clue as to who had done it. The entire staff serving Talala's floor had been sequestered. But none of them could come up with an answer. Finally, Leskov had turned over the interrogations to his subordinates so he could return to the officers' dormitory and try to think clearly. And to sleep a little, if possible. He had not slept at all in two days, and he had slept precious little in the preceding weeks, living on adrenaline as Talala revealed layer after layer of corruption, astonishing him with the veracity of each detail.

The building was unusually quiet. Trouble in the air. Leskov laid his hand over the cardboard file on his chest, pressing it against his heart. His notes. Talala's confession. Raw. He had promised Kerbitsky he would destroy everything. But for the first time in his career, he had lied to a superior.

Talala had seemed so important at first. But the Uzbek had been only a tool. They were all tools. But Leskov still could not figure out the end result that the hands behind the tools were trying to achieve. It was far more than a matter of simply getting rid of a figure who had become too much bother. It was much bigger. It sickened him, making him feel amateurish and incompetent, that he could not figure it all out.

Footsteps marched down the hall, but Leskov paid them no heed. Until a fist struck his door.

Leskov leapt to his feet, making himself dizzy. He hurriedly thrust the file of notes under the bedclothes, further appalled at his ineptness. Then he ironed his shirt with flattened palms and opened the door.

It was the duty orderly.

"Comrade Colonel, you have a visitor downstairs."

"Who is it?"

"He claims he's your brother."

Sasha and his brother walked the first few blocks in silence. Sasha felt awkward, unaccustomed to having the other man at his side, yet struck by an old familiarity that would never quite die. Once, during Sunday outings, they had done everything together—they had even worked together to lift their drunken father into the backseat of the automobile while their mother made laughable excuses to them. Sasha recalled how he had looked up to his brother, who had seemed so strong and capable, skilled in all of the things that were important to boys in between leaving the cradle and discovering sex. The hair atop his brother's head was coming to the end of a long retreat now, and the close-cropped temples bristled with gray. All of the dusty afternoons and boyish conspiracies had come to this. Sasha had sworn he would never ask his brother for anything. After Pavel had betrayed everything by joining the KGB. He had sworn he would never forgive him. Yet here he was. Ready to beg. Simmering in desperation and stale anger.

"How's your hand?" Pavel finally asked. They waited for a streetlight to change, although the dark avenue was deserted.

"Fine. Just fine."

"I was going to come visit you at your apartment."

"I don't live there anymore. The Artists' Union decided my lease was up."

"You have a place? In the meantime?"

"I'm all right."

"Maybe I could help?"

Sasha almost snapped that he didn't want any help. But it was untrue. He wanted his brother's help badly.

They crossed the overlit boulevard. On the far sidewalk, Sasha stopped and grasped the sleeve of his brother's coat with his good hand.

"Where is she?"

"Who?" Pavel genuinely looked surprised. Then the first recognition deepened his eyes.

"Shirin. Shirin Talala. Where is she?"

"Sasha, listen to me—"

"*Please.*" Weakness, shame—none of it mattered anymore. "Pasha," he said, using the childhood nickname for the first time in nearly two decades, "please, tell me where she is."

"Sasha, she's bad business."

"I don't care."

"It's dangerous. You don't know how dangerous. Her father was—"

"I don't care about her father. I want to know where Shirin is. And I know that you know."

"Sasha, listen to me. I need to apologize to you. I was wrong about something. She wasn't trying to get at me through you. But it was natural for me to think—"

"Where *is* she, Pasha? For God's sake."

"People have died. A lot of people. And I suspect it isn't over. Sasha, she's caught up in the middle of something—"

"I'll take her away."

"Sasha, listen—"

"*No,*" Sasha shouted. "You listen to me. You've never loved anybody. You don't know what it's like. I *love* her. I love her more than you could ever understand. Nothing matters except her. And I don't care what happens." He could feel his facial muscles moving like played-out rubber. Inspired, he got down on his knees on the sidewalk, clutching his brother's sleeve. "You want me to beg? You want me to crawl, Pasha? Is that what you wanted all these years?"

"No. Don't be ridiculous. Get up."

Big hands reached down.

"Tell me where she is. I beg you."

"Get up, for God's sake."

But Sasha remained on his knees, shaking like a drunkard.

"Sasha. Get up. And I'll tell you."

It took a moment for the words to register. Then Sasha hurried to his feet like an obedient younger brother. The brother who stood by the brown river, under the green trees. Where the afternoons never ended.

"Where is she?"

"Tashkent. In an apartment that belonged to her father."

"Is she all right?"

"For now."

"I need the address, I need—"

"And now you know," Pavel said suddenly in a grave voice. There was an odd hint of satisfaction, too. "Now you finally know."

"Know what?"

"What it's like." Then Pavel changed expressions. "I don't remember the address offhand. I'll get it for you, though. But I want you to listen to me, to really listen for once. It's dangerous. This is no joke." Their eyes met in the lamp-chased night, and Sasha wondered what had happened to the bright boy's eyes he had seen the last time he really looked into his brother's face. "And your Shirin . . . is different now."

"What do you mean?"

"She thinks . . . she thinks she's found God. The first thing she did when she returned to Tashkent was to get in touch with a fundamentalist Islamic group. A Sufi Brotherhood sect. They're bad business. The girl's playing with fire."

"I'll take her away."

"She may not want to go."

"She'll go. She'll go with me," Sasha said with a child's conviction.

"Sasha . . ."

"You've got to help me, Pasha. Get me an airline ticket. For tomorrow. You can do it. I've got money. I can pay anything."

"I don't want your money."

"Anything. You can have anything."

"I want your promise."

"Anything."

"I want you to promise me that . . . if she won't leave with you after one week . . . you'll never try to see her again."

"I promise. I swear it."

"And I want you to promise you'll do exactly what I ask of you, that you'll go exactly where I tell you to go."

"If she won't come with me, you mean?"

"She can go along with you, if she wants. But with her or without her, you're going to go where I send you, no questions, no arguments."

"It's a deal."

Before Sasha could react, Pavel threw his arms around him. Pavel kissed him clumsily on both cheeks, then held him in his arms.

"Be careful, little brother," Pavel said. "Be careful."

22

MAMUN ERSARI WAS A MAN OF GOD. HIS BRANCH OF the Ersari clan had long produced men who heard God's whispers in the dead of night, and they had often paid dearly for it. Persecuted by degenerate emirs and satanic commissars, they had survived only through God's infinite mercy, hidden among His people, ever waiting for the day when the One True Religion would return to the deserts and mountains that had given them life.

Mamun Ersari was a realist, within the terms of his vocation. He knew the rule of Islam would not return to his people overnight. Too much had been broken, too many knots needed to be retied in the fabric of Faith, and the infidel had spread his power widely over the blighted land. Once, there had been twenty thousand mosques within these borders. Now there were less than one hundred. But at last, the numbers were waxing, not waning.

The current demonstrations and those to come would not drive out the Russian and his pack of hired dogs. But the longest journeys were accomplished one step at a time. Now, with the Russian doubting himself, struggling to swim against a tide of troubles of his own making—now was the time to begin. The hour had come to force the legalization of religious organizations already clandestinely in existence, to expand them, to found more, to force the allowance of more Koran schools and more students, to broaden the teaching of the language of the Book, simply to widen the availability of the Koran itself.

All this could be done. Ersari had studied his enemies closely, every day of his life as a man. He understood the contradictory stance of the Russian and Communist toward Islam. All religion, the Slav beast cried, was backward, foul, oppressive, benighted. Yet Moscow had never been able to change the way of life of the Asian peoples under its heel, even when the authorities turned holy shrines into granaries and forbade belief. To forbid belief was to forbid the sun from shining. And the Slav, with his discarded wintry faith, never understood that. For the true believer, God was present in each action and inaction, in each moment. Eventually, the Communists had grown more tolerant of the vestiges of Islam than of their own lost religion, maneuvering to take advantage of Islam's respect for temporal authority, of a perceived subservience, just as they allowed the clan system to survive after early and futile attempts to break it. The Russian wanted only to maintain his earthly power, and he was willing to compromise all of his professed beliefs to do so. Moscow would compromise this time, too.

The men of his blood, sitting in the Party offices in Tashkent and elsewhere, would help. They, too, were greedy for power, anxious to impress upon Moscow their importance, their indispensability. They had been frightened by the new man's attempt to change the old ways of doing business, and now they were anxious to impress upon him the need to give them ever more freedom of action so that the empire would not break apart. Ersari understood them well. The Uzbek and Turkomen Party officials were emirs in vassalage to a distant sultan—and they wanted to wrest as many privileges as possible from the sultan's throne. And this new sultan himself, this Red czar with the mark of the outcast on his forehead, walked in the devil's shadow. These were evil times, times when men of God must act.

Mamun Ersari was a just man, as he understood justice. It troubled him that, in order to do God's will, men sometimes had to engage in acts that in themselves could not please God. At times, a man even had to soil himself by grasping the unclean hands of other men—men such as Mustafa Gogandaev.

Mamun Ersari regretted the taking of life. But it was clear that, in accordance with Holy Law, Ali Talala had deserved no less than death. The sacrifice of his family—tainted blood—was cruel and troubling, yet necessary to a good end. Mamun Ersari believed that God had willed it, yet there was compassion in his heart for all those who suffered. Even for Ali Talala, who had done the devil's work on earth. Ali Talala would never see the Gates of Paradise, not even from afar. Mamun Ersari had acquiesced in the spilling of blood because the blood ran with guilt and it was to God's end. But it troubled him to deal with Mustafa Gogandaev, to be required to feign friendship, to be forced to agree with each disagreeable word he uttered.

Now Mamun Ersari had reached the limits of agreement. He sat quietly as one of his best Koran students poured tea for all of the men present, and he waited for the resumption of the diatribe he knew would be forthcoming from Gogandaev. Evil men, in the final, Satan-devoured stages of their evil, grew transparent. Still it amazed Mamun Ersari that God should allow so much evil to be wrapped in such attractive flesh. Gogandaev looked like the perfect figure of a man. Strong, tall, with features as clear as the desert. Yet, behind those eyes lurked a thirst for blood that Mamun Ersari could no more understand than he could countenance. He knew of Gogandaev's perversions, his betrayals, his infinite lies, and he knew that this man would betray him or even his God as readily as he had betrayed Ali Talala, who had been a father to him. Gogandaev fouled the tea glass from which he drank, the carpet upon which he sat, the air he breathed. And the time would arrive when he, too, would find justice.

But the hour had not yet struck. Great events were unfolding. Mamun Ersari could not break with Gogandaev at this delicate stage, and he was willing to compromise with the defiled young man to a point. But Gogandaev's bloodthirst was truly sickening, and there were some things that Mamun Ersari could not allow before the eyes of God.

Gogandaev reached across the oversize brass tray that served as a table and picked out two cubes of sugar with his right hand. Mamun Ersari decided that he would drink his tea without sugar this day. And any sugar that remained in the little dish would be thrown away.

"The whore must die," Gogandaev said suddenly. "Until she is dead, the earth will not be free of this taint."

Ersari marveled again that so fair a human form could harbor such a depth of hatred. Gogandaev was diseased. Not in his head, as the infidels would have it, but in his soul.

"God is great," Ersari said, answered by the muttered agreement of the other guests and conspirators. "Shirin Talala, the daughter of Ali Talala, professes to have found her way back to the One True Faith. She wishes to live a purified life. Must she pay for this?"

"It's a lie," Gogandaev said. His face reddened with anger. "The whore lies. She's afraid. Desperate. She doesn't believe. It's a lie that soils the Faith."

"She voluntarily cleans the latrines of the Koran school. She does whatever is needed. She asks for nothing but God's forgiveness. If she is feigning belief," Ersari said, "then God in His infinite wisdom will know. I cannot tell."

"But you agreed that all of her breed should die."

"I am a man, and men err. I could not foresee that God would reveal a path to this one girl."

"She has to die."

"I cannot countenance it."

Gogandaev appeared as if he might rise and physically attack the source of disagreement. His rage was formidable. Satanic. Yet he mastered himself a little.

"And if . . . if I can prove to you that her faith is a lie? That she mocks us? That she mocks God? That her black soul remains with the infidels?"

Mamun Ersari answered slowly, unsure of what Gogandaev was up to. "If this were so . . . then we would have to think on these things again. But, my brother, how would you prove such a thing?"

"I don't know," Gogandaev said bluntly. "But she's lying. She'll make a mistake."

"Then we are agreed," Ersari said quickly. "Shirin Talala shall mourn her father undisturbed. The rest is the will of God."

The assembly echoed Ersari's final words. There was a passage of silence as Gogandaev sulked, beautiful in his anger.

This time it was Ersari who broke the spell of sipped tea and cracked pistachios. "We may rejoice. All things go according to God's plan, and He favors the faithful. Tomorrow will be a great day, the following day still greater. The eyes of the infidel will be opened at last."

"The faithless have no eyes to see what is before them," a voice offered.

"Truly," Ersari said, "the faithless are as blind men. But tomorrow they will begin to see. Peace be now unto the spirit of Ali Talala, who serves the faithful in death as he never did in life."

"They will come by thousands," a voice said.

"By tens of thousands," another added.

"The people will come as God wills," Mamun Ersari said.

"They'll come because their betters damn well told them to come," Gogandaev concluded, his voice still glowing with hatred.

Samsonov sat in his office. It was midday, but the light in the windowless cubicle was always the same. The office was as bare now as on the first day he had entered it. The remnants of his library had been packed and sent off to Vera's parents along with his meager assortment of personal possessions. The painting that Sasha had given him had been stored with an acquaintance. He still could not bring himself to share it with Vera. On this last day, the exposed light overhead showed only a scattering of paperwork on his desk and a tin-framed photo of Vera taken on their wedding day. The picture would go into his rucksack. The papers had to be dropped off at regiment before the trucks came to take him and his men to the airport.

Saying good-bye to Vera had been difficult because it was so different from what he had expected. She did not cry. Rather, she was oddly listless, resigned almost to the point of seeming uncaring. Pregnant women had their moods, of course. Their bodies took over their emotions. Still, he had been disappointed by the perfunctory feel of their last kiss.

But that was behind him now. He had to concentrate on his mission and his men. The mission remained unclear—just get to Tashkent and you'll receive further instructions. And his men were half-trained and half-hearted. Nonetheless,

Samsonov felt the old excitement coming over him, the quickening of the senses that only the soldier knows, the urge to run toward the sound of the guns. He loved Vera, and he was sorry to leave her. But the promise of some meaningful activity after the months of garrison plodding filled him with sharp anticipation.

He was, after all, a soldier. You could change the unit designations, the uniforms, the rhetoric. But he remained a soldier. And he was needed for work that only a soldier could do.

He was putting the last signature on his company's fuel account when someone knocked on the frame of the open door.

Samsonov looked up quickly, wondering what new problem his soldiers had discovered or created. But it wasn't Lieutenant Bedny or any of his men in the threshold. It was the warrant officer who had so nearly destroyed the company: Kuzba.

Samsonov felt an instant surge of anger, compounded because he knew that Kuzba had managed to wiggle out of deploying with the rest of them. He was to remain in charge of the home party, caring for the barracks and for all of the supply stockage the unit had to leave behind. They were leaving the wolf in charge of the henhouse.

"What do you want?"

"Easy there, Captain." Kuzba stepped into better light. He had a tentative smile on his face. "I'm not here to do you any harm."

"You've done harm enough."

"I just want a minute of your time," the warrant officer insisted. "There's something I want to tell you. Although I'm damned well not sure why."

Exasperated, Samsonov threw down his pen and rocked back in his chair. "All right. What's on your mind?"

Kuzba closed the distance to the front of the desk. He discarded the smile now, and his face looked unaccustomedly earnest, almost a bit afraid.

"I won't for the life of me pretend I like you, Captain," he said in a lowered voice. "I think you're a fool, and an asshole, to boot. But I just wanted to tell you that . . . maybe if there were more fools and assholes like you . . . well, maybe a lot of things would be different." He shook his head, going inward for a moment. "This here's a world where the big fish eat the little fish, you know? And all of the fishes, big and little, got to swim with the tide. Anyway, I'm glad I ain't going with you. I wouldn't trust this outfit in action any more than—"

A sudden noise of heavy trucks pulling up in front of the barracks startled both men. This was it. Time to go.

Samsonov reached for the framed photograph.

Kuzba reached out and caught him by the wrist. Then the warrant officer bent still lower, closer, and Samsonov could smell the alcohol on his breath.

"Listen," Kuzba said, whispering. "What I really wanted to tell you is this. You're too damned trusting, Captain. Don't trust *anybody*. And watch your back."

The two men stared at one another, suspended in a place between thought and action. Samsonov wondered whether he should be grateful for the advice or if this was just a particularly malicious display of Kuzba's wickedness, an attempt to frighten him.

The warrant officer let go of Samsonov's arm and backed away. Kuzba's body was unsteady and his face bore an expression of uncertainty the like of which Samsonov had never seen on him before. He could not shake the feeling that Kuzba was genuinely afraid of something.

"*Comrade Captain,*" a voice called from the doorway.

Kuzba jumped as though he had been bitten by a spider.

But it was only Lieutenant Bedny, looking young, half-starved, and jittery.

"Comrade Captain," the lieutenant addressed Samsonov again in his perennially nervous voice, "it's time to go."

"We go around. We go far around," the taxi driver told Sasha in broken Russian. The man's face and forearms shone with sweat.

"Why? What's the matter?" Sasha strained to see through the muggy twilight.

"Big trouble," the taxi driver said. "You stay away. All Russians stay away."

Coming in from the airport, the streets had been nearly

deserted. But it was more than the hot, cottony air that kept the people from showing themselves tonight.

The taxi driver made another abrupt turn. He was a heavy, brown-skinned man, with a scared scent.

"Very bad," he said. "You know me, mister. Russians just fine with me. Everybody just fine. But here is big trouble. You be careful with these peoples."

Sasha had read the Moscow papers on the flight. There had been nothing about disturbances in Tashkent. Then he got off the plane and the atmosphere of uneasiness, of dislocation, struck him with the first breath of the hot, dead air. The airport had been swarming with troops, the runway aprons crowded with military transports.

"What's going on here?" Sasha asked. "I don't understand."

"Demonstrations happen."

"You said that."

"Yesterday only small. Today very big. Tomorrow bigger."

The cab turned down an empty street, moving away from the first knots of locals clustered along the main boulevard.

"*Why* are they demonstrating?"

The taxi driver gave his passenger a worried look. As if he might have said too much already. But the Uzbek was the sort of man who loves to talk and cannot help himself. He drove a few hundred meters in silence then said:

"People say KGB killed great man of Uzbek people. Murder, you know. People become very angry. Religious peoples angry, Communists angry, everybody." The driver shook his head, setting off a chain reaction in his double chins that was visible even in the failing light. "Not me, mister. No trouble, please. Drive my taxi. That's all."

"Has there been violence?"

The driver shot another glance through the thick air sweltering between them. It was already summer in Central Asia, and Sasha was soaked through just from sitting in the cab. But there were more important things in the world now than a clean shirt.

"Not today. Maybe tomorrow. Big trouble. Tomorrow I drive no place with my taxi. Better stay home. Now your hotel."

They had made a long loop around the central boulevard,

remaining always in the part of the city that appeared new and lush. Ahead of them loomed a single towering building set apart by a cordon of broad streets. The hotel dominated the skyline in the heart of the city.

"Very good hotel," the taxi driver said. "No foreigners to bother. No trouble. But if you want girls, I know best girls. Not so much money."

"I don't want girls."

Good-naturedly, the man waved a hand in admonition, almost dusting Sasha's nose. He had a ripe summer smell that had sunk deep into the machine he drove.

"Very good. Tomorrow you stay in hotel."

The taxi shot up a ramp. The vast concrete deck before the hotel was empty except for a few derelict tables and chairs and a shuttered soft-drink stand. But as soon as the taxi came to a halt, Sasha could hear the noise of an enormous crowd in the distance, as though they were a ten-minute walk from a soccer game in its final phase. Sasha counted out the fare, with the driver obviously in a hurry to be gone.

There was no attendant at the door, although two militiamen had posted themselves just inside. They looked Sasha over, saying nothing. The lobby smelled of countless strong cigarettes smoked down to the nub. But it was as empty as the parking deck.

Behind the long reception counter a single Uzbek girl sat with a blank expression on her face. Her eyes lazily registered Sasha's approach, then turned away in unconcern.

"You have a room for me," Sasha said. Pavel had arranged everything, the flight, the room. As though it were the easiest thing in the world.

"The hotel is closed for repairs."

"That's impossible."

"Emergency repairs," the girl said flatly. She looked away, as though watching an invisible television off to the side.

"You have a room for me," Sasha insisted. He drew out his internal passport. "Leskov, Pavel Ivanovich. From Moscow. Check your book."

Resentfully, the girl opened the ledger. After a few moments she looked up. There was something approaching hatred in her eyes.

"Oh, yes, Comrade Leskov. For you we have a room."

* * *

"What in the hell is going on out there?"

Leskov had never seen General Kerbitsky so agitated. The old man stood in the middle of the KGB communications center in the subbasement of the old yellow building. He clutched a dead telephone receiver in one hand, with the other full of half-read message traffic. The communications room was packed with officers, many with heavy stubble betraying the fact that they had been working long past the scheduled end of their shifts.

"They beat us," Leskov said calmly. "They've made fools of us all."

"Those blackassed bastards," the general fumed. "Those obscene Asian sons of bitches."

"I should have seen it coming," Leskov said. "I knew something was wrong. It all makes perfect sense now. But I couldn't see it."

With a jerk of his arm, Kerbitsky hurled the telephone to the floor. "Somebody get me Tashkent," he barked. "I want to talk to Sholobotkin."

"Comrade General," a young officer said, extending yet another message. "The latest crowd estimates. Sixty thousand in Tashkent. Twenty thousand in Samarkand. More anticipated—"

"*Is anybody listening to me?*" Kerbitsky shouted. "I said I want a line held open to Tashkent."

He had been such a fool, Leskov realized. And on top of it all, he had sent Sasha out there. And now it was too late. The best he could hope for would be that the officers watching over Shirin Talala would alert to any danger to Sasha as well. It rang of iron fate.

"Goddamnit," Kerbitsky said. "Nobody listens to me. What do they think these shoulder straps are for? Decoration?" But his voice was marginally calmer now. He pawed over the pockets of his tunic, hunting for a cigar. "I don't understand it," he went on, talking only to Leskov now. "I just don't understand it."

"It's clear as day," Leskov answered matter-of-factly. "There was never going to be a trial. Closed or otherwise. But they were being absolutely honest with us when they passed on the word that they wanted Talala taken alive. He had to die in KGB custody, you see. It made it all perfect. Everybody wanted to get rid of Talala. He was too much trouble. But this way they kept their hands clean. And beat us over the ears for good measure."

"*Who? Why?* What the hell's going on?"

"Whoever the voices belonged to that whispered in the ears of the people who gave the orders. I don't know yet. Not precisely. But I don't think the show's over, either. There's more to come. It's all being carefully managed."

"And what's your hunch? You've always got a hunch."

"I think," Leskov said, "the ultimate point was to make Moscow—and the KGB—look bad. I believe the Central Asians, certainly the Uzbeks, are out to teach us a lesson. It's their answer to the anticorruption campaign, to our interference in the way they do business. A warning to stay out of local affairs. They're showing us our impotence, how much we need the local Party infrastructure—the traditional bosses—to keep things under control out there. My hunch is that they'll call off the demonstrations as soon as they've made their point."

"You're saying the Uzbek Party's involved? The Uzbek Communist Party?"

"Of course. That much is obvious. But there are others involved, as well. Religious fundamentalist groups. Nationalists. To some extent it's a question of who's using who. The only thing they all agree on is that they don't like us and our meddling."

"They never did," Kerbitsky said.

"Yes. But they never dared say it before."

The general shook his head in disgust. "You know, Pavel Ivanovich, it's all going to end badly. No matter what we do. Even I can see it now. You can't reform this system. First the Caucasus, the Baltics. Now this. It doesn't mend, it just comes apart." He looked off into the distance. "I worry that the men with the big fists will come back."

But I won't be one of them, Leskov thought. I can't go along. Not anymore.

"Comrade General," Leskov said, "the best thing we could do now would be to halt all movements of military and paramilitary forces into the region. The nuclear evacuation operations can wait. There's no real danger on that front. But there is a danger of appearing to overreact. The demonstrations will end when the local bosses figure they've made their point. But if we seem like we're trying to face them down, the whole thing could run out of control. The Uzbeks are just telling us to let them manage their own affairs, that they can do it a hell of a lot better than we can. Once the Interior Ministry acknowledges that it can't control the situation, the local authorities will ride to the rescue, showing us that, in the end, the people love them and trust them and listen to them and so on. They're giving us a taste of what might appear in their place, if we undercut them. That's why they've given the religious fundamentalists such a long leash. To frighten us. You know, the dangers of a new Iran within the borders of the Soviet Union and that sort of thing. I say let them play out their little theater piece. God knows, they've managed it beautifully so far. But let's stop the troop deployments. Sending in Russians and Ukrainians in uniform just now is the worst thing we could possibly do. The Uzbeks will be obliged to go one step further. And then we could have blood in the streets that would take a long time to wash away. Comrade General, if there's anyone you can contact, anyone who'll listen . . . let the nukes sleep a little longer. Don't send in any more troops."

Kerbitsky looked at his subordinate with tired eyes. A duty officer offered him a phone on a long cable, but the general waved it aside for the moment.

"You're right, Pavel Ivanovich," Kerbitsky said. "I believe you're absolutely right." His unlit cigar hung down in a fallen hand.

"Then try to stop them."

The general shook his head and sighed. "It's too late. It's already too late."

Shirin tried to sleep. But the itching, intensified by the heat, would not give her any rest. She had thought that her vaginitis was cured, but it had rushed back with a merciless intensity upon her arrival in Tashkent. She went to a gynecologist she had visited years before, but the woman only opened her hands in a gesture of helplessness. Shirin had a serious infection. The doctor knew what medicine to prescribe. But it was not available at present. Not even for hard currency.

Maybe in Moscow. As a consolation, the gynecologist offered Shirin a lotion made from herbs that women used on their hands and forearms after a day in the cotton fields.

Shirin tried to sleep, but the bloody corpse of her father appeared to her, smiling, with open arms. The night was full of screams that no one else could hear. The night was a desert unlike any she had ever known, full of vicious creatures scuttling underfoot and slithering beasts with human eyes. She had never thought of the desert as a lonely place. She had loved its clarity, its peace, the way the horizon called a horse's name, drawing mount and rider into the eternal distance. But this desert was lonely. Cold. She lay writhing and soaked in her sweat in an apartment that still smelled of her father's life, rising only to wash herself desperately, soothing herself for a moment with cold water splashed over raw, swollen flesh. She was being punished, she knew. She longed to suffer for her sins. But not this way. Her soul longed for a righteous agony, not for this discomfort that reduced her being to the smutty and trivial.

She was being humiliated. And her father came toward her, smiling, with blood pouring from a dozen wounds. They rode headlong into a bloodred sky and they could not see the cliff before them and she could not cry out because the hot wind filled her mouth with sand each time she tried to open it. So she rode onward, face down low in the mane of her pony, rubbing herself against its back. Sometimes, the doctor had told her, such ailments simply went away on their own. It was important to be very clean.

She was so unclean. She scrubbed the filth from ancient stone, choking at the stench. The old women laughed at her, as though they knew far more about her than decency allowed, and Shirin imagined that she could see her lurid history reflected in the eyes of crones made of leather and twigs. The old women laughed and Shirin tried to clean away the filth she had made of her life.

The buses and trams and the subway had all stopped running, and the streets were full of dead men and women going silently about their business. Everyone on earth was dead. But they were trapped in the ghosts of their old lives, haunted remorselessly by all that they had been, because the new heavens that they had been promised and promised and promised were a lie. The old hells were not a lie. But they were full. So everyone was trapped on the sidewalk, forced to go through the rituals of living.

A beautiful man raised a sword above a child's neck.

Sasha could have saved her. From all the devils. She could not believe even now that he was one of them. He had made her burn. But with such a good, cleansing fire.

No. All lies. *Lies, lies, lies.* Sasha had laughed at her and he had broken her. He rode beside her, laughing like a fool and whipping the hindquarters of her horse, and the cliff was so near and she didn't care. She only wanted to know if he would come with her. Over the edge of the cliff at the end of the world. Why couldn't he let her alone even now? When all she wanted was time to mourn and embrace the suffering she deserved? Why did he have to be the one? The only one?

Shirin woke in the darkness, ready to claw herself in her misery. She automatically lurched toward the bathroom to wash herself again, spirit ruined with lack of sleep, when the doorbell rang a second time.

She wrapped herself in a man's robe, a traditional Uzbek garment that had belonged to her father and still carried his scent. She drew her long, free hair out from under the collar and let it fall down between her shoulder blades, then hurried awkwardly toward the door, eyes still crazed with the sudden light.

She was collapsing inside. Her soul was breaking into fragments that would flake off and litter the floor until someone swept them away. The canyon's rim was only hoofbeats away.

She had believed she was awake. But it was still only a dream. And in this dream Sasha stood in her doorway in Tashkent, opening his mouth to speak. He looked older. Worn. As though he had not slept for weeks, as though he had stopped caring about the manifestations of everyday life. His physical decline mirrored the process at work inside her soul. They were, after all, two halves of the same being.

In this dream Sasha stood in the ill-lit hallway, wrist and hand encased in dirty plaster with metal protuberances under the fingers jutting like girders from an unfinished building. He wore jeans and a khaki shirt ruined with sweat, and his scent was instantly familiar, though tainted slightly by the sweet rot off the flesh imprisoned by the cast. This ruined dream version of her love held a hyperreality possible only in the realm of sleep. This was the vengeance of a mean and morbid God.

The dream lips moved and said:

"Shirin."

The dream voice reached down into her, sneaking behind all of the pain and disillusion to the place that always loved. It was the worst of nightmares. Because she knew she would wake from it. That she was fated to be forever waking. From exactly this dream.

In that instant Shirin knew that heaven was eternally beyond her reach. She was in hell, and hell was a place of marvelous subtlety, of a refinement so vicious that it was only natural that mankind struggled to persuade itself that hell was only a place of fire and clawed devils.

"Shirin," the ghost said again. It reached a hand toward her. Slowly, as if this apparition, too, was afraid.

She recoiled, taking a step backward, deeper into her own world.

The figure in the hallway withdrew its hand.

"Go away," Shirin said.

"Shirin, please. I'm sorry. I'm sorry for everything. I love you."

Shirin closed her eyes. Poisoned by the dream light. Sick.

"Go away," she repeated. "I don't want to see you. Ever."

"Shirin, I was so wrong. I've never been so wrong in my life. Can't you forgive me? I can't believe that you don't love me."

"You have to go. The neighbors—"

"Please. At least let me come in. To talk. I've come a long way."

"*No.* You have no right to come here. It's all over. Finished."

"You still love me. You *have* to love me."

"Go away. You're evil."

The ghost in the doorway put on a mask of terror.

"Shirin . . . that's crazy . . . that's . . ." He rested his good hand on the doorframe as if he needed to support himself, as if growing dizzy.

Shirin calmly placed her hand over the splayed fingers and removed them. It was astonishing how real a dream could feel. She remembered that flesh so precisely. Even this way, clammy with sweat.

The spectral hand tried to turn and clutch her hand. But Shirin was too quick, moving with the brilliant speed of nerves.

"Go away. Don't ever come back here."

"Shirin . . . please. I know this is a shock. I'm sorry. I couldn't wait until morning. As soon as I found out where you were—"

"You're dead to me. I've cut you out of my soul. Don't ever come back here."

"Please. I'm at the Hotel Moscow. If you want—"

She shut the door firmly, locking it. Then she fell to her knees, trying to support herself with hands and arms from which the bones seemed to have disappeared. Cold acid filled her stomach. She thought she would be sick and she tried to crawl across the rugs, sweat streaming off her forehead into her eyebrows, her eyes.

She only wanted it all to stop. She wanted to sleep again. For the moment, she even forgot the physical discomfort that had kept her in a half-sleep. It was such a minor thing now. She felt an infernal craving, matched with a fear, imagining that the dream lover in the hallway was pulling her into his arms, kissing her, damning her forever.

She wanted to sleep. To hurry the morning. So that she could put the nightmare behind her.

23

COMING INTO TASHKENT WAS A NIGHTMARE FOR SAMSONOV. His company's flight had experienced a delay on the ground at the airbase outside Moscow, and it was almost midnight when they touched down in Uzbekistan. The plane landed at the civil airport, which had been taken over by a fleet of military transports. The entire area was floodlit, and range cars with their canvas tops stripped away darted between the taxiing aircraft. The tower directed Samsonov's plane first to one apron, then another. A terse radio message ordered him to march his men to a collection point, but as soon as he had assembled them on the tarmac, an air force officer came stumbling down from the cockpit to say that another message had canceled the order and Samsonov was to wait over on the grass beyond the apron. His men were tired and grumpy, they had not been fed since morning, and despite the late hour, the sudden heat pounded them.

Samsonov marched his column of platoons to the designated spot and let them sit down with their kit. The troops carried only the most basic gear and their empty rifles. Everything else was to be provided upon arrival, from food to tactical radios. The other companies and his battalion staff were to follow within twenty-four hours.

An ambulance blared by, hunting down the line of transports, just as another jet shrieked to life. It reminded Samsonov of Bagram airbase in Afghanistan at the start of an operation: the same dust, and the heat that punished the body well into the darkness until, in a matter of minutes, the world turned cold, chilling your sweat and making you long for the morning and the return of the heat you so hated. During the flight he had continued scribbling through the endless paperwork a military deployment required. By his side, Lieutenant Bedny had dozed, calling twice for his mother as he rolled his sleeping head from side to side. It was all the same as in Afghanistan. Except that Bedny's body was still whole, while the other boys whom Samsonov had heard calling for their mothers had had all of their adulthood and adolescence shot out of them or blown away by a mine. They had become children again, dying children, smeared red in the dusty brown universe of that particular war.

A range car with a hard-shell top pulled up and braked noisily, followed by two buses. An officer in tropical dress and a saucer cap jumped out and demanded to know the unit's designation.

Samsonov saluted, identifying himself and his men. Then he said:

"Comrade Colonel, my men haven't even had a drink of water since—"

"No time, no time," the officer half-shouted. "Get them onto the buses."

"Where—"

"Later. You can ride with me. It's a terrible mess."

The officer projected an anarchic urgency that Samsonov had repeatedly encountered in rear-area types when they got their first look at combat up close.

"Comrade Colonel," Samsonov said in a controlled voice, "these troops are subject to the Interior Ministry. They've been sent here for a specific purpose. Please tell me where you intend to take us and on whose authority."

The colonel looked at Samsonov as though he had been confronted with a madman.

"Captain . . . Sokolov?"

"Samsonov."

"Captain Samsonov, we're in a state of emergency. There are tens of thousands of . . . of locals in the streets. There have already been acts of vandalism, of violence. Your men are needed to help control the crowds, to—"

"Comrade Colonel, my men and I are here on a mission related to special weapons. We have no crowd control equipment and no authorization—"

"You have your personal weapons."

Samsonov shook his head, smiling despite himself. "But no bullets. I'm the only one with live ammunition. Five rounds for my pistol."

"It doesn't matter. We're wasting time."

"Comrade Colonel, my men don't even have helmets."

"They'll be issued everything."

"Without the proper authority . . ."

The colonel's nerves were gone. He did not try the normal course of shouting a more junior officer into submission. Instead, he produced a sweat-marred letter with a hand that shook as though he were shivering in the Arctic.

Samsonov read the document in the headlights of the range car. It was an emergency decree signed by the military district commander. Based on a directive from Moscow, it authorized the bearer to countermand all other orders and to commandeer all arriving military and paramilitary units for the purpose of controlling public disturbances in the environs of Tashkent.

The authority was clear. But Samsonov did not like it one bit. Without protective headgear, riot shields, truncheons . . . all he could do would be to put on a display. And Samsonov did not trust displays.

"Comrade Colonel, I hope you realize the limitations of a unit such as this. And without the proper equip—"

"There's no time," the colonel repeated. "You've read the letter. There's no time. Get your men on board the vehicles."

Laden with their gear, the men had to cram themselves in tightly to fit aboard the two city buses. Samsonov put Lieutenant Bedny in charge of the rear vehicle, designated a senior sergeant as commander of the lead bus, then climbed into the back of the colonel's range car.

"*Turn up the radio, turn up the radio,*" the colonel demanded. And the little convoy pulled away, racing past the lines of aircraft, past the guards with their automatic weapons primed.

The first few radio transmissions he monitored almost put

Samsonov in a panic. The voices were frightened, demanding support. But soon his ears shook out the peacetime dust and he was able to listen through the fear to get at the events the voices sought to describe. It was evident that large crowds were in the streets. But it also sounded as though the mob either did not know its power or had no genuinely menacing intentions. None of the troops were involved in actual violence. They simply felt overwhelmed by the immensity of the numbers before them. The crowds moved where they wanted to go, with the security forces backing off whenever it appeared they might truly become threatened. Again and again, a calmer, older voice directed the units to withdraw and reform at a different intersection or public building.

"How long has this been going on?" Samsonov asked, leaning forward to speak over the colonel's shoulder boards.

"Only today. Since this morning. There were smaller demonstrations before. But nothing like this. It all went crazy today."

It's not crazy yet, Samsonov thought. The poor bugger doesn't know what crazy means. When the ragged men overrun your position in the darkness, when they get in among you and you can't even fire because your best friend is trapped behind your enemy—that's when it starts getting crazy. When the rifle becomes a club and you drink in the last stunned breath of the man you're bludgeoning to death . . . that was crazy. When you hammered men to a pulp with a piece of machinery intended to keep the killing and dying at a remove, when, in terror, someone from one side or the other hurled a grenade into the midst of friend and foe alike, when the men you killed or whom your brothers killed left their traces all over your uniform, over your bare, ripped forearms, your knuckles. That was crazy. When you looked down in horror at the blood soaking your uniform, when you thought in a lightning instant of animal fear that you must be dying—just before you realized that all of the blood belonged to your victims. *That* was crazy. Like the time he had briefly gone mad, stripping himself naked in the dead of night, in the cold mountain air, so he could check his white skin with a pocket lamp, convinced that so much gore could only mean that he, too, had been touched by steel or lead or sharpened stone.

When you had no choice but to wear your bloodied uniform for days on end, a feast for the flies . . .

"What's it all about?" Samsonov asked calmly. "Why are they demonstrating?"

"Oh, some black bastard got himself killed. Some gangster type. And the locals think the KGB did it—and who knows? Maybe they did. Anyway, the locals are carrying on like we just killed their collective father." The colonel resettled his oversize cap on the back of his head. "You just can't understand these people. After all these years . . ."

The colonel looked down at the floorboards in a gesture that said this was his last assignment, that he was going home after this one and be damned to the lost privileges.

"And what," Samsonov asked, "do you expect my men to do?"

"You'll be stationed by the officers' club in town. At the east end of the downtown area. At the *Russian* end. Got to keep the mob from starting some kind of pogrom."

"But what, exactly, are the parameters of the mission? Are we authorized to use force? What are the rules of engagement? Will we be issued ammunition?"

The colonel waved a hand at the dashboard. "It'll all be clear. Don't worry. Everything will be provided."

"My men need to eat. They need fresh water."

"Everything will be provided."

Samsonov knew it was not true. But he also knew that the colonel believed it. It was all so familiar. The officer who, confronted by a situation he could neither comprehend nor control, sincerely believed that the greater system would somehow fix it all up. The system would take care of everything, as it always had. Then you found yourself kicked out of a helicopter door in the darkness at the wrong landing zone, with half of the birds lost in the dark and the enemy waking up snarling and hungry all around you.

The streets of Tashkent hurried by, lined by strict apartment buildings erected in the first decade after the earthquake. In this district, everything was still. It was difficult to believe that this city was in a state of emergency.

"Comrade Colonel, please. Listen to me. We'll do our duty. But you have to help us. The best thing would be riot-control gear. If that's an unrealistic request, at least get me some ammunition so I can issue it to the NCOs. In case things really get out of hand. And my men have to have something to eat and drink."

The colonel did not move his head. The beak of his saucer cap pointed straight ahead as if he were on parade.

"I'll do everything I can," he said in a tone of voice that left Samsonov feeling utterly without hope.

The convoy sped through an artificially green section of the city, where leafy temperate-zone trees masked the street-lamps, promising that this place was, after all, not so different from Novgorod or Suzdal. A brightly lit modern hotel rose suddenly on the right-hand side, then the vehicles veered left around a small park in a long slow turn and pulled in to the curb in front of a two-story colonial building that had survived the great earthquake.

"That's the officers' club," the colonel said. "You're to close off this street and the boulevard on the other side of the park, as well." He gestured into the distance.

"Comrade Colonel, we don't have any radios. I can't co-ordinate my unit's actions across that distance."

"It doesn't matter. Everything will be fine."

Samsonov sensed that the colonel was anxious to be on his way again. To lull himself with motion, with the illusion of doing something meaningful.

"That hotel back there," Samsonov said. "That's for the foreigners. Isn't it?"

The colonel nodded, then hunched forward to let Samsonov climb out. But Samsonov was not quite ready.

"So our real mission is to keep the crowd away from the hotel. Away from the foreign tourists and businessmen. That's why you're putting us here."

"Can't have a scandal," the colonel said impatiently, annoyed. "Can't have an international scandal, now can we? Of course we don't want them getting at the hotel. Of course not."

"And what kind of security do you have at the other big hotel?" Samsonov asked, remembering the city. "The one for our own people?"

"We can't be everywhere. We're doing our best."

It was all right. Samsonov understood the logic of it. But he could not help wondering why, even now, even after all the changes, an officer of the colonel's generation simply could not bring himself to speak honestly and clearly. He had once heard Afghanistan called the "War of Official Lies." But that wasn't quite right. For him, it had been the "War of the Officers' Lies." About success and failure, about casualties, deeds of bravery and cowardice, about black marketing, disease, and the mission itself.

Samsonov crawled out from behind the colonel. The older man did not even get out of the range car to make it easy on his passenger. He wanted to be gone.

As soon as Samsonov's ears reached the night beyond the confines of the vehicle, the sound of the distant crowd swamped the little gasping noise of the engine. Yes. Indeed. Tens of thousands of them.

Different war, he told himself. Different war.

But he was not at all certain of it.

The colonel tugged at the door to pull it shut. But Samsonov held the panel firmly in his grip a moment longer.

"The ammunition," he said, hoping against hope. "Please just send us some rifle ammunition."

"Of course."

Samsonov released the door. A few seconds later the colonel was gone, disappearing into the darkness without even waiting for his buses to unload and follow him.

Samsonov began barking orders. He was determined to get his men's attention before the crowd noise got to them. It was important to maintain control, to hold it tight in your fist.

"Everybody off the buses," he shouted. "Platoon formations. *Let's go.* Sergeants to me. Let's *go.*"

Flat-footed, Lieutenant Bedny jogged up from the trail bus.

"What is it? What's going on?" he asked. He looked young, too thin and foolish in the black beret that just would not sit properly on his head.

"It's going to be very simple," Samsonov lied. "We've drawn an easy mission. Let's get the NCOs together and I'll brief everyone at the same time."

As soon as he had his subordinate leaders assembled, Samsonov took a moment to look into their faces. The crowd noise was huge, even at a distance of a kilometer or more. It was, indeed, a terrifying thing. Calling up the most primitive fears. He wondered how it sounded in the ears of these boys who not so long before had been the cocks of their street corners, bashers and bullies. Perhaps some of these faces had been waiting for him that night in the darkened hallway of the barracks. How tough did they feel now?

The faces showed markedly different responses. Some were frightened to a paleness aggravated by the glow of the street-lamps. Others narrowed their eyes as they leaned forward to hear, anticipating a new kind of excitement. A few were just exhausted, displaying the special tiredness that came over young men who were still partly children, willing to let the others pull them along in a waking dream.

Samsonov explained what seemed to be happening in the streets of the city and the role they were to play. The rest had to be improvised:

"Listen to me. Here are the rules. No one is to do anything to antagonize members of the crowd—*if* we actually come into contact with them. No one is to heckle them or to allow the initiation of a dialogue between us and them. Don't send one goddamned syllable in their direction. Be disciplined. Violence is only to be used in self-defense. And I mean that. This is not some kind of fucking game." Samsonov looked from face to face, wearing the mask he had carved for himself in Afghanistan. "Remember your drills. And make sure at least half of your men are resting at any given time as long as it stays quiet around here. First Platoon, with one squad from Third, is going to pull duty across the park under Lieutenant Bedny. Second Platoon and the rest of Third will stay here with me. The mission is to discourage the crowd from passing behind the park and entering the vicinity of that hotel over there. This is *not*, however, a fight-to-the-last-man mission. We are a deterrent. That's all. We can't prevent twenty or thirty thousand people from going where they want to go."

"Especially without bullets," a junior sergeant said. Scarred face, acne and fights. Bad teeth and no future. Samsonov almost snapped at him, but caught himself in time. After all, the kid was right.

"I'm working on the bullets," Samsonov said. "But that's really neither here nor there. We're not going to gun down our own people."

He hoped he really felt that way. In his heart he still feared the hangover from Afghanistan. The hatred of brown skin. The irrational fear. And now this. He felt that Vera had changed him, softened him, saved him. But he couldn't be sure. Perhaps it was better without bullets, after all.

"Any chance of some chow, Comrade Commander?" another NCO asked.

"I'm working on that, too. Now go back to your men and brief them. Lieutenant Bedny, I need to talk to you a little longer."

The pack of sergeants dispersed with sufficient crispness and sense of purpose to satisfy Samsonov. He had given up expecting miracles. He turned to Bedny, who was gulping back a yawn.

"Just tired, Kolya?" Samsonov asked. "Or a little scared, too?"

Bedny looked at him in the broken darkness, unsure of what the right answer might be.

"You'll be on your own over there. But you're ready for the job," Samsonov lied. "Just keep the men under control and don't let them do anything foolish. Keep an eye on Kordalaev. He thinks he can take on the whole world with his bare knuckles."

Bedny looked confused. Tired. And yes, scared. His mouth hung open and he tapped the toe of his boot at the surface of the street as though anxious to urinate.

"Comrade Commander? What can we really do? I mean, there's only a handful of us. What if they really do come this way? What can we do about it?"

Samsonov looked at the younger man. Bedny was the sort who would never have made it in Afghanistan, the kind who would have frozen at the moment of truth, gripping frozen-fingered to the hatch as his personnel carrier plummeted into a mountain gorge.

"Not much," Samsonov said.

In Moscow the night was windblown, with clouds filtering the glow of the moon as they raced on to rain elsewhere. The streets were empty, the parks emptier still. It was no longer safe to walk out at night.

Colonel Leskov did not act furtively. He did not glance over his shoulder or trace an arabesque of detours through the streets. He walked sternly and directly, with the satchel on display under his arm.

In the park, puddles from an afternoon rain mirrored the glow of the occasional unbroken lamp. Squirrels launched themselves across the pathway, but no human forms showed themselves. Not a single pair of desperate lovers. Not a solitary drunk. Thick and dark with spring, the park still hung on to a feeling of mortality, as though it were still winter and all the verdure a set of elaborate stage props, as though the leaves lifting in the wind had been glued to the branches for a Party congress.

His contact waited at the designated spot, a bit slump-shouldered, hands burrowed into the pockets of his raincoat. He gave no sign of noticing Leskov's approach.

Leskov's heart beat furiously. A part of him had hoped that the man would not show up.

The fountain had been derelict for years. It was half-filled with rainwater. The other man stared into it as if peering into a crystal ball.

Leskov stepped up beside him and waited.

"Colonel Leskov?"

"Yes."

"Shall we do this in Russian? Or in English?"

"It does not matter to me."

The man nodded and sighed. "Good. Then let's go with English. What do you want?"

"I have something for you."

The man's expression did not change. He reached a finger toward the fountain as if to stir the water. Then he reversed the gesture and put his hand back in his pocket.

"What?" he asked.

"Notes. I have notes from an interrogation I have made. With a man named Talala."

The man's eyebrows went up. The Americans were never very good at concealing their interest.

"*Ali* Talala? People's deputy and People's gangster?"

"Yes. The late Ali Talala, as you would say."

The American whistled. "Boy, you sure got your hands full with that one. So who killed him, anyhow?"

"I don't know. Truly. Certainly someone in the employ of the Central Asian administrators. But it does not matter."

"And you want to give me the records of his interrogation? Just like that?"

"Yes. You will find many names. Some of them must be a surprise to you. There is so much of corruption."

The man took his hands out of his pockets as if ready to grab the packet and run. But he only said:

"And you're doing this out of the goodness of your heart, right? And every word will be the gospel truth and so on?"

"I do not know if every word is true. I know only what Talala has said to me."

The American turned away, inspecting the fountain's far side. It was a black night, a night when honest men stayed home behind locked doors.

Suddenly the American turned to look him in the eyes.

"Okay, Colonel. So what is this? A setup? I take the package then your thugs jump out of the bushes? I thought we were getting past all that."

"There is nothing false in what I offer you. And you are protected with the immunity of the diplomat."

"That's no big secret."

"This is why I have contacted you personally. So you would have no fear. Many of your people outside the embassy are not clever. Those without the full immunity. They are not careful."

"Okay. Out of the goodness of your heart, you're giving me an inside scoop on corruption in the Kremlin or wherever. I'm supposed to believe that?"

"In the Kremlin. And elsewhere. But it is not from this goodness of my heart."

"Then why?"

It was Leskov's turn to stare down into the murky water. "You are not very good at accepting a gift. You are a man who is not gracious. But I will tell you, in the best words I have. It is only that I have lost my faith. I have thought I am a man who can do good, who can make the better changes. But I find out that I am a fool. All of my life, I have been a fool. And this is not an easy thing to see." Leskov clutched the packet under his upper arm and interlocked his fingers behind his back. To keep them from shaking. "Everything I have tried to do, it has been—how do you say it in English, *shutka?*"

"A joke."

"Yes. A joke. And you see it is the dishonesty I cannot carry on my shoulders. It becomes too heavy for me. So I want you to take this." Leskov undid his fingers and impulsively held out the packet. "When you are done with it, I hope you will give it to the journalists and to the people of the American radio station in Munich. So the facts will come at last into the light of the day. I want my people to know who lies to them. I want my country to know who makes it dirty."

The American took the packet in both hands, then quickly tucked it into his raincoat. It made a great bulge. But it would be all right. No one was watching them. Only the criminals were out tonight. And they were after other things.

"Listen," the American said, "if this isn't some kind of bullshit deal . . . if this is serious—and we'll be able to tell —we'll owe you one. You name it, Colonel. Money? Easy. In dollars. Or if you want to defect, we'll get you out."

"I have no wish to defect. This is my country."

"Then you could help us a little more." The American added quickly, "To help your country."

"I am not a spy. And I do not wish to become one."

"Oh, for Christ's sake, nobody said anything about spying. We're talking about a simple exchange of information. You know. In the spirit of glasnost and all."

Leskov held up his hand. "Please. I am not so foolish. At least not in this way. I will not spy for you. I make this gift to you one time. But I do have a favor to ask of you. *If* you find the material worth the time of reading."

"Anything. I'll get you anything you want."

"It will be a matter of great meaning to me personally. It is a matter that is impossible for me, but I think it will be a very simple thing for you."

The American smiled. "If this stuff stands up, you can name your price."

Leskov stared into the black water. The wind sent ripples across the surface.

"My price will not be so high," he said sadly.

Nine men sat in a circle on a litter of carpets. Before them lay gleaming brass trays from the workshops of Bukhara, laden with grapes, figs, dates, paper-wrapped candies, and glasses of tea. The men sat under the artificial heaven of a vast Czech chandelier—a souvenir of Rashidov's heyday, when the Soviet empire had been in proper order. The men were dressed, without exception, in Western-style suits. But they sat cross-legged in their stocking feet and wore small squared-off caps stitched with silver and gold. These were the nine most powerful men in Uzbekistan. All of them were officials of the Communist Party, although titular rank did not always correspond to their actual power. They were not young men, and the weariness of the predawn hour showed on their faces, told in the offhanded slowness of their speech and sounded in the rasp of their voices as though the sands of the Black Desert had caught in their throats.

A servant refilled their tea glasses with silent speed and disappeared. A man who had once been sharply handsome looked up from a snake of computer paper that had curled around his knees.

"Moscow," he said, "has accepted all of our recommendations." Then he smiled.

"*All* of them?" another man asked in disbelief.

"Every one."

There were more smiles, murmurings of approval.

"It is hard to believe," one man said suddenly, "that they have grown so weak."

The man with the computer printout nodded. "But it is so. And their fear is understandable. They cannot control the Caucasus. Or the Baltics. They pray that it will remain quiet in Central Asia. That the cotton will be delivered on time. That, here at least, passivity will prevail."

"Yes," a voice said bitterly. "The cotton."

"All in good time," the once-handsome man said, laughing. "It is such a game. The Russians see clearly what we have done, but cannot say it out loud. The fiction of unity must be preserved at all costs. They know they have been deceived, but the Russian prefers to cover over the truth when the truth disturbs his rest. So we have an agreement. To keep the fiction of a spontaneous uprising alive." He had always been a proud man, but now he looked at his colleagues with a confidence as fresh as it was full. "We are well positioned. They need us. And now, for the first time, they have an inkling just how *much* they need us. Whenever the other republics riot and rebel, we shall profit from it."

"And they will truly recall all of their Slavic appointees?"

"All of the important ones. All those who could have an effect."

"And they will stop this . . . this interference?"

"We will again control our own criminal investigations. And our own government accounting. It will all be as it was before."

"And Moscow will stop the campaign—"

The once-handsome man with the computer paper held up his hand. "All of it. They have met every demand. The demonstrations made it clear to them that they are in no position to control the situation. The people will answer only to their own leaders, not to those imposed by Moscow. Tomorrow, we will give the Slavs further evidence of this truth. The demonstrations will end. I have warned Moscow that we are putting all of our credibility on the line with the people and that there will be a terrible cost if they try to renege on any of our agreements."

"You believe the Russians can be trusted? Knowing we've led them by the nose?"

"Of course not. But for the moment, they see that our interests coincide. Let them clean their own house before they come here with their brooms."

"So the demonstrations will end today?"

"As the sun rises."

One of the men, a Party lord from an outlying region, had not yet smiled. With an expression of ill-concealed worry, he said:

"I have told you how it is in my district. The fundamentalists are strong there. The demonstrations in Karambul have turned violent. The people have heard about the Russians' plan to remove the nuclear warheads from the local storage site. There has been rioting. And I cannot simply call it off. I fear the people would not listen."

The man with the printout thought for a moment. "But the local agitators have been demanding the removal of the nuclear weapons and the closure of the storage area for months. This was their goal."

The district boss shrugged. "Yes. But now they see it all

as a devious plot. You understand how the common mind works. . . ."

"Yes. Well, perhaps we can turn it to our advantage." The man with the printout smiled again, marveling at the folly of the Russians. "Personally, I am not at all sorry to see the nuclear weapons taken away. We can present this to our people as our own initiative, as the establishment of a nuclear-free zone in the region. It suits the times. But the rioting will be more difficult to exploit. It no longer fits the plan."

"Perhaps," one of the oldest men said, "we should simply let the drama run its course in Karambul. We will show our strength by clearing the streets of the major cities with a word. But the nuclear weapons removal—that was another unilateral action on the part of Moscow. Perhaps we should let them see what happens when we are not consulted, when our approval is not sought. And perhaps matters in Karambul will come to nothing. The Slavs are sending many troops, as I understand it: KGB units, Interior Ministry forces. Perhaps the show of strength will work. But if blood is shed in Karambul, it will be solely on the Russians' hands. In fact, I think we should warn them that, due to their heavy-handedness, *we* cannot control *this* particular situation. Let Karambul be a last lesson to them."

The men in the circle rustled and sounded their agreement.

"Good advice," the once-handsome man said, "always comes from the lips of age."

The older man smiled, pleased, and said, "And now you'll be telling me I'm so old I should retire. You young men have learned so well how to flatter and kill."

The leader of leaders smiled in return. "We all know that age has not diminished you, stealer of wives."

The boss from the Karambul district was visibly relieved. He would not bear the responsibility if things ran out of control.

"So," the leader said, dropping the printout to the carpet, "that's it. We've won."

"For now."

"Only the desert is forever. The Russians have learned their lesson. And we shall teach it to them again, when the times require."

A small, fine-featured man sighed. "And Talala's out of the way."

The leader slackened his smile, lowering his black eyebrows. "Yes. He broke the rules. A tragedy of pride, of too much vanity, too much ambition." He turned to the man sitting next to him. "Has the plaque been commissioned?"

"It will be a fine monument," his neighbor said. "The people will not forget the martyr Ali Talala."

The once-handsome man grew thoughtful. "Our brother was the stuff of which those conquerors were made who rode down out of the desert mountains to conquer the world. But he could not see that the stars had not aligned themselves for such deeds in our time. We have also known the ages of living in between foreign empires, when the battle was simply for each possible measure of freedom under the shield of the stronger power. We have had to reconcile ourselves to days of learning to enjoy the largesse of our fathers' conquerors. We have had to learn the art of waiting. . . ."

"And a man wonders," one of the youngest members of the circle said, "how long we must wait this time. There are hours when I feel we are balanced on a razor's edge between Moscow and madmen."

"Speaking of madmen," the leader of all these leaders said, "there are still a few strands frayed from the carpet. Ali Talala, may his soul find a peace in death it never knew in life, was only the most obvious, the most immediate of these strands."

"Gogandaev?"

The leader took a sip of his cooling tea, spilling a drop on the computer sheets. "A wicked man. A man none of us could ever trust. And a man who has served his purpose."

"How soon?"

"When the time is right."

"And Ersari?"

The leader shook his head. "Too powerful. Too useful. And finally, Ersari is a man with whom one can barter. In any case, I fear who might take his place." He glanced at his watch. "Another morning."

"I'll begin putting out the word," one of the men said from the far side of the circle. "The demonstrations will vanish like a dream upon waking."

The leader nodded. Then he turned sharply to the district boss from Karambul. It was the movement of a man who would never be as tired as his neighbor imagined him to be. With a clear, hard voice that telegraphed a warning for the future, he said:

"But *not* in Karambul. Let the river find its own way to the sea. If the people of Karambul decided to kill a Russian or two as a lesson, we could not blame them."

Tensing, the district boss asked, "Shall I help guide the people?"

"*No*. You are to do nothing." Then the leader smiled. "After all, it will be a minor affair, a last echo. Karambul is of little importance. And it will be instructive to see how the Russians handle the situation."

Samsonov felt the lack of sleep as a physical weight, as though all of the pockets of his uniform and his boots had been filled with wet sand, slowing his steps and forever tugging him downward. It was a familiar feeling, remembered from the days and nights when closing your eyes meant death. He could handle it. He could stay awake for a long time, if he had to. The real struggle was to keep your mind clear, to make good decisions even as your body slowly quit on you. He had forced himself to stay awake in mountains far more lethal than these steel and concrete precipices lining the boulevards of Tashkent. He could make it. But the boy-men under his command were another matter.

Without the electricity of responsibility shocking through their synapses, his troops needed rest in order to function. He had fashioned a rotation system in which each squad took a two-hour turn on watch while the other squads of each platoon slept as best they could on the porch of the officers' club or in the shadows of the nearby park. From the position he had chosen at the junction of boulevards and streets, Samsonov could see the misshapen clusters of bodies under the pastel walls of the officers' club. He could not help thinking that they looked like corpses.

He commanded himself not to think that way. Refusing to think too much of the past now, of the war in which he had lost something irreplaceable from his soul. To reassure himself, he walked over to the clots of sleeping boys, comforting himself with their dream moans or snores, with the little movements of healthy breathing the eyes eventually found in the darkness. He promised himself that he would keep each of these boys alive, even exaggerating their innocence as they slept. Even the worst of the roughnecks and bullies lay so vulnerably disarranged. It had always impressed Samsonov that each last man was ultimately so very weak and small.

The mob was another matter. Even now, in the dead morning hours, the collective beast grumbled in the distance. The noise was not as big, the outbursts did not come as regularly, but it was apparent that some thousands of demonstrators remained active. Samsonov read it to mean that someone, some power, had firm control of the multitude. Except when looting was rampant, demonstrations usually dispersed in the hours between midnight and dawn, beaten by the needs of human biology. The continuing eruptions of voice noise wore on the nerves, but Samsonov's reason told him it was probably better this way. If someone had control of the mob, matters were less likely to get out of hand. He had a very bad half hour after a lone shot sounded from an adjoining street. But nothing came of it, and he decided it was probably just some nervous or clumsy boy-soldier in a neighboring unit.

He wandered from one bleary-eyed sentry to the next, often passing by without speaking, content to show himself to his men and to keep himself awake through motion. There was a false, fresh chill in the air now and it brought the sweet musk of flowers from the park. He thought of Vera. With the child blooming in her belly. What kind of a world could he offer that child? What kind of a life?

He had been so concerned with the fate of nations, with the future of his homeland. It seemed to him now that he had been very naive. In the end, all a man could do was to live for the beating heart that slept and woke beside him and for the fragile creatures that separated from her womb. And perhaps a man could not make much difference there, either. But he could hope.

Two military vehicles hurried down the street, paying Samsonov's thin line of pickets no heed, disappearing with snorts of exhaust and the fading glow of taillights. Samsonov decided it was time to check on Lieutenant Bedny's detachment again. If only to make sure that someone was still awake over there.

He explained to the senior sergeant on duty where he was going, trying to give the boy confidence along with clear instructions. But he could see that the sergeant did not want him to leave, that the boy, who was one of the swaggering, blustering sort, was afraid now. Samsonov did not think less of the sergeant for that. He knew too well how it felt. Jammed into a plane, then shoved out in a strange place in the middle of the night. Standing guard over some vague object with an empty rifle and no food or fresh water. While *out there*, out in the mammoth darkness, a creature with a thousand eyes and a thousand metal claws waited to devour you. Samsonov understood the feeling well. It was the real essence of soldiering.

Walking through the park, Samsonov wondered again which of his men, if any, had ambushed him that night in the hallway. He recalled Kuzba's warning not to trust anybody, and the perfume of Tashkent's flowers reeked sweet as disguised poison.

He wiped the matter from his mind. He was too tired to think rationally and healthily about such things. And it was all in the past now. This—the night, the crowd, the weariness and fear—had matured them all to a new grasp of reality. They were all in it together. Samsonov knew how that went, too: the braggart soldiers who mocked their officers in camp looked beseechingly at those same officers when the guns began to sound, waiting for the officers to make the decisions that would save their lives. And God help them if they truly didn't have good officers.

He had not quite reached Bedny's position when his instincts told him that something was wrong. A few steps later he began to hear not-quite-identifiable sounds from the street beyond the enclosure of the park. He broke into a jog.

Bedny's men were not sleeping. They stood gathered into a pack beneath a streetlamp, squeezing in on one another to get a better look at whatever was going on in the center of the group.

Samsonov ran out through the open iron gates of the park, heading straight for the action.

Quick-eyed, he noted that not a single sentry remained on duty. Each man had abandoned his post to join the miniature mob.

He heard Lieutenant Bedny's voice, high-strung and girlish: "Don't *kill* them. For God's sake, don't *kill* them."

A few soldiers looked around, startled at the sound of Samsonov's boots coming at a run. At the sight of their leader, they instantly peeled away from the pack, eyeing him with expressions ranging from uncertainty to alarm.

It was wrong. Whatever was going on, Samsonov knew with certainty that it was wrong.

"*You're killing them,*" Bedny cried.

Samsonov tore at the shoulders of the soldiers still blocking his path. His presence telegraphed through the platoon and the crowd began to open up. He shoved the last few bodies out of his way.

Two of his men, Sergeant Kordalaev and another NCO, had a pair of Uzbek teenagers down on the sidewalk. The sergeants were kicking them with all their might, boots thudding into spines, snapping heads.

Samsonov caught a glimpse of Bedny's white, terrified face.

Furious, Samsonov shoved Kordalaev so hard the NCO tripped over his victim and sprawled belly down on the pavement. The air groaned out of his lungs. The other NCO tried to retrieve a kick and get out of the way, but Samsonov knocked him down, too.

"What the hell is this? What's going on?"

The two kids, perhaps thirteen or fourteen years old, lay unconscious. Streaked with blood. Only twitching limbs and the pink foam feathering off their lips promised that they were still alive.

Samsonov bent over them. The two boys had been clutching one another in terror as their captors beat them. They were small, and this time, it did not matter in the least that they were brown skinned. They were hurt children. And the blood was on his hands.

Samsonov looked up, searching the faces of his soldiers. He finally settled his gaze on Kordalaev. Hate-faced, the NCO was rubbing a knee through a brand-new hole in the leg of his trousers.

"*You.* What's the meaning of this?"

Kordalaev retrieved his hand and straightened. There was blood on his fingers, but he didn't notice. He drew the hand across his mouth, then across his forehead. Panting.

"They were trying to sneak by us. The little blackassed terrorists."

Samsonov could read the lines of the bodies beneath the teenagers' clothing. They had more than a few broken bones. Their noses and lips had been pulped. With all the blood and swelling, it was impossible to tell if they had any teeth left.

"They're just fucking kids, for God's sake."

"We thought they were terrorists."

"And where are their weapons? I don't see any bombs."

"They must've thrown them away. Before we caught them."

He could tell that Kordalaev had gone a little drunk with the violence, that he'd got up a taste for blood. Samsonov half hoped the NCO would make a move in his direction. He knew he could have the sergeant down and unconscious before anybody could move to interfere.

But Kordalaev just stood there, heavy-breathed, with his eyes gone mad.

Samsonov snapped back into control of himself.

"Lieutenant Bedny, what happened?"

Bedny looked afraid. As though Samsonov might begin to beat him as punishment for what had been done to the boys.

"They . . . tried to run past us," Bedny said. "They kept on running. I yelled at them to stop, but they just kept running. And Sergeant Kordalaev . . ."

A good thing, Samsonov thought, that they had no bullets. Whom on earth had he been fooling? His slivers of training had made no difference. The interior troops had selected exactly the draftees they wanted: apprentice thugs and hooligans, boys who would not shy from violence. The plan was to convert them to the faith, to exploit their muscle. But there had been no conversion. They did not want to become soldiers. They still just wanted to be hoodlums, big men in a bad neighborhood.

And Bedny was hopeless. The lieutenant looked as though he were about to break into tears. All around, the platoon members waited sullenly for a final resolution of the confrontation. The unit had gone sour as a cat from whom someone had just rescued a captive bird. Disappointed hatred pitched the air. And Samsonov understood clearly that he was the target of that hatred.

He looked down at the beaten boys. They were still unconscious, certainly with concussions, possibly with permanent damage. This was exactly what the other mob, the real mob, needed to see to drive it wild. They'd tear these little punks in uniform apart. God Almighty, you were supposed to love your soldiers. But how could you love sons of bitches like these?

This, he realized years later, was why the old Russian Army had always needed iron discipline. This was why the Red Army had turned the screws even tighter. With men such as these there were only two possibilities: discipline that cut until it reached the bone, or savagery. Behind all the beautiful words, it all came down to just that.

In Afghanistan, most of his men had been different. But those had been airborne troops, volunteers. Those men had formed easily into a fine tool. Until they died in the wake of a staff blunder or a blunder of his own making. Now, at last, he understood the atrocities that other, less elite units had committed. Units in which the officers only differed from the men because of a scrap of education and occasional dental care.

"You," Samsonov told a nearby soldier. "Run over to the other position and get the medic." His voice was hard as stone. "Make it quick."

The boy took off at a run.

Samsonov knelt over the Uzbek boys. Couldn't even move them. Impossible to tell exactly which bones were broken. He wondered how in the hell he could raise an ambulance. In a strange city. Without a radio. Without so much as a street map. He did not want to advertise the event, but he decided he would just start banging on doors, if need be. Until he woke somebody with a telephone.

He had never been so disgusted with himself. He had tried to hang on to some scrap of an officer's career, compromising himself on all sides. He had wanted to keep on soldiering, on any terms. And the result of his ambition was this.

A range car with the top stripped off pulled around the corner, almost plowing into the broken mob of soldiers. With a shriek of worn brakes, the vehicle stopped just a few meters from Samsonov. A lieutenant colonel in an Interior Ministry uniform leapt out.

The officer had sharply cut Tartar eyes and a hint of Asia in his complexion that was even visible in the poorly lit street. Half a millennium of mixed bloodlines. The lieutenant colonel glanced at the two bodies on the sidewalk then turned his attention back to Samsonov without even a flicker of interest in what had happened.

"Samsonov?"

"Yes, Comrade Lieutenant Colonel."

"Damn it, man, you're supposed to be heading downcountry. I've been looking for you half the night. What kind of a whorehouse operation is this? What the hell are you doing here?"

"We were ordered here. A colonel met us at the airfield and said there was a crisis. He had a letter authorizing—"

The lieutenant colonel made a disgusted face. "It's all just a total mess. Everybody's in a panic. Commandeering troops and vehicles. There's no order, no method—why didn't you tell whoever it was that you were on a sensitive mission?"

"I explained it to him. But he had an authorization—"

"Forget it. Damn it. It's done now. But all this"—he waved his hand toward the heart of the city, the drone of the lingering mob—"this isn't donkey piss. We've got some real action out where you're going. They beat a KGB officer to death yesterday afternoon. I don't know what the hell's gotten into Moscow. Pulling out the nukes at a time like this. They're just throwing gasoline on the fire."

"Comrade Lieutenant Colonel, my men have no food, no water, and no ammunition."

The other officer put on a grimace that might have been intended as a reassuring smile. "You'll get everything you need. Especially the bullets. You'll have all you can carry. Just let me radio for your trucks."

"And we need an ambulance. For those two kids."

The lieutenant colonel made an annoyed face. "Yeah. Well. I'll bet those two little buggers wish they'd stayed in and done their homework. Don't worry. We'll get their asses out of sight." He turned back toward his range car, motioning for Samsonov to follow. "First let me radio for the trucks. We need to get your men moving. It's a long way to Karambul."

24

AND MUSTAFA GOGANDAEV WENT TO SHIRIN. HE found a thin young woman with deep circles under her eyes. The severity with which she had bound back her hair accented the angularity of her face, and her skin appeared painfully tight, with an unaccustomed yellow tinge. She attempted a smile at the sight of an old family friend and bid him enter her world—an apartment her father had used as a way station between visits to the republic's parliament and calls on his wasting whore.

Gogandaev looked at Shirin the way a man might observe a small animal he has the power to butcher and devour. He knew so much about her. All the filthy details of her life, down to her visit to a local doctor for a revolting woman's problem and the arrival in the city of her Russian lover. She had turned the Russian away, and that had complicated things a bit. But in the end, it was merely a matter of further elaborating the script he had written for her. Shirin Talala would die. And her death would be sanctioned. In a sense, she would kill herself.

Mustafa Gogandaev entered the apartment where Shirin had hidden herself and closed the door with exaggerated haste, taking the action out of her hands. He painted a look of deep worry on his face and said:

"Sister, we must talk."

Shirin asked if he would like a glass of tea, but he waved away the offer.

"Sister, there is no time."

He looked at Shirin, who slowly lowered herself onto a tumble of cushions.

"What's wrong?" she asked. "I've told them I want no part of the demonstrations. Can't they understand that?"

Even now, with the look of a refugee, her vanity forgotten, Gogandaev sensed that he was sitting before a woman who was, objectively speaking, very beautiful. It repelled him. There was nothing worse than the power such a satanic creature exercised over mankind. With that black, infernal sewer between her legs.

Gogandaev smiled the smile of a troubled brother.

"My sister . . . I worry so. I almost did not come to you today. I asked myself what your beloved father would think as he watches over us even now. Would he approve of my visit? Knowing that it could put his cherished daughter, his ruby, his sapphire, in jeopardy?" Gogandaev dropped his eyes to the deep red of the carpet. There were black, abstracted scorpions woven into its border, caught forever in the knots of a long-dead nomad woman. He shifted so that the edge of his heel rested over the nearest animal image. "I think your father would not approve of this. But I have also asked myself—what burns in the living heart of my sister? What has value to Shirin in this desert of life?"

Shirin looked at him with no outward sign of emotion. But he could feel her soul slipping out from behind its fortress walls, coming nervously into the plain where it would stand defenseless.

Gogandaev constructed a pained look for his features. "Shirin . . . I must admit that it troubles me that you have . . . shown such an interest in a Russian."

Shirin alerted. Her eyes changed. Gogandaev saw fear. And he felt a hunter's joy as he closed on his quarry.

"They are not of our kind," he went on. "Frankly, they are our enemies. And they always will be our enemies. This troubles my conscience. No—please—you don't have to say anything. Remember, your father trusted me to look after you whenever he was absent. But there were some things I could never bring myself to tell him. It is difficult. But I know I must accept your choices, my sister. After all, we are nearing the end of the twentieth century. We must not behave as though we are deep in the Middle Ages. So, although I cannot approve of your choice, I must accept it. As a loving brother. Although perhaps not without a twinge of jealousy. . . ."

"Is he in danger?"

Yes. There was fear in her eyes. And she deserved to be afraid. To fear the clutches of the devils to whom she had consigned herself for eternity.

"Yes. I always forget how clever you are, my sister. You've guessed my purpose." Gogandaev leaned toward her, grinding his heel into the rug-bound scorpion and advancing his jaw conspiratorially over the dark red sea of wool. "The demonstrations . . . will seem to be stopping. But it is only a lull, a gathering of strength. The fundamentalists are out of control. Tomorrow, in the evening hours—or perhaps sooner—there will be organized attacks on Russian citizens," he lied. "Some, perhaps many, will be killed. As an example. Now, you must excuse my prying into your life—I know how proud you are, my sister—but this hotel in which your 'friend' is staying . . . it's in a very vulnerable location. It's too close to the native quarter. And it is a symbol. Even the name is hateful to these people. I fear it will be the first place where the mob begins looking for Russians."

"I have no further attachment to this man." Shirin spoke in a cold, clear voice. But Gogandaev knew her better than she knew herself. He could hear the beginning desperation behind her attempt to hold fate at bay with a pair of words. He knew that she would run to her Russian lover, anxious to betray these fictive secrets, and that she would be observed by the men he had invited to observe her—although not by her KGB guards, who had been ordered off by the local administration in order to help cope with the disturbances in the city. She would run to her Russian, to warn him, and it would be evidence that her conversion was not sincere, that she was, in the end, nothing but a whore of the Slavs. And Shirin Talala would join her father in hell.

"I'm glad," Gogandaev said, smiling in mock relief. "If this is so, I am relieved. My heart ached to think that you had . . . chosen one of them. I merely wanted to be certain that I did not wrong you by withholding information. If, for instance, you truly loved this man . . . and if my silence proved responsible for his death . . ."

He could see deep into her now. She was collapsing into a tempest of confusion, into the cyclonic blindness brought on by her submission to the whims of the flesh. Her weakness was the weakness of a diseased soul.

"Thank you, my brother," Shirin said slowly. "Thank you for your concern." Her voice told him to go.

He did not mind. He was glad. He wanted to leave, to escape the physical smell and spiritual stench of her. He *wanted* to go. So she could have time alone with her demons.

Gogandaev rose.

"My sister . . . I have only one request of you. Should you . . . from the gentleness of your heart . . . decide to say to this Russian what I have said to you . . . then I ask only that you take great care." He gestured toward the shrouded windows. "There is evil in this city now. You can smell it in the streets, the alleys. It haunts the air. There is a darkness that the sun cannot burn away, and there is great danger in that darkness. I am afraid that these walls might prove too thin, too flimsy, to keep it out."

"Thank you, my brother."

Gogandaev headed obediently for the door, turning back only for a brief moment so that he would remember exactly how she looked in the hours before her death.

"Be careful, my sister. And trust no one."

Shirin did not trust herself. But she had made her decision. She clothed herself for the street, for the twilight, unwilling to admit her joy that she had found an excuse to release herself from her vows. At least for a little while.

It was quite likely that Gogandaev was right, she knew. He had connections everywhere. If there was going to be trouble, he would know about it. Oh, she didn't like him. And she resented his prying into her private life. But after all, he was trying to do her a good turn.

For her part, she could not sit by idly while Sasha's life was in danger. No matter how much he had disappointed her.

With her heart burning and the humbling sickness in her body forgotten for the moment, she hurried through back streets where men's eyes followed every female movement from the shadows, where the smell of offal wasting in the heat and the odors of an inadequate sewage system blended with cooking spices and engine fumes. She had forgotten everything but Sasha. She neither knew nor cared whether there were demonstrations or dangers, any more than she could spiritually connect such matters with the death of her father. Mankind was mad, and no mortal of interest was left to her beyond the man who had disappointed her heart's expectation.

What had she really expected? She asked herself what right she had had to expect perfection from a man when she herself was so imperfect a creature. The problem, she decided, was that she had always wanted it all, ever suspecting that the next of anything would be better than the last. She had been greedy in her sins. Now she was paying.

She did not yet fantasize a full reconciliation with Sasha. She was still too confused. She needed to be apart for a time, to think. To cleanse herself. And on the practical side, to heal her body. There was no question of sleeping with Sasha like this.

Besides, she wanted to do one thing in her life that truly sang of goodness. To give her beloved a gift, perhaps even the gift of his life, with no direct reward. She wanted to prove herself worthy, although she remained unsure of what it was she must be worthy.

And she would never give up her religion. She had found real comfort there, even if the essence of it still seemed to lie behind a thousand closed doors. She would never discard her rediscovered beliefs. Sasha would have to accept that.

He had come to her. After all. He was sorry. And she had made him come such a long way. It was a great love, a love worthy of the old tales. He had driven a path through the mountains for her, as had Farhad for another Shirin. Even now, he was risking his life to love her. She had always laughed at the old tales and poems, even as she secretly longed to be so loved. Now her Kosrou had come to her. In a frayed shirt, with body salt crusted on his lips. What more could she desire?

Perhaps there was some hope of enduring mortal beauty. If only Sasha could be patient with her a little longer. He would need to overcome obstacles, like the princes in the old legends. But at the end of it all, perhaps there was some hope. For the first time in her life she thought about the possibility of having children.

The doorkeeper at Sasha's hotel refused to admit her without a resident's pass. She gave him money.

He let her enter, judging her a prostitute.

The girl at the desk was determinedly inattentive at first. But Shirin had not forgotten how to be imperious. To her great relief, she found that Sasha was still in the hotel, forgetting for the moment that the purpose of her visit was to persuade him to leave Tashkent as soon as possible.

He did not answer the first knock on his door. Then, at the second knock, there was a muffled response. He had likely gone to bed, she decided. Struggling to sleep in a heat to which he was not accustomed.

The door opened. Sasha stood before her, bare chested, jeans hurriedly tugged up toward his waist with his undamaged hand. His hair was mussed. But his eyes lost their drowsiness in an instant, and he was again the dream man who had filled her doorway the night before, who had filled her life.

"Shirin . . ."

"I have to talk to you."

"Come in, please . . ."

"No." No, she could not go in. She did not trust herself to enter that room. Afraid she would forget herself, her illness, her promise and plans. And after all, she did not want Sasha to linger. She wanted him to go, to remain alive and healthy. For tomorrow.

There was so much to say. But the time was wrong, it was still too soon. Besides, such things could not be said in an unmopped hotel hallway with the floor matron barely out of earshot. No, she would save those words for a better time, for a time when her body was clean and her soul at peace. And she knew now, in her heart, that the better time would come, that she and Sasha were fated to be together. There was no helping it.

"Just come in for a moment. For God's sake. Where it's private."

"No," she repeated, whispering. "Listen to me. Please, Sasha. You have to leave. Go to the airport. Wait for a flight. Any flight. Go anywhere. But *go*."

Her alarm was instantly infectious. He reached out his good hand to catch her by the sleeve. But she was always too quick. She backed away. All of that would come later. In the better days.

"Shirin, what's the matter? Are you in danger? Tell me—"

"*No.* There's no danger for me. It's you. You're in danger. Please, you have to trust me. They're planning to attack the Russians. All the Slavs. Everything's going crazy. You have to leave this place." She was on the verge of tears. Now that he was standing before her, she wished him away. So that he might go on ahead and prepare a better place for the two of them. She had only needed to see him. Now she wanted him to fly off to safety. She had never feared anything in her life the way she now feared losing her beloved forever.

Sasha put on an unexpected expression, a small cynical smile.

"You really want to get rid of me that badly?" He shook his head. "Did I embarrass you by coming here, or—"

"*Please.*" The last of her mighty pride disappeared now. Pride was such an inconsequential thing, after all. "I love you. Sasha, I *love* you." The words were bits of iron, cutting her mouth. "I just want you to be safe."

His face turned grave, as though she had spoken different words entirely.

"Then come with me. If you love me, come with me."

Yes. She could go with him. They could run away. From everything and everyone. Forever.

"No," she said. "I can't. Not yet."

It was all such a mess. Her father and family dead. The world in chaos all around her. And yet . . . she would have gone with him except for her vaginitis. When they finally came together again, she wanted it to be beautiful. Not a matter of excuses and frayed tempers. And men were so squeamish about certain things. No, she would wait. Until a decent interval had passed. Until she was healthy again. Until things were clearer.

"If you love me, come with me."

She was crying and she did not even realize it.

"I *can't.* Please. Not yet. But I'll come. I swear it. I'll go anywhere you want."

He moved toward her again. She backed away still farther. They both stood in the hallway now.

"Promise me you'll leave," she begged. "That you'll leave right now. And I'll do anything you want."

"I want you to come away with me."

"Anything but that. Not now. Please."

"Shirin . . ."

"Promise me you'll leave."

"Shirin, this is crazy. If you love me, come with me." He shook his head as if trying to clear his eyes of something. "I can't live without you. I'm . . . so afraid of losing you."

"You won't lose me. You'll never lose me. But you have to go."

"For God's sake . . ."

"Promise me."

"Shirin . . ."

"Promise me. And say that you love me."

"I love you. *I love you.*"

"And tell me you'll leave."

Sasha had the look of a man overwhelmed. "I'll leave. If you promise to come soon."

"Soon," she said.

"Very soon."

"As soon as I can."

He moved again. "And kiss me."

But she was already backing down the hall. The swift girl who had ridden her small desert horse through the waterless hills. She wanted to kiss him. She wanted to kiss him with an intensity that had no precedent in her life. But she was afraid. Afraid that, if she kissed him, the last of her resolve would vanish. And the dream of a better place and time would be ruined. She would destroy everything with her usual impatience and selfishness.

There was too much distance between them now. He could not reach her. A look of panic swept over his face.

"Shirin, I'm not at the apartment anymore. I lost it and—"

"I'll find you."

"You remember Rachel? You can always find me through her. Rachel Traum, at the sales gallery off Nyegleenaya, she'll know—"

"I'll always find you."

Then she hurried away. Because even a moment's pause now could destroy it all. She trusted herself less with each passing second.

She ran down the stairs, afraid that the elevator would be too slow to arrive and that Sasha would follow her. This time, this one time in her life, she was determined to do things right. She would only have to wait a little while. Then they could begin to rebuild heaven here on earth.

She did not see where she was going. Her feet took her automatically in the right direction. But passing through the darkened alleyways of the old bazaar, she felt a chill at odds with the summer weather.

She straightened her back. Empty streets could not terrorize her now. Her only fear was of losing Sasha. She worried that he would leave too slowly. Or that he might not leave at all. Perhaps he would try to follow her.

For a time she imagined that someone *was* following her. And when a stray dog rustled out of a mound of garbage, she jumped. But no hand reached out to seize her.

If anything, the city was unusually quiet. As if the great demonstrations had exhausted it. Everyone seemed to have gone to sleep earlier than usual.

" 'O my beloved,' " she recited, dreaming again, " 'take my hand in thine and we will make this garden our paradise . . .' "

Yes. Paradise. In her straying vision she and Sasha lay magically apart from the rest of the world. Where no one could ever touch them.

Again, she had the sudden feeling that she was being followed. But when she turned to look, there was only the empty, broken pavement and a trickle of waste water gleaming under the stars.

A child cried, near and sharp against the big stillness of the night. Behind the walls of a hovel, a mother hushed the flesh of her flesh.

It was all so simple, really. She had always confused love with desire. Ruining the two emotions by running them together. Desire had its own sweetness. But love . . . was the delicious obliteration of the self. Surrender. Giving of yourself until you were empty and clean as the sky. They were wrong when they said that God was love. It was the other way around. Love was God. And God was no more nor less than the sum of the love loved in a given instant. You could never find God. You had to make Him.

She did not feel tired anymore. She felt refreshed, renewed. She wished she could share her vision of love with all the world.

She let herself into the peculiar silence of her apartment building. Usually, a security man sat dozing just inside the door, a retired Interior Ministry officer supplementing his pension by controlling access to this refuge of the privileged. But the entranceway was empty tonight. And dark. It felt as though all of the life had been drained out of the building, as though it had been abandoned.

Buoyed by revelation, Shirin took the elevator to her father's apartment. On her floor, the hallway lights were on and she imagined that she felt some hint of life and warmth again. She was going to wash herself. And then she was going to go to sleep. She believed she would finally be able to sleep properly. Now that she had found her peace.

As soon as she opened the door, a confusion of hands grabbed her and hurled her through the little foyer into the reception room with its pillows and carpets and brass. The room was not well lit. The men who had been waiting for her did not want too much light to shine on their work. But there was enough illumination for her to see that there were at least a dozen of them.

As she looked up from the deep red carpet, Shirin knew that she was going to die. The men were silent for a moment, staring down at her. But she knew what was going to happen. And she accepted it. She only wondered how long it was going to take and how much it was going to hurt.

25

SAMSONOV REMEMBERED THIS KIND OF HEAT FROM AFghanistan. In the summer, in the waterless hills and on the high baked plains, the heat took possession of the landscape and extracted a fierce price from any man who sought to use it as a stage for mortal action. The parched surface of the earth broke away under your boots, dusting the leather, but underneath the top layer the earth was hard, as if slowly turning to stone. The earth was hard, the Afghans said, and heaven was far away. The blue, vacant sky flickered golden at the rim of vision, and it was impossible to judge distances accurately in the enormous vacancy. The heat pressed down on your neck and shoulders as though you were carrying the sun in your pack. Your lips caked and cracked and your dry tongue moved over them like a lizard skittering over dead bark. The heat was a second enemy, a third party to the struggle. You sweated inside your too-heavy uniform until the brine added weight to your trousers and slowly chafed your inner thighs until they were raw and pink as the flesh of a sunburned child. Your sweat burned over you and made you wonder why on earth any man would choose such a life of his own free will.

This was the unit's second day at Karambul, the second day under this sun without shade, and the third day without proper rest. Samsonov's grimy, unshaven soldiers manned their positions in silence, too miserable to talk. The day before they had taken up positions just at the edge of the small desert city, ordered to wait for further orders. Periodically they heard pecks of gunfire from streets and alleys beyond their range of vision, but no one had approached them. They waited astride the main road leading into the city, but it had gone barren of commerce, as though everyone had taken their vacations at once and left the place deserted.

It seemed as though the chain of command had forgotten them. Then, late in the afternoon, a range car raced out of the heart of town, followed by a line of trucks. The vehicles were full of local Interior Ministry troops and militiamen. An officer with smeared glasses dismounted long enough to tell Samsonov:

"They're coming. They're coming this way. Do what you have to do. But don't let them reach the north-south highway."

"Where are *you* going?" Samsonov asked, watching the laden trucks grind by.

"We're being withdrawn. We're regrouping. Just don't let the bastards reach the north-south highway."

The officer remounted his vehicle. Instantly, the driver took off in pursuit of the column of trucks.

And that was the last guidance Samsonov received.

The mob arrived in its own good time. But it wasn't as bad as Samsonov had feared. No one brandished weapons and the vanguard halted well short of Samsonov's line of riflemen, contenting themselves with chanted threats and awkwardly waved placards. As soon as he had taken the crowd's measure, Samsonov's primary concern shifted to the control of his own men. He trooped the line again and again, steadying his soldiers, reassuring them that there was no real danger yet and reminding them that no one was to chamber a round until ordered to do so.

As the hour approached for the evening meal, the crowd began to thin, and as darkness fell, only a handful of demonstrators remained to observe the actions of the contingent of interior troops. At that point, Samsonov carefully began to withdraw his men to a hillock a kilometer back from the edge of the first settlement, where the road climbed and fell again as it reached for the main highway.

The new position was better. Although the low ridge wasn't much more than a ripple in the earth, it was commanding. And the fields of observation were clear on all sides. No one would be able to outflank his line without being detected. Further, should the demonstrators come after them in the morning, it would take a great deal more resolve for them to initiate anything serious. The crowd would have no cover, nowhere to run except back toward the city—and that was a long, bare way.

All night he sat or lay awake under the stars, listening to the intermittent throb of helicopters back where the north-south highway ran. Those would be KGB helicopters, shepherding the vehicle convoys as they laboriously shifted the warheads in special vans. He wondered how much longer the operation would take, how much longer his men would need to remain in position, how much longer he would have to struggle to maintain discipline in the pretense that these boys were trained troops. The only advantage he could see in his present situation was that nobody was likely to desert. There was no place to go.

Then the sun came up, slowly revealing a city that did not resemble anything in Afghanistan. Karambul was one of those sudden initiatives of distant planners, a city conjured from nothing to provide a work force to mine and process ore found under the desert. The inevitable shabby hovels had grown up around the city's edges, but mostly the eye saw rows of high-rise apartments, not quite as tall as those in Kiev or Moscow, due to the danger of earthquakes, but of the same general design as apartments throughout the land. As the light firmed, Samsonov could see huge cracks in the walls of the apartment blocks, but no sign of concern from the residents—only balconies hung with colored rugs and linen.

The morning haze never completely disappeared. The city remained under a cloud of brown chemical smoke. In the left distance, huge slag heaps marked the site of open-pit mining, while, on the right, pearly fumes rose from industrial minarets.

The heat began to gather and the smell of the city intensified. Even separated from the city by a kilometer, out in the open, Samsonov's eyes and nose began to burn. It seemed as though the pollution should evaporate into the great expanse of desert. Instead, it hung densely over Karambul, as though the pollutants had a natural affinity for each other. Samsonov knew from hearsay how hard life was in these out-of-the-way industrial sites. Conditions were especially bad for the children, and when they were examined for the draft, an extraordinary proportion of the young males proved unfit for service due to respiratory problems. Lives in these cities were desperately empty, and often short. In their attempt to design an earthly paradise, men had created an urban desert worse than the desert they had intended to conquer.

As the morning progressed, the crowd slowly began to reassemble at the city's edge. Only when several hundred demonstrators had gathered did they tentatively begin to make their way toward Samsonov's position.

He didn't worry. He could feel their irresolution. He realized it could always take a turn for the worse. But for now, the confrontation would be containable. The demonstrators simply needed a target for their protest, someone to see them and hear them.

The crowd halted as soon as it came within shouting distance. The poorly lettered placards began to wave again. But all Samsonov could feel was weariness and pity.

He was so lucky, really. He imagined how horrible it would be if he and Vera and the child had to live in a pit like this. It was nothing more than a penal colony for citizens who had committed no crime. Once you entered this world, it was almost impossible to leave. Where else would you get an apartment? Where else would you even find a job? Samsonov believed that he understood the anger of the men shaking their fists down the long slope, and he tried to imagine what it was like to be on the other side, looking up the road into the barrel of a gun.

Behind his back, a helicopter chopped through the sky. At first it sounded as though it were flying toward his position, but the sound quickly faded again. The warheads were still moving.

In Moscow he had watched a television interview with an American expert on the Soviet Union. The American had been far more circumspect and reluctant to offend than the

Soviet interviewer, who had seemed bent on insulting his own country at every turn. But the American said one thing that had stayed with Samsonov and that penetrated him now: the tragedy of this country was that the people had no choices. Looking at the man-made stain on the desert, Samsonov realized that the American had been right. It was, indeed, a land without choices, a land of single fates and no alternatives. Everything was predetermined. And the men and women who lived in those crumbling housing blocks and plumbingless shanties had to reconcile themselves to it. The Soviet Union, the American had said, was a land without hope, where hope sickened into dormant rage. The American had spoken better Russian than many of the troops the Soviet Army had sent to Afghanistan. Of course, in Afghanistan, there had at least been hope—the hope of going home someday, alive and whole. You never thought of the sorrows that might be awaiting you upon your return. In that killing heat, in the relentless danger, home had been flawlessly beautiful, and all wives and girlfriends were true.

Samsonov squatted in the heat. His boots were discolored with salt stains and his battle tunic clung to his back like a glue-soaked rag. He judged the number of demonstrators at nearly a thousand now. But they continued to maintain a respectful distance from the skirmish line of his troops. Once in a while he could catch an insult formed in bad Russian, but much of the chanting and yelling was in a language he did not understand. Not so long before, the sound would have given him cold sweats, would have made his fingers tighten on his weapon. But it was all right now. The brown faces shining full of anger were no worse than any others.

He thought of Vera, unspeakably grateful that she had taught him how to love. It was a debt he would need a lifetime to repay. She had lifted him out of his nightmares into dreams of flesh and devotion.

Surely, he thought, Dostoevsky and Tolstoy each had been right in his own way. Love's redeeming power could triumph over anything. He watched the lackadaisical, heat-punished assembly down the slope and knew that only Vera's love had fitted him for this duty, this hour. Slow knots of stragglers joined the crowd. New chants began. But Samsonov remained so calm that he surprised himself.

The crowd gave a sudden snarl, then lulled back into disorganization. Competing speakers each drew their own groups of listeners, and the most threatening gestures were the advances of lone young men who, after separating themselves from the safety of the group by a few paces, would make an obscene gesture or wave a sign and shout something unintelligible then retreat, swollen with heroism, back into the ranks of their brethren.

Samsonov heard a number of helicopters trace the highway in sequence. He wished one of them would fly to his position and land, if only to show his soldiers that they were not entirely forgotten. But, he judged, the KGB boys were probably doing everything they possibly could to clean out the storage depot as quickly as possible. Morale support visits to the interior troops would not be high on the list of priorities.

Another young man, identical to the rest in his pale shirt and dark trousers, pranced out from the crowd and began a tirade that only his compatriots could hear. He gestured angrily, threateningly. But it was only theater, Samsonov knew. The action of a young man who felt great powers in himself, but who was impotent of possibilities.

So many of my dreams, Samsonov thought, were the wrong dreams.

The sun seemed to have stopped overhead, filling the sky. His soldiers sat or knelt exhaustedly on the sandy soil, positioned at intervals of a few meters, silent. The unit already had several cases of severe sunburn. But there was nothing to be done about it for the moment. All Samsonov could do was to keep the men inactive, delaying the first heat casualties as long as possible.

Lieutenant Bedny ambled up from the makeshift command post they had rigged behind the crest of the hillock.

"Comrade Commander?"

Samsonov turned his full attention to the lieutenant. Sweat-soaked and thin, the boy's bony shoulders were never meant to carry a uniform. Bedny clutched an assault rifle that was by far the most serious thing about him.

"Think we'll have to stay here much longer?" the lieutenant asked.

Samsonov shrugged. "Hard to say."

"We did a radio check. Nobody answers."

Samsonov looked off into the distance. En route to Karambul, they had been provided with bullets, but he did not want to use them. They had been provided with a radio. But the chain of command ignored their calls. At least the rations were put to good use.

"We're not of much concern to anybody at the moment," Samsonov said. "They've got their hands full with the nukes. They'll come up on the radio when they're ready."

"But according to procedures, they should be monitoring at all times. What if something happened? What if that mob—"

"It's not a mob. Not yet. It's just a crowd today. And we'll do what we can to keep it that way." Samsonov laid a hand on the lieutenant's briny shoulder. "Don't worry. I'll worry for both of us. They can see that we're armed."

"But . . . they're fanatics."

Samsonov smiled. He couldn't help himself. "I doubt if it's going to get all that serious. They're just blowing off steam."

"You really think it's going to be all right?"

"Probably."

"Still, they should answer the radio."

"Yes."

"The men are running low on water."

"They've got enough. For now."

"Maybe somebody should go back? And try to establish contact?"

"We'll wait a while."

"It's so hot," Bedny said weakly.

Yes. It was hot. So hot you dreamed of winter. And in the winter, you dreamed of the sun. Life was nothing but a dream of other, better times.

"It'll get hotter," Samsonov said. "Late afternoon's always the worst." He decided he would troop the line again and warn each man one more time to conserve the water in his canteen.

A single shot sounded. It was an enormous sound, echoing for a long time over the scrub desert. A shocked silence followed in its wake. The soldiers were bewildered, the crowd stunned. The speakers broke off, the ranks congealed, unsure of what was coming. A few men threw themselves to the ground, but most were too amazed.

A lone member of the crowd lay in the roadway. A moment before he had been standing forward of his comrades, shouting and gesturing up the incline to where Samsonov's men waited. The spreading redness on his white shirt was visible across the distance that separated the two groups of men.

Samsonov had recognized the sound of the weapon. It was a standard-issue Kalashnikov of the caliber carried by his men.

He stood up to his full height.

"*Hold your fire,*" he shouted. He hurried down the line of prone or sprawled soldiers in the direction from which he believed the shot had come. "*Who fired that shot? Who fired, goddamnit?*"

No one answered. The soldiers either looked at him with the faces of sheep or carefully looked away.

Down the slope, some members of the crowd took off at a run toward the edge of the city. But those who remained had undergone a chemical change.

Now they were a mob.

Within seconds, weapons appeared down the slope and pistol shots cracked out from the anonymity of the mass. More people ran. A few of Samsonov's men fired back from the far end of the line. It was contagious. Others began to shoot.

"*Cease fire, cease fire,*" Samsonov screamed, running, raging. He kicked the rifle from the arms of one of his men, tore a weapon from the next man's grip.

"*Cease fire.*"

The air sang with pistol rounds fired off by the mob. But the distance was too great for handguns and the shots went wide of the mark. The shooting was more of a gesture of defiance and anger than a real threat.

But the weapons in the hands of his own men were far more potent. Two other members of the crowd crumpled to the dust.

Most of the locals either lay hugging the earth or had taken flight. But a few remained on their feet, milling about in astonishment and wonder.

"*No more shooting, goddamn it to hell.*"

At last, his men began to obey him. The firing thinned, then ceased. A donkey bleated in the fresh silence.

Abruptly, Samsonov realized it wasn't a donkey. The sound was coming from a wounded man down the slope.

"Lieutenant Bedny," Samsonov barked. "Run the line. Make sure everybody's all right."

But the lieutenant did not respond. He had thrown himself flat on the earth, hugging his rifle as though it were a doll. He did not even look in Samsonov's direction.

"Sergeant Malashov, Sergeant Krupka. To me. *Now.*"

But no one moved. Samsonov clenched his fists over his weapon.

"I said get over here, damn you." He looked down the line of riflemen. "Krupka. Malashov. Podyenny."

No one responded to his commands. He stood alone on the crest. Down the hill, the remaining members of the mob watched the little drama, assessing the situation. A few demonstrators got to their knees, while others crawled to take better cover behind their neighbors.

Samsonov could feel it. He knew what was coming. You put guns in men's hands and then gave them the least excuse for hating. And they used the guns. He knew he had to do something very quickly, before the firing resumed and a mistake turned into a massacre.

Down the slope, a few brave souls had gathered around the wounded. The man lying in the road still made his absurd donkey cries. But they sounded weaker now.

Samsonov realized that he was afraid. More afraid than he had been in a long, long time. Vera had done that to him, too. He so wanted to return to her, to rest in her arms, to smell her golden hair in the darkness of a bed. It was a terrible thing to be so afraid.

He walked back to the huddle of soldiers constituting his command post. The sky was remarkably blue and clear, a porcelain heaven.

"Try to get a response on the radio," he ordered the blank faces. "Tell them we need immediate medical support." Then he turned to his medic. "Give me your kit."

Samsonov did not wait for a response. He dropped the rifle from his hands and seized the aid bag by the strap, slinging it over his shoulder. He removed his beret, used it to wipe the sweat from his forehead, then stuffed it into one of his cargo pockets.

He hoped there would be time. He could feel the second-to-second shifts in tension, the wanting to shoot on both sides, the itch to help destiny along. He marched slowly back through the thin line of his soldiers, going without a backward glance. He took the road down toward the first of the wounded.

The locals watched him come in silence. He made his way deeper into the no-man's-land and a few members of the crowd got back to their feet.

That was good. You had to ease the fear. To impress on everybody that the danger lay in the past, not in the future. That it had all been an error.

He shifted the aid bag around so the demonstrators could see the little red cross on the white field. Still more of them rose silently to their feet, while others got up to their knees, compromising between curiosity and fear.

It was a long way in the heat. He hoped he would actually be able to do some good with the junk in the medical bag. He tried to remember the first-aid procedures perfunctorily taught in the service schools then desperately applied in a far-off war.

He glanced briefly beyond the mob to the city with its chemical halo, then raised his eyes higher to the distant mountains and the sky. If you walked in a perfectly straight line and kept going, he thought to himself, you would be in China.

Sometimes, when she was nervous or in a hurry, Vera pushed invisible strands of hair out of her eyes, as if she had felt something beyond the realm of the normal senses. Why did she remind him of lilacs?

He felt a powerful blow between his shoulders. As if a truck had driven into him at a very high speed. He lay on the ground with no memory of falling, and very late, he registered the sound of the shot. It had come from one of his own men.

The bullet had severed an artery, but in the moments before Samsonov bled to death, he heard the ripple of automatic weapons turned loose and he knew that it was going to be a massacre.

Lieutenant Bedny was shaking. He could not believe he had done such a thing. But the evidence lay in the roadway: a still body in uniform.

He had amazed himself. But he was not sorry. The bastard had deserved it. Life had been so good. Then this stuck-up prick had fallen from the sky. Now they were all in the middle of nowhere, with bloodthirsty niggers all around them. A man could get killed out here.

Before Samsonov arrived, he had been on the verge of getting his own automobile. But without Kuzba around, everything had fallen apart. Now he was sweating to death with a mob of blackasses after his blood.

"*Fire,*" Bedny screamed, voice cracking. *"For God's sake, fire."*

Most of the men obeyed him.

"She's dead," Pavel Leskov repeated. "It's true."

His brother sat beside him on a bench overlooking the river. The weather was splendid, warm but with a freshening breeze, and the gilded spires of the Kremlin caught the sun across the water.

Sasha had been silent for a long time, eyes fixed straight ahead. There had been no outburst of grief, only silence. Almost as if he had expected such a turn of events.

"She's dead," Pavel told him, "and I'm sorry." It was true. He was sorry. In failing to protect the girl, he had robbed his brother of a love unexpectedly genuine and he had broken his promise to Ali Talala. And a promise was a promise, no matter to whom it was given. So the remorse in his voice was genuine. But then he began to lie:

"You're next. They've associated you with the whole business. You're going to have to leave."

Sasha watched the brown water flowing under the old wrought-iron bridge.

"You have to listen to me," Pavel went on. "I can get you out of here. But I can't help you if you stay. People owe me favors. I can help you leave. But there's no time to lose."

But there was, in fact, a little time, and Pavel sat back and let the sun reach down into his cheekbones. A pair of disoriented tourists strolled by, the man dangling a camera and fooling with a map done in accordion folds. The woman's face showed more temperament than intelligence.

Suddenly, without turning his head, Sasha spoke:

"How did she die? I want to know."

"They shot her," Pavel said quickly. He had already prepared all the necessary lies. "They shot her down in the street. It was over in an instant."

"All because of her father?" Sasha said, voice dull.

"Things are different out there. Clans. Blood feuds. They're not our kind."

Two pigeons settled on the grass by an overflowing waste container. The birds waddled about drunkenly, pecking at the ground.

"I loved her," Sasha said in his dead voice. "I still love her. I can sit here calmly on this bench, listening to you. But you know I can't quite believe it. Intellectually, I understand the words. But the meaning . . . hasn't quite reached me yet." He turned his head slightly, regarding his brother. "It's so strange, Pasha. I can feel it outside me, waiting to get in. I can see it. Like I'm looking through a window. Because the reality's still outside. And I expect her to come walking along this embankment at any moment."

"It couldn't have lasted, Sasha. It wasn't that kind of love."

"I know."

"Perhaps we just have to be grateful for what we're given."

Sasha looked off into the river again. "It's not that way with me."

"In any case, you have to go. It would be senseless to stay here. I'm sure Shirin would have wanted you to leave."

To Leskov's surprise, Sasha grinned, almost laughing. He shook his head at the wonder of the world.

"It's just so odd," Sasha explained. "Hearing her name. From you. Like that."

"I'm sorry."

"You have nothing to be sorry for."

"But she would have wanted you to go."

Sasha nodded. "Yes."

They sat for a bit longer, with time melting in the wonderful sunlight. Down the embankment, a fisherman tried his luck in the near-dead river.

"Will your hand be all right?" Pavel asked. "I mean, will you be able to paint?"

"That's the least of my worries."

"You see, I want to send you where you can paint. Where you can really paint."

Sasha looked at his brother quizzically.

"You're going to America. It's all arranged. But you can't tell anyone. You'll just go. When you're safe, you can write back to your friends."

Sasha snorted. "I'm not very lucky for friends, anyway."

Why had it taken so long? Pavel wondered. Why had it been so hard? Why couldn't they just have been brothers, real brothers? Before it was too late.

"You agree? You'll go?"

"It's a godsend. Of course I'll go. I'd go anywhere, Pasha. The farther away the better." Sasha cleaned the corners of his eyes with his fingers. "Because, if I stay here, I'll spend my life waiting to see her in the street or in a subway car. Maybe I'll be able to believe—"

Pavel recognized that his brother had reached the point where he would agree to anything. It was as if he had undergone a particularly harsh interrogation.

No matter. His brother would be safe. In a different, perhaps a better, country. Where men understood about the rule of law. Perhaps they understood about painting, too.

You had to be grateful for that which was given you. And Pavel Leskov was grateful for this beautiful day on the banks of the Moscow River. At least it hadn't ended badly.

Neither of the brothers wanted to go, but they had reached the limit of the words that could be spoken in that place, at that time. They let the sun warm them and let the breeze off the water clean them. After a little while, Sasha took Pavel by the hand, and recovering from his initial surprise, Pavel returned the grip firmly. They stared at the traffic on the far bank, the golden spires, the luckless fisherman.

"Just one thing," Sasha said suddenly.

Pavel looked inquiringly into his brother's exhausted features.

"I won't go without my cat."

Epilogue

VERA LIVED FOR HER CHILD. BLESSED WITH THE NAME of a dead, false father, the baby resembled no one but Vera—blond, strong, and wide faced, with no trace of that precocious intelligence that guarantees a girl a life of unhappiness. Vera was not unhappy. Her father died of a heart attack, and her mother, instead of remaining in the country with its food and familiarity, migrated to the city to share the single room her daughter had been awarded upon the death of her husband in action. The old woman tended the baby during the workday, completing the matriarchal circle of sacrifice that seems to bring so much more happiness to Russian women than could any imaginable sexual intoxication. The women lived together amicably, cherishing regrets that none could speak aloud and pondering the inevitable fate of the child born into a world pocked with such vain and foolish men.

Occasionally, Vera went out with a male coworker or acquaintance for an evening, but nothing came of it. A hand on an arm, a blundered kiss followed by a harsh word disciplining a man sweating with alcohol—that was the reach of her adventures. She accompanied these men into the slow Moscow evenings more from force of habit than from any genuine interest. Then she returned home to the room that smelled of dinner and the baby's wastes and undressed slowly and carefully, musking the air with her unused body and rhyming out the same lullabies her mother's mother had once poured over her.

It was all the same, and it was not bad, so long as you did not feel any sharp urge to think, and so long as you could watch your child grow and tell yourself that no inconvenience was in vain. Food grew ever scarcer in Moscow, and inflation gulped Vera's salary. The women had to rely on the charity of relatives back on the privatizing state farm. But none of this was truly important.

Vera never thought of Sasha now. Her lost husband was a far more comfortable and appropriate object for an intermittent reverie, having made himself perfect by dying.

Sometimes the grandmother would look at the mother and child and weep slowly and luxuriously at the harshness of life. Whenever that happened, Vera smiled close-lipped, priding herself on her youth, vigor, and strength, rich in the novelty of motherhood, and waiting, with quiet anxiousness, to grow old.

Ashi limped among the dead. The Moslem cemetery lay untended, all weeds, dust, and unvisited monuments. One day a week, the man who had bought her for his brothel allowed her to go, unsupervised, to the gravesite. With a brilliant eye for women's souls, her keeper had judged her early on. She would not flee with some enraptured suitor any more than she would make trouble in the house—as long as she was permitted this single freedom. Growing wealthy on the ruin of her bones, the man even taught her how to determine which bus would save her the agony of walking on the hard pavement under the equally hard sun.

Still, there was a little way to walk at the end of the ride. She levered herself along on two wooden canes, a young woman who, in a year or two, would not be able to walk at all. But she did not really understand that any more than she understood what all the men were about. Sometimes, if they came back often enough, she half-recognized a face or the eccentric gesture of a hand catching at her collapse to better position her for ecstasy. But none of it mattered. She did as she was told, by anyone inclined to tell her, and waited for the day of the week when she could come and sit by the side of her beloved.

It was not the custom to visit a gravesite so often or so soon. But Ashi didn't know that. For her, the journey to Talala's half-hidden burial place was almost a biological impulse, like the will to lift food to her mouth. She had loved him beyond words and reason when he was alive, and it would never have occurred to her to cease loving or revering him now that he was dead. Death itself was not a very clear thing to her.

She sat down in the dust, lowering herself until she lost control and fell the rest of the way, already thinking of how difficult it would be to regain her feet when it was time to go. She laid out the food she had brought for the dead man: bread, apricots, water flavored with cherries, a tomato, and a bit of cheese, and she watched untroubled as the ants discovered it. In the trance of memories and poetry, she sang those interminable songs of a golden past, singing all of her beloved's favorites, forgetting the soreness left behind by the infinite men with their clumsiness, nights, weeks, months, and seasons of strangers, forgetting everything but the song of the moment and the recollected beauty of the fountain by the roses and the hand of the single man for whom God had enlivened her.

Mustafa Gogandaev was murdered in his office. He had been waiting alone, after hours, for a promised telephone call. The assassins shot, stabbed, and hacked him until his body was nearly unrecognizable. The assailants were never identified.

Because of administrative exigencies, it was found appropriate to bury Gogandaev at the side of the unfaithful wife he had killed in defense of his honor.

Colonel Pavel Ivanovich Leskov shot himself on the first day of the attempted coup in August 1991, assuming it would succeed. The documents that he had delivered to the Americans, detailing the whole sordid business associated with the Talala case and its Moscow connections, had not been released to the Western press as he had requested. Instead, the Americans had kept the information for their own intelligence purposes, and the great exposé Leskov had envisioned had never materialized. He had betrayed his country for nothing. The only good that had come of it was Sasha's rescue. The boy—in the most important moments Leskov still thought of his younger brother as "the boy"—was in California, with a new, better life.

Before he killed himself, Leskov took his brother's painting down from the wall beyond his bed, wrapped it in newspaper, and carried it to the home of the crippled Jewish girl with whom Sasha had deposited most of the paintings he had not been able to take with him to America. Leskov had never been introduced to the girl and she was startled to see a KGB uniform in her doorway on such a day, but as soon as he explained who he was, she grew radiant, almost beautiful in an inexplicable way, and invited him in to admire his brother's work.

Leskov accepted the invitation and followed the girl to her bedroom, which she had turned into a combination gallery and shrine. The walls were literally covered with Sasha's works, while still more of his paintings lay carefully stacked against the furniture. There were watercolors propped up on a chest of drawers, sketches on a nightstand. The light was bad, but it didn't matter. The power of the color and form was overwhelming. Leskov stayed longer than he meant to, silently wondering why none of their lives had been more successful, wondering why men so overvalued trivial things until it was too late. The girl brought him a cup of tea but did not bother him with words. A good, proud curator, she allowed her visitor to sink into the wonder of the treasures that had been entrusted to her.

When he could bear no more, Leskov thanked her and left. He drove himself out of town in an automobile he had commandeered from the service motor pool, explaining that he did not want a driver since the matter of his errand was too sensitive. It was a day on which anything was possible and no one asked too many questions.

Leaving the city, he passed long lines of waiting tanks, their crews perched blank-faced on the turrets. He believed that this was the end of his dreams. There would never be a rule of law in this country.

He drove to a green spot along the Moscow River where

he had first gone with his wife and then with his sons. He thought about the boys, of how they had naturally, perhaps wisely, gravitated toward their mother, no matter what device he'd employed to try to reach them, and he thought about his parents until, finally, as always, he thought about Sasha. He wept for a little while, then, imagining that he heard another vehicle approaching, he drew out his pistol and laid the barrel over his tongue.

Sasha's only problem in America came from the other Russian émigrés. They welcomed him, expecting him to share in their instant nostalgia for a homeland he could not recognize in their wantonly embellished memories. They invited him to parties where they played Visotsky's record albums, discussed the great, interminable intellectual projects upon which they were embarked, drank too much, and marveled at the Americans' superficiality and appalling lack of culture.

Sasha began evading all such invitations, visiting only with Lev Birman, who was doing very well as an artist. His friend already had a history of exhibitions in San Francisco, Los Angeles, and Seattle. But even Lev sometimes forgot how miserable so much of their daily lives had been. Living with a Japanese American girl who kept his life in order, Lev seemed to have forgotten how lonely he had been, how ignored, how ragged and insecure. He rented videos of Soviet films neither of them would have dreamed of watching while still in the Soviet Union, and he had acquired a fondness for the slovenly, hungover writings of Shukshin.

Sasha wasn't having any of it. Money provided by his brother's mysterious friends, followed by a small advance from a San Francisco gallery, enabled him to rent an apartment in Pacific Grove, and he energetically embarked on a program of avoiding other émigrés, improving his English, and becoming American. He spent a great deal of time walking the streets and wandering through the shops. The abundance was magnificent, but best of all he liked the color. He would walk up the hill to the Safe-Way supermarket just to rejoice in the fruit and vegetable sections. It was as if the colors of the whole world had come to America. Far from going teary-eyed over Visotsky's gutter snarling, he bought himself a portable cassette player and went to the nearest music store, where he asked the girl behind the register what music he should listen to in order to understand Americans. He left the shop armed with tapes by the Grateful Dead, the Beach Boys, Madonna, and Emmylou Harris.

He swam in the cold bay, grew slowly brown under the misty sun, and tried to forget. He did not allow himself to sketch or paint Shirin from memory. Instead, he painted his first American girlfriend, a remarkably tanned woman who worked in a gallery in Carmel, jogged, did aerobics, and fed her little boy health foods. The portrait was such a great success that two of the woman's best friends phoned him with offers that were astonishingly clear. Yet, even this tall, golden woman, with her good muscles and clear eyes, was more a matter of habit than anything else. His body might still be aimed at women, but his soul wandered off. For all her beauty and sexual flair, the American woman finally seemed as flat as her portrait. Divorced, with a child, she remained phenomenally naive and unscarred by life. She smiled over nothing. He did not know how much of himself he could ultimately share with such a woman.

But he steadfastly refused to fall into the trap of mulling over Shirin's fate. She was dead, and that was that. You could not let yourself collapse into the worship of yesterdays and lost possibilities like some slobbering alcoholic. You had to paint and swim and walk and memorize long lists of new words in your new language. You listened to the new music of your new homeland, struggling to catch the words and sometimes suspecting that it was better you did not understand them all just yet.

Vrubel was happy. California was a cat's paradise, a landscape with the feel of a tamed jungle, safe, yet full of the illusion of wildness. Vrubel prowled through the brush outside the little apartment, staying far from the road, and grew fat on cat food that looked and smelled better than most of the meat Sasha had eaten in his own earlier life. Vrubel's single difficulty in adjusting was a dense infestation of fleas, but a local veterinarian who drove up in response to a telephone call was glad to help remedy the problem for a breathtaking amount of money. So a largely flealess Vrubel flopped down on the artist's bed and purred, dreaming a living dream of the small birds of California.

Of course, Sasha was happy, as well. It would have been impossible not to be happy in such a beautiful place, surrounded by so much abundance. He never forgot the disorder, the hypocrisy, and the daily meanness he had left behind. He was grateful to his brother for all of this, wishing he could write him. But Pavel had warned him against it. It would hardly do for an émigré in America to correspond with a colonel of the KGB. Still, as Sasha watched the Soviet Union dissolving on the television news, he hoped that he might one day see his brother again.

When the August coup came, Sasha was both appalled and oddly satisfied at first. He was only surprised that it collapsed so quickly. He wondered which side his brother had been on, then decided that it didn't matter. Pavel was just another bureaucrat, and bureaucrats always survived. Sasha figured his brother had probably transitioned, smoothly and cynically, to the new Russian security apparatus. Pavel, for all his undeniable good points, was the sort of man who would put his career above everything.

Sasha was happy. Still, there were evenings when his girlfriend had to work late or tend her child, evenings when the television pictures from his homeland were too depressing and his painting was not going well. Then he would boil water and take down the single tea bowl that had survived the journey from Moscow, and he would take out the edition of Akhmatova's poems a friend had inscribed to him. If tea and verses didn't help, he would leave Vrubel to his dinner and dreams and go down the long streets to the sea. There was even a path you could take down through the cypresses into the enclave of the rich, where the big homes sat back and you could find a quiet place to sit on the rocks above the sea.

He loved this wild sea, so different from the tame waters beside which his grandmother had led him by the hand. He loved the explosions of spray on the boulders and the way the sea otters spread their dinner on their upturned bellies, paddling and eating. He loved the sun's descent and the dwindling away of the tourists, the eternally fresh air and the feeling of spirituality that might or might not have been an illusion. The last brightly clad men left the golf course by the ocean and the lights came on in the great houses hiding in the trees. Then you were alone, with the lightest spray reaching your face, and perhaps with a little more time on your hands than you really wanted.

Then he would think helplessly of Moscow, annoyed with himself at first, telling himself it was a dirty, fouled, ruined city, a place of despair and eternal lies. But he could not help remembering the evening light at the end of the first really warm June days, how the scabbed buildings became young again, ocher softening to lemon, while blue, green, and rose facades refreshed themselves in the gloaming. Young girls leaned brazenly over balconies, watching, waiting. Old women fanned themselves on wobbly chairs. Teenagers laughed in the streets, smart enough not to think beyond the possibilities of that one night. The angles and lines of the roofs grew surreal, while the shabby classical pillars and balustrades recalled better times with the struggling dignity of dowagers. A drunk curled up on the sidewalk and a young woman hurried home, clutching a stuffed plastic bag, her eyes vacant with thoughts of her real life beyond the streets, beyond the subway and the sour stairwells. They were such wonderful girls, the ones who retreated within, begging you to follow them, those gorgeously serious girls reading books on a crowded bus, looking up suddenly with their eyes full of tomorrow.

Even the despised Arbat filled his memory now. Not the tourist-plagued daytime Arbat, with its bad art scorching the eye, but the Arbat of late summer evenings, full of young lovers, tired cops, and music. A beggar-violinist played "Scheherazade" a few buildings down from a jazz band honking away like a gathering of melodious automobiles. Two young girls played classical guitars in a doorway, and a young man with a deep, sweet voice sang unaccompanied folk songs from the band shell of a passage. At ten o'clock on a June evening, the light clung to the buildings, unwilling to quit the sky. He remembered the light, the light, and the light, and the smells of exhaust, of bodies, of girls. Then he would think inevitably of Shirin, who had nothing to do with the Arbat and everything to do with the enormous emptiness he felt underneath his happiness, and he would sit for a long, long time remembering.

* * *

Rachel, too, remembered. She recalled a time when her life had been full of friends. They were all gone now, but she did not despair. She only hoped that they were happier than they had been when they had all been together. It was so very hard for people to be happy. She could never understand that, convinced that she might be happy with very little.

She lived in the world of Sasha's paintings, shutting herself in her room for hours on end, staring, dreaming, and trying to understand how there could be so much wonder in the world. Sasha had written to her, twice, from California. But she could not bring herself to reply, although she had plenty of time for writing letters. The gallery where she had worked had been transformed into a joint venture with a German firm, and the first thing the new management did was to replace the old staff with attractive young women who understood makeup far better than art. Rachel had time to write, but she always found something else to do. She rearranged Sasha's pictures, seeking to be fair, to give each canvas its share of the good light. She had her favorites, of course. But all of them were Sasha's works. She had a sacred trust to guard them, until the day when they might finally be appreciated. Or until the day when Sasha would return.

Her father had raised the prospect of emigrating to Israel. So many of their acquaintances were leaving now. There was nothing to eat for those who did honest work, and the streets were full of viciousness and spite. But at the mention of leaving the country, Moscow, the apartment, Rachel collapsed and had to remain in bed for three days. Surrounded by her collection of paintings, she had slowly regained her strength and her father never mentioned Israel again.

There were portraits of women, of course. But they, too, somehow made her feel closer to Sasha, or at least to his history, and they, too, received their share of the light. On her bad days, her weak days, Rachel sometimes wept, excusing her tears with the argument that the pain in her back was too much to endure. But she never really gave in to despair. It would have been too silly, too selfish. She had only to look at Sasha's pictures, perhaps holding a sip of sugared tea in her mouth, to know how lucky she was.

She felt so much wiser now. She had always dreamed of a better world, when, in fact, the beautiful world of which she had dreamed had been all around her, all the time. You had to learn to see beyond that which did not matter. And then you could experience the glory, the richness, the nearly infinite mortal capacity for joy. The world was so full of beauty that it was almost a punishment for mankind. It was a splendid, shining world, full of love, where no end of wonderful things might happen.